Praise For
The Wizard W[...]
Chronicle[...]

☆

"The picaresque adventures [...]t, hapless
Togura Poulaan . . . a somew[...] Quixoteish
figure. . . . Togura escapes [...]risonment and
encounters spirits, pirates, [...]s, talking rocks
and pagan tribes. The result[...] shifts in
tone—sardonic, philosophic, pragmatic and
pedagogic—keep the reader interested and off-
balance."
—*Publishers Weekly*

———————

"An engaging read, racily told, and with new
magical twists for the fantasy reader who wants
something different."
—**Susan Shwartz,**
author of *Byzantium's Crown*

———————

"A fast-paced fantasy of epic scope."
—**P.C. Hodgell,**
author of *Godstalk* and *Dark of the Moon*

———————

"Superior sword and sorcery. . . . A stylish and
horrific fantasy adventure awash with heroic
derring-do and some of the most ingenious magic
I've come across in many a moon."
—**Julian May,**
author of *The Pliocene Exile*

———————

"Well-crafted . . . thoroughly enjoyable. I happily
recommend it to everyone who enjoys the
wonderment of magical worlds where only pure
fantasy roams."
—**Gary Gygax,**
co-creator of the *Dungeons & Dragons*®
fantasy role-playing game

———————

Books by Hugh Cook

THE WIZARD WAR CHRONICLES:

Wizard War
The Questing Hero
The Hero's Return
The Oracle

Published by
POPULAR LIBRARY

THE ORACLE

WIZARD WAR CHRONICLES IV

HUGH COOK

Published in the United Kingdom as
The Women and the Warlords

POPULAR LIBRARY

An Imprint of Warner Books, Inc.

A Warner Communications Company

Gendormargensis

Yolantarath River

Stranagor

TAMERAN

HAUMA

RAVLISH

CENTRAL

LANDS

HAUMA SEA

Locontareth

Favanosin

SWELAWAY SEA

OCEAN

THE PALE

Ork

Skua

Lesser Teeth

ARGAN

Greater Teeth

Distance in leagues

0   200   400   600   800   1000

1 league = 2000 paces

Drum

Larbster Bay

Razorwind Pass

Lake Armansis

D'Waith

THE PALE

Skua

TREST

Hollern River

Lorp

Lorford

ESTARI

CENTRAL OCEAN

0 20 40 60 80 100
leagues

• selected communities

∧ mountains
∩ hills
↓ swamp
≈ sea
···· road

CHAPTER
<u>One</u>

Name: Yen Olass Ampadara
Birthplace: Monogail
Occupation: oracle
Status: slave
Description: heavy-built female of Skanagool race, age 30, hair black, eyes slate, height 11 qua, diamond tattoo on left inner thigh
Residence: room 7, height 3 of tooth 44, Moon Stallion Strait, Eastern Quadrant, Gendormargensis

* * *

It was Third Foal of Seventh Cohort in the year Khmar 18, and the season, of course, was snow. Yen Olass knew the date, but, with no sun, moon or starsign to guide her judgment, she could only guess at the time. A howling gale was blowing; the mouth of the cave offered only a prospect of indeterminate grey sky and gaunt black trees thrashing in the wind.

Though it was certainly late in the day, she thought she could still get back to the hunting lodge at Brantzyn. If she ran out of daylight, she would have to find her way in the dark. But before setting out, she had a little problem to sort out. The problem had four legs, a mouth like cast iron, and a definite will of its own.

'Come on, Snut,' said Yen Olass impatiently, slapping the problem. 'Ease up!'

But her pony obstinately held her breath, refusing to let her tighten the saddle girth.

'Infidel!' she said, punching him in the flank.

She lowered her head and butted him. Then she considered

poking him with her knife—but she was too softhearted to hurt a horse like that.

'You can't hold your breath forever,' she said.

Time proved her right. She tightened the saddle girth, packed the saddle bags, then rolled up her triple-ply soleskin horse blanket and tied it on behind the saddle. Now they were almost ready to go.

Yen Olass took a little bamboo box from one of the inner pockets of her fleece-lined league rider's weather jacket. She opened it, releasing the pungent smell of volsh, the thick niddin-grease used by the people of the north to keep out the cold and the wet. She smeared her cheeks with grease, then put away the box and pulled on her wadmal mittens. She drew the hood of the weather jacket well forward, then donned her snow-coat. The weight of its voluminous folds comforted her; she would be glad of the extra warmth out in the storm.

Now she was ready.

Yen Olass mounted up, watching her head because the roof of the cave was low. It seemed to be very gloomy. Was it her imagination, or was the light failing?

'Let's go,' said Yen Olass. 'Ya!'

Snut said nothing, did nothing.

'Ya!' said Yen Olass. 'Ya!'

She flicked the reins and kicked the horse with her heels, but Snut took no notice.

'Son of a tortoise,' said Yen Olass. 'Move yourself!'

And she slapped him, hard.

When that got no results, Yen Olass dismounted, grabbed the reins and hauled Snut toward the daylight. He resisted strenuously, but she forced him to the cavemouth. Then he baulked absolutely, and no exercise of brute force would get him outside.

'What are you?' said Yen Olass. 'A horse or a mule?'

She knew very well what he was: intelligent. It was no day to be travelling.

'It won't get any better if we wait,' said Yen Olass.

She should have left for the hunting lodge that morning, but had delayed, hoping the weather would improve. It had not. Tortured trees creaked and groaned in the wind. The sky was darkening: obviously it was later than she had thought.

'Come on,' said Yen Olass. 'We can do it.'

Snut was a shag pony, and the shag pony was the indomitable

mount of the riders of the far north; for endurance in the cold, only the grenderstrander could better it. If they set out for the hunting lodge now, they might just make it.

'Do you really want to spend the night here?' said Yen Olass.

Snut obviously did. All things being equal, Yen Olass would also have chosen to stay. But she was a slave, and could not set her own schedule. She was not supposed to be here at all. Instead, she was meant to be in Gendormargensis, a day's ride to the south, and there would be the most fearful trouble if it was discovered that she was missing. Extending her absence by a further day would increase the risk beyond reason.

Outside, there was an appalling graunch of rending wood. A tree came crashing down.

'I respect your judgment,' said Yen Olass to Snut, 'but I'm late already.'

The sky was thickening to thunder. The driving wind slashed sideways and lashed her face with snow. Out in the gathering darkness, another tree crashed down dead.

'On the other hand,' said Yen Olass, 'better late than never.'

And she led Snut back into the gloom of the cave, back to her woodstock and the ruins of her camp fire. Feeding the hot embers with a little bark, she got the fire going again, avoiding the need to fumble with her tinder-box in the numbing cold.

With the fire burning brightly in its circle of rocks, Yen Olass unloaded Snut, took off the saddle and removed the harness, wondering vaguely what kind of relief her horse felt when she took the bit from his mouth. She kept her snow-coat on, intending to sleep in it. She also kept the hood of her jacket pulled forward, but that did not stop Snut from licking at the volsh on her cheeks, liking the salt in the grease.

'Stop that!' said Yen Olass, pushing him away.

He nickered, and nuzzled her.

'What do you want?' said Yen Olass. 'An apple. An apple, huh? Is that right! And why should you get an apple? You men are all the same, you know. You think you can get away with anything. Well, it's just not so.'

But, when Snut persisted, she gave him an apple—a wizened little thing, which he crunched down greedily. She now had three apples, plus some oats in a nosebag. When that was gone, there would be nothing left for the horse, who could hardly share her own survival rations—pemican and evil-smelling milk curds. Snut knew how to dig in the snow with his hooves to uncover dried grass and moss, but since there was little forage in the woods at the best of times, he was unlikely to find much now.

'I hope you realize,' said Yen Olass, 'if we get snowed in, I'm going to have to eat you.'

Snut made no reply, but tried for another apple.

'No,' said Yen Olass. 'I'm saving the apples to have with roast horsemeat.'

Then she hugged him, crowding in to his warmth, to his strength, to his comfort.

'But I won't eat you unless I really have to. You're my only horse in the world.'

Strictly speaking, Snut was not hers at all. The shag pony belonged to Lord Pentalon Alagrace, the Lawmaker of Gendormargensis during the absence of the Lord Emperor Khmar. It was Alagrace who owned the hunting lodge at Brantzyn, and who made it possible for Yen Olass to escape into the wilderness every now and again for a few days' hunting. He took a considerable risk by extending such illegal privileges to her; he would be angered by her late return.

'Well,' said Yen Olass, 'if he doesn't like it, he can go and eat himself.'

Defiance was easy when she was far from Gendormargensis and the world of men, safe in this cave which was hers and hers alone.

She would have to spend at least another night in the cave, so she did a quick stocktake, estimating how much wood was left. On discovering the cave in the spring, she had named it Bear Barrow, though no bears had been in residence. She had bullied two of Lord Alagrace's league riders into helping her lay in a big supply of wood. Subsequent visits had diminished it, but enough remained for a couple of nights—or longer, if she was frugal.

'Sleep for all bad horses,' said Yen Olass, covering Snut with the horseblanket.

Then she settled herself down on the floor of the cave, heavyweight geltskin leggings protecting her from the cold. She took off her helm boots and undid her foot bindings. In recent years, many people had taken to wearing socks, but Yen Olass had no time for such outlandish foreign fashions. Foot bindings were simple, cheap, and always gave a perfect fit—and, more to the point, they were what the Sisterhood issued to its oracles.

Yen Olass slipped her feet into a fleece-lined luffle bag and tightened the drawstrings, securing them with a slipknot. Her feet, now safe inside the luffle bag, said hello to each other, and started to get really warm.

Darkness was swamping the mouth of the cave.

The onset of night brought no fears, for Yen Olass knew she was safe. The wild animals of the forest had learned long ago to shun human beings, while no bandits would be abroad in a howling storm. Her horse was one of her friends, and her fire was another; the cave would protect them all, even though the gale was rapidly becoming a blizzard.

However, when Yen Olass pillowed her head on her boots, she reached behind her head and felt for the hilt of her boot-sheath knife. It was well placed for a quick draw. Then— though she felt this was slightly ridiculous—she sat up, strung her bow, took an arrow from her closecapped waterproof quiver, and laid both bow and arrow within easy reach.

Having taken these precautions, Yen Olass settled herself for sleep. She was not tired, but knew that sleep was the easiest way to ride out the storm. She was slightly hungry, but made no move to appease her hunger, choosing instead to forget about it. Flames talked to the wind, discussing the chemistry of the wood on which they banqueted. The fire was over-generous; Yen Olass warned herself to economize. Then she closed her eyes, and went to sleep.

*   *   *

Yen Olass lay sleeping, dreaming of a long line of concubines sitting in pairs in the middle of Moon Stallion Strait. The concubines were chained neck to neck. Their placid smiles contained just a hint of senility. Lord Alagrace prowled up and down the road with a sword in his hand. His face dispersed itself into a disc of shadow. He snarled in a foreign language. His hands multiplied. The sky was blue then green. It tasted of violets.

As Yen Olass slept, wandering in the world of dreams, an intruder entered her cave. Snut snorted. The intruder, mounted on horseback, cracked his head on the roof of the cave, and swore.

Yen Olass woke, eyes startling wide.

The fire was burning low, scarcely more than a circle of

embers. Shadows lurched in the gloom beyond. Yen Olass snatched her knife and rolled from the fire. A sharp tug unravelled the slipknot securing the luffle bag. She kicked her feet free and scuttled into the deeper dark behind her woodpile. She remembered, too late, that she had left her bow behind.

Yen Olass watched as horse and rider came forward. The horse was a shag pony like her own. The rider dismounted. He was a Yarglat tribesman of indeterminate age—forty, perhaps? Lit from below by the dying firelight, his face was the domain of all kinds of sinister evil. Initiation scars on his cheeks suggested he had been raised in the old ways, in the tribal homelands far to the north. The skull of a rat dangled on a braided cord outside his furs. His face was marked by fatigue, and there was snow in his shaggy hair.

The man coughed, hawked, then spat into the low-burning fire. If the fire hissed when he spat, then the sound was lost in the wind. He nudged the bow and arrow with his foot, then peered into the darkness where Yen Olass was hiding. She could smell him. He reeked of horse, grease, stale sweat and woodsmoke, as if he never washed from one year to the next.

'Show yourself,' said the man.

Yen Olass clenched her knife fiercely. When she had wanted to learn how to kill people, one of Lord Alagrace's league riders—more than a little amused at such a foible—had indulged her for an entire afternoon. She had left his care thinking herself the complete expert, but now she would only remember a single command: stab upwards. Stab upwards!

'If you don't want to come out,' said the man, 'you can stay there and freeze for all I care.'

He beat at his furs, knocking off the worst of the snow, then threw up a couple of pieces of wood on the fire, sending up showers of sparks. Yen Olass was surprised to see he was not wearing any gloves. He rubbed his hands and blew on his fingers, then tucked his hands into his armpits.

Stealthily, Yen Olass reached for a piece of wood, then chucked it into the darkness off to one side. It clattered noisily against the wall of the cave, but the stranger was not distracted.

'Play all the childish tricks you want,' he said. 'It makes no difference to me.'

As he did not seem to be about to attack her, Yen Olass put down her knife and started to massage her feet, which were already getting freezing cold.

'They told me I'd find you here,' said the stranger, squatting down by the fire. 'Though they made it sound easier than it was. I lost my way twice, getting here. Come on, little girl. Don't you recognize me? I'm Losh Negis, the Ondrask of Noth.'

Yen Olass had never seen him before; she knew the high priest of the horse cult only by reputation. She had never attended a horse sacrifice, and never wanted to. Killing horses then burning them—now that was really barbarous.

Little flames were crawling over the bits of wood the Ondrask had thrown on the fire. Her feet were getting colder and colder; the fire looked very inviting. Yen Olass picked up her knife. Uncertainly, she advanced into the firelight, raised her free hand and gave the formal greeting:

'Yesh-la, Ondrask.'

He nodded, but did not bother to make a formal response. He threw more wood on the fire. She resented the way he made so free and easy with her wood, her fire, her cave. Without bothering with her foot bindings, she shoved her feet into her boots. She left the boot laces loose, just tucking them in beside her ankles. She was sure she could make it to the cavemouth—but would Snut come when she called? He was encumbered by the horse blanket: she would have to get that off him.

'You can't ride him bareback, little Yenolass,' said the Ondrask, following her thinking.

'Can't I?' said Yen Olass.

She resented the epithet 'little', which was a deliberate insult. There was nothing little about her: she was as big and as heavy as most men, and certainly taller than the Ondrask.

'Sit down, Yenolass,' said the Ondrask. 'I'm not going to hurt you. I didn't come all this way just to rape a woman.'

Yen Olass sat, but kept hold of her knife.

'The name is Yen Olass,' she said, emphasizing the way her name broke into two entirely separate words. 'Not Yenolass. If you wish to call me something else, then use my full title: Yen Olass Ampadara.'

'I'll call you Yen,' said the Ondrask. 'Dogs and slaves only rate a single name.'

'You call me Yen and I'll call you Losh-losh,' said Yen Olass.

'Watch your tongue,' growled the Ondrask. 'If you were mine, I'd teach you what a woman calls a man—and when.'

'Contrary to popular belief,' said Yen Olass, in a conversational tone of voice, as if apropos of nothing, 'it takes very little strength to stab a man to death.'

'Whose experience speaks?' jeered the Ondrask.

'I killed my first man at the age of twelve,' said Yen Olass in a level voice.

She told her lie in the tones of truth. At the age of twelve, there had been many times when she wanted to kill herself a man—one man or many. Hatred gave her voice conviction.

'So you killed a man,' said the Ondrask. 'And what good did that do you?'

'Find his bones and ask him,' said Yen Olass.

The Ondrask grunted. He got to his feet and snapped his fingers. His horse came to him, and he began to unsaddle it. Yen Olass was unsure of his intentions. If she ran, he could probably catch her. If they fought, he could probably take her and break her, then work his will with her afterwards. Best to get some control over him, then—so that, if necessary, she could disable him with a word. She knew how to do it. All she needed was an opening, which was swift in coming.

'This is a slave's job, really,' said the Ondrask, loosening the saddle girth.

'I was not born to be an ostler,' said Yen Olass. 'Hear the omens. I was born in a blizzard. I was born with a clot of blood clenched in my fist. My mother walked in places beyond your imagination. My conception was immaculate.'

'Listen to the female thing,' said the Ondrask to his horse.

'When I was conceived, the stars shone white,' said Yen Olass, her voice becoming a lilting chant. 'Out beyond the stars, the darkness. They say it's cold in the darkness; you die, they say.'

For the words 'you die', she dropped her voice, saying those two words in a lower tone. Most people would never have noticed the drop in tone which marked those two words out as different from the rest. But the Ondrask did.

'Stop that!' he said sharply.

Yen Olass ended her spiel then and there, immediately. She was shaken. She had never been caught out before.

'I play those games myself,' said the Ondrask. 'A very minor part of my art—but, no doubt, the sum and total of yours.'

Yen Olass said nothing, watching as the Ondrask dumped saddle and harness on the floor of the cave. Clumsiness betrayed his fatigue. He tried to hide his weariness, but she saw he was exhausted. She suspected he had been lucky to find the cave at all—lucky, indeed, that the storm had not claimed his life. He had no baggage. Knowing she would have to feed and shelter him, she now saw him not as a potential rapist, but as a danger of a different order—the incompetent traveller whose failings put the lives of others at risk.

'You came unprepared,' said Yen Olass.

'I expected to find you quickly,' said the Ondrask. 'It was further than they led me to believe—and the way was tricky.'

'Excuses never saved lives,' said Yen Olass.

It was a telling criticism which he did not try to answer, because he could not. Though he was of the Yarglat and she of the people of Monogail, both were children of the barrens of the far north, the lands, as Serek has it, 'beyond all maps, and cold beyond belief.' Both had learnt the same lessons in early childhood.

The Ondrask seated himself by the fire again. Yen Olass sheathed her knife and took the horse blanket off Snut. She draped it round the Ondrask's shoulders. He shook it off.

'I never asked for that,' he said, with anger.

'But you need it.'

'I'll get by without it.'

'Heat is strength,' said Yen Olass, quoting an old survival maxim. 'And one who weakens serves to weaken all.'

Her position was unassailable. The Ondrask yielded, allowing her to wrap the horse blanket around him. He pulled its warmth close to his body, shrouding himself in its comfort.

Yen Olass offered him pemican. He hesitated. Then spoke, loudly, harshly:

'Skak, give me food.'

'I have already offered,' said Yen Olass serenely. 'How can you demand what has been offered?'

She knew he had blundered badly. Of her own free will, she had offered to share her survival rations. The rigid survival ethic of the Yarglat gave him only two choices: to accept or decline. Acceptance would formalize their relationship, making him her guest, and placing him under obligations.

'I was tired,' said the Ondrask, by way of apology. 'I will eat.'

And he accepted her gift of pemican, which put him in a very uncomfortable position, since she was both a woman and a slave.

As the Ondrask ate, Yen Olass got a cooking pot out of her baggage and took it to the mouth of the cave. The night was now as black as hell, and every bit as cold. The wind, demented, raged across the land. Yen Olass packed the pot with snow, tamping it down to a little water. Bringing the pot back to the fire, she balanced it on two fresh logs. When she had hot water, she would reconstitute some of her dried milk curds.

The Ondrask huddled by the fire. His filthy locks were wet with melted snow; he reached behind his head and wiped away some water which was running down his neck.

'Why did you ride so light?' said Yen Olass.

'Because anger rode me all the way from Gendormargensis.'

'They would have given you food at Brantzyn, if you'd asked.'

'They offered. I told them to set tables for two.'

'You thought to eat with a woman?' said Yen Olass, mocking him ever so gently. 'To eat with a slave?'

'The tables,' said the Ondrask, 'were not going to be in the same room. But . . . here I've no objection.'

Though he made that concession, he could not bring himself to thank her outright for her hospitality.

Yen Olass knew they might be in bad trouble. A storm like this could last for weeks, leaving impassable snow drifts more than head high. Having got one concession from the Ondrask, she went hunting for another:

'If we have to kill a horse,' said Yen Olass, 'we kill yours first.'

'Agreed,' said the Ondrask.

'That way,' said Yen Olass, watching him carefully, 'you may lose a horse when you sought to recover one.'

The Ondrask eyed her in silence, then said: 'I'm not as impressed as you might expect me to be.'

When the Yarglat quarrelled, it was usually over horses or women. Gendormargensis was glutted with women, the spoils of recent conquests, but good horses were still hard to come by. As Yen Olass had guessed, a problem with horses had sent the Ondrask raging down the road from Gendormargensis. But why had he come to her? What made him think she could help?

'Now tell me the details,' said Yen Olass.

'No,' said the Ondrask. 'Let's see how you ride blindfolded.'

'Just one question then,' said Yen Olass, exchanging boots for luffle bag. 'How many horses?'

'Three.'

Yen Olass knew the Ondrask was an old friend of the Lord Emperor Khmar. The two were as close as brothers. Lord Alagrace, the Lawmaker of Gendormargensis, did his best to keep on the good side of Khmar, who had once come close to killing him. Alagrace would supply any horses the Ondrask needed. And, if those horses went missing, Alagrace would have no trouble replacing them. Unless . . .

'The horses were stolen . . .' said Yen Olass slowly.

'Yes.'

'And the horses . . . the horses had been consecrated for sacrifice.'

'In a public ceremony,' said the Ondrask.

'I know how it's done,' said Yen Olass. 'If taken anonymously, they'd be gone for good. But you didn't ride all this way for nothing. So you know who took them. And you want them back.'

'You ride well,' said the Ondrask. 'You're very close to the truth. Tell me who took them.'

Yen Olass checked the cooking pot. The snow had melted, but the water was not yet hot. She sat back, thinking, taking her time.

'You know who it is,' said Yen Olass. 'So Lord Alagrace should have the thief cut up and killed. But some people he won't dare touch.'

'But he's Lawmaker!' said the Ondrask, his rage sparking to life.

'Come on,' said Yen Olass, quietly. 'You know his position.'

Obviously some high-born Yarglat clansman had made off with the Ondrask's horses, and Lord Alagrace, always reluctant to make enemies amongst the Yarglat, was procrastinating, hoping the problem would resolve itself.

'He's Sharla vermin!' said the Ondrask. 'We should have killed them all in the Blood Purge.'

'You did kill them all,' said Yen Olass, 'or nearly all. Lord Alagrace was one of the few survivors.'

'Yes,' said the Ondrask. 'And who let him live? That's what I'd like to know.'

'He was away in Ashmolea,' said Yen Olass. 'Didn't you know that? No, I don't suppose you would.'

The Ondrask was known to keep very much to his yashram,

which was usually somewhere in the countryside beyond the walls of Gendormargensis; she doubted if he knew half as much about the politics of the city as she did.

Who might have taken the horses?

While the water heated, Yen Olass reviewed the names of potential culprits. Yoz Doy? No, he was in the south, with Khmar. What about Ulan Ti? No, he was too old, and too sensible. Chonjara, perhaps? Chonjara was wild enough . . . but it could not possibly be him. Though many of the Yarglat had succumbed to the cosmopolitan trends of agnosticism or outright atheism, Chonjara remained true to the beliefs of his northern homelands. He had even suggested that the horse cult of Noth should become the state religion of the Collosnon Empire, replacing the multitude of faiths which now lay within its borders—though even the Lord Emperor Khmar had not been prepared to go that far.

When the water had boiled, and Yen Olass had heated up some milk curds, she gave her only spoon to the Ondrask, letting him eat first. She watched while he ate. He left her less than half. To let a slave witness such a breach of etiquette, he must have been very hungry indeed. When Yen Olass had finished what was left, she asked him directly:

'So what did happen to your horses?'

'Chonjara ate them,' said the Ondrask.

'I beg your pardon?'

'Chonjara ate them!'

'So you tell me,' said Yen Olass politely, knowing an impossibility when she heard one.

'Chonjara held a banquet to celebrate his father's year seventy. He was in the market for some horsemeat. Only the best for his father! Haveros sold him three horses—my horses!'

'Ah,' said Yen Olass, for now all was explained.

Over the protests of his father Lonth Denesk, Haveros had abandoned the worship of the horse gods, and had espoused some trivial little local religion. Chonjara had criticized him for that in public, and now Haveros had taken revenge.

'Since you can't get your horses back . . .'

'I want an apology. And not in private, either. I want Haveros muck-down grovelling, with the whole city watching.'

'That might be difficult,' said Yen Olass.

'But you'll arrange it.'

'My writ doesn't run that far,' said Yen Olass. 'In fact, my writ doesn't run at all.'

'Lord Alagrace said you'd help.'

'Any oracle can give you a reading,' said Yen Olass. 'There's no need to come chasing out here just for a reading.'

'I told Alagrace an oracle couldn't help me. I told him I wasn't interested in a reading. But he told me you'd do better than that. He told me you'd fix it.'

'What?' said Yen Olass.

She was genuinely shocked, and it took a lot to shock her. How old was Lord Alagrace? Sixty-five? Not old enough to be going senile, surely?

'I'm sure Lord Alagrace couldn't have said anything like that,' said Yen Olass.

'He said exactly that,' said the Ondrask. 'His very words were: she will fix it.'

The words quoted by the Ondrask were unambiguous: 'Sklo do-pla san t'lay', translating as 'Originating from her will be a fixing.' The word used for 'fixing' implied the use of money, blackmail, trickery or political influence. Or black magic. Yen Olass was furious. Was Alagrace stark staring raving mad? There was no way she could possibly help the Ondrask, who, when he discovered the truth, was going to be very, very angry.

'So what are you going to do about Haveros?' said the Ondrask.

This was very difficult.

'There are always possibilities,' said Yen Olass. 'Your knife may know at least one of them already.'

'My blade has been consecrated to a higher purpose,' said the Ondrask. 'We have to find another way.'

'And we will,' said Yen Olass.

Though her chances of solving the problem were close to zero, she could hardly tell the Ondrask to horse off backwards until he bogged himself. She had to show willing.

'Let's hear the details,' said Yen Olass. 'Start right from the very beginning.'

'The beginning,' said the Ondrask, staring into the fire. 'The beginning was . . . when I came south.'

'Oh, I'm sure you can start further back than that,' said Yen Olass.

The Ondrask, failing to catch the mild note of sarcasm in her voice, raised his head and looked at her.

'Where should I start then?'

'If you're really stuck for an opening,' said Yen Olass easily, 'start with the beginning of time, for all I care.'

The Ondrask closed his eyes. He was very weary. At first, she thought he was going to drift off into dreamland then and there, but after a while he opened his eyes again. When he spoke, his voice was low; she had to lean forward to hear it, because the wind was competing in the background.

'Not many people ask about the first things,' said the Ondrask, in the voice of a man who has a story to tell. 'Not many people care to know any more.'

Yen Olass began to suspect that her little joke about the beginning of time had been unwise.

'Not many people care to know, but the knowledge is there for those who wish to know. This is the way it was. In the beginning, there was a barren plain where the wind moved from itself and to itself, and the wind was dark and light in one. The wind was both horse and rider.'

Yen Olass recognised the creation myth of the Yarglat. He really had started at the beginning. Having asked for this, she dared not complain as the Ondrask slowly worked his way through the tale of the First Things and the genealogies of the Horse who was Horse and the Rider who was Rider. It took quite some time.

As the Ondrask talked, telling now of the Last Ride of the Horse who was Horse and the Rider who was Rider, Yen Olass began to hear in his voice a measure of loss, of sorrow, of homesickness. And while she was not of the Yarglat, she was most certainly of the north, and she too began to yearn for those empty horizons, those high-hunting stars, those skies where the night veils infinity with curtains of green light, purple, red. She too yearned for the campfire where the talk goes back and forward in the long winter night, man and woman and horse and child all gathered together in the same communal warmth.

While the Ondrask talked, Yen Olass began to remember names and faces gone from her life for almost two decades. She realised now the true source of the Ondrask's rage. The high priest of the horse cult was suffering not just for the loss of his three horses, but for the loss of an entire way of life.

The Ondrask had reviewed an entire culture by the time he got to the story of his own birth.

'They named me Losh Negis. I was born in a tent on the barrens where the wind rolls forever, thinking the world downhill. I was weaned on mare's milk and billet. By the time I could walk, I was learning to ride, clinging to the fleece of a sheep.'

Bit by bit, he created his world for her.

'At the age of fourteen, I was initiated into a raiding party. Six years after my spear was first blooded, I endured a vision. I knew the power then, or thought I did. What I knew was the shadow of a shadow. But I followed the Old One thereafter. I learnt of the Powers That Walk and then became them.

'My people listened to me when voices gathered. I both gave and received. For them, I endured the darkness. I talked with those who have no bones. I brought back much wisdom, and shared. In those days, my very shadow was worth more than a man. In the city here in the south, people looked on me as if I was an animal—and a poorbred animal at that.'

The Ondrask paused. Yen Olass made no grunts of approval, no small encouraging sounds, no conversational noises. The Ondrask did not need them, and would not have welcomed them. He brooded for a long time, staring into the dying heart of the dying fire.

'The fathers of our grandfathers came south to conquer an empire,' said the Ondrask, 'but the empire conquered us. The Blood Purge changed nothing. We slaughtered real men, thinking to kill our enemy, but it was already too late for that. We were defeated by our victory, and Haveros is the measure of our defeat.'

The Ondrask said nothing more, and Yen Olass saw that his tale was at an end. He had still not answered her original question, but she knew he would no longer welcome being quizzed on the trivial details of who said what to whom and where and when. He had spoken of first and last things, and he had talked himself out.

But Yen Olass did have one question to ask before they slept. She had always wondered about it, but, till now, she had never met anyone who might know the answer. She dared her question.

'You were born in the north,' said Yen Olass, 'and so was Khmar. What does Khmar believe?'

'Khmar?' said the Ondrask, looking at her, as if seeing her for the first time. 'Khmar believes in Khmar.'

Listening to the wind, Yen Olass thought it was dying down a little, but she was now too tired to be certain.

*   *   *

Yen Olass woke to find daylight filtering into the cave. The Ondrask was huddled under the horse blanket, snoring. The two shag ponies were awake. Sometimes, on other hunting trips, she had woken in the night to find Snut sleeping standing up. She had never been able to figure out how horses could do that; whichever way she looked at it, it seemed contrary to reason. She thought it was very clever of them.

Yen Olass took her feet out of the luffle bag. They were not happy about that at all. Swiftly, she put on her foot bindings, then pulled on her boots and laced them up. Going to the mouth of the cave, she found a bright cold sun shining from a clear sky on silent snowdrifts. The drifted snow was deep enough to slow them down a bit, but too shallow to stop a determined horse and rider.

Here and there, trees showed vivid yellow wounds where branches had scabbed away. The rest of the world was white and black: white snow, black trees. So many trees. The corpses of the dead ones hulked out of the snow.

Though these woods were fairly open, and riders were seldom hindered by undergrowth, Yen Olass still felt there were far too many trees. There was something weird and unnatural about those columns of wood shafting up from the earth. Something rather evil about those gaunt grasping branches. Out riding, you always had to keep a sharp lookout in case a branch tore your head off. Then, stopping in a strange place, you could never tell whether something was hiding close by, watching. In the woods, she always felt enclosed, denied the open horizons of unlimited freedom which were her birthright.

As she stood there watching, she saw a small bird perch briefly on a bough, then fly away. In the snow there was a neat set of little paw marks: a fox had passed by that morning.

She heard the Ondrask grunt as he woke; a little later, he joined her at the cavemouth.

'Yesh-la, Ondrask,' said Yen Olass.

'Darjan-kray, Yen Olass,' he said, giving her both the formal response and the courtesy of her name.

They stood there shoulder to shoulder. Now that they had slept out the night in the same cave, she hardly noticed his odour; his smell was hers. Though she knew she would be fearfully late in getting back to Gendormargensis, that hardly seemed to matter. She felt . . . she felt almost happy. She would have felt better still if they could have stayed. She hated going back to the city.

'How has the hunting been?' said the Ondrask.

'Not so good,' said Yen Olass.

Game was scarce, but Yen Olass hardly cared. She came here to be free, not to kill things.

The sun glared on the absolute white of the snow. She had better smear her cheeks and eyelids with ashes before they set out. On a day like this, a day's riding could leave an unprotected person snowblind. She had better grease her boots, too; she had meant to do it the day before, but had forgotten.

Snut came to her for an apple, and she gave him one, then gave another to the Ondrask's horse. Both horses and humans would eat properly once they reached the hunting lodge at Brantzyn. Then they would push south, heading for Gendormargensis.

CHAPTER
Two

Name: Lord Pentalon Alagrace
Birth title: sal Pentalon Sorvolosa dan Alagrace nal Swedek quen Larsh
Family: Swedek quen Larsh, one of the High Houses of Sharla. Great-grandfather was Arnak Menster, Warmaster in Gendormargensis during the Wars of Dominion in which the Sharla Alliance was defeated by the northern horse tribes

Career: graduating from the Military Academy, spent twenty years with the Battle Corps in the Eastern Marches, ultimately having command of the Grey Cohorts. Subsequent service almost exclusively in the Diplomatic Service

In the year of the Blood Purge, Khmar 15, was in the Embassy which travelled to Molothair to negotiate an exchange of hostages with the Witchlord, Onosh Gulkan. Declined to return to Tameran, going into exile in Ashmolea, but in Khmar 17 accepted an invitation to become Lawmaker in Gendormargensis

*   *   *

Lord Alagrace urgently needed to find Yen Olass, but the oracle was missing.

He knew she had returned to Gendormargensis, as her shag pony was back in the stables attached to his city residence. Her weapons were back in the stable loft. By law, no woman was entitled to be in possession of weapons, so Yen Olass could not risk keeping bows, arrows or knives in her own quarters.

According to the stable hands, Yen Olass had returned the day before, shortly after dusk. Where she had gone thereafter, nobody knew. She had not checked in with Lord Alagrace's office, as she usually did, and a servant sent to her quarters in Moon Stallion Strait had returned without finding her. Now Lord Alagrace himself had come to tooth 44, Moon Stallion Strait, to see if he could find any clue which would tell him where the missing oracle was.

Lord Alagrace had never visited this street before, and had no idea what he might find. When Yen Olass had demanded quarters outside the reach of the Sisterhood, a little more than half a year earlier, Lord Alagrace had told his secretary to arrange it, and when Yen Olass had pronounced herself satisfied, he had not bothered himself about it further.

Tooth 44 turned out to be a cold, massive building in white marble. In the foyer, three old women were sorting dirty linen into baskets, which would later be picked up and taken to the Central Washhouse. And, on the stairway leading upwards, two soldiers were gaming with dice.

The soldiers leapt to attention when they saw Lord Alagrace. But it was far too late for that. Their helmets, their ceremonial shields and their spears were cluttered together in a corner; it was impossible for them to pretend they had been attending to their duty. Lord Alagrace took their names, then asked them what their duty was.

The soldiers told him the names of a dozen dependents of the last emperor, Onosh Gulkan, the Witchlord, who were now living in this building under what was supposed to be house arrest.

'And what really happens?' said Lord Alagrace.

'We make sure they're all in the building by evening. Other than that, nobody worries.'

'I see,' said Lord Alagrace.

This explained a lot. At least twice since his return from Ashmolea, he had thought he had been seeing ghosts when he had glimpsed people whom he had thought dead or banished long ago. When he had the time, he should really have an inventory made of the more important captives held in Gendormargensis.

'Who else lives here?' said Lord Alagrace.

The guards were able to tell him a few names. He vaguely recognised some of them. They were hostages and ambassadors from states which had now ceased to exist, indigent old generals who were waiting for the Lord Emperor Khmar to attend to their petitions for pensions, a couple of Khmar's distant relations from the far north—the place was a veritable bureaucratic rubbish bin for dumping problems which were not worth solving.

Lord Alagrace asked the guards a few more questions, then went upstairs. On the way up, he passed a group of old women who were going down, and one or two of them looked at him strangely. Puzzling over those glances, he realised he remembered them for the years when they had been young and beautiful—famous hetairai, the playthings of the powerful. Unless his memories deceived him, in his youth he himself had lusted after at least one of them—though always from a distance.

On reaching height 3, Lord Alagrace soon found room 7. Yen Olass, as a slave, was not permitted a door which could be closed against the world; instead, the interior of the room was guarded only by a free-standing screen, which he could walk around if he chose.

'Yen Olass?'

No answer.

Lord Alagrace went in and looked around. There was a bed, a chair, a window. Little else. A brazier, which was cold. A linen basket with a few soiled oddments sitting in the bottom of it. A linen chest for clean clothing. A battered old klon. A wobbly side table with a few oddments on it—some stones, a couple of broken shells, a scrap of cheap amber with some dirt flaws running through it—he couldn't imagine why she kept such rubbish. On the bed, folded sheets, folded blankets and a scruffy quilt, which was leaking feathers.

Looking under the bed—his knees creaked alarmingly as he knelt down—Lord Alagrace discovered an oracle's nordigin. There was also a felt-lined box containing a copy of the Book of the Sisterhood. Lord Alagrace, who had never perused this classic statement of the Sisterhood's doctrine, took it out and had a look at it. But the script was too small for him to read. These days, relays of scribes were kept busy copying out vital documents in a big, bold hand, so he could consult them at his leisure.

Disappointed, Lord Alagrace returned the Book of the Sisterhood to its box. He knew he could always requisition a copy, then have it read aloud to him, or copied out in a hand big enough for his deteriorating vision to cope with, but he would never do that, because he would have been ashamed to show so much interest in a woman thing.

When Lord Alagrace left the room he saw, some distance down the corridor, a rheumatic old woman standing in the doorway of her quarters, leaning on a stick and watching him. On the off-chance, he went down the corridor to ask her if she knew where Yen Olass was.

She invited him into her room, which was small, and crowded with antiquated furniture, tapestries and carpets. She claimed that she did indeed know Yen Olass. She pointed to a large, amber-coloured cat which was asleep on her bed. The cat, she claimed, belonged to Yen Olass. Once the oracle came back from 'the world of her wandering', she would reclaim the cat, which was called Lefrey. No, Yen Olass had not been in the building for the last few days. No, nobody could say where she might be.

The woman then started to get querulous, complaining about the cold of the building, the irregular linen service, the state of the communal ablutions, the rats she had seen in the latrines. Lord Alagrace excused himself.

Leaving the building, he passed a blank-faced woman who walked with an odd, jerking shuffle. He shuddered. Someone unfamiliar with the history of Gendormargensis might have mistaken the woman for a cripple or a victim of terminal syphilis, but Lord Alagrace knew exactly what was responsible for that peculiar gait—and that face washed clean of all character and emotion. The woman was an ofika, the first he had seen for years.

During the reign of Onosh Gulkan, the emperor who had earned himself the title of Witchlord, the running of Gendormargensis had been left very much in the hands of the powerful dralkosh Bao Gahai. Drawing strength from a liaison with the powers of the dead, she could destroy anyone who opposed her, turning them into an ofika, a semi-sentient automaton which would, to the best of its remaining ability, obey without question.

Bao Gahai, who must be at least sixty by now, was said to be still alive, living in the court of Onosh Gulkan in the city of Molothair on the island of Alozay, one of the Safrak Islands of the inland waters known as the Swelaway Sea.

Thinking of Bao Gahai, Lord Alagrace realised who the old woman with the amber cat was. Her name was . . . no, her name still escaped him. But he remembered when he had seen her last. She had been one of Bao Gahai's servants and, once, at great personal danger, and seeking no reward for herself, she had sheltered him from the wrath of the dralkosh.

Lord Alagrace hesitated, and thought about going back. But the demands of the day were many, and he could not linger any longer.

*   *   *

When Lord Alagrace got back to Valslada, his city residence, he found a messenger waiting. The messenger had come from Lord Alagrace's office in Karling Drask.

'So what have you got to tell me?' said Lord Alagrace.

'My lord, your secretary has sent me to tell you that an important communication is waiting for you at Karling Drask.'

Lord Alagrace swore, more from habit than anything else, and set out for Karling Drask. His secretary had received his basic training many years ago in the secret police of the Witchlord Onosh Gulkan, and had never been able to shake his obsession with secrecy.

Arriving at Karling Drask, Lord Alagrace found the communication was a letter from the Ondrask of Noth, demanding that he come personally to the Ondrask's yashram to collect Yen Olass. Lord Alagrace recognized the handwriting. The Ondrask was every bit as illiterate as the Lord Emperor Khmar. He had dictated the letter to Yen Olass Ampadara, who had written it out in a large, bold hand, knowing that Lord Alagrace was no longer able to focus well enough at short distances to read small handwriting.

With Khmar in the south, Lord Alagrace was the supreme authority in and around Gendormargensis. The Ondrask had no right to give him orders. Furthermore, Lord Alagrace was busy. He had all the responsibilities which went with the Lawmaker's office, and, while the Lord Commander of the Imperial City was ostensibly Volaine Persaga Haveros, that was only a matter of form, and Lord Alagrace handled all the administrative decisions which went with that position, too. However, the Ondrask called, and the Ondrask had influence with Khmar—so Lord Alagrace went.

Now, at least, he knew where to find the oracle Yen Olass Ampadara.

*   *   *

At the Ondrask's yashram, Lord Alagrace found Yen Olass sharing a meal with Losh Negis. He could hardly believe his eyes. However, Losh Negis explained that Yen Olass had given him hospitality in the wilderness, which made everything clear; a true Yarglat, like the Ondrask, had to repay such a debt, even if the debt was to a female slave.

'But when you come back,' said Losh Negis to Lord Alagrace, 'she will be cooking, not eating. I will make her my skona-pana-tay.'

Yen Olass flinched when the Ondrask made that little joke, and the Ondrask's women—or those of them who were within hearing—muttered amongst themselves. In Eparget, 'skona-pana-tay' meant, literally, 'young silk triangle'; the words were usually translated into other languages as 'silk girl', and formed the courtesy title of a particular type of whore.

Lord Alagrace got the impression that Yen Olass was glad to leave with him.

*   *   *

Lord Alagrace and Yen Olass argued all the way to the city of Gendormargensis. Yen Olass, for her part, was still upset because Lord Alagrace had earlier told the Ondrask that she had the power to fix the problem he had with Haveros and the horses.

Lord Alagrace was furious with the solution Yen Olass had found. She had persuaded the Ondrask to tell his follower Chonjara to watch Haveros until he got the chance to destroy his enemy—perhaps by challenging him to a duel.

'I do not want any more duels!' said Lord Alagrace.

'That,' said Yen Olass, 'is not my problem.'

'Wrong,' said Lord Alagrace. 'I've been looking for you all day so you can help me to stop a duel.'

'Is that so?' said Yen Olass. 'And who are the fighters?'

'Lord Denesk and Tonaganuk.'

Lonth Denesk was the father of Volaine Persaga Haveros, the apostate Yarglat clansman who had been daring enough to steal horses which the Ondrask had dedicated for sacrifice. Tonaganuk was the father of Chonjara, the Ondrask's follower who had, all unknowingly, bought those horses and butchered them for his banquet.

'Tell me,' said Yen Olass, 'how did the fathers come to be involved in the quarrel of the sons?'

'It all started when I tried to solve our little problem . . .'

'Yes,' said Yen Olass. 'I thought it might be something like that.'

'There are women in Gendormargensis,' said Lord Alagrace, 'who have had their tongues torn out for less than that.'

'The Sisterhood,' said Yen Olass tartly, 'would not approve of such damage to the Sisterhood's property.'

She was reminding him that they were not master and slave. They were, if anything, partners in crime. Lord Alagrace sighed. When he had to work with flawed tools like Yen Olass, it made things very difficult. But then, everything was difficult these days.

During the Blood Purge, in which the Yarglat had run amok in Gendormargensis and elsewhere, they had killed out almost the entire intellectual elite of the Collosnon Empire. The administration of the capital had gone into the hands of one of Khmar's cousins—briefly. Lord Alagrace was still trying to repair the damage.

'Tell me about the fight,' said Yen Olass. 'Are they going to use axes?'

'They're not going to fight,' said Lord Alagrace. 'They're going to apologise to each other, then go back home and behave themselves.'

'After they've hugged and kissed,' said Yen Olass, in one of the moments of whimsy which she usually hid from him.

'If you can make them hug and kiss, then go ahead,' said Lord Alagrace. 'But first let me tell you the problem . . .'

CHAPTER
Three

Gendormargensis: capital of Collosnon Empire; military and administrative city situated on Yolantarath River, commanding strategic gap between Sarapine Ranges and Balardade Massif. Extensive fortifications and notable archives; centre of fur trade; famous for annual horse fair and river tournament; pop. (est. Khmar 18) 273,460.

*   *   *

In the eighteenth year of his reign, the Lord Emperor Khmar was absent from the city of Gendormargensis. Accompanied by his second son, Meddon, he was at war, forcing the command of the Collosnon Empire south to the shores of the Pale. Nevertheless, even though the Lord Emperor rode elsewhere, the customary intrigues of court life continued.

Most secret and most scandalous of all those intrigues was the liaison between Volaine Persaga Haveros and the Princess Quenerain. By now, many people knew that Haveros had taken the Ondrask's horses, but few would have thought him rash enough to bed the Princess Quenerain.

Haveros, a high-caste warrior and the hero of seven campaigns, was Lord Commander of the Imperial City, answering only to the Lawmaker Lord Alagrace during Khmar's absence. Haveros was a big man with a big-built appetite for food, laughter, song and bawdry. He was also a drinking man, with a drinker's broken-red veins in his battle-scarred face: but his alcoholic thirst had yet to destroy his virility.

The Princess Quenerain, nineteen years old, and virginal more in deed than in thought, had pearl-smooth hands and milk-warm thighs. When she conspired with Haveros, her eyes did all the talking; before their first words kissed, they knew their destiny.

And so it came to pass.

While her father was at war in the south of the continent of Tameran, the Princess Quenerain lay with the warrior Haveros, offending against both law and custom.

The princess had already been ordained as head of the Rite of Purification, which was important for both war and peace, as it served to absolve soldiers from war guilt; the dignity of the Rite demanded an unblemished virgin to oversee its rituals.

But the Princess Quenerain did not think of this as she grappled with Haveros, her breathing flushed, his flesh defying gravity, lips closing, heat clenching, thighs thrusting, her hands clutching his rhythm home to hers.

And afterwards, fever relapsing toward sleep, neither of these two drowsy and sated animals thought of anything in particular as they lay there, heat declining, pulse slackening, sweat cooling, vague disconnected images already prefiguring their dreams.

This act of copulation was rash but not suicidal. The lovers had secured their privacy by choosing to fornicate within the confines of the Princess Quenerain's private quarters in Karling Drask, the War Archives complex; for contraceptive protection, Haveros had consented to wear a hand-tailored condom fashioned from a section of the intestines of a reindeer.

And so they slept in peace, untroubled by an intimations of disaster; they both knew exactly what they could get away with —or thought they did.

Elsewhere, snuggled down under her dreamquilt, her body burdened by the encroaching weight of her cat Lefrey, Yen

Olass Ampadara was already asleep. And dreaming. No man lay beside her, and no lover figured in her dreams; though she was now officially a virgin, as a child she had been gang-raped by a dozen of Khmar's soldiers, and had subsequently failed to develop romantic yearnings.

Yen Olass was dreaming of a rabbit. This small, frightened animal lay mewling in the snow. It had been skinned; thin purple veins obtruded from its rasp-raw flesh.

Yen Olass dreamt that she cradled this hubbly little thing deep within her comfort, snuggled it down into the feather-warm quilting of her weather jacket, and soothed the air with a growing song which made the raw flesh renew its bond with a pelt of luxuriant fur.

Floating from dreamsleep toward wakefulness, Yen Olass imagined herself, for a moment, as Earthmother, healer of the hurts and pains of the universe, infinitely tender and unstintingly generous.

Then she woke, and knew otherwise.

*   *   *

Dawn.

The Yolantarath River lay empty-wide outside the battlements of Gendormargensis. Sheer-frozen, as it had been since Winterblade, it lay beneath drifts of snow; the rising sun spiked both ice and snow with that blinding dazzle known, in Yarglat parlance, as 'caltrops'.

Sentries guarding the walls of the Imperial City stamped their feet, and watched a few early-rising fishermen trooping onto the river to reopen holes which the night cold would have sealed.

Engulfed in a warrior's embrace, the Princess Quenerain slept, dreaming of pumping honey.

The warrior, Volaine Persaga Haveros, woke, and sniffed first the hair then the flesh of the woman who slept in his arms. Disentangling himself from her embrace, he dressed; he had no intention of washing on a morning as cold as this one. He armed himself, then left.

The corridors of Karling Drask were utterly silent. Haveros strode along those deserted marble avenues, paying no attention to the mosaics which adorned the walls. He was thinking of all the things he had to do that morning. His father, Lonth Denesk, was due to fight Tonaganuk later that morning. The fight might spark off a clan battle within Gendormargensis. If that happened, Haveros wanted to win the war. Even now, his people would be assembling in the clan drillhall; Haveros would see that they were properly armed and instructed before the duel started.

Haveros wished Lord Alagrace had not involved his father in this business. What had the old fool been thinking of, calling Lonth Denesk and Tonaganuk together? He should have realised that was the worst possible thing he could have done. The old man was slipping.

Haveros reached the exit, and departed from Karling Drask, scarcely acknowledging the salutes of the guards on duty there. The sun was bright, the sky high: it was a good day to die.

*   *   *

Alone in a frost-cold room, Yen Olass woke. There was someone outside the screen.

'Who is it?' she said.

Was someone about to demand a reading? That would be unusual. While Yen Olass sometimes gave readings of other people living in tooth 44, most of them observed the conventions and made appointments well in advance. Nevertheless, while unusual, it would not be unprecedented; Yen Olass had no right to deny any patron at any hour of the day or night.

Her visitor slipped round the screen, entering the room: it was only Nuana.

'Where have you been?' said Nuana.

'Molychosh,' said Yen Olass curtly, using the Eparget word which meant 'pasturing', and, by extension, denoted retirement or a holiday.

'Sa?!' said Nuana, using the generalized expression for surprise and disbelief. 'An oracle, pasturing? Since when did the Sisterhood treat you so sweetly?'

'What do you want?' said Yen Olass.

Her voice was sharp. She had more than enough to cope with today, without being bothered by Nuana.

'You know what I want.'

'I haven't got it.'

'You must get it!'

'I don't for you or anyone,' said Yen Olass, stretching, allowing herself to luxuriate in the quilted warmth of her bed.

'He beats me,' said Nuana. 'Because you don't get it, he beats me.'

'Get out,' said Yen Olass.

But Nuana Nanalako, a sun-dark Southsearcher woman, was not disposed of that easily.

'He doesn't just beat me either,' said Nuana.

'You heard me,' said Yen Olass. 'Get out!'

Her cat Lefrey, awakened by these female voices, stirred, stretched, then curled down deeper into the layered warmth of the featherbed dreamquilt.

'You're the lucky one,' said Nuana, advancing. 'He gave you away. You never had to . . .'

'What?'

'He's a filthy old man,' said Nuana.

Yen Olass got out of bed and stood on the stone floor in her sleep-shift, shivering in the biting morning chill.

'You get out of here,' said Yen Olass, 'or I'll rip your face apart.'

Yen Olass was bigger and stronger than Nuana. And she was angry. After being nagged by Nuana for half a season, Yen Olass had had enough. Unless Nuana retreated—now!—there would be a regular scratching match.

Nuana, confronted by an angry and advancing oracle, broke and ran. They were both slaves, but if they were caught brawling, Nuana would be the one who went under the spikes. Even the high-born could not lay hands on an oracle with impunity. When Nuana had gone, Yen Olass stood trembling with anger.

Not for the first time, Yen Olass wished she had a proper door which she could close and bolt against the world.

*　　　*　　　*

Elsewhere, the warrior Chonjara was already up and about. He had been sharpening a battle-axe. Now he tested the blade: and was satisfied.

*　　　*　　　*

Alone in her room, Yen Olass attended to her ablutions, then broke her fast with a barley-meal cake. All things considered, she would rather have been in her cave to the north, eking out a bare existence with pemican and milk curds.

With breakfast over, Yen Olass settled her mind by meditation, contemplating the everspan slumber of the bubbles of light encapsulated in her piece of amber, which was one of the few beautiful things she owned.

Her day was commanded by a single duty, which was to attend a duel at the Enskandalon Square. Seeking to disarm a possible conflict between Haveros and Chonjara, Lord Alagrace had banqueted the fathers of those two famous warriors, hoping that he could persuade the fathers to tell the sons to end their quarrel. Instead, the fathers had taken up that quarrel themselves, and were now preparing to fight to the death.

Before combat, Yen Olass would give a reading for the fighters. This was no delicate matter of statecraft or high politics; she only had to provide two arrogant old men with an excuse to apologise to each other, and thus to evade the intolerable demands of honour.

With her meditations finished, Yen Olass donned her outdoor clothes, tucked a rug under her arm and picked up her nordigin, the lacquered carrier box safeguarding her Casting Board and her 365 Indicators. Thus equipped, she made her way to the Enskandalon Square. She was the first to arrive: there was no other life in the square except for a few old women, dressed in black, who were sweeping away the snow on the far side of that empty expanse of white.

Yen Olass had arrived very early, because that was her duty: the Sisterhood believed that an oracle should avoid the temptation of making a grand entrance, and accordingly ruled that an oracle should arrive first, wherever possible. She unfolded her rug of double-layer yaquern fur, and settled herself to wait.

After a while, someone entered on the far side of the Enskandalon Square. Slowly, the figure trekked across the snow, eventually revealing itself as the text-master Eldegen Terzanagel. That worthy was dressed in grey furs; his hair was cropped short and dyed grey if it was not grey by nature; he wore a severely-disciplined short-cropped grey beard, and about his garments hung a rope of grey beads, a tuft of grey feathers and one skull, painted grey.

'Is that you?' said Terzanagel.

'Whom were you seeking?' said Yen Olass coldly.

'So it's you,' said Terzanagel, her voice having confirmed an identity which had been put in doubt by snuggling furs and three wrap-around scarves. 'Did Nuana speak to you?'

'Your whorebit slave intruded on my quarters this morning,' said Yen Olass. 'Send her again, and you'll get her back with her face torn off.'

'Yen Olass,' said Terzanagel, managing to sound hurt. 'Why so fierce? Haven't I always done well by you?'

In a sense, he had. When Yen Olass had arrived in Gendor-margensis as part of the plunder from Monogail, Terzanagel had purchased her at auction. This wilful slavegirl had then resisted his advances—to be precise, she had bitten his penis, drawing blood, and had punched him in the testicles. he could have had her skinned alive for that, and many men would have done so without hesitation; however, instead of taking revenge, he had donated her to the sisterhood, and had paid for the five years of study at the Imperial School needed to equip her to be an oracle instead of just one of the Sisterhood's working slaves.

However, Yen Olass had suffered badly when she had been initiated into the Sisterhood. Besides:

'Anything you did was for your own purposes,' said Yen Olass.

She knew very well that Terzanagel's lifetime ambition was to journey to the Stepping Stone Islands of the southern continent, Argan, so he could complete his research on the life and times of that famous poet of antiquity, Saba Yavendar. Nuana Nanalako came from that region, and Terzanagel, needing someone to teach him the local dialect, had spent two years and a lot of money acquiring that Southsearcher woman.

Unfortunately for Terzanagel, the law forbade text-masters to leave Tameran; to fulfil his ambitions, he constantly sought favour and influence, and his every act of good citizenship was calculated to further this quest. It was said that the Sisterhood could not be bribed; nevertheless, ambitious men did well to ingratiate themselves with that school of oracles.

'Yen Olass, I'm not asking much. All I want is a map.'

'Patience melts snow,' said Yen Olass, which was a local idiom meaning all things come to those who wait.

'Yen Olass, I don't have much time. I'm an old man.'

'Tratz!' said Yen Olass, using a word meaning gelding's testicles—or, to translate idiom into idiom, horse feathers.

'I'm sixty years old!'

'My great grandfather was ninety on the day he died—and he died fighting. I saw.'

Terzanagel obviously had more to say, but was silent, for

someone else was approaching. Footsteps crunched over the snow behind Yen Olass; she did not move, but as the newcomer entered her field of vision she saw it was the Ondrask of Noth.

Today, the high priest of the horse cult was dressed in his full ceremonial regalia. He wore animal skins garnished with a gaudy array of rainbow feathers, beads, skulls, miniature knives and obsidian arrowheads, and, even on a day like this, when the cold tended to subdue most smells, he stank generously. Today, the smell of rancid fat was dominant.

'Brother!' said the Ondrask, embracing Terzanagel.

'Brother,' responded Terzanagel, as ritual required; he engaged the Ondrask's embrace with something less than enthusiasm.

They were brothers in name only; the ritual demanding their embrace celebrated the historical links between the priesthood of Noth and the modern-day text-master, links which the text-masters, for their part, would have been happy to forget.

While the Ondrask did his best to prolong the embrace—knowing exactly how it discomforted the text-master—General Chonjara arrived. This fierce, broad-shouldered man of thirty-five was overshadowed by a hulking heavy-weight bruiser—Karahaj Nan Nulador, his bodyguard. Nan Nulador now dropped down on one knee in front of Yen Olass.

'No,' said Yen Olass.

'Give him what he wants,' said Chonjara.

Earlier, the text-master Eldegen Terzanagel had been unable to tell that Yen Olass was Yen Olass because of all her winter-weight clothing. But Chonjara and his bodyguard knew her for an oracle: the lacquered box at her side betrayed her calling. Reluctantly, Yen Olass reached out and touched Karahaj Nan Nulador on the forehead, dabbing at him lightly with her layers of wool. And she said, as the Sura Woman does:

'Peace for your daylight.'

And Nan Nulador was content.

Yen Olass would happily have spent all day handing out blessings and doing other forbidden things—reading fortunes, interpreting dreams and making charms—but the Sisterhood rigorously discouraged any and all involvement in the kind of occult practices which might lead an oracle to become mistaken for a dralkosh.

An oracle's work must necessarily have a gloss of mystery—men accepted the intervention of magic when they would have

crucified any woman who dared present herself as an arbitrator
—but the Sisterhood was determined that the order must not
become entangled with religion, superstition or the practice of
evil arts.

As the Book of the Sisterhood put it:

'The Method is not a way of Power or a way of Decision.
The Method calls on nothing outside itself, for the oracle exer-
cises no Power and makes no Decision. Instead, when a patron
so requests, an oracle enters a conflict at the centre, making of
herself a pivot. The Art is no Summoning, no Shaping. It serves
only to reveal possibilities.'

Now more people were starting to arrive. Some of them were
Yarglat clansmen, bearing weapons, and clearly spoiling for a
fight. Others were league riders, foreign mercenaries who gave
their loyalty to Lord Alagrace alone. Today, Lord Alagrace
could not use the army to keep order, since most of the army's
officers were men of the Yarglat. However, his league riders
were reliable, and their presence would lessen the possibility of
outright slaughter in Enskandalon Square.

Yen Olass looked for the two old men, Lonth Denesk and
Tonaganuk. Neither had yet arrived. Yen Olass closed her eyes,
and imagined:

Snow.

Wafting snow beneath ricepaper skies. A world of frozen
mud, silence, and bloodless horizons stretching away across
leagues of ice and tundra toward distant infinities of cloud. Between her thighs, the bulk of a long-haired grender-strander, its
travelling rhythm urging past a herd of musk ox, past huge
browsing beasts with snorting breath—

'Lord Alagrace ordered you here, didn't he?' said Chonjara.

Yen Olass, her reveries thus interrupted, opened her eyes.

'I am here,' she said.

'My father certainly didn't ask for you,' said Chonjara. 'So it
must have been Alagrace. Unless Lonth Denesk . . .'

'Haveros, maybe,' said Nan Nulador.

'No,' said Chonjara. 'He was boasting last night about how
his father would kill mine. It must have been Alagrace. Isn't
that so, girl?'

As they were speaking Eparget, the dominant dialect of the
northern horse tribes, and thus the ruling language of Gendormargensis, the word Chonjara used for 'girl' was 'lakux', a

word also meaning 'fully', and carrying implications of naivety, inexperience and frivolity.

And Yen Olass could hardly answer 'I am a woman', for the word for woman, 'Narinii'—a word also meaning 'mare'—implied a mature, sexually experienced female of proven fertility.

Yen Olass felt hurt. She did not analyse her pain—the Sisterhood discouraged introspection—but the dynamic producing her pain could reasonably be stated like this:

I am Yen Olass. I am not a girl. But not a woman (narinii). Language has no word for me. Unless I choose to call myself fench oddock ('thinning blood', meaning 'old maid' or 'crone', or—sometimes in a different context, and sometimes not—'soup stock'.) But I'm not that. So what am I? Myself. Alone.

'Why so silent, girl?' said Chonjara.

'Do you wish for a reading?' said Yen Olass, who saw that he was one of those who hated the Sisterhood, and that she could match insult for insult by treating him as if he were a patron.

'In another time and another place, I'd rip you open and rape you,' said Chonjara.

'My lord!' said Nan Nulador—and Yen Olass saw that General Chonjara's bodyguard was shocked.

For that matter, she was shocked herself.

And so, perhaps, was Chonjara, for he looked around uneasily, seeing who might have overheard him. The Ondrask of Noth certainly had, but that hardly mattered, for the high priest of the horse cult had no love for the Sisterhood. Yen Olass doubted that the brief time they had shared together counted for anything now that they were back in Gendormargensis. Who else had heard? The text-master, Eldegen Terzanagel. That, for Chonjara, might be unfortunate.

Sensing her advantage, Yen Olass pressed it home:

'In another time, another place, healthy young sons might take care of their senile old fathers instead of encouraging them to hack each other to pieces with battleaxes.'

Chonjara turned on her, and now it was Yen Olass's turn to realise she had gone too far. Chonjara's face was white with anger, for she had insulted his father with an unpardonable expression: in Eparget, 'shasha', the word for 'senile', meant not just old and weak-minded, but also implied impotence, incontinence, coprophagic habits and a tendency to indulge in a desire to practise fellatio on dead sheep. Among other things.

A confrontation was prevented by the arrival of Lord Ala-grace, Lonth Denesk and Tonaganuk, together with a crowd of underlings, onlookers, friends and functionaries. Amongst the new arrivals was Haveros, Lonth Denesk's son, who looked around, frowning when he saw how many league riders were on the scene.

Lonth Denesk and Tonaganuk were relaxed and jovial, and seemed to have been drinking a little. Yen Olass realized Lord Alagrace had settled the matter with some last-minute diplo-macy; in all probability, the old men had been draining a cup of friendship just before coming to the Enskandalon Square.

Yen Olass knew Lord Alagrace would be pleased with his success. Any duel amongst the Yarglat was dangerous to the peace of Gendormargensis. And, in itself, duelling claimed the lives of too°many bright young officers, and allowing old men to kill each other encouraged the young.

Yen Olass knew that Lonth Denesk and Tonaganuk must be every bit as glad as Lord Alagrace. When the Lawmaker had banqueted them, they had got drunk; siding with their sons, they had called each other 'liar', 'coward' and 'woman', and then they had called each other out. Sober, they must have cursed their stupidity—they had been comrades in battle for twenty years in their younger days.

Nevertheless, unrelenting shame would ride the man who shied away from combat; an excuse was needed to avoid a fight to the death, and Yen Olass, at Lord Alagrace's request, was going to provide that excuse.

The two old men composed themselves while a herald de-clared the details of the challenge; then Lord Alagrace, surpris-ing nobody, intervened:

'Fight if you wish,' said Lord Alagrace, 'but before combat, please give your consideration to a reading.'

Lonth Denesk and Tonaganuk both agreed. General Chonjara scowled. For the reading, Yen Olass threw back her hood, unwrapped her scarves and took off her mittens; she opened her laquered box, took out the Casting Board and slotted its two halves together, shook the 365 Indicators in their leather bag, then began.

Yen Olass placed sixteen Indicators on the Casting Board. What did those sixteen ivory tablets tell her? Nothing. The Book of the Sisterhood taught methods and ways of reading the Indicators, but those were only for the guidance of novices;

most skilled oracles used the Indicators only as the starting point, and completed the reading by intuition.

Yen Olass used neither Indicators nor intuition; she had planned her campaign beforehand, devising four sequences of pointless destruction and two of reconciliation. Now, with her planning done, she let these images possess her, and become visions; as a skilled orator, she submitted to the eloquence of her own words, permitting them their own life of passion.

Nobody would dare interrupt until she was finished; here, in the public eye, she was guaranteed absolute freedom from intrusion. Her own room in Moon Stallion Strait had never provided her such security.

'A horse,' said Yen Olass. 'A stallion. Rider of winds. Women tremble before him. A rider. Woman-master. Who can say which is which? Masters of all horizons. Only the sun can ride them out. Rider tells the horse to stay—now! Stay still. A fly. What? Nothing. No, a fly.'

And now she no longer saw the Casting Board, the Indicators, Chonjara's fur-lined boots or the people in the Enskandalon Square. Her eyes were unfocused, staring through reality. Her head was lifted, her voice pitched to carry over the heads of those who listened. Talking to whom? To what? She saw the horse, and she saw the fly.

'Just that. No more. A fly. Tail. A whisk of a tail to brush away—what? It was nothing. No, a fly. But the horse moved. And the rider, suddenly angry—gashed home. Red blade. Scream choked on blood rolled up and over, four legs, gone. Dead meat. All for a fly. Blood on the blade, blood—'

Yen Olass screamed.

A cry of horror broke loose from her throat as something shattered her vision.

What?

She saw Chonjara's foot still in the air, still rising, her Casting Board breaking apart, the ivory Indicators scattering.

And she heard Lord Alagrace, his voice a roar of outrage:

'Chonjara!'

'Children play girl-games,' said Chonjara, his voice thick with anger—and with something close to hatred. 'Men have other ways to work the world.'

Lord Alagrace now had no choice. The Law of Readings compelled him, as the most senior person present—Lawmaker in the absence of the Lord Emperor Khmar, and hence senior even to Volaine Haveros, the Lord Commander of Gendormargensis—to ask the patrons to name the doom of the criminal who had interrupted the oracle.

'Lonth Denesk,' said Lord Alagrace. 'Tonaganuk. This individual has interrupted your reading. I ask you—'

'There is no reading,' said Tonaganuk.

And with those words he committed himself to mortal combat.

There was nothing else he could have done.

For the reading to continue, Chonjara's fate would first have to be settled. For interrupting a reading, he could be killed out of hand, if the patrons so desired. Tonaganuk could only spare his son from punishment if Lonth Denesk agreed. Doubtless Lonth Denesk would agree to pardon Chonjara—but then Chonjara would be shamed for life by the fact that he had been pardoned by a man who was, officially, his father's enemy.

So to save his son's good name, Tonaganuk was now forced to declare the reading at an end, and fight Lonth Denesk, as was his privilege; the conventions governing readings allowed any patron to break off the proceedings at any point.

Lord Alagrace did not swear, but he came close to doing so. It was well known that Lord Alagrace was the mentor of Celadric, Khmar's son, the young man who was now proving himself such a master of the skills of negotiation, arbitration and diplomacy; Lord Alagrace, although he was an old man, was committed to the new order which he saw would in time replace the reckless combat-law of the horse tribes.

Now, despite his best efforts, Lord Alagrace was about to see two old men hack each other to death for the sake of a system of blood and honour already at least a generation out of date.

Yen Olass sat on her yaquern fur rug, weeping quietly, more from shock than from anything else. The crowd fell back; General Chonjara stepped forward to present his father Tonaganuk with battle-axe and shield. Volaine Haveros carried similar gifts to his own father, Lonth Denesk. Chonjara's bodyguard, Karahaj Nan Nulador, was down on his hands and knees in the snow, gathering the scattered Indicators.

'Thank you,' said Yen Olass, as Nan Nulador laid the ivory tablets before her.

Nan Nulador made a sign of reverence—a fist unfolding to five fingers, meaning 'this (all) which I have is yours'—and then withdrew.

And Yen Olass ceased weeping.

And watched.

The two old men had taken off their gloves and had shed their heavy coats. Lord Alagrace was trying to talk to Tonaganuk, pitching his voice too low for anyone else to hear; unfortunately, Tonaganuk was somewhat deaf, and was finding it hard to make any sense whatsoever out of what Lord Alagrace was saying. Lonth Denesk peered at them with rheumy eyes, clutching the haft of his battle-axe in swollen earthroot fingers.

'Come on,' said a voice from the crowd of spectators. 'What are we waiting for?'

Yen Olass identified the speaker immediately: York, the youngest of Khmar's four sons. Eighteen years old, an uncouth brawler with a passion for hunting and fighting. Lord Alagrace abandoned his efforts to avert violence, and withdrew; the duel commenced.

First, silence.

A pause.

And Yen Olass waited for York to speak again—but he knew better than that, and held his tongue.

A little snow feathered down on the light wind. The old men glowered at each other and began to circle, slowly, moving their feet deliberately. In the cold air, their breath snorted out in little puffs of steam. Both were having trouble supporting the weight of shield and battle-axe. Light glittered as the spur-bright axe blades wavered.

Then they swung at each other. Both stumbled as blades clattered against shields. They clashed again, neither strong enough nor fast enough to strike a decisive blow. A third clash left both unblooded. Lumbering forward, labouring axes through the air, brunting attack after attack with their shields, they hacked and parried.

The old men began to sweat. Both were gasping now, gasping like drowning men. Their faces were wet, white hair dripping with sweat, sweat running down into white beards. Then Tonaganuk mustered enough strength to strike one formidable blow which drove his opponent's shield back.

First blood.

Lonth Denesk bled from his upper lip, just slightly injured by the shield jolting backwards into his face. But now Tonaganuk sensed his weakness. This was the moment. They clashed again, axe against shield, shield against axe. But now, instead of drawing back to strike again, Tonaganuk pushed forward, using his shield to shove Lonth Denesk backwards.

Taken by surprise, Lonth Denesk tried to brace himself—but slipped, and went down. Tonaganuk gashed his axe home. There was the sharp sound of shattering teeth. Lonth Denesk struggled, trying to rise, his limbs flailing. Tonaganuk brought his axe down, ripping his enemy's scalp open. Lonth Denesk, blood streaming down his face and straining through his beard, struggled up into a sitting position, tried to say something. But the axe hacked into his throat.

And Yen Olass, watching with fascination—she could not help herself—saw, to her amazement, that Lonth Denesk was still alive, though blood was flowing freely and his wound gaped his trachea open. Lonth Denesk rolled over, got to his hands and knees, tried to rise—

But—

Yen Olass squeezed her eyes shut. But nothing could shut out the sounds. Lonth Denesk did not cry out—could not, with his throat hacked open—but she heard the butchering thuds of heavy steel cleaving home to bone. It went on for what seemed like a long time.

Then it was over.

Slowly, Yen Olass opened her eyes.

Lonth Denesk lay dead in bloodstained snow. Tonaganuk stood alone. He had dropped his shield, he had dropped his battle-axe, and he was—clutching his chest. As she watched, Tonaganuk sank to the ground, crushed down to his knees by disabling agony. Chonjara stepped forward.

'Leave him!' said Haveros.

If Haveros had stayed silent, nobody would have objected if Chonjara had gone to his father's aid. But now that Haveros had spoken, Chonjara could not intervene—Haveros was insisting that the tradition be followed, and the tradition was that a duel was not over until both men were dead or one had walked away, a victor, without any assistance.

Back in the old days, when the horse tribes had been nomadic wanderers instead of the rulers of an empire, this tradition had sometimes meant that a wounded victor died slowly in full view of the witnesses, unable to crawl away from the body of the man he had killed. But those were the old days: in Gendormargensis, it was unusual for anyone to enforce that ruling.

But now Haveros did.

And so it was that Tonaganuk died, slowly, of a heart attack, expiring in the Enskandalon Square under the eyes of his son Chonjara, who was forbidden to take those few paces forward to be by his father's side.

CHAPTER
Four

A light snow was falling; the spectators were starting to disperse. Lonth Denesk's bloodstained corpse was an ugly sight, so Haveros removed his cloak and used it to shroud his father's body. Haveros looked strangely lost.

It was very quiet.

Chonjara gathered his father's body into his arms, surprised to find it weighed so little. All his life, Tonaganuk had seemed to him the ultimate warlord, and now . . .

As Karahaj Nan Nulador joined his master, Chonjara quietly ordered him to take the body to the house of Quenstain Garkers, an old family friend living close to the Enskandalon Square. Nan Nulador bowed, took Tonaganuk's body in his own arms, then departed, carrying his burden lightly.

Chonjara strode away, determined to be the first to reach his mother with the news. That was his duty. And since his father was dead, it was now also his duty to take over his father's place, and become in his own right the ultimate warlord . . .

Seeing Chonjara leaving, Lord Alagrace hesitated, uncertain as to his priorities. It was vital that he speak with both Chonjara and Haveros as soon as possible, to make sure they understood he would have their heads if their two clans went to war with each other in Gendormargensis. He also wanted to protect his tame oracle by making an immediate personal report to the Sisterhood, explaining that the fault lay with Chonjara. Otherwise, Yen Olass might be interrogated by the Silent One, and that formidable lady, reviewing Yen Olass's performance, might uncover some very embarrassing facts.

Lord Alagrace, disturbed to see how shocked and shaken Yen Olass looked, went to her first, though he knew he had little time to spare to comfort her. As he reached her, the Ondrask of Noth came to his side.

'You're needed elsewhere,' said the Ondrask, fully aware that today's killing might precipitate a disastrous feud. 'I'll take her home.'

Lord Alagrace was surprised. The Ondrask was a most unexpected ally.

'If you want to help,' said Lord Alagrace, 'come with me when I talk to Chonjara.'

'Talk to him yourself,' said the Ondrask, suddenly turning rude and abrupt.

'As you wish,' said Lord Alagrace, who was sure he could cope with or without the Ondrask's help.

Yen Olass allowed herself to be led from the Enskandalon Square. She was in a daze. To her surprise, she found herself walking along hand in hand with the Ondrask. She so seldom touched another human being that this was something of a shock. The Ondrask had never touched her when they were together in the cave or at his yashram.

'Have you got my things?' said Yen Olass.

'Here,' said the Ondrask.

He had her rug tucked under his free arm, and he was carrying her nordigin containing her Casting Board and Indicators.

When they reached room 7 on height 3 of tooth 44 on Moon Stallion Strait, Yen Olass realized that the Ondrask had known exactly where they were going, anticipating every turning, and leading the way into her room without being told it was hers.

He had known where she lived.

'Thank you for carrying my things,' said Yen Olass.

Her thanks were sincere. When the high priest of a powerful religion plays porter for a female slave, he is making a considerable concession.

'My pleasure,' said the Ondrask.

The response was odd, and so was the way he looked at her. Yen Olass was not really sure how to handle the situation. In the wilderness, where the Ondrask had been a refugee from the storm, things had been easy enough. At his yashram, when she had been advising him on his problem with Haveros, she had felt confident in her professional role. But now?

Yen Olass wished he would vanish, but he lingered.

'Do you wish for a reading?' said Yen Olass.

'No,' said the Ondrask.

The room was as cold as a morgue. Yen Olass got out her tinderbox and tried to light her brazier. Her hands were shaking, and not just from the cold. Performing as an oracle was how she justified her existence in Gendormargensis; her professional abilities validated her right to live and eat, and Chonjara, by attacking her in public, seemed to her to have threatened the entire basis of her life.

'Can I help you with that?' said the Ondrask.

'You can help me by bringing Chonjara to heel,' said Yen Olass. 'He's your dog.'

'Don't worry about him,' said the Ondrask. 'If there's any trouble from today's events, well . . . if you got into too much trouble, I could—'

'Don't say it,' said Yen Olass.

She suspected that he was about to offer to buy her from the Sisterhood. She doubted if he would find that possible. However, with the help from the Lord Emperor Khmar, maybe he would—and to be bought by a man was the last thing she wanted.

She watched as yet another spark from steel and flint landed on a bit of tinder and promptly went out. As she persevered, the Ondrask fingered her seven-stringed klon. His long dirty fingernails plucked at one of the strings. It rattled discordantly against the sounding board. In the small room, where the Ondrask's stench was given little chance to dissipate, he was not pleasant company.

Yen Olass wanted to tell him to leave, but did not dare be so direct.

'It's not proper for you to be here,' said Yen Olass.

'Don't you have time to talk a little?' said the Ondrask.

Touching, fingering, staring, he looked like someone appraising an inheritance. Out in the wilderness they had, if only briefly, seemed like kindred spirits. But they were back in the city now. Here this bizarre shaman, with his greasy hair and his gaudy feathers, his dangling skulls and his primitive talismans, seemed like something out of another world. He had no place in her room.

'I am constrained by the Rule,' said Yen Olass.

'People cannot live by the rules,' said the high priest of the horse cult. 'What is a rule? A word that tries to ride a person. Is that fitting? Do you ride a horse, or does the horse ride you?'

'I live to obey,' said Yen Olass.

'You do have a choice, you know,' said the Ondrask.

A choice? What on earth was he trying to tell her? Yen Olass saw him start to finger her laundry. He came upon one of the pads which she used to . . .

'Get out!' screamed Yen Olass.

She had been through too much that day. To have this stinking animal exploring the intimacies of her laundry was more than she could bear.

In the face of her anger, the Ondrask retreated, leaving her room without another word.

It had been a disastrous day. She had failed Lord Alagrace. The debacle in the Enskandalon Square might well cause the Silent One of the Sisterhood to ask questions about her competence. She seemed to have made an enemy in Chonjara. And now, by losing control for just a moment, she had grievously offended the high priest of the horse cult.

When she had been at the Ondrask's yashram, Yen Olass had prided herself on her cultivation of a new and valuable political contact, but now all her efforts had gone to waste. She knew the enormous size and tenderness of the typical male ego; she could only guess at what the Ondrask might do now. Maybe he might try to buy her just for the pleasure of subjecting her to his discipline.

Yen Olass got the brazier going at last. Then, in defiance of the Rule, she went to bed, and stayed there for the rest of the day. Her cat Lefrey soon joined her; during the winter weather, he was never away from her room for long. As a special treat, she allowed him to sleep in the bed rather than on it; he was her only friend, and she treasured him.

CHAPTER
Five

A month after the duel, Lefrey disappeared.

Yen Olass immediately suspected what had happened, and challenged Nuana Nanalako accordingly. She readily admitted complicity.

'We've got him,' said Nuana, 'and you won't get him back till you bring us the map.'

This was blackmail.

What Yen Olass felt about the half-inching of her cat need not be described; civilized people, having cats of their own, will understand immediately, whereas doglicking barbarians are beyond enlightenment. However, after the initial shock had worn off, Yen Olass stopped sentimentalising over the loss of Lefrey and began to consider the wider implications.

Though cats may well be considered as people, ultimately cats are expendable, but there was a lot more at stake than a cat. Nuana could take everything Yen Olass owned—and Yen Olass would never dare complain.

'An oracle has no attachments.'

So ran the Rule.

But Yen Olass, a hoarding creature by nature, found it impossible to conform to the Rule. By possessing a cat she was in breach of the Rule; her dreamquilt was against the Rule, and so was her seven-stringed klon and her collection of shells and her amber thankskeep.

However, the problem did not end there.

Yen Olass could say a parting for her cat; she could even live with the confiscation of her comforts and fripperies. But if Nuana went one step further and laid an Information with the Sisterhood, then Yen Olass really would be in trouble.

In a dormitory in the Woman Sanctuary in the Western quadrant, there was a bed assigned to Yen Olass Ampadara. The wardmistress had never reported her absence, for, as Yen Olass well knew, that greedy old woman was more than happy to lay claim to an extra food allotment. However, if the Sisterhood investigated their oracle, they would soon discover the truth—and ask questions.

How did Yen Olass come to have her own room in tooth 44, Moon Stallion Strait? Who arranged eating privileges for her at the Canoozerie? What quid pro quo earned her a seat of her own in the Hall of Heavenly Music? Was it true that a horse in Lord Alagrace's stables was permanently assigned to Yen Olass? If so, what did she use it for? Was it true that she sometimes actually rode out hunting?

There was, in short, much more than the fate of a cat in question. A whole way of life was threatened.

Any investigation would soon lead the Sisterhood to suspect —correctly—that Yen Olass had earned these unlawful privileges by performing political favours for Lord Alagrace. When making a reading, an oracle was only supposed to conjure up images, fables, tales or parables suggesting alternatives to the patrons; to attempt conscious persuasion was forbidden by the Rule.

And there was no doubt that Yen Olass had sinned against the rule for years now. Even before the Blood Purge, Lord Alagrace had made occasional use of her talents. Since he had returned from exile in Ashmolea, she had served him on a daily basis, and had benefited accordingly. By now, he rarely had to instruct her, for she knew his purposes as well as any of his chief ministers, and could serve his will even when a crisis arose in his absence.

If the Sisterhood investigated Yen Olass, she might be stripped of her powers as an oracle and put to work in the kitchens. At the very least, steps would be taken to ensure that she did live in the Woman Sanctuary from now on—and that in itself would be unbearable. Yen Olass hated the wetwater smell of the female quarters, the cloistering walls which encouraged the captive women to engage in feuds and jealousies; she remembered the meals of scange and rotten lanks, which sometimes stank like vomit.

In her own quarters in Moon Stallion Strait, Yen Olass enjoyed many luxuries, and the finest was her privacy. There were no secrets in the Woman Sanctuary, that place where close-quartered women combined their body chemistry to make themselves one single animal, celebrating this mystery by menstruating in unison once in every moon.

Seeing how much damage could be done if she continued to resist, Yen Olass went to the text-master Eldegen Terzanagel and promised to get the map for him; he instructed her accordingly.

*   *   *

The War Archives was a relatively young institution; it had been established twenty years previously by Lord Pentalon Alagrace. Originally it had been a modest establishment devoted to the study of logistics, for Lord Alagrace believed that most campaigns were decided, to a large extent, by the degree to which logistical requirements could be satisfied.

However, in twenty years the War Archives had grown considerably. Staffed mainly by past and present army officers, it had survived the Blood Purge intact, and had profited from the chaos which followed.

It now controlled the previously independent House of Cartographers; it had taken over the Guild of Praise Singers; after a direct appeal to the Lord Emperor Khmar, it had even won permission to establish its own cadre of interrogators in direct competition with the traditional School of Executioners.

Strong, confident and aggressive, the War Archives bureaucracy was now contending for one of the richest prizes of all: the regulation of Ordhar, the command language of the Collosnon Empire. Ordhar had been previously developed and administered by the text-masters, who bitterly resented the War Archives' effort to deprive them of their prestige, salaries, offices and assistants; the relentless infighting had now reached its peak, with the text-masters accusing the War Archives of complicity in the fire which had badly damaged the Pranzalstrud, the chief library of the text-masters.

If the text-master Eldegen Terzanagel had gone anywhere near the War Archives complex now dominating King's Honour Crescent—only four years old, that complex contained the finest architecture in all of Gendormargensis—then the consequences of such a foolish move would quite possibly have been the immediate and permanent disappearance of the said text-master. However, nobody challenged Yen Olass as she passed through the portal giving access to the complex. Nobody would ever challenge an oracle, or even think of doing so.

On her way to the map room, Yen Olass walked down wide corridors where floors and walls were decorated with mosaics in the Drayling Style, which depends for its effects on the interweaving of different seasons, blending pools of fruited sunlight with frozen ponds, banks of burning autumn with snowdrifts and youngbud trees. She knew the way; she had visited the War Archives often enough before, when summoned by Lord Alagrace or some other worthy.

To get to the map room, she had to pass outside the Naquotal Conference Room; it must have been in use, for in the wide corridor outside there were bodyguards and other retainers lounging against the walls or seated on wooden benches. A number of edged weapons, banned from the Conference Room, were stacked up against one wall.

As Yen Olass drew near, a man moved to intercept her; inwardly, Yen Olass quailed, fearing discovery, yet she maintained her poise.

The man was Karahaj Nan Nulador, General Chonjara's bodyguard; he dropped down on one knee, as he had in the Enskandalon Square.

'Peace for your daylight,' said Yen Olass, blessing him.

'Whom do you read for today?' said Nan Nulador.

Again Yen Olass was panic-stricken. She could hardly answer 'nobody'; on the other hand, if she named any particular individual, it was entirely possible that person might be inside the Conference Room, in which case it would look very odd if she failed to stay and wait for them.

'A reading has just been concluded,' said Yen Olass, finding the way out of her difficulties.

'Then . . . please.'

Nan Nulador gestured at the door to a side room. He was asking for a reading! And now Yen Olass was really in trouble, for her laquered box, which should have contained her Casting Board and her 365 Indicators, was entirely empty—she planned to use it to carry away the map she intended to steal.

'An oracle does not refuse a patron.'

So ran the Rule.

And the assembled bodyguards and retainers, bored, idle, watching and listening, would be sure to note any refusal, however she phrased it. Mutely, Yen Olass walked into the side room; Nan Nulador closed the door, and they were alone.

The room was a bare box of stone, generously lit by a series of tall, narrow windows which admitted a draught of ice-cold air. Yen Olass walked to the windows, wondering if she could drop her empty nordigin out of a window; she looked down and saw an empty courtyard below. If she managed to slip and fall and drop her carrier box, the first thing Nan Nulador would do would be to run down to that courtyard to rescue it. And he would find it empty.

Yen Olass turned and faced her danger.

'You want a reading,' said Yen Olass. 'Where does the conflict lie?'

'With my wife,' said Nan Nulador. 'It was . . . there was . . . there was one child born dead. Then another. Both my sons, born dead. I have to know. Has someone put a curse on her. Or is she—'

'Do not name it,' said Yen Olass sharply, knowing what the next word would be.

'Is she a dralkosh?'

There. It was out. It had been said. And Nan Nulador stood trembling, waiting, frightened by the accusation he had made against his wife—for nobody suggests that a woman may be a dralkosh unless they believe she is—yet eager to know the answer, to know the truth, to have it settled.

'Dralkosh,' said Yen Olass, repeating the word Nan Nulador had spoken.

It was an ugly word, denoting a woman who drew power from a liaison with the dead. It was a matter of record that every woman with a legitimate claim to the title had long ago fled into exile with the Witchlord Onosh Gulkan and his chief dralkosh Bao Gahai. Nevertheless, in any given year, in the city of Gendormargensis at least a dozen women were named as 'dralkosh', and stoned to death.

'Is she?' said Nan Nulador. 'Aren't you going to do a reading?'

And now there was more at stake than the discovery that Yen Olass had brought an empty carrier box into the precincts of Karling Drask. A woman's life was at stake.

'We will discover the truth for you,' said Yen Olass, with a serene confidence she did not actually feel. 'But a reading may not be the best way. Tell me: what did you dream of last night?'

'I don't dream,' said Nan Nulador stolidly.

So much for that idea.

In fact, as Yen Olass knew very well, all human beings dream, for like all other god-created creatures they partake of the nature of gods, and the function of dreams is to allow even the humblest of all animals to create freely, as the gods themselves do. But if Nan Nulador refused to remember his dreams, Yen Olass could hardly interpret them for him. Yet she had to find some way to satisfy him without opening her carrier box.

'You will dream tonight,' said Yen Olass, her voice clear and penetrating, two parts of desperation to one part of calculation —a very powerful recipe.

'You say—'

'Believe me,' said Yen Olass.

And Nan Nulador did.

So it was that Yen Olass ventured into the territory of the Sura Woman, the sly-voiced old crone whom the traveller will find reading fortunes, interpreting dreams and selling charms in any market in the lands round Gendormargensis.

'But you need a dream now,' said Yen Olass, 'So I will tell you one. This is a dream which I have from the inner air, by a method which may not be revealed.'

She was venturing further and further into occult territory, knowing full well what a scandal this would cause if the Sisterhood came to hear of it. The Sisterhood, drawing on the histories of other places, other times, knew that the development of the Collosnon Empire would lead it to discard the traditions of the past; for the time being, the Sisterhood would operate with the paraphernalia of Casting Board and Indicators, but the order planned in due course to abandon these trappings of superstition, and to work frankly as a Guild of Arbitrators.

Yen Olass, by claiming to create a dream, was laying claim to paranormal powers in a way the Sisterhood could never countenance; as Nan Nulador settled himself at her feet, listening in wide-eyed fascination like a child hearing some tale of dwarfs and dragon-slaying heroes, it was clear that this hulking fighting man was convinced that magic was being worked for his benefit.

'A dream,' said Yen Olass. 'A rabbit. Snow. No skin. Rabbit with no skin. Cries. Rabbit cries. A woman comes. She loves. Picks up the rabbit. Comforts it. A woman's nature. A rabbit. A ic

child. This is the snow falling. You will remember. As she comforts, fur. Grows. Rabbit grows fur. Is comforted.'

And spinning out this spiel, Yen Olass dropped her voice, speaking in a lower tone for certain key phrases: she loves, a child, you will remember.

In Monogail, Yen Olass had learnt certain disciplines from her mother, who had been a powerful healer of minds, and had instructed her from the earliest age. She was now making use of that training.

Spinning her spiel, Yen Olass slid a stream of words into Nan Nulador's mind; as they were very close to nonsense, he resisted none of them; as he sat there following the story of the rabbit saved from the snow, Yen Olass infiltrated his mind with a message given segment by segment, each segment marked out for the attention of his 'menthout', his peripheral mind, that part of the mind which monitors all the things happening outside the tiny area on which operational consciousness, 'yokthout', is actually focused.

'Those two then,' said Yen Olass. 'Close together in the snow. All around. The rabbit knows to sleep with her. Yet is it enough? More snow falls. Surely to cover her. But what is this? A feather. Falling. The snow is feathers. All the world is falling with feathers. Enough.

'The woman waits. Downfalling feathers. Time. The feathers are warm. Night comes. The woman is warm. Sooner or later, there will be dawn. Sunlight. Birdwine pouring. Mother and child. Yes. An outlook of sunlight.'

Bit by bit, marking each part of her message with that drop in tone, Yen Olass gave him his orders, thus: sleep with her, sooner or later, child.

Her story ran on, telling of how the woman and the rabbit survived the feather snow, went on a journey, found a house, and—

'But how it ends, I don't know,' said Yen Olass. 'That's all the dream I remember. When you dream you will know more than you know now, and more than I can tell you.'

And with those final words, she slipped in the final command to pull all those carefully marked phrases together, and make them one message: remember when you dream.

Would it work?

The chances are good. If Nan Nulador had wanted to dispose of his wife, he would already have named her as a dralkosh, and she would already be dead. So, despite the fact that she had given him two dead children, he wanted her to live.

The door opened; General Chonjara entered the room.

'What's this?' said Chonjara.

'We've just concluded a reading,' said Yen Olass coolly.

Chonjara grunted; Nan Nulador rose to his feet, and made reverence to Yen Olass, this time using not a simple hand gesture, but a more elaborate and courtly form, thus: the right fist, clenched to the chest at heart-height, rolls open as the arm sweeps down, fist flowering into fingers as the upper half of the body bows forward.

'Come on,' said Chonjara, and Nan Nulador followed him out of the room.

Yen Olass stretched, easing the tension from her muscles, easing the tension from her bones. She picked up her empty carrier box. Outside, in the corridor, there was the sound of voices and footsteps, a clatter as a bench was pushed back against a wall. The Naquotal Conference Room was emptying.

Yen Olass waited till the corridor was quiet, then she resumed her journey.

*　　　*　　　*

The map was some thousands of years old. If chance favours them, vellum, parchment and papyrus will outlast the centuries, but cannot be expected to do so without suffering the insults of time; this map, on the other hand, was as clear and bright as if it had been made yesterday. However, there was no mystery in this, for it was made of twenty-five ceramic tiles, and its colours were high-temperature glazes. It is often the weakest things which outlast the cities of power: clay and poetry.

The map showed the Far South and the Deep South, the Stepping Stone Islands and the Inner Waters; in the lands south of the Inner Waters, within territory now commanded by the monsters of the Swarms, the map showed roads and cities. This map had been in the possession of the Sanctuary of Gendormargensis for centuries before the arrival of the horse tribes; however, during the Blood Purge, the Sanctuary had been destroyed, and its treasures had gone to the War Archives.

Not that the Archives had any use for the map—even the Collosnon Empire was not likely to match its strength against the Swarms, and, besides, the map was long out of date. However, on the strength of possessing 27,542 maps—nearly all of them uselesss—the War Archives had recently been able to acquire funding for another seven map curators.

Despite the number of people who derived their income from looking after maps, nobody appeared to be on duty when Yen Olass entered the map room; as the Ceramics Section held only a handful of maps, Yen Olass found what she was looking for without any trouble at all; she packed the twenty-five tiles into her carrier box, and left the map room.

She had not gone very far before she heard a bellow of anger: 'You!'

Shocked, she wheeled—and saw only an empty corridor behind her. But she knew who had shouted: General Chonjara. So she was discovered. 'How dare you! Whore! I'll kill you!'

Yen Olass began to run.

She fled down the corridor, slid round a corner, and crashed into a squad of soldiers, who were running toward the shouting.

'What's this?' said one, grabbing her.

'Unhand me!' shouted Yen Olass.

At any other time, the outrage of an oracle would have led to her immediate release. However, in view of the shouts and screams now coming down the corridor—and one of the screams was that of a woman—the soldier was not going to release anyone caught fleeing from the scene.

'Come,' said the soldier.

And Yen Olass, surrendering when he started to hurt her, was hustled down the corridor. The uproar grew louder. Rounding a corner, they came upon a most extraordinary sight. The Lord Commander of the Imperial City of Gendormargensis, Volaine Persaga Haveros, was fighting with General Chonjara. Haveros was stark naked; Chonjara was fully dressed. They were on the ground, wrestling, each seeking a stranglehold. The Princess Quenerain, also stark naked, was trying to demolish Chonjara's bodyguard with a chair; unwilling to damage the head of the Rite of Purification, Karahaj Nan Nulador was doing no more than defending himself.

'Break!' shouted one of the soldiers.

The combatants paid no attention, so the newcomers intervened. One of them made the mistake of grabbing the Princess Quenerain by the hair; appalled that anyone should manhandle such a sacred person, Nan Nulador went to her aid. He snatched

52 / Hugh Cook

up one of the lighter soldiers and began to batter the others with this convenient weapon.

More soldiers arrived. Seeing the brawl, they pitched in, choosing sides at random. Yen Olass was released as her captor waded into the fray. She fled—and was stiff-armed by a short-sighted street-fighter, the veteran of a thousand tavern fights. She sat down suddenly, the breath knocked out of her. A man landed on top of her. Someone kicked for his head. Yen Olass fought free, grabbed for her carrier box—and swore as someone kicked it and it burst open.

Sheltering the tiles with her body, as she might have sheltered a child from a herd of stampeding horses, Yen Olass jammed them back into her carrier box. Some were intact, others in pieces; she did her best, then closed the box.

General Chonjara, torn away from Haveros, struggled to his feet and shouted for order, raising his voice above the raucous shouts of battle-drunk soldiers. The Princess Quenerain hit him with a chair, and he went down. Someone sat on him. Seizing her opportunity, Yen Olass bit him on the ankle, getting a good grip and sinking her teeth deep into the general's flesh. He kicked her in the head.

Yen Olass was knocked backwards. A soldier grabbed her by the scruff of the neck, dragged her to her feet and drew back his fist to slug her—but Yen Olass smashed him in the jaw, and he went down. The women of Monogail were a sturdy breed. She grabbed her carrier box, and, seeing a break in the scrum, she lowered her head and charged.

A man got in her way, but Yen Olass won through to freedom; the man woke up later in the day with a sore head and a vague memory of losing an argument with a stone wall.

*   *   *

Lord Pentalon Alagrace, Lawmaker in Gendormargensis during the absence of the Lord Emperor Khmar, did his best. Those soldiers who had been found unconscious, disabled or too badly damaged to hide were flogged in public, each getting twenty lashes. The Resident Commander of Karling Drask, the War Archives complex, was demoted for failing to maintain good discipline. For good measure, all the soldiers working in Karling Drask were confined to barracks for sixty days.

That left Lord Alagrace with four people to deal with: the

Princess Quenerain, Volaine Haveros, General Chonjara and Karahaj Nan Nulador. Lord Alagrace excused Nan Nulador from punishment; bodyguards are chosen for loyalty and fighting ability rather than discrimination, and it would have set a dangerous precedent to have brought sanctions against a bodyguard who had fulfilled his obligations for fighting alongside his lord.

As for the others . . .

General Chonjara claimed to have broken into the Princess Quenerain's quarters in order to catch Haveros indulging himself with the supposedly virginal head of the Rite of Purification; Chonjara claimed to have been successful, and certainly both his targets had been naked when the subsequent fight had spilled out into the corridor.

For her part, the princess claimed that Haveros had been manhandled into her room by Nan Nulador, and that Chonjara had raped her before Haveros managed to break free and come to her rescue. However, the time factor militated against this story; having attended a conference shortly before the fight, Chonjara could hardly have found time to do all he was charged with. The silks worn by the princess were undamaged, so they must have been removed from her body with care; at the time of the fight, Chonjara's lust had been confined by the constraints of half-armour, which took time to take off and put on again.

Since Haveros, Chonjara and the Princess Quenerain were all high-born Yarglat, Lord Alagrace himself had to decide their fate. Only the Lawmaker could pass judgment on a high-born Yarglat. He did not want to avoid his duty—but his situation was impossible.

Only a fool would have brought the Rite of Purification into question by laying charges against the Princess Quenerain—who was, besides, Khmar's daughter. Haveros was high in the favour of the Lord Emperor Khmar, who had made him Lord Commander of the Imperial City. Khmar did not love Chonjara so much—but Chonjara's protector was the Ondrask of Noth, who had more influence with Khmar than anyone else in the empire.

What was Lord Alagrace to do?

As a descendant of the High Houses of Sharla, the ancient enemies of the Yarglat, Lord Alagrace was hated by virtually everyone of any importance. The Blood Purge, which had claimed most of his friends and relations, had destroyed his power base. The Lord Emperor Khmar, finding that a competent bureaucrat was necessary to run a city of a quarter of a million people, had summoned Lord Alagrace out of his self-imposed exile in Ashmolea—but it remained to see whether Khmar would back Alagrace against a high-born Yarglat.

Lord Alagrace consulted with Yen Olass who gave him direct and honest advice, telling him to flee to Ashmolea. He refused. He had come to Gendormargensis because he knew he still had high standing with one person: Celadric. At the moment, Khmar's eldest son was powerless, but on Khmar's death Celadric would become emperor. If Lord Alagrace managed to survive that long, there was a good chance that he would become Celadric's chief minister, and would effectively end up running the Collosnon Empire.

For such a prize, he was willing to gamble with his life. It was, besides, the only prize that would justify his life: the only prize that would justify his service to the emperor who had killed the people who were dearest to him. Granted control of the empire, Lord Alagrace could found a high civilisation in Tameran, and end the barbaric rule of the Yarglat.

It was the last dream which remained to him.

Lord Alagrace, in his wisdom, did as little as possible. He cautioned the Princess Quenerain to maintain her silence; he exiled Haveros and Chonjara to hunting lodges north and south of Gendormargensis; he assumed the title of Lord Commander of the Imperial City, and in his own name made all those administrative decisions which he had previously made for Haveros; he let it be known that he would not permit rumour or innuendo relating to the personnel of the Rite of Purification; he drafted a despatch to the Lord Emperor Khmar and sent it south on the long and difficult journey across the snowbound land.

The reply came back in the spring, brought by boat to Gendormargensis which, as always, had been turned into an island when the thaw caused the river to flood.

This was the reply:

'Greetings, gaplax. The masters fight and the dogs are punished. Did you think you could silence rumour? You'd be the first. Half the army knows already. Give the dogs their show. Quenerain's head on the battlements, if you see fit. Are you Lawmaker? Are you even lord of your own lice? I can see you now, standing in your own shit, shivering. As I say. Write it down. Every word. Melish. That's all.'

Lord Alagrace only had to read the message once to know it was, indisputably, a communication from the Lord Emperor Khmar. The obscenity at the beginning was definitely intended for him; that at the end might have been intended for him, or for the scribe taking dictation from the illiterate horse lord, or for both of them.

A temperate ruler would have smoothed over the scandal by exiling Chonjara and Haveros to different parts of the empire. However, Khmar was obviously prepared to accept even the death of his daughter—and the destruction of the Rite of Purification, an institution which Khmar had never really liked. What had roused Khmar to fury was the fact that his Lawmaker had come running for help, instead of settling the matter himself.

Lord Alagrace realised that he had been out of the company of the emperor for too long. Khmar had been raised by his grandmother, in the far north, far from the civilising influences of Gendormargensis. He was as reckless as his grandfather Nol Umu, and had never learnt to prefer compromise to the joys of chaos.

Now, at least, Lord Alagrace had a clear statement of Khmar's position. It seemed Khmar would back him to the hilt, whatever he decided to do. So who should he move against? Haveros or Chonjara? To strike a blow against Chonjara would be, indirectly, to strike a blow against the Ondrask. The more Lord Alagrace could diminish the Ondrask's prestige now, the easier it would be to get rid of him when Celadric came to power.

By the next day, Lord Alagrace had given Chonjara an ultimatum: accept this judgment or die.

The judgment was that General Chonjara should make public penance for slandering the Princess Quenerain. If Chonjara pleaded guilty to slander, that would do something to quell the rumours now abroad in the wide world. Chonjara deserved punishment in any case, for spying on the Princess Quenerain and intruding on her quarters in Karling Drask: Lord Alagrace did not look kindly upon such lawbreaking, even in the name of vigilante justice.

After an interview in which Lord Alagrace converted his own

fears into anger—and Lord Alagrace, when angry, was a formidable force—Chonjara accepted his fate.

The judgment was made public, and so, on a warm spring day when the floodwaters were receding, General Chonjara, his body stripped naked, presented himself at the Enskandalon Square, where a fully laden manure cart was waiting for him. There was also a large audience out to enjoy the fun.

Chonjara, his face frozen, did not seem to hear the jeers and catcalls. Among the Yarglat, public nudity was taboo, yet Chonjara showed no shame; he carried himself with arrogance, if not with pride. His chest was matted with black hairs; Yen Olass, who would not have missed the occasion for anything, thought he looked rather like a bear. Since most of the game within easy riding of Gendormargensis had been killed out, she had never seen a bear, and this was one of the minor sorrows of her life.

Chonjara turned to face Lord Alagrace.

'My lord,' said Chonjara.

His voice was flat, heavy, expressionless. Was he going to ask for a reading? Yen Olass, standing beside Lord Alagrace, had already been briefed, and had prepared a reading that would bring Chonjara more shame than any physical humiliation possibly could. Her reading began like this: 'A bear. A honey pot. Bear looks at the honeypot. Little bear. Can't have. Angry now...'

She waited. She was ready.

'I will remember this.'

So spoke Chonjara. And that was all he said. He turned his back on them, and Yen Olass saw the muscles rippling under his skin. He was a strong man—yet once he shouldered the heavy yoke, even he had trouble in getting the manure cart to move. His procession through the city took half a day, and the worst part came when he went past the fishing works.

At the fishing works, young yerkels on the roof poured out a barrel of sluck, and down it came, a cascade of greasy water, floor scrapings, fish heads, disintegrating bits of flesh and bone, decayed rags and rotten sawdust. Chonjara walked on, like an animated statue, his face immobile, his eyes fixed on horizons elsewhere.

And Lord Alagrace, hearing of it—he had not followed the procession past its beginning—remembered Chonjara's words. And began practising his swordplay.

CHAPTER
Six

In the early days of spring, when the city of Gendormargensis was still talking about the public humiliation of General Chonjara, a patron asked Yen Olass Ampadara for a reading. The patron was Volaine Persaga Haveros.

'I want to know my fate,' said Haveros.

'I am not a fortune teller,' said Yen Olass.

'But you will tell me what I want to know,' said Haveros, and laid before her a fragment of blue tile.

Yen Olass knew exactly what it was. On taking the twenty-five tile map to the text-master Eldegen Terzanagel, she had found him excited, his face lit by the avid, shining greed of a newly married husband about to lay hands on his virgin (or, to be precise, his face had worn the expression Yen Olass imagined such a newly married husband might display). But when the carrier box had opened to reveal the wreckage inside, Terzanagel had been dismayed, then furious. Only six tiles had been broken, and only four were incomplete, but Terzanagel had made it seem like the end of the world. Yen Olass knew the shape and size of every missing piece—and saw them often in her dreams.

So now, seeing this fragment, Yen Olass knew she was discovered. She looked at the broken bit of tile, then raised her eyes to find Haveros staring at her with an expression of . . . rage? Madness? She had seen that look before. What was it? Why had he not denounced her already as a thief, a spy, an enemy of the state? Considering that expression, Yen Olass admitted that she knew what it was: lust. Yet, unlike the text-master, Haveros was not the kind of man to lust after knowledge. What he wanted was . . .

57

Yen Olass remembered Monogail. She remembered the soldiers. Their hands scrabbling over her body. The weight of their stinking breath. She could not speak.

'Well?' said Haveros.

Yen Olass did the only thing she could do. She opened her carrier box and took out her Casting Board, slotting the two halves together. She took out the leather bag containing the 365 Indicators; she shook the bag then extracted sixteen tablets and laid them out on the Casting Board, placing four rows of four tablets in a foursquare design.

'These are the quadrants of north, south, east and west,' said Yen Olass, endeavouring to impress Haveros with the mystery, for she was about to give a reading to try and save herself. 'In order, they are the quadrants of snow, sky, sun and moon, or alternatively, stasis, change, action and thought.'

She thought of telling him more, then saw his sardonic smile. Yen Olass looked down at the cool ivory tablets, each decorated with an exquisite pattern etched in black, blue, red or green. Even though she assigned no occult powers to this apparatus, his mockery still seemed tainted with sacrilege. Yen Olass looked at Haveros and said:

'What's so funny?'

'You look like . . .'

He was amused. She could hear it in his voice.

'Like what?' said Yen Olass, starting to get angry. 'What do I look like?'

'As if you thought I was going to . . . to eat you. Or to do something I shouldn't. You don't think I'd touch you, do you?'

It was too much to endure. The urbane, scornful amusement. Years of careful, diplomatic campaigning had allowed Yen Olass to make something of a life for herself, and now, with a tiny bit of broken pottery, this big ugly man was going to abolish her entire world. And—worse!—he mocked her for being proud enough to imagine that he might want to possess her. Carefully, Yen Olass raised one side of the Casting Board. The Indicators shuffled onto the floor. Haveros started to speak:

'You can't get out of it—'

Yen Olass picked up the Casting Board and hurled it at him. He ducked—too slow! The board clipped his head. As it spun away, Yen Olass snarled, her mouth locking open in something which was almost a scream. Haveros stared at her, then reached up gingerly and touched his head. He examined the blood on his fingers. Then smiled—and laughed.

At that laugh, Yen Olass felt her resistance collapse. It was no good. Whatever she did. They were too strong, too sure of themselves. She could never hurt them. This was their city, and she was their slave. But, even in defeat, she would make no concessions. She would not beg. She would not plead. If he was here to bring her death sentence, she would not give him the satisfaction of seeing her grovel at his feet.

Haveros licked the blood from his fingers, then held up the little bit of tile.

'Where does this belong?'

'I don't know,' said Yen Olass.

'I saw what happened,' said Haveros.

'So what did you see?'

'Enough to make me think. What would an oracle steal? Plates from the kitchen of Karling Drask? Tiles from the roof? Wall panels from the bathroom in the Riverside Suite? By the time Lord Alagrace let me return to the city, I'd worked it out.'

'Clever,' said Yen Olass, admitting nothing, even though she realised that she had already betrayed herself.

Only the certainty of personal destruction could have set an oracle free to attack a warrior like Haveros; by her own actions, she had demonstrated her guilt, and condemned herself.

'It has to be a text-master,' said Haveros.

'What has to be?'

'No more games now,' said Haveros. 'I know which map has gone missing. The catalogue tells me it's an old, old map with inscriptions in the High Speech. Only a text-master would want a useless thing like that.'

Texts in the High Speech of the wizards of Argan were not in fact without their uses, for the text-masters had spent the last ten years endeavouring to master that language so they would be able to serve as translators when the Collosnon Empire invaded Argan.

'Why should I tell you?' said Yen Olass. 'It makes no difference to me.'

'Why?' said Haveros. 'What do you think I'm here for? To bring you your death warrant? To amuse myself a little at your expense? No, it's not like that at all. Of course, it could be . . . but I'm sure we can reach an agreement.'

'It's a trick,' said Yen Olass.

And she was sure it was. Once Haveros knew which text-master had suborned her, he could complete his rehabilitation by denouncing her.

'Listen,' said Haveros. 'Listen very carefully, and I'll explain in little little words that even a little mouse like you can under-stand.'

Yen Olass, who was not little at all, swallowed the insult nevertheless, and listened. And began to understand.

*   *   *

Eldegen Terzanagel lived in Tangzkez Nesh in the purlieus of the Lutzuke tenement area, just to the east of the horse market. This was one of the oldest parts of Gendormargensis; the streets were narrow, noisome and unfashionable. Nevertheless, Ter-zanagel had made himself very comfortable; Yen Olass envied his ground floor quarters, for she often grew tired of climbing up and down the stairs in tooth 44, Moon Stallion Strait.

Volaine Persaga Haveros came to Tangzkez Nesh disguised as a beggar. He had no aristocratic beauty to conceal. A little dirt, a lurch, a limp, a shrouding cowl, a mouthful of strong liquor to flush his breath, a mutter, the occasional obscenity—he was perfect. And when he reached the rendezvous, it took only a change of clothes, some clean water and some mintwash to refashion him in the image of love.

The Princess Quenerain, on the other hand, arrived in a closed palanquin, a shabby equipage such as any moderately successful merchant household might have maintained. She came dressed in her finery—silks, perfumes, jewels and gold. When entering Tangzkez Nesh, the princess never said a word to Yen Olass—never acknowledged her existence.

Yen Olass was always there, keeping watch with Nuana Nan-alako. The text-master Eldegen Terzanagel, though he had al-lowed himself to be blackmailed into making his house available for this illicit liaison, always absented himself when the lovers arrived, leaving his slave girl to help the oracle keep watch.

At first these two women attended to their guard duties with scrupulous care, expecting General Chonjara to appear at any moment at the head of a squad of armed men. However, as the days went by their anxieties receded, and curiosity began to dominate fear. One day, Nuana showed Yen Olass a ventilation slit which overlooked the sleeping quarters and allowed them to watch and hear all that took place between Haveros and the Princess Quenerain.

Soon, their guard duties became notional, and they amused themselves by spying on the trysting couple. They watched honey being applied to the most tender places, then licked off; they watched hands grappling with flesh and sweat; they watched two people becoming desperate, straining creatures, biting, groaning, moaning, writhing. Stifling giggles, they listened to the shameless dialogues of infatuation:

'Son-son, is your little medi-vedi weary? Here, let me wake him up . . . what? Does that tickle? Come on, don't be . . . yes, he's a brave little soldier, isn't he? . . . oh, that's quite . . . ah . . .'

'Does your little teni like that, Suggy?'

'Oh yes, oh it's so . . . oh, it's slipped out. Oh, Son-son, it's so slippery . . . here, let me help you put it back in . . . ah, that's better . . . oh . . . push . . . oh . . .'

At which point it was standard for Nuana to open her mouth in an orgasmic 'O', thus threatening an immediate detonation of laughter, and forcing both voyeurs to withdraw to the cellar, where they could allow their mirth its free and unrestricted expression. Their laughter was not just a response to the human comedy: it was also a form of revenge. For these two women, who endured all the minor and major humiliations that slave status brought, there was something exquisite in the spectacle of this high-caste lord and his high-caste lady pawing each other's bodies, licking each other, sharing saliva, and first baby-talking then swearing and imploring as they struggled toward the brink of the apotheosis of friction.

It was only in her dreams that Yen Olass knew she envied them.

* * *

It lasted for a month. Then the lovers were betrayed. The textmaster Eldegen Terzanagel went to see Lord Alagrace, and told all—or nearly all. Terzanagel did not admit that he had been blackmailed, but simply said that Haveros had threatened him.

'You have my sympathies,' said Lord Alagrace, knowing that Haveros was a determined and sometimes violent man.

'My lord . . .'

'We will arrest him, of course.'

'But . . .'

'But what?'

'His friends will still be . . .'

'Are you afraid of revenge?' said Lord Alagrace. 'I won't call you as a witness when I grant him his trial. If we can catch him in the building with the Princess Quenerain, that will be enough.'

'But he will know—or guess. And his friends . . . my lord, I request permission to . . . to absent myself from Gendormargensis while this . . .'

Sensing that the text-master was truly afraid, Lord Alagrace gave him permission to make a journey to the south-east, to inspect the archives in the Atka Castle at Port Domax. As Port Domax was a free port beyond the rule of the Collosnon Empire, there would then be nothing to stop Terzanagel going further if he wished—but Lord Alagrace did not care.

Lord Alagrace provided the text-master with horses and travel documents, together with some money for the journey, and a squad of league riders to accompany him on the first stage of his travels.

Lord Alagrace went to this trouble because he believed that justice should be done, if that was at all possible; that those who witnessed crimes should be encouraged to come forward, and should be protected when they did; and that the Lawmaker should go to special pains to prosecute criminals in positions of high responsibility, for they have betrayed a trust as well as breaking the law.

To him, it was a source of secret shame and sorrow that he found himself forced to manipulate justice on occasion for the most cynical of political purposes. However, this did not make him more tolerant; instead, he became even more determined to perfect the processes of the law as they applied to other people.

And so it came to pass that the text-master Eldegen Terzanagel slipped out of Gendormargensis one evening with his slave girl Nuana Nanalako. Accompanied by their military escort, they rode through the night, and by morning they were well and truly launched on a journey which, of course, would not end at Port Domax, but would take them south by sea to Ashmolea and then to the Stepping Stone Islands, where Terzanagel would be able to complete his researches into the life and works of Saba Yavendar, creator of the Winesong.

THE ORACLE / 63

When morning came, Yen Olass arrived at Tangzkez Nesh—and found Lord Alagrace waiting for her. He briefed her, cautioned her and calmed her fears, and asked some questions. Yen Olass showed him where he could hide and watch.

Haveros arrived a little later.

'Nuana!' said Yen Olass. 'Our visitor's here.'

She went into the empty kitchen and picked up a bowl of water.

'Thank you, Nuana.'

She returned to Haveros, bearing the bowl of water. He washed his face, then withdrew to change his clothes. When the Princess Quenerain arrived, Haveros was waiting in the sleeping quarters. The princess said nothing to Yen Olass, but went straight in. They were always just a little rushed for time, because Haveros always had to inspect a ceremonial guard at noon, and the Princess Quenerain had to conduct a service of the Rite of Purification at the same time—and Yen Olass herself often had an appointment with a patron in the later part of the morning.

From the observation point, Lord Alagrace watched. He did not interrupt the couple: he wanted to see. He had to see to believe. When they were finished, Lord Alagrace retreated; Yen Olass showed him the way out.

The Princess Quenerain left first. Lord Alagrace made no move to stop her, but, when she had gone, he stormed Tangzkez Nesh, leading a force of twenty league riders who had been ordered to kill anyone who resisted. Lord Alagrace hoped Haveros would put a fight and die in combat, thus sparing the city and the regime the shame of a public trial. But Haveros, too much in love with his life to commit suicide, surrendered without a struggle.

Lord Alagrace visited him later in the East Tower Jail.

'Why?' said Lord Alagrace.

And Haveros, his hands and feet in shackles, made no reply, but looked out of the window at the world beyond, where the wind kicked up waves on the river and the clouds clawed south.

'Why her?' said Lord Alagrace. 'The city is full of slaves and whores. So why her?'

'Love,' said Haveros.

When a grown man talks of love, there is no hope for him; Lord Alagrace turned away in disgust.

'I raped her,' said Haveros.

'Who believes that?'

'The people will.'

'Khmar won't,' said Lord Alagrace. 'And even if he did . . .'

The Lord Emperor Khmar would be extremely angry if Lord Alagrace was to execute Haveros just for a little matter like rape, particularly when the only supporting evidence was a confession which Khmar would never believe.

'If you don't want to punish me,' said Haveros, 'why did you arrest me?'

'So that justice can be done. Nobody can be allowed to stand outside the law.'

'But now you've arrested me, you're too frightened to enforce that law,' said Haveros. 'You're a coward.'

Lord Alagrace bowed his head. It was true. He had really expected Haveros to fight and die in Tangzkez Nesh—had really expected that a sense of honour would compel the warrior to meet his death at swordpoint. He had not anticipated the complications of a trial.

When Haveros and Chonjara had fought earlier in the year, they had brought trouble upon themselves by quarrelling in the public eye. But when Haveros had conducted his affair with the Princess Quenerain, he had been entirely discreet. The public disclosure of the affair was Lord Alagrace's responsibility, and the Lord Emperor Khmar was likely to see that as a case of his Sharla Lawmaker making war on Yarglat clansmen. If Lord Alagrace had Haveros executed, Khmar was likely to delete his head with a hammer.

'If you think you've made a mistake,' said Haveros, 'then let me go. Forget about it. I can, if you will.'

'Not possible,' said Lord Alagrace. 'Chonjara's heard of your arrest.'

'Oh.'

There was no need to say more. If Lord Alagrace abandoned the trial, Chonjara would protest, and the law would be brought into disrepute. More seriously, Chonjara might challenge Lord Alagrace, giving him a choice between public shame and death. If Lord Alagrace followed the matter through and allowed it to come to trial, he was likely to incur the wrath of the Lord Khmar.

There was no way out.

Or was there?

'A dralkosh,' said Lord Alagrace.

'What?' said Haveros.

'The mob has a woman in a cage in the northern marketplace. They're going to stone her to death tomorrow.'

'Then she's got nothing to lose.'

'They're going to stone her baby, too.'

'Ah,' said Haveros.

Sensing hope. He would live; he would be free of these shackles, free to rejoin the world of horses and women, wine and song.

'This dralkosh,' said Lord Alagrace. 'She worked magic on many men ... deluded their senses. Turned them against the law. Made them mad. And you ... you were one of the victims.'

'But the princess?'

'You drugged her. People will believe that. But even so ...'

'I know what the punishment is,' said Haveros. 'I can live with that.'

Even for a man seduced from the righteous path by the occult arts of a dralkosh, there was still punishment in store. Otherwise men would constantly have yielded to such seduction without a struggle. Ruefully, Haveros rubbed his left ear, which would soon be missing; then he gave a little grin. He was going to live: he could not subdue his high spirits.

'An exile's life is a hard one,' said Lord Alagrace.

'Oh, I'll survive,' said Haveros.

He already knew where he would go and whom he would turn to, but he had no intention of telling Lord Alagrace, who would have been extremely alarmed to know that Haveros planned to seek help from the Lord Emperor Khmar.

'Done, then,' said Lord Alagrace.

'Done,' said Haveros.

And they bowed to each other, and Lord Alagrace departed to attend to the necessary business. The dralkosh was extracted from the mob; after negotiations, she confessed to bewitching Haveros, among others; the baby was put into the care of a good family, and the dralkosh was stoned to death.

Haveros admitted succumbing to the madness engendered by the dralkosh; his left ear was cut off and he left the city in an ignominious fashion, with whips chasing him as he rode out on a broomstick like a child riding an imaginary horse. The law allowed him twenty days of grace in which he could flee without hindrance; after that, every man's hand would be against him, and it would be death for him to be caught within the boundaries of the empire until ten years had elapsed.

For the Princess Quenerain, there was a special Ceremony of Cleansing, at the end of which she was once more officially a virgin, and free to continue as head of the Rite of Purification.

Yen Olass escaped without punishment: her involvement in the scandal did not become public knowledge. Haveros and the Princess Quenerain had nothing to gain by naming someone privy to their intimacies, while Lord Alagrace dared not risk an inquiry that might find he had suborned an oracle for his own political purposes.

Lord Alagrace dispatched a report on the affair to the Lord Emperor Khmar, requesting direction regarding the vacant position of Lord Commander of the Imperial City of Gendormargensis; that duty done, he was free to brood about his own failings, among which he numbered fear, indecisiveness and a small but undeniable degree of ineptitude.

CHAPTER
Seven

Midsummer's Day initiated a new year, Khmar 19, which did not get off to an auspicious start. Drought fostered forest fires and brought a water shortage to the surrounding region; stones fell from the heavens, and then a comet appeared in the northern sky, causing an outbreak of dralkosh hunting; the Yolantarath River fell below memory's lowest level; there was a rumour of cholera, an outbreak of equine enteritis and a plague of mice; a child was bitten by a mad dog and died of rabies, and a cat by the name of Lefrey succumbed to a virulent form of influenza and passed away, a tragedy which greatly distressed an oracle by the name of Yen Olass Ampadara.

Things could have got worse, but improved instead. Rain fell; the river rose; a new holy man appeared, and had some success in persuading Gendormargensis that the habit of stoning women to death had got out of hand; the leader of a long-standing slave rebellion was captured and crucified, and his remains fed raw to some of his followers who had been detained in the starvation cages; from the south came news of success, conquest and victory.

Then, when all seemed to be going well—the autumn promised a bumper harvest—dispatches arrived from the Lord Emperor Khmar. Lord Pentalon Alagrace was ordered south to the newly conquered port of Favanosin, where the emperor would be waiting for him. General Chonjara and the Princess Quenerain were to travel with him. Khmar did not say why he wanted these three, but Lord Alagrace could guess. Doubtless Khmar, unhappy with the administration of justice in Gendormargensis, was ordering all three south for punishment.

What else could it be?

Khmar specifically ordered Lord Alagrace to 'leave your tame league riders in Gendormargensis', which was ominous, to say the least.

Lord Alagrace informed Chonjara and the princess of the emperor's wishes, then revised his will. Khmar, who was not the world's most responsible administrator, had failed to make two vital appointments, so Lord Alagrace nominated two of the more sober-headed high-born Yarglat clansmen to act as Lawmaker and Imperial Commander of the city until further notice.

While a staff officer organized a convoy for the journey south, Lord Alagrace completed his personal business then conferred with Yen Olass Ampadara. He explained his position. He was going south; he would have to face the emperor; Khmar was a ruthless and unpredictable judge. If faced with the prospect of immediate death, Lord Alagrace planned to ask the emperor to listen to a reading. It was known that Khmar did not travel in the company of oracles; would Yen Olass consent to go south to Favanosin to give a reading?

Yen Olass once again advised Lord Alagrace to flee the empire; when he refused, she agreed to travel south with him to risk Khmar's anger.

Any mission to the emperor was dangerous, because Khmar was given to extravagant outbursts of rage and violence. Nevertheless, he was capable of generosity, and sometimes indulged his own sly sense of humour in remarkable ways. It would be difficult for an oracle to manipulate Khmar, but not impossible; he could never be led by the nose, but ways might be found to give him a little nudge in the right direction. It was, in a way, the ultimate challenge; the thought of it made Yen Olass afraid, and that was one reason why she accepted.

Her actions were also conditioned by her awareness of discreet enquiries which the Sisterhood was making about her activities. Her Midsummer Report, detailing her activity for Khmar 18, had come back to her with lists of questions; after many days of waiting, she was not yet certain if her answers had proved acceptable. All things considered, it seemed a good idea to get out of Gendormargensis.

Lord Alagrace was, in many ways, her protector; if he left then Yen Olass would lose many of her privileges, and would be vulnerable to any investigation which challenged her behaviour. If he died, she could seek some other protector in the south; if he was exiled, perhaps he would take her into exile with her. Yen Olass began to wonder what Lord Alagrace would be like as a lover, a bedmate, a husband. He was old, yes, but he would be better than what she had at the moment—which, since Lefrey died, was nothing.

Yen Olass quit her quarters in Moon Stallion Strait, and moved into Lord Alagrace's residence for her last few days in Gendormargensis. She spent whole evenings in the stables, packing and repacking her saddle bags. Her klon, her dream-quilt and a few other oddments went into a storeroom under lock and key, and Yen Olass made the housekeeper swear to guard those valuables with her life. Yen Olass wheedled a sabre out of the armoury, and cut herself three times sharpening it.

She was leaving Gendormargensis!

She extracted some money out of Lord Alagrace and bought new boots, new foot bindings and lightweight coat of rabbit skin which she could wear over her fleece-lined weather jacket when it was too warm to wear a snow-coat. There was more than a little money left over—Lord Alagrace had only a vague idea of what things cost, and Yen Olass was ferocious when in pursuit of a bargain—so she indulged herself outrageously by spending some of it on a piece of a cone of sugar, which came from the south and was extremely expensive.

Since she might never return to Gendormargensis, Yen Olass now, for the first time, actually got round to visiting the Vel-pliski Statue Gardens, famous throughout much of the surrounding territory, but patronized by few of the inhabitants of the city itself. It was a quiet place, full of grass, moss, sunshine, flowers, olum trees, groves of grey sprite bamboo, plum trees, and of course, statues—of men, of women, of children and of animals. Including bears.

The largest statues were those of a dragon and a whale. The whale looked like a bulbous log with a few half-defined excrescences growing from its body. This monster was said to live in the sea, a ship-length of quiescent blubber, feeding on driftwood, seaweed and landlost gnats. Yen Olass was not convinced; the whale was hardly a credible creature. For that matter, she was not convinced that the sea existed, at least not as it had been described to her; she suspected that the sea was half extravagant imagination and half irresponsible exaggeration.

The dragon, on the other hand, carved from stone but painted in the colours of flowers and fire, was so powerful and vibrant that it insisted on the autonomous drama of its own life. Besides, the dragon was not just a credible creature, but also a necessary creature, for each element has its own animal, and the dragon was the beast dedicated to fire, as the worm is to earth, the bird is to sky and the fish is to water.

There were some children playing on the dragon, and for a while Yen Olass watched them. Then one fell over and grazed her knee. A mother appeared, but scolded the child instead of comforting her:

'Look what you've done! Didn't I tell you? Didn't you listen to me? I just can't trust you. Now you—listen—next— time . . .'

This said while shaking the child.

Which started to cry, a hopeless sobbing wail.

'It's no good crying. It's your own fault. Didn't I tell you? Come along now.'

And the child was dragged off, still crying.

And Yen Olass wished she could have intervened, because the child was so little, and it was only being itself. Yen Olass— vulnerable because her own world was breaking up around her —was quite upset by what she had seen.

She returned to the bears, which were shown fishing in the river. Yen Olass was an expert on bears, or thought she was. They are the laziest and most comfortable creatures in all of creation; they go fishing and honey-eating, and never get told off for getting their feet wet.

'So you like bears, do you?' said a voice.

And Yen Olass discovered she was being observed by a street derelict, some old soldier without a pension.

She let him tell her all about bears, about how to build bear traps, how to track a bear, the diseases bears carry and how bear meat should be cooked; at the end of his lecture he clearly expected a little money, but instead she gave him rather more.

As she left the statue garden, Yen Olass thought about the children she could have if she was exiled with Lord Alagrace, and married him. She would not be cruel to them; she would dress them in bearskin, and they would live some place where they could run free . . .

Returning to Lord Alagrace's residence, Yen Olass found a letter of summons waiting for her. She was required to present herself to the Library, immediately, with all her equipment.

Yen Olass was irritated. The last time she had been ordered to the Library, they had gone through her copy of the Book of the Sisterhood page by page, checking every flaw and blemish against their damage records, and they had spent half a day doing it. Never mind. Soon she would be out of the city, and free from such petty harassment.

She went along to the Library and took all her equipment to the Head Librarian for scrutiny; her nordigin, her Casting Board, her Indicators and her copy of the Book. The Head Librarian took them away from her.

'We're keeping these.'

'For how long?' said Yen Olass.

'They're confiscated.'

'But I'm leaving the city tomorrow!'

'Are you?'

'It's all arranged.'

'I have instructions here,' said the Head Librarian. 'You are to report to the Silent One. Immediately.'

Yen Olass obeyed, trembling.

When she was ushered into the presence of the Silent One of the Sisterhood, she found herself in a room of ivory and pearl, white as snow and cirrus cloud. Yen Olass made reverence to the enthroned entity who sat veiled in silk, waiting. For what? For a confession? Well, she was not going to get one that easily.

Finally, the Silent One spoke. Her voice was clear, well-modulate and imbued with an imperious anger.

'Yen Olass Ampadara, you have dared altogether too much.'

Yen Olass held her tongue. She would wait for a bill of particulars before she started to defend herself, otherwise she might betray herself by disclosing crimes which the Silent One could not even guess at.

'Why have you taken it upon yourself to move your place of abode to Valslada?' said the Silent One.

'I have been accommodated in Lord Alagrace's city residence because I leave with his convoy tomorrow, for the south.'

'Who has directed you to go south?'

'I am the loyal servant of the Sisterhood,' said Yen Olass. 'I exist only to serve.'

'Well spoken,' said the Silent One. 'We will now give you your chance to serve. Lord Alagrace has made a written application requesting your services for his journey south; this application has been refused.'

Yen Olass stood there in silence, feeling her throat choking up. She was so disappointed. Back to the Woman Sanctuary! She would have to watch out, or somebody would be sure to steal her new boots. It would probably be best to take them to bed with her. And what about her brand new coat? What was she going to do with that? It was definitely against the Rule.

'Another fate has been decreed for you,' said the Silent One. 'We are selling you to Losh Negis, the Ondrask of Noth. He wishes to breed from you.'

'What!'

The Silent One sat in a manner true to her name, letting the cry of outrage which Yen Olass had given die away.

'I'd rather die,' said Yen Olass.

'You have our permission to withdraw and commit suicide,' said the Silent One, without emotion.

That last answer left Yen Olass entirely defenceless. She knew that if she was prepared to die she would have killed herself at the age of twelve. She knew that she wanted to live, even if she had to eat shit for breakfast for the rest of her life. But the Ondrask? He stank. He was a barbarian. He was illiterate. He would treat her like a dog. And he had other women already, she had seen them at his yashram, they would hate her and steal her boots. And when he grew tired of her, what then?

'Does he know . . . ?'

'The Sisterhood does not ask what the Ondrask does know or does not know,' said the Silent One. 'We are satisfied that to serve his wants in his instance will be to serve our own best purposes. We no longer regard you as an asset to our organization.'

Yen Olass bowed her head, fighting down tears. She did not want to be smothered by a stinking barbarian, to chew furs and sew clothes, to live in a yashram with dogs and lice and squalling children and alien women who hated her.

'Return to Lord Alagrace and advise him of our decision,' said the Silent One. 'Another oracle can be supplied to him for the journey south if he so desires.'

Yen Olass, not wanting to make her situation any worse, made reverence to the Silent One, then fled.

Lord Alagrace was not at Valslada. She sought him in Karling Drask, and found him in the office of the Lord Commander of the Imperial City; he was trying to instruct the new incumbent on how to conduct the census planned for the coming winter, and was not pleased to be interrupted.

When Yen Olass made it clear her need was urgent, Lord Alagrace took her into a side room, where she poured out the troubles of her heart.

'Well,' said the Lord Alagrace, when she had finished, 'there it is. It's not what we wanted, but we'll just have to live with it.'

'It's me who has to live with it!' said Yen Olass.

'I don't see what you're making such a fuss about,' said Lord Alagrace. 'Coming south with me, you were likely to get yourself killed. This way, you get a man, a house, some children.'

'I can't have children!' wailed Yen Olass.

That was not true. Despite what the Sisterhood had done to her at the age of twelve, she was still entirely capable of breeding. However, Lord Alagrace, who had no precise knowledge of the messy details, had no reason to think she was lying. He thought of childbearing as the essence of a woman's estate; to his own mind, the inability to bear children must necessarily be a tragedy for a woman.

'If you can't have children,' said Lord Alagrace, 'the Ondrask will just have to endure the disappointment.'

'But he'll beat me!'

'A slave's estate is a hard one,' said Lord Alagrace, unmoved.

'If we go now we can get away,' said Yen Olass. 'I can come with you. I can help you. I can be very, very good. You'll die without me.'

'You'd be a help when I met Khmar,' said Lord Alagrace, 'but I can't take you south. A hundred yahooing Yarglat would ride us down. You don't seem to realize that my authority in Gendormargensis is finished. Everyone knows or thinks that Khmar is displeased with me. If I give them a chance, the Yarglat will be more than happy to kill the last surviving member of the High Houses of Sharla. By the same token, it doesn't matter if you tell all the world what we've done together in the past. I'm not likely to come back here as Lawmaker—or as anything else.'

'You mean you want to die?'

'I mean I accept my fate, whatever that may be. Yen Olass, we can only struggle so much against what life has in store for us. Now remove yourself. I have business to conduct.'

Yen Olass left Karling Drask, crying, and not caring who saw it. But on her way back to Valslada, she dried her eyes, and began to think. She realised now why the Silent One had directed her to take the news to Lord Alagrace. The Silent One had guessed, more or less, what would take place. It had been done deliberately, to show Yen Olass that there really was nobody in all the world who would help her or defend her.

Now she had no friends in all the world.

She wished she could run away somewhere. She wished she could run away to the cave near the hunting lodge at Brantzyn. She had really enjoyed herself there, with her fire as her friend and her horse as her friend.

Well? Why not run away?

She had a horse, and her saddle bags were all packed. She could not run north: the bandits in the Sarapine Ranges would get her if the pursuit failed. But south . . . south was Khmar. The lord emperor, terrible and entirely unpredictable. Could a slave petition the lord emperor? She would find out, by asking him.

At Valslada, Yen Olass saddled Snut and loaded him up for her journey. She put on her league rider's weather jacket and her new lightweight fur coat. She armed herself with her weapons.

She was ready to go. She would camp out that night, sleeping in her snow-coat, safe under a horse blanket with Snut.

Yen Olass mounted up.

'Ya!' said Yen Olass.

And Snut made for the stable door.

'Hey, you!' said a voice.

It was one of the stable hands. Yen Olass could have explained herself with any of a thousand lies, but instead she panicked.

'Ya!' said Yen Olass. 'Ya!'

As Snut raced past the stable hand, he grabbed one of her boots and pulled her out of the saddle. She fell heavily. Getting to her feet, she slugged the stable hand as he grabbed her, and he staggered backwards. As Snut came back to see what was wrong, Yen Olass snatched her sabre from its saddleside sheath.

'You want to play rough, huh?' said the stable hand, and picked up a pitchfork.

Yen Olass hesitated. He frightened her.

'What's this?' said a familiar voice. 'What's going on here?

It was a league rider, the one who had once spent an afternoon teaching her how to kill people.

'The slave was trying to steal a horse,' said the stable hand.

'I was riding on business for Lord Alagrace,' said Yen Olass.

'A slave does not ride with weapons,' said the stable hand.

'I'll settle this,' said the league rider. 'Girl, come with me. And you—get back to your work.'

Out in the grounds, away from the stable, the league rider talked with Yen Olass. Not knowing what else to do, and with no percentage left in telling lies, she told him the truth. He was young, and bored after months of idle peacetime duty; he had already been paid off by Lord Alagrace, and his service would end when Alagrace departed from the city. A good gallop wouldn't do him any harm at all.

'I'll get your horse,' he said, 'and mine. I'll tell them you persuaded me you had a legitimate mission to Brantzyn, that I accompanied you half the distance for your protection, and last saw you heading north.'

Yen Olass was sure he was going to rape her, kill her, steal her horse or sell her to a slaver down the river, but what could she do? To go might be disastrous, but to stay was impossible.

'Thank you,' she said.

CHAPTER
Eight

Lord Alagrace was annoyed when Yen Olass disappeared, particularly after a casual enquiry established that there was ultimately nothing to stop an oracle from having children just like any other woman. As he saw it, Yen Olass had turned down a chance for her life to end happily ever after. Now she was a runaway slave, and likely to go under the spikes when she was caught. He was disappointed in her.

A three-day womanhunt failed to locate Yen Olass. After an ugly interview with the Silent One, and an acrimonious argument with the Ondrask, Lord Alagrace left Gendormargensis with Chonjara, the Princess Quenerain, some servants, a contingent of thirty soldiers and some mules.

They voyaged in a ferry boat down the Yolantarath River, which first winds south as it flows from Gendormargensis toward the western coast of Tameran; at the southernmost point of the river, they picked up the Yangrit Highway and travelled thereafter by land.

Travelling at the personal command of the emperor, they could demand horses from the way stations along the highway. These served the imperial couriers, and consequently stocked only the best animals. However, as they could seldom provide more than half a dozen mounts, the convoy travelled at the marching pace of the infantry.

They journeyed south at a leisurely pace, for Lord Alagrace was in no hurry to face the emperor. Sometimes they halted by night in a town or a village, and sometimes a way station accommodated them; on occasion, failing to reach a way station before dark, they halted in woods or by fields, put up tents, and cooked over open fires, sleeping with guards on watch for gypsies and thieves.

Every evening, Lord Alagrace practised with the sword, preparing himself for the confrontation at Favanosin. He did not contemplate challenging his emperor; rather, he was perfecting himself for his death.

Sometimes they halted at a place large enough to support its own tea pavilion. Always there was water, for this was a land of streams and small rivers, and no community built its houses far from running water. At every tea pavilion, Lord Alagrace indulged himself with the silk girls. He rather enjoyed these melancholy autumn evenings: the wine mellow, the sunlight fading, a faint smell of cooking smoke on the air, and a girl with a klon playing in the plankenyi style, one note allowed to die away before the next started.

He indulged himself shamelessly in regret. He had served the Yarglat faithfully, believing that the ends justify the means. Then, in the Blood Purge, the ends had disappeared—so how was he to justify the means he had used? There were still his hopes of succeeding through Celadric, of course, but those hopes were a pale shadow of the glory of his original ambitions. The high civilization of the High Houses of Sharla was now lost forever, the people who could have rebuilt it buried in mass graves . . .

And now, since Khmar was probably going to kill him, even his hopes for Celadric were at an end . . .

Lord Alagrace knew he had failed, and therefore he was released from the demands of ambition. For those of us ruthless enough to discipline ourselves according to the dictates of our unlimited ambitions, to fail becomes the ultimate luxury. and so it was with Lord Alagrace: like a man bleeding to death in a warm bath, he felt slow, comfortable, languid, unable any longer to summon sufficient passion to lament his own fate.

Where had he gone wrong? To find the answer, he reviewed his past. He had studied the evolution of empires, consulting old texts and modern histories derived from the same. He had placed his faith in a future of rational administration where the stable bureaucrat would be more important than any warlord with his sword imbrued with slaughter. Though Khmar had seemed a disaster to civilization, Lord Alagrace had taken the opportunity to become mentor to Celadric, Khmar's eldest son; as the boy grew, Lord Alagrace had taught him a new ethic in which planning, negotiation and consulation were more important than battle, glory and conquest.

His fault, really, was that he had indulged himself in the

present by postponing his struggles to an indefinite future. Celadric might die, or might come to power when Alagrace was dead. Lord Alagrace should have tried to wrest the empire from Khmar. There were ways. A mercenary army, a conspiracy, an alliance with the Witchlord . . . he could have tried. Attempting to overthrow the horse lord would proably have meant his death, but he was doomed to die anyway . . .

And now that it was all over, for the moment . . . life was sweet. The wine, the notes of the klon, the voice of a silk girl lifted in a plaintive song . . . a leaf falling toward running water . . . evening, and a fish taking an insect, clearing the water in a smooth curve . . . a metal, with the savour of sauces, recalling other places, other times . . . then the darkness, and perfume against his skin, hands nourishing his flesh, eyelashes whispering against his cheek . . . smooth hair, warm lips, a sigh . . .

A girl who says she loves you . . .

Sometimes, his flesh striving toward spasm, he would almost allow himself to be convinced that there was some revelation to be discovered in this crisis of desire. Sometimes, afterwards, he almost allowed himself to be persuaded that he was a great lover, and that the girl did, indeed, love him . . . at least a little. Yet he never quite managed either of these feats, for failure did nothing to strengthen his powers of self-delusion.

The silk girls were a cadre of desirable whores reserved for the higher castes in an effort to save them from the diseases the common soldiers shared in the stews—diseases which often meant, eventually, not just buboes and genital warts, not just sterility, stinking discharges and the inconvenience of pissing through an ulcerated urethra, but, with time, blindness, paralysis, insanity and death.

Despite medical inspections, this method of quarantine was not foolproof, but it afforded the high-born with a degree of protection. The silk girls for their part were glad enough to escape from the routines of army brothels; while they were safer from the classic venereal diseases, the advantages of being a silk girl did not end there.

As silk girls, they enjoyed better food, clothes and accommodation; they were protected from violence, and saw only one client in an evening, instead of twenty. Their smaller clientele made them less likely to develop the cervical cancers encouraged by the rampole efforts of hundreds of dirty penises; the link between the dirty penis and cervical cancer had been demonstrated just ten years previously by the great medical statistician, the First Honour Inspector of Human Biology, Tarlor Poutan na Venski (another victim of the Blood Purge), who had begun his elegant and exhaustive study after discovering that oracles, being virgins by law and necessity, never suffered from this kind of cancer.

Together with these advantages, the silk girls benefited from better contraceptive methods—sponges soaked in olive oil were the most reliable, and both these products were imported at great expense by way of Ashmolea. When these methods failed, they enjoyed the services of a better class of abortionist.

Furthermore, clients were free to buy the silk girls from the state, thus releasing them from the nightly routine of enticement, excitement and surrender. No matter how enchanting the entertainer, Lord Alagrace knew that calculation ruled every gesture, every murmur, every touch which treasured his flesh. For these girls, as their charms declined with age, would be returned to the army brothels; if nobody intervened, they would end their lives as old, diseased slave women, sorting coal from rock in the screening sheds of a mine, or working dawn to dusk spinning hemp to rope.

Whenever a girl mimed passion, or said—as if confessing a secret none other had been privileged to hear—that he had gratified her desire. Lord Alagrace always reminded himself that for any of these slaves of the state he would be a desirable owner. He was old, and at least a little soft-hearted; it was even odds that he would leave a girl her freedom in his will, and a little money to sweeten that freedom. And he knew himself to be old-fashioned and straightforward, an easy customer, his usual satisfactions being suggested mostly by biology; unlike some, he had no wish to have a woman sewn up tighter, to push his fist into her privacy, to see her satisfy a dog, to mark her neck and watch her mouth gape.

Possessed of such knowledge, he succumbed to no infatuations; the blandishments designed to satisfy that most subtle sexual organ, the ego, never persuaded him to believe that he was in love. Yet, even so, he allowed himself to enjoy those blandishments. It gave him pleasure to listen to some melodious, faintly fevered voice massaging his sense of mastery:

'. . . You're the first man I've met who's been able to touch me like that . . . I don't know what it is, but I can't resist—this . . . do you like this? Does it make you happy? I want to make you happy, you're the most beautiful person I've ever met in my life . . .'

Often he would fall asleep with some woman gentling his body; at the end of the day he was sometimes very tired. But sometimes, if the girl was drowsy and fell asleep before he did, Lord Alagrace would lie awake and allow himself to think about his lifelong service to the empire.

In his youth, fighting in the armies of the Collosnon Empire, he had allowed himself to believe that he pursued power only in order to rise to a position where he could serve the higher purposes of civilisation. But in fact, he had existed as a function of his own ambition, which had been gratified time after time; on first leading his own troops to victory, he had felt like a young god, strong, powerful and immortal.

Now in his declining years, he sometimes doubted even the existence of the 'higher purposes' which had been the excuse for his drive to power. It was generally agreed that an empire was the highest expression of civilisation. Yet, supporting the glory of the greatest empire was the grubby, commonplace suffering: a woman in the sweating darkness of an army brothel closing her eyes as a soldier shoved his penis into her vagina, a sewn-up oracle falling asleep in a cold bed in a solitary room, a legless soldier begging bone-sustenance in the streets of Gendormargensis . . .

Yet surely it would all be worth it if Celadric became emperor and brought about a new form of government, more reasonable, more humane . . . yet what if reasonable, human government only created reasonable, humane nightmares? . . . down from the hills comes tribes of fratricidal barbarians, battering each other's skulls with jagged rocks, then eating the corpses so produced. Settling in the cities, they become reasonable, humane and civilised, learning to prefer cats instead of dogs. Their wars are fought in accordance with rules designed to make them reasonable, humane . . .

Half-remembering half-translated pieces of the Book of the Remnant, that ancient and fragmentary account of the Days of Wrath, Lord Alagrace would sometimes fall asleep to dream of reasonable, humane wars fought with weapons which never killed, but, instead, softened the skull, ate out the eyes, turned the finger joints to jelly . . .

Discovering such doubts in his old age, he did not struggle for answers, but instead indulged himself, to a degree, in self-pity, in a sense of futility. Perhaps all his life had been for nothing... no matter. Defeated, he had nothing more to live for, therefore... these final days were sweet.

His contemplative calm allowed him to enjoy sunlight and cloud, landscape and skyline, a cup of wine and the heat of a woman's body, and, every day, the rituals of the blades. Working with his sword, perfecting techniques of balance and timing, attack and evasion, feint and follow-through, he sometimes recaptured, just for a moment, the sense of godlike strength which had possessed him at times in his youth.

And often, at the end of a perfect autumn day, he thought to himself: this day has been enough. It has been enough to have lived just for this day, this one perfect day...

And so, travelling south toward Favanosin, Lord Alagrace reconciled himself to death, and made himself ready for it.

CHAPTER *Nine*

The slave Yerzerdayla was sold down the river by the dralkosh Bao Gahai, who was jealous of her beauty and who needed the money. Since the collapse of the Safrak Bank, the economy of the Safrak Islands was marginal; even as chief confidant of the Witchlord Onosh Gulkan, Bao Gahai could not live in the style to which she had once been very much accustomed.

Gendormargensis was known to be glutted with women, so the slaver who bought Yerzerdayla, and a string of half a dozen other women besides, took them south. Khmar was in the south. If you had the best in the world, then an emperor's court was the best place to sell it, and the slaver was confident that Yerzerdayla was the best.

At the river port of Locontareth, he picked up a couple of guards for the journey down the Yangrit Highway. One was a semi-alcoholic drifter from some distant place by the name of Rovac. The other was Yarglat the Yarglat, a morose, solidly-built warrior from the north. Both had their own horses, and hired themselves out on the cheap; the slaver was uncertain of their fighting ability, but wanted them more to scare people off than for anything else.

Everyone rode. The slaver had no fear of his property escaping on horseback, for where would the women go without male protectors? And what fate could improve on a place in the imperial court?

When the slaver caught Yarglat the Yarglat casting long glances at the elegant Yerzerdayla, he cautioned the guard about property rights. But when Yerzerdayla herself chose to ride beside Yarglat, the slaver did not intervene.

Many leagues down the Yangrit Highway, when the tall and slender Yerzerdayla was riding beside Yarglat—it was a fine day, with gleaners following the harvest on either side of the road, and a hawk wheeling overhead—the female slave addressed herself to the warrior:

'You know, I first met you when you were twelve years old.'

'You would have been in your cradle then,' said Yarglat the Yarglat.

'No, I was twenty years of age,' said Yerzerdayla.

'That would make you close to forty now. You can't be more than twenty-five.'

'I'm twenty-five exactly. But I've suffered the prisons of Bao Gahai, which lie beyond the realm of time.'

'What's that like?'

'It's like it was before you were born. It's like nothing at all. When you come out, the whole world has changed, but you're not even a single day older.'

'That's hardly a punishment.'

'You find yourself in the future—which is not the world you were born to. Nevertheless, not everything is strange. You, for instance . . . you're the woman I saw in the child.'

Yarglat the Yarglat was silent, watching their shadows ride shadows down the highway in the westering sunlight of an autumn afternoon.

'I brought you a piece of a cone of sugar . . . afterwards. Don't you remember, Yen Olass?'

'There was a woman,' said Yarglat the Yarglat, reluctantly. 'I thought there was something about you, when I first set eyes on you. But I couldn't think what . . .'

'Well,' said Yerzerdayla, 'it's been close to twenty years for you, and scarcely five for me.'

'Even so . . .'

'It was your walk which first gave you away. Did you ever see a Yarglat tribesman who wasn't slightly bowlegged? Right from the first, I wondered what you really were. I watched you closely. You made mistakes, you know. A Yarglat horseman talks to his mount, and sometimes claims to hear it talking back. He might stroke it or kiss it—but no Yarglat ever hugged a horse.'

Yarglat the Yarglat blushed.

'Your voice betrayed you, too. Not every man has a low voice, and yours was scarcely soprano. But your voice penetrated. It was that of a trained speaker. That gave me something to work on. I saw you never drank grain spirits—only wine. Now, did you ever meet a Yarglat clansman with a taste for wine?'

'Perhaps I'm the first.'

'And perhaps not. Yesterday, when we passed that convoy of high-born Yarglat clansmen going north, you hid your face. I was watching you. I saw. So here's a mystery. Someone who is not of the Yarglat yet may be recognized by them and does not wish to be, someone with a professional voice and a taste for wine . . .

'Not much to go on.'

'No. But I worried the problem all through the day; the answer came in my dreams. When I woke this morning, I knew. Yen Olass, what are you running from? Where are you going to?'

But Yen Olass, chagrined at being discovered, was in no mood to trust strangers—particularly not strangers who were tainted by association with the dralkosh Bao Gahai.

As they rode south, she waited to see how Yerzerdayla would use this weapon against her. In Gendormargensis, she had learnt that nobody ever obtains an advantage without trying to exploit it. Yerzerdayla was virtually powerless, and therefore, in the way of those who lack power, must be prepared to use vicious means to obtain her own ends.

Now Yen Olass watched Yerzerdayla not out of curiosity but out of fear, hating the alien woman, hating her tall and slender beauty, and hating the insights of her acute intelligence which had discovered who and what Yen Olass was.

*   *   *

Nearing the borders of the old empire, they were warned that the newly conquered territories further south were as yet not entirely subdued. Partisan bands harried the roads, making travel dangerous for small groups. The slaver put up a tea pavilion, to wait until they could join a larger convoy; he idled away his days drinking and gambling with the Rovac guard, and was usually dead drunk by nightfall.

While they were waiting there, a brawling group of Yarglat officers came north. They filled the tea pavilion with their noise and their boasting, talking of slaughter and rape, of dawn attacks, of fugitives hunted and caught, of torture, arson and pillage. Yen Olass knew that if she was caught, these were the people who would subject her to their justice. She could imagine all too precisely what they would do to a runaway slave.

Yen Olass fled to the safety of the stables. There, she discovered Snut was not being looked after properly. She was furious. She started making life hell for the stable hands. These slaves were all the same—except the further south you got, the idler they got.

She was interrupted by Yerzerdayla, who called her outside. Yen Olass supposed that Yerzerdayla had chosen this moment to blackmail her. So what should she do? Run? Or kill her enemy?

'Yen Olass,' said Yerzerdayla, 'you mustn't treat people like that. How can you behave like that? Aren't you ashamed of yourself? Kicking that poor little hunchback dwarf!'

'He's a worthless stinking slave,' said Yen Olass, viciously.

'A slave, is he?' said Yerzerdayla quietly. 'And what are we?'

'Don't you lecture me, you whore,' said Yen Olass. 'You skak! You filthy female inlet!'

Yerzerdayla slapped her, smashing an open hand across her face.

'Don't you ever talk to me like that again!' said Yerzerdayla, her voice hissing with fury. 'Don't you ever, ever talk to me like that again!'

Yen Olass, her eyes smarting with tears, turned on her heel and stalked away.

'You come back here!' said Yerzerdayla. 'You come back here this very instant!'

But Yen Olass kept going, quitting the tea pavilion for the

comparative safety of the small town nearby. Should she stay? If she did, Yerzerdayla might have her killed. Should she run? She had to go south, because only Khmar could grant her absolution; without Khmar's pardon, she would live the rest of her life as a runaway slave under sentence of death. But the roads were too dangerous for her to travel alone. She had to stay with the convoy, no matter what the risk.

To console her sorrows, Yen Olass indulged herself outrageously, spending half her money on a string of amber beads. They were very beautiful. She suspected they were loot, the price knocked down because the market was flooded with plunder from the south, so she felt guilty about buying them— but she could not resist them, all the same.

At a tavern, she bought herself just a little red wine. It was Lord Alagrace who had introduced her to wine. In the tavern she found, to her disgust, men eating huge bright-red insects. It sickened her: the gross size of the insects and the gusto of the men who were demolishing them. The insects, clad with grotesque armour and sprouting huge feelers, were hideous.

One of the men saw her disgust, and, laughing at the ignorance of the people from the north, offered her a bit. Yen Olass could not bring herself to be rude enough to refuse hospitality. She accepted: and was surprised.

'What is it?' she said.

'Gaplax,' said the man.

Yen Olass smashed her fist down on the table as she rose to her feet: Yarglat the Yarglat could do no less when someone used such an obscenity to his face. This brought a roar of laughter from the whole table.

'Sit down,' said someone. 'Have a drink.'

'I only drink wine,' said Yen Olass coldly.

'That's fine, for that's all we've got.'

They sat the foreigner down amongst them, and explained that 'gaplax' was the name the insect owned in one of the languages of the south. No insult was intended.

'That's just as well,' said Yen Olass, 'for I've killed a man for less.'

This brought more laughter.

'Laugh as you will,' said Yen Olass. 'I killed my first man at the age of twelve. I've killed many since.'

That sobered them up a little, for here at the southern border of the old empire it was well known that northerners were casual killers, not to be trifled with lightly. However . . . there was wine, bread and gaplax, the weather was fine . . .

'This is no day for fighting,' said one of the southerners. 'Share a gaplax with us. Better still, have one yourself.'

'How much do they cost?'

'It's on us. Make yourself comfortable. Come on now, take off your coat.'

'I can't.'

'And why not?'

'Because,' said Yen Olass, sweating, 'the killer of my father rides south, I have vowed to suffer until I have killed him.'

'Where in the south would this gentleman be?'

'With Khmar.'

Conversation faltered. In Gendormargensis, imperial politics was the commonplace of gossip, but under provincial interpretations of the law it was very easy to get oneself accidentally convicted of treason—so one did not speak lightly of the emperor.

Still, the death-vow made the northern stranger even more fascinating to the southerners than before. While they demolished a skin of wine and a brace of gaplax between them, Yen Olass told of the death-fight between Tonaganuk and Lonth Denesk, Chonjara's public penance, the exile of Haveros, and the day the Ondrask of Noth disgraced himself by throwing his mother-in-law in the river.

The last tale was a vile and gratuitous slander, but none of these southerners was to know that. Indeed, they were so ignorant, no naive, so ready to swallow down even the most outrageous improbabilities, that Yen Olass yielded to temptation and indulged in a number of staggering untruths concerning certain high-born Yarglat clansmen.

It was evening when Yen Olass made her way back to the tea pavilion, mellow with wine, and stuffed with bread and gaplax. She knew now that the gaplax lives in the shallowest waters of the sea, the males hiding themselves under rocks while the females recline in nests made of water-twigs, comforting a brood of eggs. If you whistle in a certain way—and Yen Olass had mastered the certain way of whistling—they will march out of the water and line up on the shore before you. Alternatively, they can be secured by knocking two stones together: the sound stuns them, and they float to the surface, paralysed.

The tea pavilion was gaily lit with lanterns. It was crowded with Yarglat officers, heavy with drink, their brawling energies now replaced by drunken nostalgia.

Yen Olass did not want to venture into the company of those drunken animals. She stayed in the gardens, wandering by herself, wishing there was enough light left for her to admire the trees and the fish ponds. Wishing, too, that she could stop being a man, at least for a little while, since she took no pleasure in keeping her breasts bound up, in shrouding her body in concealing furs, in conjuring up aggression to handle minor social contingencies which would have been easily dealt with by way of little diplomacy.

Alone in the garden, she listened to the music from the tea pavilion. She listened to the music of zither, klon and slubvox, to the atonic wail of a woman's song pitched to heartbreak, and it seemed the song spoke to her, to her alone:

> In the river I glimpse my lover's face,
> Gone passing, many moons;
> In the smoke I glimpse horizons elsewhere,
> Gone passing, many moons;
> Homeland of my children never born.

And now the moon itself was rising, tangled in the branches of the trees. Yellow moon rising. Yen Olass stretched out her hands to the moon, and said the Old Words, as her mother had taught her:

'Allmother moon . . .'

That was as far as she got. She could not remember the rest. She had forgotten. She had entirely forgotten. The Old Words were gone, forever. How could she have been so careless?

Yellow moon . . . yellow moon . . . a woman singing . . . wine, which disarms us . . .

Yen Olass stretched out her arms just one more time, and said, to the moon, to the yellow autumn moon (is it so much to ask?):

'Allmother moon . . .'

But it was no good. She could not remember. She had lost her mother, and now she had lost even her mother's words.

And suddenly the ground swayed, her legs buckled, and she collapsed. Wracked by agony, she wept, crushed down to the ground, down to the dank of the earth and the smell of loam and leaves.

'Yen Olass . . .'

With gentle hands, Yerzerdayla raised her to her feet. Yen Olass allowed herself to be folded into the arms of the tall, gentle woman who smelt of the distant spicelands. She clung there, sobbing, while Yerzerdayla soothed her hair, her voice low, a hush of comfort.

Yen Olass wept, as if she would die.

Yerzerdayla held her, protected her, sheltered her, until time and comfort calmed her.

Then:

'Come,' said Yerzerdayla. 'We must talk.'

CHAPTER
Ten

Counselled by Yerzerdayla, Yen Olass stayed behind when the slaver moved on. She recognised the truth of the points Yerzerdayla had made. Khmar was capricious, true, and it might amuse the emperor to receive a petition from a woman. However, Khmar would never be free to indulge himself like that.

This was how Yerzerdayla put it:

'A man lives by his image of men. Khmar has spent his life being more a man than other men. Therefore, he is no longer free to be anything else, even if he wants to.

'You must not come to him as a woman alone. He likes people who dare, but he could never allow himself to like a woman who dares in her own right. If you come to him, you must do so under the shield of a man. Lord Alagrace must be that man.'

So Yen Olass waited for Lord Alagrace.

When Lord Alagrace finally came down the Yangrit Highway, Yarglat of the Yarglat was waiting for him, and Alagrace of course recognised her immediately. So did Chonjara and the Princess Quenerain, who were all for denouncing her and having her put to death. But Lord Alagrace overruled them.

As Yerzerdayla had predicted, while Lord Alagrace might have been resigned to death when he left Gendormargensis, death would grow less and less attractive as he approached it. He had not been prepared to raise a finger to help Yen Olass in the north, but, since she had helped herself, he was now prepared to exploit her for his own advantage.

Pleased to be exploited if it meant she would survive, Yen Olass outlined the campaign she had worked out with the help of Yerzerdayla.

Lord Alagrace should write a report and send it on ahead by courier to the Lord Emperor Khmar. In the report, Lord Alagrace should say that after thinking about the problems in Gendormargensis, he had come to realize that they had all resulted because some high-born Yarglat clansmen had been denied the natural outlet for their energies which should be seen as part of their birthright: war.

If Khmar was angry with events in Gendormargensis, the line of defence chosen would appeal to him more than any groveling apology.

As a footnote, Lord Alagrace could note that a band of women had dared to thwart the Lord Emperor's Lawmaker by denying him the oracle of his choice. However, thinking it would reflect badly on the emperor if his Lawmaker yielded to the Sisterhood, Lord Alagrace had taken the oracle south with him regardless . . .

As plans went, this one was shaky. However, it might serve to blunt Khmar's wrath, and Lord Alagrace, who had been unable to think of anything better, drafted the report and sent it on ahead—hoping it would reach its destination, and not be seized by the partisans who were managing to kill one courier in seven.

*   *   *

Travelling south, they entered recently occupied territory, and the pleasures of travel diminished. The countryside was restless; as thirty men could not guarantee their safety, they travelled with a hundred. They passed burnt-out ruins, body-pits and crucifixes burdened with bodies.

The road was passable, with slaves hard at work upgrading it to military standard. In many places, waystones had yet to be erected; it felt strange to travel without seeing those monoliths

carved with glyphs proclaiming the texts of the Law. The southerners here were dour, sullen, alien—and, naturally enough,
they had been conquered too recently to have learnt Eparget,
though some of the people had picked up a few words of Ordhar
from the troops.

In such situations, the command language ran a great risk of
contamination. Despite the best efforts of imperial discipline,
Ordhar refused to conform to the laws laid down for it, and was
forever acquiring souvenirs from foreign lands, developing eso-
teric slang and allowing bits of alien tongues to be spliced into
its fabric.

It was important that Ordhar be kept pure and simple, for it
had been designed as a standard language for all the armies of
the Red Emperor, Khmar. Where waystones had been erected,
text-masters attached to the conquering armies posted lists of
forbidden words, such as 'okaberry', a local word meaning
'rotten' or 'unsatisfactory', and now apparently increasingly
used by the troops when speaking of their food, their officers
and the weather.

The common soldiers were contaminated with such words
when they slept with the local women, which they found easy
enough to arrange, since there was a shortage of food usual in a
war-ravaged countryside, and many women were selling their
bodies to keep themselves and their families alive. Here there
were no tea pavilions and no perfumed silk girls with downcast
eyes and smooth-oiled thighs; Lord Alagrace found nothing to
tempt him, and abstained.

While travelling, Lord Alagrace scarcely saw General Chonjara, who preferred to travel in the rearguard. When there had
been tea pavilions, Chonjara had never patronized them; he had
no taste for silk girls, preferring to slip away and find something else, although Lord Alagrace was not exactly sure what,
and chose not to find out. Now that they were in hostile territory, Chonjara sat up late with the soldiers, drinking, singing
and telling jokes. This raucous carousing kept the Princess
Quenerain awake, so she complained bitterly. Lord Alagrace
ignored her complaints, for the princess had not endeared herself to him on this journey; nothing was good enough for her,
and she treated every inconvenience of the road and the weather
as if it were a personal insult.

Yen Olass enjoyed the journey. To the south lay danger, but
also hope. To the south, too, lay the sea. Every evening she

practised the whistle she would use to summon the gaplax out of the water, and imagined how impressed everyone would be when they came trooping out of the sea to line up in front of her. Everyone would eat well, when they got to the sea.

Occasionally soldiers came to ask for a reading, so Yen Olass begged some paper from Lord Alagrace, and, using his writing brushes, she marked out a Casting Board and made 365 paper Indicators. Though the Sisterhood had withdrawn her right to practise as an oracle, the soldiers were scarcely concerned with the legal issues involved, and, this far from Gendormargensis, there were no other oracles to give her any competition.

Chonjara's bodyguard, Karahaj Nan Nulador, came to ask about his wife; she had been pregnant when he had said good-bye to her in Gendormargensis, and he was worried about her. He found it hard to sleep at nights. Yen Olass tried to reassure him. Failing, she worked on him with her hypnotic skills, reaching the point where she could put him to sleep with a word, and his worries were gone by the time they drew near the sea.

Yen Olass now began to get very excited. She regretted the professional dignity which prevented her from pestering people with questions: is it really salty? is it really wide as the cattle plains? are there really waves the size of houses? will there really be whales? do whales really exist?

But the sea, when they got there, turned out to be a cheat. It was a dull piece of water looking like a narrow lake. Yen Olass rode ahead of the convoy, following the highway down to the waterside. She dismounted, and scrambled over the shore, wrinkling her nose as she caught the smell of the water.

It did not look very promising.

The rocks were damp. Green stuff like moss grew on them, and they were very slippery. Yen Olass did her whistle, then waited. Nothing happened. She tried again. Maybe there weren't any gaplax on this part of the coast. She turned over a rock, to look for a male gaplax. To her great excitement, she found all kinds of tiny insects under the rock. But they were not like the gaplax. Some were green and some were brown, and they had claws like a scorpion she had once seen in a book. They scuttled away into hiding. When she tried to grab one, it bit her with its pincers, then held on relentlessly; finally, her eyes smarting, she had to smash it with a rock.

That made her remember about banging rocks together to call

out the gaplax. She pounded stones together—to no effect. Finally, she took off her boots, waded into the sea, and started manhandling some of the larger rocks. But she never saw a gaplax, or even the empty nest of a gaplax.

Wet, frustrated and disappointed, Yen Olass gave up, and turned back toward the shore. Looking inland, she saw the entire convoy drawn up on the highway, watching her in silent amazement. She put on her foot bindings, put on her boots, then stumped over the stones toward her horse.

'Have you been enjoying yourself?' said Lord Alagrace.

'The sea stinks,' said Yen Olass, mounting up.

Then she galloped off down the road, swearing to herself. Later in the day, when Lord Alagrace caught up with her, he explained that the sea was much bigger than the part they had seen so far, and much cleaner.

'What?' said Yen Olass. 'Is it only this part that stinks?'

'All the sewage from Favanosin rides the tides into this fiord,' said Lord Alagrace. 'When we travel over the hills ahead . . .'

He told her what they would see, but Yen Olass did not believe him until her horse finally crested the heights, and there before her lay the sea—a vast plain of pewter stretching away to a southern horizon where thunderclouds black as coal dust were brewing one of the storms that the Pale was so notorious for.

'Down there,' said Lord Alagrace riding beside her, 'that's Favanosin.'

But Yen Olass had no eyes yet for the town: she was still gaping at the sea.

'If you're impressed by natural phenomena,' said Lord Alagrace, 'then you've got a new treat in store. The Lord Emperor Khmar is down there, waiting for us.'

He was reminding her of the task at hand, and the challenge that awaited them.

'I'm ready for him,' said Yen Olass, sounding as confident as she felt—for some reason she always felt more confident when she was riding a horse, lording it over the world beneath her.

However, when the time came to actually face the emperor, some of that confidence disappeared: this would not have surprised anyone who knew Khmar.

CHAPTER
Eleven

The Lord Emperor Khmar hated living inside buildings. Enclosed by four walls, he became uneasy, disturbed by the dead air, the muted sounds, the diminished contact with the weather. Appreciating the benefits of impressing the populace with his wealth and power, he allowed architects to build him palaces, but he refused to inhabit them; the glorious Retzet t'Dektez in Gendormargensis was empty but for guards and caretakers, as Khmar had never so much as stepped inside it.

It was, therefore, hardly surprising that Khmar chose to live outside Favanosin, in tents pitched on good grazing land. There he received reports from the commanders trying to sanitize the mountains to the east and the west, and consulted those officers now trying to plan the next major campaign—an invasion of the southern continent, Argan.

Khmar still had time free to plan a reception for Lord Alagrace, a man he had little liking for; he had saved up some pirates especially, so he could intimidate Alagrace by making an example of them.

When Lord Alagrace reached Favansin, he was not immediately invited to present himself to the emperor; instead, Khmar interviewed his daughter, then spent two days closeted with General Chonjara. Only then was Lord Alagrace allowed to approach the imperial presence.

Khmar's tents were made of leather supported by bamboo poles. They were not utilitarian survival shelters, but impressive pieces of architecture in their own right; a mounted warrior could have entered the main tent without ducking his head. Guarding Khmar's home was a bizarre bodyguard, an indication of the true nature of the emperor.

Some rulers like to pretend that the exercise of power is an aesthetic enterprise. Approaching their thrones, one enters into an ordered and denatured universe where every care has been taken to exclude any hint of pain or suffering. Khmar needed no such pretences; he travelled light, owning few possessions and no illusions, and saw no need to conceal what he was or how he had come to be what he was. His bodyguards were all veterans who had been crippled or mutilated in battle. Some were minus a hand or an arm, others lacked an eye or a nose, and one—the victim of enemy torture—endured his days without any cheeks, these having been cut away, thus making it difficult for him to drink and impossible for him to chew food in the ordinary way. These bodyguards were tough, arrogant men, confident of their fighting ability; they were armed to the teeth with whips, ropes, bolas, throwing knives, spikes, swords and battles-axes.

When Lord Alagrace, accompanied by Yen Olass Ampadara, arrived for his audience, he was shown inside by a spearman who stumped around on a peg leg. In the main tent, Lord Alagrace and Yen Olass seated themselves on leather cushions in the presence of guards, scribes and a foodtaster. The two scribes were both legless; the foodtaster was blind. There was no doubt that Khmar was a barbarian: but he honoured his obligations.

As Khmar did not immediately manifest himself, Lord Alagrace and Yen Olass had plenty of time to meditate upon the less pleasant aspects of war—and the possible consequences of Khmar's displeasure. Both were acutely aware that the Princess Quenerain and General Chonjara had been given ample opportunity to poison the emperor against them.

After they had waited for some time, a young man entered, looked them over, then withdrew. Yen Olass did not recognize him, but Lord Alagrace did: Exedrist, the drunkard. Khmar had four sons, Celadric, Meddon, Exedrist and York; Exedrist lived with his father and served more or less as a messenger boy.

A little later, Exedrist returned:

'The Lord Khmar regrets that he will be delayed, but invites you to indulge your appetites while you wait. He recently had the leading citizens of this town barbecued for conspiring to conceal their wealth—would you care for a choice portion?'

'Thank the Lord Emperor for his consideration,' said Lord Alagrace, 'but we have already eaten.'

Perhaps Khmar had arranged for one or more people to be cooked alive, and perhaps not; if they accepted his invitation, perhaps they would be served human flesh, and perhaps just pork, but Lord Alagrace, who had both personal and religious objections to cannibalism, did not wish to take chances. Exedrist smiled, and Lord Alagrace realized that Yen Olass had lost much of her colouring.

'Khmar is not a monster,' murmured Lord Alagrace, as Exedrist withdrew. 'He simply has unusual enthusiasms.'

Yen Olass, feeling slightly ill, said nothing. However, she had composed herself again by the time the Lord Emperor made his entrance, striding into the tent with an easy, rolling gait.

Khmar was a squat, ugly, blow-legged man with calloused, muscular hands, big bony fingers and thick, horny fingernails. His dark eyes glittered, hunched in shadow beneath lumbering brows. Scalps dangled from his big skullknuckle belt. A respectful two paces behind came a svelte young man with a cool, calculating gaze. This was Celadric; Yen Olass had seen him before in Gendormargensis.

'Alagrace,' said Khmar, without ceremony. When he spoke, Yen Olass saw his teeth were filed to points.

'My lord.'

'A good journey?'

'Excellent, my lord.'

'But you chose lame horses. Yes? Why so slow? Because I was waiting to chop your head off? Believe me, I was tempted when I found out how you were dawdling. Here—look at this. See what they've made of my son.'

Seizing Celadric, Khmar pulled him forward like a slaver leading an auction piece to the block. Celadric, the ultimate diplomat, remained unruffled, preserving his dignity. At twenty-three years of age, he was already a power in his own right, having obtained port privileges for the empire in Ashmolea, and having successfully negotiated valuable trading concessions in the Ravlish Lands.

'See!'

'He's grown tall, my lord,' said Lord Alagrace.

'Yes. Tall and beautiful. Like his mother. He gives tentspace to tame poets, who sing the praises of his flesh. Eyes like limpid olives—hands as soft as dead men's cocks. I am my father's son—but my son is his mother's little girl.'

Celadric shook off his father's grip.

'As an instrument of state policy,' said Celadric, 'rape has its limitations. Sometimes it's better to teach a foreign power to love us.'

'Hear him!' said Khmar, showing his scorn.

'I've succeeded where you've never ventured, and never will,' said Celadric.

His tone was not one of defiance, but one of certainty; Yen Olass realised Celadric had no fear of his father, and this knowledge comforted her. Perhaps, if something terrible happened, she could throw herself on Celadric's mercy. Perhaps he would help her.

'Oh yes,' said Khmar. 'Some we must love. And why? Because we can't ride horses over water, that's why. Or so the past tells us. But that changes. Now! We're learning to walk on water, even now. We'll take them. First Argan. Then Ashmolea.'

'What do we need it for?' said Celadric.

'Listen to my son!' said Khmar. 'What do we need it for? We need as a man needs a woman. My age must conquer—now!—because his age never will. Isn't that so, Yen Olass?'

Hearing the Lord Emperor pronounce her own name, Yen Olass flinched as if she had been hit.

'Why did you run away, Yen Olass?' said Khmar.

'Lord Alagrace wanted me to south with him,' said Yen Olass, 'but the Sisterhood refused. When the Sisterhood defies the Lawmaker, surely my duty is to serve the Lawmaker, who holds power as your personal appointment.'

'Who asked you to play politics?' said Khmar.

His voice was savage. In his voice, Yen Olass heard the lash, the knives, the spikes. Yen Olass quailed.

'My lord, I exist only to serve,' said Yen Olass, trembling.

In her voice was complete and total surrender. She hoped surrender would be sufficient. But it was not.

'You defied the man who had been made your master,' said Khmar, relentlessly. 'Why? Surely Losh Negis was man enough.'

'I first met him when we were hunting,' said Yen Olass. 'He prided himself on his skill. Was it wrong to give him a chance to prove it? Was it wrong for me to want a man to hunt me down? Do you think I never looked behind me, in the hope of his dust? I hoped for much, but the way was too easy.'

Yen Olass was playing the part of one of the archetypal women of Yarglat mythology: the highblooded female who runs and resists in the hope of being hunted down and raped. Khmar was not immune to the appeal of the myth.

'He was a man,' said Yen Olass, her voice now strong and vibrant. 'Or so I thought. The man to take me. The man to master me. I trembled for his touch. Yet the horizon lay empty behind me.'

Khmar grunted.

'You came south. You followed the same road as Alagrace.'

'Did I make the chase too easy then?' said Yen Olass. 'Should I have gone to east or to west?'

Khmar grunted again.

'You talk of Losh Negis, but when you get here, it's Alagrace you've chosen as your master.'

'A woman must have a man to serve,' said Yen Olass. 'Since Losh Negis will not master me to his purpose, I must serve what man demands me.'

'You are not a woman yet,' said Khmar. 'Just a girl. Perhaps you feared to be made a woman.'

Yen Olass lowered her eyes.

'I hoped with fear. I will not say I was not afraid. This filly feared, yet hoped for a stallion. She has not been gratified.'

'Losh Negis,' said Khmar, 'has sat by the fire too long. There is a disease. Men call it civilisation. He has begun to suffer. He needs something wild enough to cure him. I'll send you north, and he can face the consequences. If he really needs me to break his women to service, there's something wrong with him.'

And Khmar reached out, and touched her. His hand was warm against her cheek. Yen Olass did not know emotion was appropriate, and therefore showed none.

'A man should have had you sooner,' said Khmar. 'In my grandfather's day, you would not have waited so long. There was no Sisterhood then. No sewing up.'

'The empire was smaller then,' said Celadric, his voice oboe-smooth. 'Simplicities sufficed.'

'Then and now,' said Khmar.

'We are faced with the case of a slave who ran away from the Sisterhood,' said Celadric.

'From Losh Negis.'

'From the Sisterhood,' said Celadric. 'She had not been handed over to the Ondrask when she fled.'

'A quibble,' said Khmar.

'No,' said Celadric. 'A point in law. You have seen the correspondence. It is the Sisterhood which demands that she go under the spikes.'

Khmar grunted, and glared at his son. He had not, of course, read any correspondence on the matter, though he might have had some read out loud to him.

'The law is my law,' said Khmar. 'The Sisterhood obeys me.'

'You can enforce your law in Gendormargensis as you wish,' said Celadric. 'But at what cost? The Sisterhood serves us in many ways. Since the Blood Purge, who else can we rely on for order in Gendormargensis? If this slave can challenge the Sisterhood, others will surely try it.'

'So?'

'So kill this worthless female inlet, otherwise you may one day have to kill people you value.'

Yen Olass by now had conceived a murderous hatred for Celadric. As she listened to the cool, elegant young man writing her life off, she wished she could tear his face off.

For a moment her life hung in the balance. Khmar was undecided. He did not like being lectured by his son. Nevertheless, there was some truth in what Celadric said.

'In my youth,' said Khmar, 'I rode females as you ride horses. The filly is far from worthless. The fault lies with Losh Negis. With some speed for the hunt, he would have made her his woman. If he chose to sit in his yashram poking his fire, he can't hope for my sympathy. He loses his woman.'

'But the Sisterhood—'

'I declare the slave sold to Losh Negis,' said Khmar. He hunted for one of the foreign words introduced into Eparget to express legal terms necessary for ruling an empire, yet lacking from the language of the Yarglat. He found what he was looking for. 'Retrospectively. A word which alters history, yes? I did not believe it, but my son once told me it was just so. Yes. Retrospectively.'

Yen Olass saw that Khmar was poking a little fun at his son, and enjoying it. Dragging out some more ponderous legalese, savouring its alien flavour, Khmar continued:

'The Sisterhood's claims to the slave are null and void. It is Losh Negis who owns her. And it is I, Khmar, who takes the woman from him. Because I love him. Because I wish to stir the man in him. Because I wish to remind him that he is too young to squat by his fireside—and to remind him what happens when he does. The woman can stay with Alagrace, as his oracle.'

'She cannot be an oracle,' said Celadric, 'for an oracle, by definition, is a servant of the Sisterhood. She—'

'She's sewn up tight enough,' said Khmar. 'That makes her oracle enough for me. Yen Olass—you will be Khmar's oracle. Khmar's own Sisterhood in the south. Till I'm dead. Then my son will kill you.'

Khmar hawked, and spat on the floor.

'You think I hawk and spit because I'm a barbarian,' said Khmar, addressing Yen Olass. 'Well, I am. And proud of it. I'm my own man, not like my son, owned by a thousand weightless talk-talk men, castrated dancing boys the lot of them.'

He glared, and pointed at Celadric.

'I can see what's coming when I'm gone. Perfume-farting hairdressers made ministers of state. Shit-soft little law-voicers snuggling up the emperor's ear, pleading discretion. Well, not till I'm dead. That's for certain. That's something.'

He turned his attention to Lord Alagrace.

'Oh, Alagrace will love it when I'm dead. Old woman-breasted Alagrace. He's waiting for it.'

'My lord—'

'I never said you'd hasten it! Only that you waited for it. Isn't that so? Well? Tell me? Is he waiting for it?'

The question was for Yen Olass. She sensed that the question was a test of some kind. She had to presume that her life depended on the answer. For the moment, Khmar had granted her life. Yet, if he executed Lord Alagrace—as a traitor, perhaps? —he might slaughter her as well. Had he planned it that way? Was he amusing himself, by giving her a hope of survival, just so he could take it away?

'Well?' said Khmar.

'The question,' said Celadric, 'is not rhetorical.'

'Who is it who asks me to play politics?' said Yen Olass. 'Is it you?'

Her question was directed at Celadric. She was hoping that whatever answer he gave would entangle father and son in an argument, distracting attention from her. She desperately needed time to think. But Celadric did not get a chance to speak.

'I do!' said Khmar.

'Am I the road or the traveller?' said Yen Olass.

Now all her training and experience as an oracle was being brought into play. She felt as if she observed the proceedings from a staggering height. She felt lucid. Weightless. She saw everything with hallucinatory clarity: Khmar's predatory eyes, Celadric's cool disdain, the relentless scrutiny of the body-guards, the intense blue of the sky framed by a flap-window, the sharp pinpricks of sunlight stabbing through the leather of the tent where a seam was tearing apart.

'You are both and neither,' said Khmar.

Her feint had been deliberately cryptic, sounding out his intentions. By the way he had parried, he had refused to hint at the answer he wanted.

'Khmar is dead,' said Yen Olass, slowly. 'Lord Alagrace and Celadric meet in conference. They had once thought to inherit an empire which they could shape at will. Now they find they are locked in a struggle of life and death with the powers of Argan. The struggle will last out their lives and beyond. They find they have not inherited an empire: they have inherited Khmar.'

There was silence. Yen Olass conjured up an image of amber. Contemplating the everspan peace of encapsulated light, she meditated.

'Who tells you of Khmar's wars?' said Khmar, frowning; the invasion of Argan was a long-standing part of the empire's policy of expansion, but the imminence of that invasion was not supposed to be common knowledge.

'The whole waterfront talks of it,' said Yen Olass. 'It is said that soldiers talk because they have tongues. That suggests a remedy, if I could name the culprits: but I cannot.'

'And what were you doing on the waterfront?' said Khmar.

The question caught Yen Olass off balance. Unable to conjure up a plausible lie—she had lied so often to save her life that by now the truth seemed lethal—she told the bare facts.

'Finding out where the gaplax come from,' said Yen Olass.

'I could tell you the answer to that,' said Khmar. 'They're spawned by sons with their cocks up their mother's bums.'

'Not that kind of gaplax. It's an insect. It's half as long as your arm. They live in the sea, and they're caught in pots. They're caught with rotten meat, not by whistling. They're bright red. Not before, but after. They're cooked in boiling water.'

Yen Olass realized she was babbling, and stopped abruptly. Then she added—she could not help herself—

'But they're very nice to eat.'

'Then we will have some cooked for us,' said Khmar, clapping his hands, once, to signify that the audience was over. 'We will eat alone. Alagrace can go. He has already eaten, and we have no wish to overfeed him.'

Yen Olass and Lord Alagrace both made reverence to the emperor, and began to withdraw.

'Yen Olass,' said Khmar, 'I said that we would eat alone. Not me. We. We is two people.'

In the mouth of an emperor, of course, 'we' can mean many things. But Yen Olass did not say this. For once, she was lost for words.

CHAPTER
Twelve

A man does not eat with a woman. A master does not eat with a slave. And the emperor most certainly does not eat with a female slave.

Yet this happened.

The kitchen did not talk of this. The kitchen talked, instead, of the gaplax. What if Khmar developed a taste for them? What if he called for a gaplax when he was a thousand leagues inland? How many chefs' heads would it take to teach him the difficulties of transporting live gaplax as far as Locontareth or Gendormargensis?

Khmar was usually content with horsemeat, and that was the way the kitchen liked it. This Yen Olass had a lot to answer for.

Halfway through the meal, the kitchen had other things to worry about. Khmar's bodyguards burst into the kitchen tent, seized the entire staff, dragged them outside and bound them to execution posts. Khmar's foodtaster was writhing on the ground, vomiting his heart out. If the same happened to Khmar, heads would roll.

Fortunately, Khmar did not suffer. The foodtaster had proved allergic to seafood, but the emperor suffered no ill effects, to the great relief of the kitchen.

Even at the best of times, the incident with the foodtaster would have spoilt the meal. Yen Olass had a very uncomfortable time. Khmar always seemed on the point of saying something—and always withdrew. What was he afraid to tell her? Perhaps he wanted to ask for a reading, yet was too . . . too embarrassed to?

The day and the danger were not yet over. On the principle that it is always best to die with a full stomach, Yen Olass ate her way through four gaplax. She had invented the principle on the spur of the moment, to justify making a pig of herself.

'You have strong appetites,' said Khmar.

'I was born biting,' said Yen Olass.

And that was as near as they came to small-talk.

*　　　*　　　*

After the meal, Khmar resumed his audience with Lord Alagrace, with Yen Olass in attendance.

'Not all your actions have pleased me,' said Khmar to Alagrace, opening his attack without ceremony.

'I have done my best in accordance with the law,' said Lord Alagrace, stiffly.

It was exactly the kind of opening Khmar was looking for. If Alagrace had not given it to him, Khmar would have created it.

'I know all about your version of law,' said Khmar. 'Warming your hands with your arse while voices clock the sun to the western horizon. That's your law—now you see mine. Bring in the pirates!'

Armed guards brought in four swarthy-faced men who were forced to the ground in front of the Red Emperor.

'They claim to be ambassadors,' said Khmar, 'going to see Ohio of Ork. Do you hear that? Ohio of Ork! Some pirate pretending to be a king. There'll be no pirates in my waters, not once I'm finished with them. We have to build seapower. Wipe them out. You've seen what they've made of my son, Alagrace, but a grease-arse diplomat like him could never get rid of the pirates. This is the way to do it!'

So saying, Khmar grabbed one of the men—scooped him up, lifted his body toward the roof of the tent, then hauled it down from the air, breaking the spine across his knee. Then he tore out the throat with his teeth. Then grinned: blood and sharpened ivory.

One of the three remaining men got to his feet and charged. He died before his second step—nine pieces of metal sticking into him. Six knives, two spears, one tomahawk. Khmar's bodyguards were the best.

That left two men.

One cowered down on the floor, but the other spoke rapidly.

'What is that rabble speaking?' said Khmar.

'He is speaking one of the southern languages,' said Celadric. 'The Galish Trading Tongue. It is one in which I have acquired some fluency. He asks for the oracle to give him a reading.'

'A reading!' said Khmar, displeased at this interruption to the outright slaughter he had planned. 'Who told him about oracles and readings? You? No, don't answer, I've no time to listen to any lies. Well—is he entitled to a reading? Yen Olass?'

'No,' said Yen Olass. 'He is an outlander. He is not entitled to a reading.'

'So what should we do with him?'

Nobody answered.

'Yen Olass? I asked you a question.'

'I am a woman,' said Yen Olass, cautiously. 'I do not dispose of the lives of men. It is not for me to say.'

Truth to tell, Yen Olass believed that girls can do anything, but she told her emperor what she thought he wanted to hear.

'Oh, most excellent of liars,' said Khmar. 'Yen Olass, you can be emperor for a moment. More: you are emperor. Decide.'

Yen Olass hesitated. What kind of game was this? She did to dare presume that the meal Khmar had given her was a sign of favour: he might turn on her in a moment, and butcher her, then joke about how he had been fattening her up for the table. As she hesitated, Celadric spoke:

'Since when did you take instruction from a female?'

'I want to see how a female rules,' said Khmar. 'Then I will know how things will be when my dear Celadric comes to power.'

Why did Khmar dart such insults at his son? Perhaps he wanted Celadric to attack him, and die in the attack. Perhaps he wanted Celadric to try and kill him—and to succeed. Celadric himself understood Khmar's bitter words as the last sport left to a dying man, and perhaps he was right.

'Speak, Yen Olass,' said Khmar. 'Silence, all. Hear the woman emperor.'

Yen Olass now held in her hands the lives of two men. She doubted if she could save them both. One of them, perhaps? Perhaps.

'Certain acts unthink certain thoughts,' said Yen Olass, pointing to a fresh-killed corpse. 'A man lies dead. Another man hears of it. His destiny was to be an assassin of great fame; instead, he earns his fame by knifing wood for block prints. This is necessary. Power must be manifest—but likewise mercy.

'A ship confronts the navy. If captured, all die. They have heard of this. With no hope, they fight to the death. Men die for no purpose. If there is the possibility of mercy, hope will disarm trapped men. Victory comes easy. Mercy is a potent weapon in the arsenals of a great power.

'Yet the emperor lives by strength. The emperor must show mercy, but must not cherish weakness. So preserve the survivor. As a free man or as a slave—by your judgment. Let them fight for the privilege.'

Khmar laughed.

'Is it true what the rumours say, Alagrace? Is it true you let this woman help you rule your city?'

'No,' said Lord Alagrace.

'Then more fool you,' said Khmar. 'Celadric—tell them. Trial by unarmed combat.'

Celadric hesitated.

'He flinches,' said Khmar. 'He'd have a woman killed, that was easy enough. But he falters when it comes to men. Celadric, you'll have three men to kill when I'm gone. York, Meddon, Exedrist. When I'm gone.'

So saying, Khmar raised his voice to a battlefield bellow:

'Do you hear that, Exedrist? Are you listening, you softbrained vermin? Do you hear me? Do your spies hear me?'

He coughed then, and spat.

'Otherwise, civil war. You'll find out, soon enough. Soon, I'm dead. No—don't say otherwise. Soon I'm dead. I'm a sick man already. Shitting blood and leaking water. You'll have your test soon enough, Celadric. Now tell them! Combat!'

Celadric spoke, and the two remaining pirates squared off. A moment later, one lay dead. The survivor withdrew his blade: a vicious little boot-knife with an oosic handle. Not much of a weapon, but still lethal in the right hands.

'Who gave him the knife?' said Khmar. 'Was it you, Celadric? Was this animal your assassin? You don't want to answer? I'm not surprised. No matter. I'll be dead soon anyway. But when we leave tomorrow for Gendormargensis, you'll be leaving some of your skin here, that's for certain.'

Celadric showed no emotion. He had excellent self-control. Khmar pointed at the surviving pirate:

'Celadric. Tell your assassin that a man who takes orders from a woman is only fit to be the slave of a woman. And the slave of a slave woman, at that. Tell him he belongs to the oracle. From now on, she is his god, and he will obey his god in all things—or die.'

Celadric translated, and thus it was that in the autumn of the year Khmar 19, the oracle Yen Olass Ampadara acquired a slave, an Orfus pirate from the Greater Teeth, a man by the name of Draven (Bluewater Draven, not to be confused with Draven the leper or Battleaxe Draven or with Draven the Womanrider, even though he'd done a little of that in his time.)

But that was not the end of the day's business. Khmar was fatigued, but he was not finished.

'Alagrace, now—I had so many, many things to say to you. We were going to have a very interesting conversation here. There were so many things you had to explain. But now . . . now I don't care for the answers.'

That was as close as Khmar could come to admitting that he was exhausted. When he said he was sick, he was telling the honest truth. He knew his own mortality.

'So let me tell you your duties. Your orders have been written down for you, in detail. You always were the best at logistics, weren't you? Argan is yours. Chonjara will help you take it— you need a good fighting general to give you some fire in your belly—but overall command, that's yours.'

Khmar held up his hand.

'No, I don't want to hear it.'

'But my lord—'

'Do it,' said Khmar. 'It is finished.'

When Khmar used that formula, everyone knew better than to argue. Lord Alagrace, granted leave to speak, would have argued for hours against the invasion of Argan. Alagrace had always argued that any move south of Tameran must be preceded by a campaign against the Ravlish Lands, which would secure ports from which the Collosnon Empire could project seapower into the Central Ocean. However, Khmar—who could not swim—had planned this war between continents by looking at a map and seeing where there was the smallest gap between landmasses. Khmar, the Master of All the Cavalry, the Horse born of the line of Horse, was not amenable to argument.

The audience was at an end.

*   *   *

The next day, Yen Olass saw Yerzerdayla at a distance, comforting Celadric after his public punishment. She realized Celadric had bought Yerzerdayla and at first she was horrified at the thought of such a cold-blooded monster owning such a warm, generous woman.

But then, when she thought about it, what better fate could Yerzerdayla have hoped for?

Yen Olass sensed that Yerzerdayla would organize Celadric, and that he would appreciate her incisive intelligence, her poise, her elegance. They might never love each other, but their relationship might, in time, become an alliance of powers: in time, Yerzerdayla might make herself empress.

Now, if Yerzerdayla had been bought by Khmar . . . that would have been a disaster.

What kind of woman would Khmar want?

Yen Olass lay awake at night, thinking about it. Thinking about the way Khmar had denied Losh Negis the right to claim the flesh of the woman he had bought from the Sisterhood. About the strange meal they had had together. About the way he had let her decide for the pirates.

The emperor could scarcely take Yen Olass to bed. Whatever her legal status, she was of the Sisterhood. The most powerful men in Khmar's empire were those from the Yarglat clans which had followed him out of the north, and those men tended, like Chonjara, to be true to the old ways. Such men might tolerate oracles, and even make use of them on occasion—but to have their emperor succumb to one? That would be a different thing again.

Everyone remembered the reign of terror of the Witchlord,

Onosh Gulkan. An oracle who captured an emperor might all too easily remind men of the wiles of the dralkosh, Bao Gahai of evil memory. In the popular imagination, the gap between an oracle and a dralkosh was not so terribly wide. A great warrior, Haveros, had recently been seduced by a dralkosh. An emperor could not be presumed to be immune . . .

Yen Olass realised Khmar had chosen the path of discretion for good and sufficient reasons. But she could not help thinking that she was better equipped to live as an empress than as a slave.

*   *   *

Lord Alagrace knew why Khmar had put him in charge of the invasion of Argan. Logistics was his speciality, in which no Yarglat clansman could match him; the invasion across the waters of the Pale was going to need an enormous amount of planning and organisation, which made Lord Alagrace the inevitable choice as supreme commander.

He accepted his fate.

But one person who did not accept her fate was the Princess Quenerain. Her father had told her she was going to go to Argan in her capacity as head of the Rite of Purification. She was appalled at the prospect. In effect, she was being exiled from Gendormargensis. She thought her father was punishing her—and she was right.

CHAPTER
Thirteen

In Favanosin, Lord Alagrace, dealing with military simplicities instead of the delicate politics of Gendormargensis, had no need of an oracle to help him. Yen Olass lived alone in a small two-room house, the property of a midwife who had fled when Khmar's troops invaded; she never saw Lord Alagrace from one week to the next. She drew food and fuel from Central Supply, eating well, for as an oracle her rations were those of a junior officer.

Winter came, and it grew cold. The days shortened, but little snow fell. Instead, pounding rain swept in from the Pale, obliterating the sun. Everything became damp and wet for days on end; fires smoked, the roads were churned to mud, mould clagged the walls, and eyesight itself faltered in the dull everwater light.

Yen Olass was homesick that winter, dreaming back to the cold, hard snows of the north, and the clear cold skies of the northern winter. The days passed slowly. She made a proper Casting Board, and fashioned 365 Indicators from pieces of wood, but few people came to ask for readings. She grew lonely.

She had nobody. Even Snut had gone off to war in the mountains, and Yen Olass had said a parting for him. She tried to make friends with some of the local fishermen, so she could go out and help catch gaplax, but women were bad luck in and around boats, so they rebuffed her.

Draven might have been company of a sort—though Yen Olass had to admit she was a little afraid of him—but Lord Alagrace had requisitioned him almost immediately, providing him with quarters elsewhere, and women and wine as well.

Draven drew maps and charts from memory, described wind tides and beaches, inspected ships, advised on rigging, and, once he had mastered sufficient Ordhar to command men in his own right, trained soldiers to be sailors. Lord Alagrace then had to intervene to protect Draven from the wrath of the textmasters, who caught him mixing foreign words with his Ordhar commands; this was unavoidable, as Ordhar lacked the vocabulary for dealing with shipboard life.

Lord Alagrace was desperately short of the equipment and expertise needed to get an army across the Pale. The navy was almost nonexistent: the empire could scarcely protect its newly conquered lands from pirate raids. Shipyards were labouring on new vessels, while agents acquired others in Ashmolea and the Ravlish Lands, but the manpower shortage had to be remedied, for the most part, by training people from scratch. It is not the easiest thing in the world to turn a soldier into a sailor. Lord Alagrace, in fact, thought it an offence against nature—but it was necessary, so he got it done.

So Lord Alagrace kept Draven, and never found time to spare so much as a thought for Yen Olass. However, when she wanted something done, she commanded it using the formula 'Lord Alagrace had decreed'. In this way, she got shipwrights to build her a nordigin in which she could keep her Casting Board and her Indicators, she got her chimney swept and she got her front door replaced. Now that she had a door at last, she was not going to settle for second-best.

Her situation was anomalous. For the moment, Central Supply treated her as an oracle attached to the army. But what would happen when the army moved on? The emperor had named her 'Khmar's own Sisterhood in the south'. But, in legal terms, what did that actually mean? When the army moved on, would anyone have a duty to feed her?

Yen Olass began to hoard food. She requisitioned an extra daily ration from Central Supply, for 'entertainment'; nobody questioned it. But, as her supply began to mount, she grew slightly guilty, and started to set aside half her extra ration for feeding beggars. At dawn and dusk she distributed a little bread and barley-meal griddle-cakes to half a dozen human scarecrows who came to her door.

Sometimes, Yen Olass thought she would rather have fed birds—or cats—but there were none to be had in Favanosin. The conquering army ate reasonably well, buying up the entire fishing catch and importing food as well, but the local population was starving. The average life expectancy for any stray animal bigger than a cockroach was now only half a day—and even cockroaches found life dangerous.

This monotonous existence ended at midwinter when Lord Alagrace, his transportation and supply problems shaping up nicely, turned his attention to minor matters such as the question of translators. Here the text-masters had failed him badly. Khmar had authorised Alagrace to take text-masters south of Tameran. However, although many were trained in the languages of Argan—including the High Speech of wizards— none was eager to chance the perilous expedition south. Demands sent to Gendormargensis brought back only excuses, most of which were of a medical nature impossible to verify or dispute at a distance. Those text-masters who had accompanied the troops to Favanosin, and had interfered ever since, zealously defending the purity of Ordhar, discreetly disappeared when in danger of being ordered south.

Lord Alagrace, as always, did not despair, but improvised. His agents had acquired, from the Ravlish Lands, two men who spoke the Galish Trading Tongue, the lingua franca for much of Argan. He would use these to teach others. Among those he requisitioned for his new cadre of translators was Yen Olass Ampadara.

Veteran soldiers are skilled foragers, with a habit of converting any portable item to their own use. Yen Olass was a natural target for Lord Alagrace's recruitment drive. She, for her part, had mixed feelings about this. On the one hand, she hated the thought of having to give up her house. On the other hand, the army would feed, clothe and shelter her, and in Argan she would be safe from the Sisterhood, from Celadric, and from the Ondrask of Noth.

Overall, she was glad to be going south.

That winter three ships were lost to the waters of the Pale, but others voyaged to Argan and returned safely. From the intelligence reports brought back by these ships, Lord Alagrace found it would be easy to take his first objective, Trest, a realm with negligible defences. However, his army would then have to cross a swamp to reach the land of Estar, which he had to secure to get a port on the west coast of Argan. Consequently, Lord Alagrace arranged for the supply of vast quantities of sprite bamboo, so his army could make a corduroy road across the swamps.

Toward spring, small, elite cavalry squads were shipped across the Pale. Their tasks included further intelligence gathering, a little raiding, and the destruction of the temple of Estar, known to be able to call on occult powers for the protection of the land. Argan, that strange and dangerous territory lying beyond the Pale, harboured many minor gods and demons, as well as wizards and other masters of power, dragons, monsters, and ancient strongholds of surpassing strength.

Shortly before the fleet sailed, a letter from the Lord Emperor Khmar told Lord Alagrace the identity of a spy who had been sent to Argan in the autumn.

'He was given the task of securing full knowledge of the defences of the nearest useful port on the western coast of Argan, or, in the event of that port being undefended, details of the defences of the ruling city or castle of the land.'

Lord Alagrace wondered who had drafted this smoothly worded communication for the emperor. How many other people knew the facts? In particular, did General Chonjara know that his enemy, Volaine Persaga Haveros, was now in Estar? Did the Princess Quenerain know? Those three must inevitably meet, and the consequences were potentially disastrous. Was Khmar deliberately putting them to a test of destruction?

(And having thought of that, Lord Alagrace had to consider this: was Khmar deliberately testing his erstwhile Lawmaker by sending him south with Chonjara as his leading subordinate? Did Khmar anticipate a clash of wills, a struggle for supremacy? And did Chonjara?)

Whatever Chonjara knew, thought or felt, he played the perfect professional soldier, dedicating his days to the training of his troops. By the time the invasion fleet was ready to sail, Lord Alagrace knew that everything possible had been done in the way of preparation. The night before they set sail, he went to bed with a good conscience—but dreamed of glowering warriors, of towering hill forts, wizards, lethal magic and dragons breathing fire.

*   *   *

Just before the invasion fleet sailed, Karahaj Nan Nulador found Yen Olass on the waterfront. He waved a letter which had come from Gendormargensis. Nan Nulador was illiterate, but someone had read him the letter, which he had committed to memory. He gave Yen Olass his rendition of the despatch.

'Is that what it says?' said Nan Nulador. 'Is it true?'

Yen Olass read the letter.

'It's true,' said Yen Olass.

And Karahaj Nan Nulador allowed himself to rejoice.

'A son! I have a son! You must give a reading for his destiny.'

So Yen Olass did. This was pure fortune telling, but she had no scruples about that. For the son she predicted life with honour, fame, children, wealth, and death on the field of battle.

'Death with honour?' asked Nan Nulador, anxiously.

'With honour,' said Yen Olass, nodding.

And Nan Nulador was satisfied.

When Yen Olass boarded her ship—all the translators were travelling together, so their taskmasters could keep them grinding away at their lessons—she thought of the child born far away in Gendormargensis. In a very real way, it was her creation: without her help, the mother would have been stoned to death as a dralkosh, and the baby would have been dead before conception.

As the ship trudged away from the coast of Tameran, a raft of sprite bamboo lubbering in its wake, Yen Olass wondered if she would ever see that child: and wished it was hers.

*   *   *

The crossing of the Pale was uneventful for those who did not get seasick. Yen Olass felt fine, but faked the symptoms to get some time free from mastering the trading tongue, which was full of so many strange words for so many weird things: camels, keflo shell, flying fish, ambergris, batador, walrus hide, elephant, mammoth, markhor, ebony, red coral, pumice.

Listening to soldiers' talk, she heard stories of battles, forced marches, sieges and sickness, mutiny, punishment, loot, women and drink. Crossbow experts boasted about how they would down the dragon said to lord it over the land of Estar. Yen Olass dreamed of that dragon—and of the soldiers and their women.

After many monotonous sealeagues, during which Yen Olass grew sick of the smell of hay—her ship was carrying some of the army's reserve supply—Argan came in sight. The southern continent proved to be dull, bleak, and larger than her imagination.

They anchored off Skua, a marginal settlement lying west of Scourside and east of the mountainous Penvash Peninsula. For two days they did nothing; Yen Olass concluded that wars were not as lively as storytellers pretended. Then they landed, finding the shore churned to mud by horses, men and loads of sprite bamboo. Skua had surrendered without a fight, and a force had gone inland to invest the High Castle of Trest; the main body of the army was already marching for Estar.

Yen Olass feared the war might end before she saw any excitement, but, riding a haywagon west, she found the main body of the army camping by the swamps, busy building a corduroy road.

While they were camped near the swamps, the Princess Quenerain came to see Yen Olass.

'I want a reading,' said the princess.

'About what?' said Yen Olass.

'About the prospects for love.'

'An oracle gives a reading only where conflict arises between two or more parties,' said Yen Olass, going very formal on her. 'An oracle does not tell fortunes.'

'I know an oracle who's whored her fortunes through half the army,' said the Princess Quenerain.

This was an exaggeration, but Khmar's daughter had a point. She could make trouble for Yen Olass if she really wanted to.

'Very well then,' said Yen Olass, 'since you insist . . ."

And she told a fortune for the princess. Out of malice, Yen Olass predicted that the Princess Quenerain would meet:

'. . . a tall dark stranger. Very tall. Strong, Vigorous. Riding a stallion, or maybe a stallion riding. Women in love with him. Envy. But he's yours—you claim him. Nobody else can have him.'

The Princess Quenerain swallowed this down like a cat swallowing cream. And believed it. Well, let her believe it. There would be no lovers for a princess here—unless she chose to lie with a common soldier. Knowing the scandal that would cause, Yen Olass hoped she would.

*   *   *

The days went slowly. The road was almost static, like a river of treacle, sogging reluctantly through the swamps at a few paces a day. But, out in the great wide world, things were happening. From usually reliable sources, Yen Olass heard that the temple of Estar had been razed, and that Estar's dragon was dead.

While intelligence reports came in with such welcome news, the corduroy road pushed on through the swamps. Progress accelerated as commanders and men mastered the necessary skills and teamwork. And then, one day, it was done: and the army advanced, leaving behind it an abandoned camp site with its network of paths, tree stumps, tent pitches, latrines, rubbish heaps, hitching posts, fireplaces, manure heaps and empty haywagons.

Crossing the corduroy road was an unsettling experience. The poles of sprite bamboo, laced together to make a road, creaked and flexed beneath the weight of men, horses, oxen and wagons. In places, the bamboo sank below the surface, and Yen

Olass had to march ankle-deep in water: for this invasion, junior interpreters did not rate horses.

When Yen Olass was on one of these waterlogged sections of the corduroy road, the army came to a halt. As they waited, the word came back down the line. Up ahead, a cart wheel had broken: there would be a delay. Yen Olass would have had the cart pushed into the swamp so the army could march on: it was ridiculous to delay the invasion while a wagon wheel was fixed. But presumably the carthands were unwilling to trash their vehicle, and there was nobody at hand with sufficient authority to give them the correct orders.

Yen Olass was not prepared to stand around in the water, even though her boots were by now soaking wet, and could hardly get worse. She pushed her way forward until she could clamber onto a marsh-island which quaked beneath her weight. There she settled herself amongst the harsh swamp grass. Yen Olass had acquired the soldier's knack of making herself at home wherever she happened to find herself. She took off her boots and wrung out her foot bindings. A soldier joined her on the island, which sagged dangerously.

'No more!' said Yen Olass sharply, 'or we'll sink!'

From up ahead, she heard the querulous voice of the Princess Quenerain complaining that there was no water. That was typical. For anyone who was really thirsty, there was plenty of swamp water, although admittedly by now it was liberally laced with the mud, spit and piss of a marching army. But besides that, anyone with any sense had acquired a water skin by now, and kept it full. Yen Olass carried such a skin everywhere, tied to her belt—and, in a small pack she carried on her back, she had emergency rations, a blanket and spare woollen clothing. Her spare foot bindings, boot grease, tinder box and various personal items were kept in the inner pockets of her league rider's weather jacket. But then, Yen Olass was used to adapting to necessity, whereas the Princess Quenerain had always been accustomed to the world changing itself to suit her own convenience.

At length—but sooner than one might have expected—the army started to move again. As they advanced, Yen Olass saw a wagon in the swamp: it had been unloaded then pushed overboard. So somebody had been thinking, after all.

*   *   *

When they camped on the western side of the swamps, rumours and stories began to circulate freely as patrols brought news to the army. Now the ordinary soldiers learnt of the casualties suffered by raiding parties which had infiltrated Estar; they had all known for some time that Estar's temple had been destroyed, but now learnt that only three of the Collosnon soldiers taking part in the attack had survived. Other raiding parties had disappeared without a trace. They learnt also of the strength of Castle Vaunting, the ruling castle of Estar, said to be commanded by a fearsome army of soldiers, adventurers, renegades of one description and another, and Rovac mercenaries from islands far to the west.

However, the army had many victories to its credit, and few of its veterans had serious qualms about the dangers that lay ahead. After days in Argan, they had seen no dragons, no monsters and no magic—in fact, everything had been remarkably commonplace. The general opinion was that the perils of the southern continent had been greatly overrated, and would be matched easily by the skill and strength of the soldiers of the Red Emperor, Khmar.

The next day, the army started for Castle Vaunting. A strong rearguard stayed to protect the corduroy road: Lord Alagrace wanted to ensure that his supply lines stayed open behind him. Patrols and foraging groups spread out into the country on either side of the main line of march, and mounted scouts rode far ahead.

While the main body of the army moved at the walking pace of the infantry, cavalry squadrons drove deep into the territory of Estar. Some were tasked with seizing control of the coastal trading route, the Salt Road, as Lord Alagrace wanted to ensure that no news of the invasion reached powers further south. To help stop news going north, along the Hollern River, some parties of infantry had been given the job of venturing into the depths of Looming Forest and setting up a blockade across the river.

As the army marched toward Castle Vaunting and the associated town of Lorford, Lord Alagrace reviewed the latest intelligence, and learnt of nothing untoward; it would be some time yet before he learnt that three wizards had recently arrived in Estar.

CHAPTER
Fourteen

The invaders were shocked by their first sight of Castle Vaunting. Its battlements seemed endless. Labouring upwards out of a hill of grass, its heights, the details shrouded by heavy rain, made a doom-dark mountain mass; shadow upon shadow, the tors and crags of the enemy stronghold strove toward the darkness of engulfing cloud. Eight towers studded the walls, while the vertiginous gatehouse keep was a fortress in itself. That hulking darkness, lording it over the centuries, had been built to hold against armies greater than theirs.

It was with some surprise that the infantry learnt that the town of Lorford had given no resistance. The cavalry had already secured the Salt Road, the town, and the approaches to the castle.

Working on the commands of short-tempered siege marshals with thunderous voices, the troops made camp, built earthworks to guard against any sally from the castle, and assembled siege equipment. The drawbridge had been pulled up, so they had no easy way into Castle Vaunting, which was ringed with a deep moat with everlasting fire smouldering at the bottom of it. However, it would take more than a ditch and a wall to stop the Collosnon army.

Before the siege marshals assigned tent pitches to the translation section, Yen Olass made sure she got lost in the confusion. She had no desire to help unload wagons and put up tents in the mud and rain. There was a lot happening, and she wanted to see some of it.

While she was inspecting the assembly of some siege catapults, she heard that a monster had been captured in a skirmish to the north, in Looming Forest. Yen Olass suspected this might be a tall story—she had already learnt that an army is a magnificent rumour machine—but decided to go and see for herself.

She found out where the monster was being held: in a tent in the security section.

A guard outside the tent challenged her, but Yen Olass told him she had been asked to inspect the monster then give a reading regarding its provenance and its nature.

The guard expressed his doubts.

'Lord Alagrace has commanded,' said Yen Olass, her voice hard and cold.

And he yielded, allowing her to go inside. Would the prisoners be a real monster—or just a big ugly man?

The first thing Yen Olass saw when she got in the tent was a woman huddled on the ground, weeping. Ignoring her, Yen Olass looked round for the monster. It was everything she could have hoped for.

It was bigger than Yen Olass, and heavier. It was green. Two arms, two legs. Skin that looked hard, almost chitinous. Gill slits on both sides of the neck, which was massive. On the sides of the body, ridges riding against ridges, perhaps protecting and concealing further gill slits. Down at the groin, a knotted complexity of tendons, muscles and raised ridges, hiding the nature of the sex organs from the inquisitive gaze.

So.

A monster—a real monster!

One of the creature's arms had been gashed. The congealed blood round the wound was red. Yen Olass was offended that a monster should have chosen red for the colour of its blood. But then, rats had red blood, and so did cats, and nobody objected to that. But rats were hardly monsters, and cats were really people. Tentatively, Yen Olass reached out and touched the wound, lightly. She was fascinated. She wondered if they would burn the monster, or if it would be stoned to death, like a dralkosh.

Suddenly the monster opened its mouth, revealing a formidable collection of teeth. Yen Olass stepped back smartly. Even though it was trussed up firmly, it might still be dangerous.

The monster made a noise:

'E'parg.'

Yen Olass was not impressed. From such a considerable monster, one could reasonably have expected something more expressive than a couple of nonsense syllables. A growl, for instance. Or a roar.

'The monster went e'parg,' said Yen Olass, 'and the cat went miaow.'

The next moment, Yen Olass was shocked to hear the monster say:

'P'tosh, and the cat went miaow.'

It was echoing her words. But then, birds did that—strange little birds with many colours, which came from Ashmolea, cost a lot of money to buy, and usually died in the winter. Yen Olass had always wanted one.

'You don't look much like a bird,' said Yen Olass to the monster.

She talked to cats and horses, so she saw nothing strange in addressing the monster, even though there was no chance that it would understand.

'E'parg,' said the monster. 'E'parg Hor-hor-hurulg-murg. P'tosh, miaow. P'tosh.'

Yen Olass was annoyed. Her monster had already forgotten all the words she had taught it. All but one.

'And the cat said miaow,' said Yen Olass, firmly.

'P'tosh, and the cat said miaow. P'tosh.'

'What's this p'tosh business?' said Yen Olass.

'P'tosh. Kana p'tosh.'

Yen Olass stared at the monster. Her eyes widened. Kana? Kana p'tosh? Wasn't that one of the phrases her language instructors had drilled her with? Was the monster talking? E'parg—what did that mean? She remembered. In the Galish Trading Tongue, 'e'parg' meant 'I bear', in the sense of 'I am burdened with'; it also meant 'I am called'.

Not sure whether she was allowing herself to hear speech in an animal's grunts, Yen Olass addressed the monster:

'E'parg Yen Olass Ampadara.'

'P'tosh, Yen Olass Ampadara. E'parg Hor-hor-hurulg-murg.'

'P'tosh, Hor-hor-hurulg-murg.'

'Skanskesh. Nordis.'

'Yol, skanskesh,' said Yen Olass, and fed the monster some water from the skin she carried at her side.

Once the monster had drunk some water, it began to speak very fluently in the Galish Trading Tongue, but Yen Olass was unable to understand. She was frustrated by her limited command of the language. She understood 'I am of the Melski' and 'help me', but little else.

To talk with the monster, Yen Olass was going to need help from her language instructors. She knew where to find them. Yet she hesitated. A speaking monster might not be the most welcome contribution to the morale of the Collosnon army. On the other hand, discovering such an interesting beast might win her a certain amount of local fame.

Then Yen Olass realized that a speaking monster would be a valuable source of intelligence. She should go and tell Lord Alagrace that the large, dangerous creature his men had captured in the forest was an intelligent entity in its own right, and could talk.

Yen Olass said goodbye to her monster, and went to find Lord Alagrace's command tent. When she found it, an aide-de-camp collared her:

'Yen Olass,' he said. 'Lord Alagrace is looking for you.'

'That's all right,' said Yen Olass, 'I'm looking for him. Let's go and talk to him.'

'Not yet!'

'But you said he wanted me.'

'He's with the wing commanders right now.'

'Talking about what?'

'Grazing.'

'Grazing!' said Yen Olass, and snorted.

But the aide-de-camp made her wait just inside the entrance of the command tent, which was crowded with officers, messengers, siege marshals and couriers, and filled with a babble of talk. Near the entrance was a torture post, to which a prisoner had been tied. He was being interrogated; an executioner stood off to one side, arms folded, disappointed to find that the prisoner was talking without needing physical coercion.

The prisoner had been stripped of his armour, a weird assortment which included an ornate helmet of polished metal, topped with an irresistible concoction of plumes. Yen Olass looked at it, looked away, looked at it again, bit her lip, hesitated, then grabbed it.

Nobody tried to take it away from her.

Yen Olass smoothed the slightly bedraggled plumes between her fingers, then let them tickle her nose. She put the helmet on, trying it for size. She was surprised how heavy her trophy felt. The padded metal cut down her field of vision and muffled her hearing. The padding was missing from the nose guard, and her nose complained about the cold touch of the bare metal.

'Yen Olass!' said the aide-de-camp. 'We're wanted now.'

Yen Olass marched forward through the gloom of the tent, and halted in front of Lord Alagrace, who was seated behind a campaign desk. Behind him was an open flap-window. On the campaign desk was a basket of bread and gaplax which some fatuous apple-polisher had rescued from the ruins of Lorford. Lord Alagrace, in no mood for gourmandizing, pushed it toward Yen Olass.

'For me?' said Yen Olass, delighted.

'No!' said Lord Alagrace. 'For a prisoner. One of the town women denounced her. She belongs to one of the castle commanders. She's his evening woman. We want her kept in good condition. We may use for her barter if the castle sends an embassy to treat with us. She's your responsibility now. Take her this.'

'Where is she?' said Yen Olass.

'At the security section, of course,' said Lord Alagrace impatiently. 'She's in the same tent as a—what was the thing?'

'A Melski,' said one of his aides. 'A monster from the forest.'

'The monster talks!' said Yen Olass, remembering why she had come to see Lord Alagrace in the first place.

'I'm sure it does,' said Lord Alagrace.

'No, really.'

'Then you can interrogate it for us,' said Lord Alagrace. 'Now go.'

'Sir!' said Yen Olass, slamming her right fist to her heart in a Collosnon soldier's salute.

Then, thinking she might have dared too much, she grabbed the basket of bread and gaplax and scuttled away.

'And Yen Olass—'

She darted between crowding bodies, hugging the basket close to her body. Lord Alagrace's voice, rising to a roar, pursued her:

'Take off that ridiculous helmet!'

*   *   *

On her way to see the prisoner, Yen Olass ducked under a cart, and skulking down low and out of sight, she gorged herself on bread and gaplax. But there was still some left when she got to the security tent. And she was still wearing her helmet.

Inside the tent, the monster appeared to be sleeping, but the woman prisoner was still weeping. Yen Olass was amazed to think that anyone could go on crying for so long. She nudged the captive with her boot.

The woman scrunched herself up into a little ball, like a hedgehog. Yen Olass nudged her again. Harder, this time.

'Hey, you,' said Yen Olass, not bothering to conceal her contempt.

Slowly, the captive uncurled, and looked up. Her face was soggy with misery. A soft, young face, with brown hair straggling down on either side of it. She might have been pretty, if she hadn't been so bedraggled. So this was the castle commander's woman. Or was it? Yen Olass hunted for a word in Galish, and found one: 'seg', meaning whore.

'Seg?' said Yen Olass, a note of interrogation in her voice.

The woman burst into tears and curled up again. Obviously that was the wrong thing to say. Seeing the damage she had done, Yen Olass began to feel a little bit guilty. Momentarily, she wondered what Yerzerdayla would have thought of this. Yerzerdayla would have been appalled to find Yen Olass terrorizing a captive woman.

'Now then,' said Yen Olass, trying to soothe her victim. 'Now then.'

She squatted down by the bundle of misery and wondered what to do next. She touched it with a soothing hand: and it flinched.

'Am I so dangerous?' said Yen Olass.

Maybe, from the captive's point of view, she was. After all, Yen Olass was a big, bulky foreigner arriving in boots and helmet, her sex anonymous beneath weather jacket and furs. In that context, 'whore' had been a disastrous word to use; realising what the prisoner must have thought, Yen Olass was now thoroughly ashamed of herself.

What was the Galish word for filly? Nom? No, that was a word for a female camel. 'Gamos' was a word for any kind of female horse. That would do. Yen Olass practised a Galish sentence in her mind, then said it:

'I am a gamos.'

Silence. Then the captive looked at her, then looked away.

'Gamos!' said Yen Olass. 'I am a gamos!'

The captive began to sniffle violently, crushing her face into her arms. Was she having a fit or something? Suddenly, Yen Olass realised the prisoner was laughing. What was so funny? Her pronunciation couldn't be that bad.

'I am a gamos,' said Yen Olass, starting to get angry. 'A gamos!'

The captive laughed and laughed and laughed. She was working herself into a state of hysteria.

'Say stanaba,' said the monster, Hor-hor-hurulg-murg, who had been listening all the time.

Yen Olass remembered now. That was the Galish word for a female human.

'Stanaba,' said Yen Olass. 'I am a stanaba.'

But she still failed to see what was so funny. She knew that, sometimes nearing the final stages of exhaustion and fear, people will laugh for no reason, sometimes following helpless laughter with a crying jag. That must be what was happening here.

The captive calmed herself and sat up. Yen Olass took off her helmet, and then introduced herself. Yen Olass Ampadara and Valicia Resbit.

'Elkordansk,' said Resbit, patting her abdomen.

'Hungry?' said Yen Olass.

Resbit said several sentences, in which Yen Olass caught only the word 'boy'. She could scarcely be hiding a boy child under her clothes.

'What?' said Yen Olass.

Resbit nursed an imaginary baby in her arms.

'Child?' said Yen Olass, pointing at Resbit's abdomen.

'Boy child,' said Resbit. 'Elkordansk.'

Was she pregnant? If so, this was very confusing, for even Yen Olass knew that a pregnant woman cannot tell the sex of her child. And what was an elkordansk?

'Eat,' said Yen Olass, pushng the remaining bread and gaplax toward Resbit.

As Resbit ate, Yen Olass helped herself to a little more, and they began to talk. Neither of them knew very much of the Galish Trading Tongue, which was not Resbit's native language, but, slowly, they began to make sense of each other, helping out language with mime, with imagination drawings done with a fingertip in the air, and with the occasional astute comment from Hor-hor-hurulg-murg.

There were really starting to get to know each other when there was a commotion outside. Going to the door of the tent, Yen Olass saw a big crowd gathering some distance away; there was a lot of shouting go on.

This looked interesting.

'I'll be back,' said Yen Olass.

But she lapsed into Eparget as she said it, so Resbit did not know what to think when her new friend disappeared.

CHAPTER
Fifteen

When Yen Olass managed to push her away into the centre of the crowd, she found a large ugly man, bound hand and foot to a pole. Yen Olass recognized him without any trouble at all: Volaine Persaga Haveros, sometime Lord Commander of the Imperial City of Gendormargensis. A violent argument was going on as to what should be done with him.

The argument ended when Lord Alagrace arrived.

'Cut him loose!' said Lord Alagrace.

Men with knives went to work. They sliced away the ropes and removed the gag from his mouth. Haveros lay in the mud with the rain falling on his face; he looked dazed, stupid. Lord Alagrace looked around. Yen Olass tried to shrink back into the crowd, but failed.

'You!' said Lord Alagrace. 'Make yourself useful. Give him some water.'

Yen Olass knelt down and began feeding Haveros some water. As he suckled on the half-empty skin, she wondered, belatedly, whether he would catch any terrible disease, as the Melski monster Hor-hor-hurulg-murg had already drunk from the same water skin.

Another woman joined Yen Olass. It was the Princess Quenerain. This high-born lady knelt down in the mud and began to massage the captive's hands, to get the circulation going. Ropes had cut deep into the skin, leaving ugly red marks, as if he had been branded.

'Haveros!' said a voice.

Yen Olass recognised that voice. It was General Chonjara. A moment later, the general grabbed her by the shoulders, pulled her away from Haveros and threw her backwards. Yen Olass landed heavily.

'Chonjara!' said Lord Alagrace. 'Have you gone mad?'

But the general paid no attention. He grabbed the Princess Quenerain by the scruff of the neck and pushed her aside. Then he drew his sword and raised it high, to strike the executioner's blow. Haveros lay helpless, waiting.

'No!' screamed the Princess Quenerain.

She punched Chonjara in the armpit. Soldiers leapt forward to overpower the general, dragging him to the ground and disarming him. Taken from behind, his sword-arm momentarily disabled by the punch to the armpit, he could do little to defend himself.

Yen Olass, still lying on the ground—she judged that was the safest place to be for the moment—was impressed. She had not credited the Princess Quenerain with enough physical initiative to take on a mouse, far less a warlord.

Lord Alagrace was calling for order. Haveros was trying to sit up. And Chonjara—struggling, biting, kicking, swearing, spitting—was going quite red in the face. How very interesting. Yen Olass propped herself up on one arm so she could get a better view.

'Are you hurt?' said a man, squatting down beside her.

She smelt his strength. It was Karahaj Nan Nulador, Chonjara's bodyguard. Although he was pledged to his master, Nan Nulador was not expected or required to assist him against a senior commander like Lord Alagrace—that would have been treason.

'I'll live,' said Yen Olass, unable to resist dramatizing her plight just a little bit. She allowed Nan Nulador to help her to her feet.

Chonjara, giving up the struggle to break free, gasped for air then shouted:

'Kill the traitor!'

'That's enough!' said Lord Alagrace.

'A traitor!' shouted Chonjara. 'Standing with the enemy! Kill him!'

Volaine Persaga Haveros, now sitting upright turned his head to one side. He vomited. The Princess Quenerain tried to help him up, but he lacked the strength to stand.

'Behold!' shouted Lord Alagrace. 'The resident interpolator sent to the imperial province of Estar by the Lord Emperor Khmar.'

'A spy?' said Chonjara, incredulously. 'A spy? Sent here by Khmar? Would the emperor recruit such a man? After what he did in Gendormargensis? Take your filthy hands off me, you whoredog chickenlice!'

The soldiers holding Chonjara released him.

'Who told you to let him go?' said Lord Alagrace, more than a little frightened to see his authority so rapidly eroded. 'Seize him!'

A soldier made a tentative effort to take hold of the general, but Chonjara knocked him aside, and nobody else took up the challenge.

'Look at that,' said Chonjara, pointing at Haveros. 'That, an imperial servant? That's a drunk. A traitor. Whoring his favour to an enemy power.'

Haveros croaked.

'Poisoned,' said Haveros.

'Poisoned!' said Chonjara. 'Drunk—that's the word.'

Lord Alagrace looked around.

'Who brought Haveros here? Who carried him here on the pole? You? Then tell us—how was Haveros taken?'

'The cavalry took him, sir. He was riding out of Lorford, on a horse. Captured, he claimed imperial warrant. Saying what you claim for him, sir. A security marshal gave him some nataquat to keep him quiet.'

'You hear that?' said Lord Alagrace, turning on Chonjara. 'He's not drunk, he's been doped with nataquat. You hear that? And he told his story before I told it for him. Understand? He's not the traitor—you are! You've defied my authority. You've defied your superior commander on the field of battle.'

This was said in a parade-ground bellow. Fear made Lord Alagrace vicious. He was acutely aware that his most senior officers were Yarglat clansmen. In a crisis, there was always the chance they would turn against him—the last survivor of the High Houses of Sharla.

Having seen his own authority stolen from him, and his men brought to the point of mutiny, Lord Alagrace was not about to give any quarter now that the power struggle had turned in his favour.

'Khmar sent this man!' said Lord Alagrace, invoking the power of the Lord Emperor. 'Just as Khmar sent me. Who here disobeys Khmar. Do you? And you? No? Then take him!'

On his command men laid rough hands on Chonjara, who put up only a token resistance. Best to finish the business now. Take Chonjara's head, before he could put it together with his cronies and cook up a full-scale rebellion.

'Traitor,' said Lord Alagrace, addressing Chonjara, 'I find you guilty of treasonous mutiny, and sentence you—'

'I demand a reading.'

'And sentence you—'

'A reading! That's my right! I demand a reading! Bear witness, he denies me my rights! He's trying to have me killed before the truth can be heard! I demand a reading!'

There was an ugly muttering from the crowd. Lord Alagrace looked around to read the surrounding faces. He saw that if he ordered someone to kill Chonjara, he would not be obeyed. His hand went to the hilt of his sword—and was restrained.

'No,' said Karahaj Nan Nulador.

'As you wish,' said Lord Alagrace.

Lord Alagrace did not believe the stories that Nan Nulador could crush rocks with his bare hands, but he was glad when Chonjara's bodyguard eased his grip. He shook himself free.

'You realize,' said Lord Alagrace, quietly, 'this is mutiny.'

'What law says you can murder him?' said Nan Nulador.

While Chonjara's bodyguard was not one of the brightest lights in the intellectual firmament, he was not as ignorant as some people took him to be. He knew that Lord Alagrace had no authority to kill a man out of hand.

'Very well,' said Lord Alagrace. 'The forms will be obeyed.'

He turned to Yen Olass, hoping she would give him a quick reading so he could get Chonjara killed. Or, alternatively, perhaps she could find some way to deny Chonjara a reading.

'Oracle,' said Lord Alagrace. 'This man asks for a reading. Is he entitled to a reading?'

'He is,' said Nan Nulador.

He was right, and Yen Olass, hearing him, knew that he knew he was right.

'There is conflict between two parties,' said Yen Olass. 'Even if his guilt is certain, he is still entitled to ask for a reading. Even if sentence has already been pronounced against him, he is still entitled to ask for a reading.'

Lord Alagrace was displeased. This was not what he had expected to hear. Still, no oracle's reading could alter the outcome, as far as he was concerned: Chonjara was guilty of trying to overthrow his authority. Guilty, and dangerous, and a candidate for immediate execution.

'Give a reading then,' said Lord Alagrace.

'I will have to get my nordigin,' said Yen Olass, for the carrier box containing her Casting Board and 365 Indicators was elsewhere. 'It's with the translators' baggage.'

'You should have it with you!' said Lord Alagrace, allowing himself to unleash some of his anger against this defenceless target. 'So you haven't got it—do without it.'

'The Rule does not permit me to,' said Yen Olass.

She wanted to take Lord Alagrace and shake him. Fear was mastering his judgment. She knew he wanted Chonjara dead straight away. She knew delay would favour Chonjara. But she also knew that delay was a necessary risk.

'In obedience to the Rule I will go for my nordigin,' said Yen Olass, seeing the danger of Lord Alagrace taking them both to destruction.

She turned to go.

'Stop her!' said Lord Alagrace.

Soldiers barred her way. She turned back to Lord Alagrace and said, her voice cold:

'In this time of danger, Khmar's oracle urges all parties to follow the forms.'

She saw Nan Nulador nod in agreement.

'I must obey the Rule,' said Yen Olass.

'You're Khmar's Sisterhood in the south,' said Lord Alagrace. 'You can make your own Rule. You'll give us a reading. Now.'

'What's this?' said Chonjara. 'A reading which isn't a reading? Are you going to have me judged by a dralkosh?'

Lord Alagrace saw his own error, too late. He tried to salvage what he could.

'She has Khmar's favour,' said Lord Alagrace.

'Khmar wouldn't be the first emperor to favour a dralkosh,' said Chonjara, shaking off the men who held him.

'I am an oracle,' said Yen Olass, raising her voice. 'An oracle, obedient to the Rule.'

'A runaway slave, and Khmar let you live,' said Chonjara. 'A slave, yet Khmar fed at your table. You poisoned his foodtaster, but you let the emperor live. Why? Because you wanted something from him. You got what you wanted.'

'She is an oracle,' said Lord Alagrace.

'You tell us yourself,' said Chonjara, 'she conjures up readings out of nothing. Out of the air itself! I saw the Witchlord! I saw his dralkosh, Bao Gahai! I know that look! You can tell it in the woman's eye! Are we going to let this dralkosh die a virgin? Form a square! Form a square!'

Lord Alagrace was jostled as excited men formed a square. Yen Olass tried to escape. Chonjara grabbed her by the hair and hauled her back. She hit him, very hard. He slammed a fist into her solar plexus, knocking the wind out of her. Then he threw her into the middle of the square, where she went sprawling in the mud.

'Who fights for the privilege?' said Chonjara.

He had everything in his favour now.

'Khmar's foodtaster is alive and well,' said Yen Olass, staunchly, picking herself up from the mud.

'And I wonder what he paid for his life,' said Chonjara. 'Come on, who fights for the woman?'

Half a dozen grinning bravos stepped forward. Then a bigger, taller man joined them: Karahaj Nan Nulador. For a moment, Yen Olass allowed herself to hope. She had a champion. He would find a way to save her: somehow. Chonjara had named her as a dralkosh, but she had given Nan Nulador a son, and he would not forget.

'Nan Nulador,' said Chonjara. 'Get out of there. You fight when I tell you to, not otherwise.'

Wordlessly, with a glance of apology at Yen Olass, Nan Nulander withdrew.

So this was it then: the end. She was going to meet the fate traditional for women who get embroiled in the affairs of men: rape, destruction and death. She was going to be fought over, then carried away and mauled and pawed and slavered over and cut open and poked then taken out and stoned to death with rocks battering her bones and her breasts and her head and smashing her face to a pulp, she had seen it done, she knew what happened.

She saw the possibility of a quicker, cleaner way. Now that she could no longer preserve herself by submitting to the ruling power, Yen Olass chose to die fighting. She spat into her right hand, and closed it into a fist. It was the traditional Yarglat gesture of contempt and defiance, and she had practised it in secret a thousand times when she was playing at being Yarglat of the Yarglat.

Could she take out Chonjara? She could try—and if she died trying, it hardly mattered. Chonjara, using all his energies and wit to dominate and control the crowd, had not yet had time to recover his sword.

'I killed my first man at the age of twelve,' said Yen Olass.

By dint of long practice, the line came out perfect.

'You can make a fist, I can see that,' said Chonjara, who, as a general, was to about to compromise his dignity by fighting with a woman. He pointed at one of the bravos who had lined up to contend for Yen Olass. 'Take her!'

The man stepped forward. Nan Nulador intercepted him and flattened him.

'Nan Nulador!' said Chonjara.

'Am I ruled by a dralkosh?' said Nan Nulador, standing over the comatose body of the man he had downed.

Chonjara hesitated. He could answer yes. He could persuade the crowd to tear Nan Nulador apart. But Chonjara valued his bodyguard; the muscle-mountain was too valuable to sacrifice lightly.

'By your oath,' said Chonjara, 'I command you to stand back and stay silent.'

Nan Nulador bowed his head and withdrew.

'You can command his body,' said Yen Olass, 'but not his judgment. There's one person who knows Khmar won't be happy about this!'

There was a murmur from the crowd, and Chonjara was not sure what it meant. He gestured at another of the bravos.

'You!'

'So that's the man you choose to face Khmar,' said Yen Olass.

And the hero hesitated.

'Khmar will take you and break you at his leisure,' said Yen

Olass, addressing Chonjara. 'As for me—when I piss again I piss on the grave of your sheep-lick shasha father.'

In the crowd, someone tittered.

'That's enough from you, whore,' said Chonjara. 'We can cut you open and rip you apart here and now.'

'We?' said Yen Olass. 'You and who else? How many others do you need to help you? I would've thought you could've managed on your own. After all, you managed all right in Mentigen.'

There was a roar of laughter from the soldiers. Yen Olass knew all the army gossip, including the rumour that a small tribe in Mentigen had made Chonjara stand at stud to a mare to save his life when he had been their prisoner.

Chonjara charged.

Yen Olass cowered down, as if in fear. Then snatched up a handful of mud and threw it. She ducked sideways as Chonjara kicked and flailed, fighting blind, bellowing, his eyes full of mud. Yen Olass took him from behind, her arm sweeping up between his legs. Crunching into his testicles. Lovely.

As Chonjara went down, Yen Olass followed through, putting in the boot. Then stopped, panting. Should she kill him? She wanted to, yes. But the army would feel obliged to destroy a woman who killed a man.

And if she let Chonjara live? Was the army ready to be persuaded that Chonjara was a fool, that Khmar would punish mutiny, that there was no evidence to condemn her?

'Take your boot off his throat,' said Volaine Persaga Haveros, stepping forward.

He looked ill; he was still shaking off the effects of the nataquat which had been used to drug him. But his voice, when he shouted, could be heard by everyone.

'There!' shouted Haveros, pointing at the looming mass of Castle Vaunting. 'That's the enemy. Armed men. Hundreds of them. But that's not all. Wizards. Three wizards have come from the south.

'So look at our heroes! Fighting in the mud! While up there —power is gathering. Every hour we delay gives those forces more time to gather their strength. I've been there. I've seen them. I can name the wizards for you: Phyphor, Garash, Miphon.

'You think I came here from choice? To Argan, from choice?

I could have fled to Ashmolea. Or to the Ravlish Lands. A hundred kingdoms would have hired my sword. But I came here. Because the Lord Khmar gave me my orders. Because he knows—and you know, if you think about it. There's powers here which might be enough to finish us.

'That's why I came. Risked my life. Across the Pale, through the forest. Months here. Learning the castle, learning the ways. And now I'm here to tell your danger. And what do I find? Mud fighting! Over a woman. An army—fighting over this. Over this?'

Haveros took hold of Yen Olass. She was wet, soggy, muddy, her hair bedraggled. Her furs, covered with mud, emphasized the unyielding broad-shouldered bulk of her heavy-boned body, so typical of women of Skanagool race.

'What are you going to fight over next?' said Haveros. 'The local washerwoman? A sack of stinking fish?'

There was laughter. Haveros gave Yen Olass a little shake. She let herself be shaken, suspecting that he might be saving her life—but she hated him all the same. She wished she could have been beautiful. And she wished she could have annihilated Haveros with a glance. And she wished she had taken her chance to kill Chonjara, who was now dragging himself up from the mud, slowly, painfully.

'The girl stays with me,' said Haveros. 'We can't have her running round on the loose, punching out our commanders. As for anything else . . . that can wait till we've taken the castle. We've got work to do.'

A siege marshal took the hint and lifted his voice in command. Slowly, the crowd began to disperse. Nan Nulador helped Chonjara away, and Lord Alagrace, his own authority at least partially restored, began to issue orders.

The army was functioning again; trampling horses, bootshod men, oxen, cartwheels and falling rain completed the transformation of the occupied ground into a quagmire. Preparations for a rapid attack got underway. The leadership crisis was temporarily resolved, and everyone was back at work.

And Yen Olass understood that Haveros had intervened precisely to obtain this result. It hardly mattered to him whether she lived or died, but he refused to allow the army to amuse itself at the expense of the business of war. In all the army, nobody cared about the ultimate fate of Yen Olass Ampadara: except perhaps Karahaj Nan Nulador.

CHAPTER
Sixteen

The army was camped on open ground between the Hollern River and Castle Vaunting. This must have been a reasonably pleasant spot when the advance guard had arrived. Now that some five thousand men had trampled over it, dug holes and fireplaces, put up earthwork defences, unloaded carts and driven in hitching posts for oxen and horses, it looked ugly. The town of Lorford, just to the west, was now mostly burnt-out ruins; what remained was being demolished for firewood. Soldiers had already crossed the bridge leading north from Lorford to fell trees for extra firewood.

What would happen once Estar had been conquered and subdued? Yen Olass knew engineers and surveyors attached to the army were investigating the possibility of digging a canal from the Pale to the Central Ocean—a canal right through Trest and Estar, so ships could journey from Tameran to the Central Ocean without daring the notoriously dangerous waters of the Penvash Channel. No doubt Estar would become a garrison town writ large, a chunk of territory consecrated to military use.

Yen Olass pitied the people who lived in Estar: but only a little. After all, they would be better off than the inhabitants of Monogail. The Yarglat had thought their land worthless, not worth a garrison, and Monogail had been depopulated. Which was why, whatever Yen Olass dreamed of, she never dreamed of going home: she had no home left to go to.

But she could not forget the cold northern wastelands of her childhood, and she could not help thinking how things would have been if the invaders had never come. Her people would have admired her black hair, her grey eyes, her strong shoulders and her eloquent speech. They would have thought her an ideal woman, perceptive, intelligent, strong enough to master animals to her will, and properly padded against the winter cold.

She would have been reindeer woman by now, or maybe a mind-healer like her mother. In any case, she would have had her own grenderstrander and her own grey hunter. No cats, of course, not in Monogail (no cats, no trees, no apples, no snakes) . . . but she might have had a man. Or she might not—it would have been for her to choose.

Above all else, she resented the loss of the right to choose. As an oracle, she had been a pivot, a device to insert into a deadlocked conflict to allow opposing forces the chance to move toward a mutually acceptable compromise. The Rule of the Sisterhood, though it had forbidden her many things, had protected her with a certain aura of holy mystery.

Now, it seemed her career as an oracle was over. The word had been spoken: 'dralkosh'. Just by saying that word, Chonjara had marked her. He had branded her. Haveros had saved her life, at least for the moment, but Yen Olass knew she would be risking her own destruction if she ever spoke again in public.

So what was she now? A slave, no more. If she managed to cling to Haveros, she might keep her life a little longer. If he died or gave her away or sent her away, then the best she could hope for was that someone would find her a useful object, to fetch and carry, to honour and obey, to worship and respect, to be mounted and fucked on demand, to bear children as her owner wished, or to be probed and aborted as he wished.

And if she stayed with Haveros, could she hope for anything better?

And even if the world forgot that she had been called a dralkosh, and even if (by a miracle) Haveros persuaded the Sisterhood and the Ondrask to renounce their claims to her life and her body—would she be free? She would be free to beg, or starve, or live in rags and work as a washerwoman, or give herself to one man or many as a wife or a whore, meaning a slave for life or a day.

In the Collosnon Empire, women did not have their own choices or their own voices. The men were trained from their earliest days to be conquerors; they practised their skills on women at home, then went off to foreign wars to use their skills against outsiders, returning to their women with those skills now perfected and in need of constant practice to keep them so.

Yen Olass knew her wit was a match for most men, and her strength a match for many. But she could not take on a whole society organized for conquest at home and abroad. She had won her fight with General Chonjara, but if Haveros had not stepped forward to end the matter, she might have lost. She might have mastered the crisis with her eloquence, if nobody opposed her. But a single shout—'Three cheers for the dral-kosh', say—would have been enough to have her torn to pieces.

No matter how strong she was, and no matter how intelligent, she was weak because convention was against her. She was a woman, hence, by definition, an object to be used in all those interesting ways men had invented.

In the Collosnon Empire, a man was a fish swimming down a great river, able to tap vast energies by a little intelligent navigation. Yen Olass, on the other hand, was a strange fish from a foreign sea, sheltering on the lee of a rock as she wondered if she could live long enough to force her way a little further upstream. Despite her intelligence and strength, she could not hope to outlast the river.

When Yen Olass dared to visit the translation section, it was made clear to her that her services were no longer wanted. She had expected this. Wiping someone else's spittle off her face, she grabbed her pack and fled.

Yen Olass stayed well clear of Lord Alagrace, who had endangered her life by his foolishness. Knowing the dynamics of ambition and hatred amongst the high caste warlords of the Collosnon Empire, Yen Olass expected that there would soon be a three-way power struggle for command of the army. Either Chonjara or Haveros would be the victor. Lord Alagrace would certainly lose, dying in a duel or a mutiny, unless he was murdered in his sleep.

Motivated by fear and necessity, Yen Olass did her best to play the woman's game and ingratiate herself with her rock, Haveros. She stayed in the background while he supervised the erection of a command tent for himself, and talked to those officers who came to greet him. There was not much Yen Olass could offer Haveros, but, once he was free of other concerns, she offered him what she had: the talking monster. To her disappointment, Haveros already knew about the Melski. So Yen Olass told him about Resbit. He laughed when she told him Resbit belonged to the prince of the castle.

'Someone's confused you,' he said. 'She's some woman one of the mercenaries used to sleep with. She's not important. But if you're worried about your friends, we'll bring them here.'

Yen Olass had not been worried at all, but supposed she should have been concerned, at least for Resbit.

'Not the monster,' said Yen Olass. 'We don't want a monster here.'

'You don't,' said Haveros, 'but I do. The Melski can be useful to us, if we treat them right. They'll work for us on the river, if we pay. If we use force they'll disappear into the wilds, never to be seen again. You say you can talk to this one?'

'It speaks Galish.'

'None of them speaks Galish,' said Haveros firmly. 'They've got their own language, which is all they speak.'

'This one is different.'

'Maybe so,' said Haveros. 'Or maybe it's a survival technique. Handy to know what people are saying when they don't think you can understand, yes?'

Yen Olass hastened to agree.

'Only I wouldn't think monsters had much trouble surviving,' she said.

'The water people are soft,' said Haveros. 'Let's go.'

And he went with her to the security section. Yen Olass expected that Resbit would be glad to see her. She looked for some sign of welcome when they entered the tent, but was not rewarded. When Resbit saw the state she was in—Yen Olass had not had a chance to clean herself or her clothes—she burst out laughing. Yen Olass was furious.

But fear replaced anger when she saw Haveros cutting the monster loose. Yen Olass, thinking that most unwise, backed away, measuring the distance to the exit.

'Don't be alarmed,' said Haveros. 'I know these people. Remember, I've lived in Estar for months. They're a peaceloving breed.'

'If you say so,' said Yen Olass, speaking in Eparget, which the Melski was most unlikely to understand. Then: 'Is it a he or a she, or is it an it?'

'A he,' said Haveros, slicing away a rope. 'The females are smoother, and they've got a slit between the legs like our own.'

'If it's a he, then where's its . . .'

'The male organ retracts when not in use,' said Haveros. 'They live much of their lives underwater, especially when they're young. They don't want dangling things for fish to bite at.'

Yen Olass laughed. The Melski now looked less like a monster and more like a sad and slightly ludicrous parody of a man. She was glad to have something to laugh at, was glad to have a little laughter to help occlude her stark vision of the use and abuse her world was going to make of her. Soon, given the chance, she would soothe herself with stories, and construct wishing-dreams in which she could take shelter; that would help keep her sane.

Haveros cut the last of the ropes free. The Melski tried to move, but could not. Resbit began to massage its limbs, working on it just as the Princess Quenerain had worked on Haveros earlier in the day.

Watching Resbit, Yen Olass felt, for the first time, some empathy with her. Now she realized why Resbit had laughed. She, too, was in an almost helpless position; she, too, needed some laughter to help her cope with the world. Tentatively, Yen Olass began to help succour the monster. Its flesh was unpleasantly rough and dry; maybe, as a water monster, its health required frequent dips in the river.

Soon the Melski could walk, and they all started out for the tent. On the way, Haveros began to ask the Melski questions about the last Galish convoy which had gone up the Hollern River toward Lake Armansis, far to the north in the Penvash Peninsula; at first he tried to use Yen Olass as a translator, but found his own Galish much better than hers.

Haveros had a small tent erected near his own for the use of Resbit and Hor-hor-hurulg-murg.

'Is it safe for a woman to sleep with a monster?' said Yen Olass.

'Melski males are incapable of sexual desire for human females,' said Haveros.

He was about to tell her more when he was interrupted by the arrival of a messenger.

'What is it?' said Haveros.

'Sir. The drawbridge had been lowered. An embassy is coming down the hill.'

Haveros acknowledged the message. Then he drew Yen Olass to one side and spoke to her quietly.

'The princess,' said Haveros.

'What about her?'

'You have to keep her away from me. When we meet this embassy—'

'I'm not coming! It's dangerous! People will spit on me and—'

'Hush,' said Haveros. 'You'll be safe. Everyone behaves themselves when the army meets an embassy. Besides, I'll be keeping an eye on you. Now, when we meet the embassy, warn the princess off if she comes near me.'

'Don't you want her?' said Yen Olass, hoping.

'Of course I want her,' said Haveros. 'But she has to be a little discreet. Take her aside and tell her so.'

So now Yen Olass knew why Haveros was being so good to her. She was going to be his mouthpiece amongst the women, bearing messages to the Princess Quenerain, arranging assignations, standing guard while Son-son stuck Suggy's teni with his slippery wet medi-vedi. Yen Olass saw it all. Still, as fates went, it was not so bad. Not bad at all, considering the alternatives.

CHAPTER
Seventeen

The embassy consisted of one man, a hard-faced professional soldier who announced himself as Morgan Gestrel Hearst, son of Avor the Hawk, veteran of the wars of the Cold West, Chevalier of the Iron Order of the city of Chi'ash-lan, warrior of Rovac, dragon-killer and bloodsworn defender of the Prince of Estar, Johan Meryl Comedo.

'... in which capacity I claim the right to meet in combat the man I see there sitting amongst you, Volaine Persaga Haveros. Oathbreaker! Sworn to the service of the prince, he proves himself a liar, a trust-breaker, a traitor. If this assembly has any regard for its own honour, it will grant me his head, either by handing it to me or by giving me the chance to take it, man against man, blade against blade.'

This, translated from Galish into Eparget for the benefit of Lord Alagrace, his senior officers and siege marshals and all their attendants and immediate subordinates, failed to make a stir. The Collosnon Empire, an immensely self-confident and self-absorbed organisation, had little regard for the accusations and the histrionics of outsiders.

'This is not the time to challenge,' said Haveros, 'whatever the provocation. We should be talking terms. We can at least arrange for you all to escape with your lives.'

'Such generosity!' said Hearst, with a sneer, 'I don't require or desire any favours from you. Once you've bloodied your-selves against the castle walls, you'll start to get a better idea of what's yours to give and dispose of.'

'I can tell you one thing that's ours to dispose of,' said Ha-veros. 'We took prisoners in Lorford.'

'Cook them and eat them for all I care,' said Hearst. 'My oath of service is to the prince, not to the earthgrubbers under his feet.'

'One of our prisoners is Valicia Resbit,' said Haveros. 'You know and I know that she's been favoured with the attentions of Elkor Alish. Your fellow Rovac warrior, your companion in your years in the Cold West.'

'Alish has said nothing of his whore,' said Hearst, speaking with tight-lipped fury, as if he had been mortally insulted. 'You can cut her up and share the bits around for all I care.'

And now it seemed that his attitude had hardened. He refused three different sets of terms, all of which would have allowed the inhabitants of the castle to depart with their lives and go elsewhere. Finally, Hearst was presented with an ultimatum to take back to Castle Vaunting:

'Lord Pentalon Alagrace, his judgment graced by the mani-fold contributions of Volaine Persage Haveros, the resident in-terpolator of the imperial province of Estar, imposes terms as follows.

'Surrender must be immediate. Any delay will mean death for all those in the province of Estar who now stand in rebellion against the imperial power. The Supreme Power of Tameran will not countenance any further insolence from those designed by nature to be his slaves. Through the grace of Lord Pentalon Alagrace, hear his commands.

'Our Lord the Emperor Khmar requires the surrender of the ruling castle of Estar, together with all horse and weapons.

Those in the castle must leave, taking with them only their clothes and their children. The ruby eye of the dragon Zenphos is to be delivered to the army of rightful inheritance. The prince of the castle is to be delivered up for execution. Any and all diviners, necromancers, sorcerers, witches, palmists, makers of spells and potions or other workers of magic are to be killed, and their heads presented to the commander of the battlefield.

'Long live the emperor!'

It was anyone's guess how much of that ultimatum would actually be carried back to Castle Vaunting; it was the common agreement of experienced observers that the warrior Morgan Hearst seemed remarkably ill-suited for the role of ambassador, and, if his intransigence was typical, the peaceful surrender of the castle could not reasonably be expected.

*   *   *

When Morgan Hearst returned to Castle Vaunting toward nightfall, the rain had eased to a drizzle. In the failing light, a ceremony was organised for those chosen for the first wave to attack the castle. The Princess Quenerain officiated.

Dressed in a robe of blue silk—blue is the colour of the unattainable sky, and hence of virginity—the princess led the assembled men through the Seven Charts, ending with the Voicing.

Rituals differ according to tribe and nation, but all have something in common. An area of ground is temporarily or permanently consecrated for the use of a selected group which has assembled to express a common purpose. Both the consecration and the common purpose may be explicit or implicit; it makes no difference.

The Collosnon Empire had learnt long ago that to command the body is also to command the mind. It used tried and trusted military rituals—drills, parades and inspections—to perfect the discipline of the armies. However, disobedience and desertion were still common, and sometimes there was outright mutiny.

These failures were, by and large, the results of lapses of leadership. High caste warlords still tended to behave with the reckless lawlessness which had characterized the chiefs of the horse tribes. The Lord Emperor Khmar tolerated these delinquencies, and was lax when it came to disciplining his commanders.

Still, when failures of discipline were investigated, the emperor himself could hardly be blamed in public, and it would not have been politic even to go so far as to blame the high caste commanders. Accordingly, desertion and mutiny produced more regulations to control the common soldiers, and more rituals to perfect their indoctrination.

The Rite led by the Princess Quenerain was an exercise in indoctrination. If it did nothing else, it persuaded the soldiers that they were important; the Rite, led by the emperor's daughter, existed for their benefit. No doubt some found other consolations in the Chants and the Voicing, but even the most cynical got something from the experience.

By the time it was completely dark, the ceremony was over; an honour guard holding aloft burning torches escorted the Princess Quenerain to her tent, and the first wave prepared for the onslaught on Castle Vaunting.

Lord Alagrace gave attack command to a junior commander, Pukegoh Novdoy. Both Chonjara and Haveros had demanded the honour of leading the assault. However, Chonjara would not have inspired his men with confidence since a woman had so recently beaten him up in public. Haveros was a natural choice, since he knew the interior of Castle Vaunting, but Lord Alagrace thought it unwise to inflame the rivalry between Chonjara and Haveros.

Under cover of darkness, big crossbows were brought up to the castle moat. Grapples with ropes attached were shot through the air. These hooked onto the battlements. Men swarmed up the ropes, their bodies buffeted by a rising wind, a five-scream drop to the glowing depths of fire yawning beneath them. Some of the invaders were to advance along the battlements to storm the gatehouse keep. Others were to abseil down to the central courtyard and try and force entry to the gatehouse keep from there.

When the first wave reached the battlements, at first there was no sign of battle. But the battlements were high and the wind strong: for all Lord Alagrace could tell, a battle might already be raging there.

Suddenly there was a rumbling roar. The ground shook. The walls of Castle Vaunting flushed sullen red with reflected light. The clouds themselves glowed with reflected fire—and, from the castle moat, blazing flames lept upward. The ropes laced across the moat crinkled into flame. Lord Alagrace swore. The first wave was cut off, trapped in the castle: they would have to fight their way to victory or die.

A moment later, a lurid blast of white lightning swept a section of the battlements near the gatehouse keep. He heard thin voices cry out. The sound was diminished by wind, height and distance, but Lord Alagrace knew he was hearing men screaming. And he suspected they were his own.

*   *   *

While the Collosnon army mounted its assault on Castle Vaunting, Yen Olass Ampadara slept with the monster Hor-hor-hurulg-murg and the woman Valicia Resbit, sometime mistress of the Rovac warrior Elkor Alish. They slept in a tent, with guards outside to make sure that the two who were prisoners could not escape.

Before sleeping, the three of them had talked for hours. Yen Olass had found out that Resbit was definitely pregnant, or thought she was, and was convinced she was going to bear a boy-child with a sword-arm like her lover's.

The hours of talk had already given Yen Olass a markedly better command of Galish. Conversation had given life to the dead forms of the language which she had laboured on, day in, day out, ever since midwinter, and she was already starting to learn new words.

Now, the two women slept huddled together for warmth, their bodies making one mound of softly breathing wool and fur, a single blanket sheltering the two of them. The Melski slept apart. Hor-hor-hurulg-murg needed no body-warmth to make him comfortable; his body was supremely adapted to the slush and wet, and, though adult Melski were accustomed to sleeping in the air, he could have got a reasonable night's sleep curled up in a hole in the bottom of a lake or a river.

All three of them, captive creatures in danger of their lives, were exhausted; they did not wake when the flames of the castle moat roared up, making the ground reverberate and shake; they slept on, dreaming, till morning came.

*   *   *

At dawn, a report came from Castle Vaunting by means of signal flags. Casualties were heavy; Pukegoh Novdoy was dead.

The enemy had repulsed all attacks on the gatehouse keep, but the Collosnon commanded the battlements. No fire, lightning or other magic had been used for hours; the strength of the defending wizards must be exhausted.

Lord Alagrace sent back a question:

'Water?'

The reply came back:

'Rain pools. Small. Enough one day.'

Lord Alagrace conferred with siege marshals. They could build a bamboo tower beside the moat, rig chains between the tower and the battlements, and send food and water to their men by means of a flying fox arrangement. But that would take days.

Lord Alagrace ordered the survivors of the first wave to rest, tend their wounded, eat, sleep, then launch a further assault on the gatehouse keep in the afternoon.

From intelligence Haveros had provided, Lord Alagrace knew he still had enough men on the battlements to have a reasonable chance of defeating the enemy absolutely by this all-out assault. If that failed, either his siege marshals would have to find some way of sending reinforcements to the battlements immediately, or some way would have to be found to reopen negotiations with the enemy.

And if that failed, Lord Alagrace could still starve out Castle Vaunting by siege. He might lose all the men of the first wave, but victory would still be his. In the end. But now—he was bone-weary, having been awake all night. Lord Alagrace retired to his tent, leaving orders for his guards to wake him if any fighting started.

Haveros made his own plans. When fighting started again, all eyes would be turned on the castle. Yen Olass took his message to the Princess Quenerain: he would come to her in the afternoon, once fighting started on the battlements. Yen Olass would stand guard while they obtained their satisfaction.

They had waited long enough.

CHAPTER
Eighteen

While the struggle for control of the battlements proceeded, two members of the besieging army seized the opportunity to indulge in some close-quarter tactics of their own. Haveros and the Princess Quenerain had been apart for too long; now, at last, they were together, secluded within the tent set aside for the princess to prepare herself for the Rite of Purification. Nobody would disturb them while the battle raged: nobody would even think of them.

The Princess Quenerain shed her clothing. Haveros stripped naked, and clutched her perfume. She shuddered, panted, gripped him with claws, receiving him into her body.

And then—

The world slurred. He clutched air and held it.

'Cluth?' she said. 'Nabeek . . .'

Her eyes widened to peacock iridescence. Light danced across her body. Her breasts enveloping.

And then:

The world snapped into hard focus. They gasped for breath, as if they had been swimming underwater.

'What happened?' said the Princess Quenerain, her voice a whisper, terrified.

'Madness. From . . .'

From what cause? He touched her, lightly, to comfort her fears. And touched her. And touched her. Grease beneath his fingers. Roast meat. He closed, bit. She wrestled him. They lurched, fell. Laughing—her laughter ripped from her lungs like a scream—she fled from the tent. He caught her just outside, and they went down together and—

Realised what they were doing.

She was bleeding. He had bitten her neck, hard, drawing blood. Armed men staggered across the ground, as if driven by heavy wind. One steadied himself, and stared at the naked lovers. He had bitten through his lower lip.

Someone was screaming.

Haveros scrabbled up handfuls of dead grass and mud, plastering it against his nakedness in a vain effort to hide his shame. The Princess Quenerain flinched from the hate in the eyes of the soldiers. Her hands, like damaged butterflies, fluttered at her face. She wanted to see, yet she wanted to hide her face from the world which was about to say—

'Dralkosh!' shouted a soldier.

'No!' bellowed Haveros.

A spear-butt took him from behind, beat him to the ground. As though it was her they were pounding, the Princess Quenerain sank to her knees in the mud. Shuddering. Other soldiers were taking up the cry of 'dralkosh' but one, standing quite near, said in a low and level voice:

'Woman, have you no shame?'

The voice was real. The cold mud was real. And her body— naked in public view. This was not a dream. The Princess Quenerain clutched her hands to her places knowing that the gesture was futile, since if this was not a dream then she was most certainly dead—or as good as dead.

Out of the corner of her eye, the Princess Quenerain noticed a figure in a battered fur coat skulking away, trying to look inconspicuous. It was Yen Olass Ampadara, who had been standing guard outside the tent. She almost made it—then someone saw who it was, and raised the alarm. Yen Olass tried to sprint away. A man stuck the butt of a spear between her legs. Down she went, face first into the mud. The man leapt onto her back, grabbed her hair and yanked it back. To cut her throat? No: all he did was scream:

'Dralkosh!'

'This,' croaked Haveros, trying to rise, 'has gone too far.'

Then someone hit him on the head, and he was knocked unconscious.

*   *   *

Lord Alagrace did his best. He quailed at the thought of returning to Tameran and telling the Lord Emperor Khmar that his daughter Quenerain had been stoned to death in the imperial province of Estar.

However, there was little Lord Alagrace could do.

The facts spoke for themselves. The survivors of the first wave had been fighting the enemy on the battlements, when a sudden spasm of communal madness had broken the impetus of the battle. That madness had swept through the entire Collosnon army, causing men to shout or throw themselves to the ground, attack each other, to mutilate themselves with weapons, to step into the flames of the castle moat or cower down to the ground, terrified of the weight of the sky.

And the madness had caused the lovers Haveros and Quener-ain to reveal themselves.

Lord Alagrace blamed wizards, but his soldiers had never seen wizards. They believed in them, certainly—after the evidence of the blazing flames of the castle moat and the lightning used against their comrades on the battlements, they could hardly disbelieve. But the figure of the dralkosh was much more familiar.

If a man was impotent with a woman, that was evidence to suggest she was a dralkosh. If her children were born deformed, or the wrong sex, or were not born at all, that too meant she could be a dralkosh. If there was flood or famine or plague or a man went mad or a dog turned rabid, someone must be to blame, and often it turned out that a dralkosh was at the root of all the trouble.

Now the army had two dubious women in its ranks. One was the Princess Quenerain, who had already once been the centre of a scandal. The princess, supposedly so pure, so virginal— yet now discovered to have been fornicating with Haveros while a battle was on. Fornicating, while another woman stood guard: Yen Olass Ampadara, known to be an oracle, known to possess occult powers, known to tell fortunes and read the future, known to be a brash and wilful woman, known to have used sorcery to help her disable General Chonjara when she humiliated him in front of the army.

Something had gone seriously wrong: madness had attacked the whole army. Someone had to be blamed: a cloven of shameless dralkosh, their unclean bodies urging and gaplax. They stood condemned.

True, there were dangers in stoning the emperor's daughter to death. However, battering women to pulp was, in the Collosnon Empire, the traditional way of working off public and private frustrations. Here the frustrations were great, for the army was stalled in this deadwater province, stalled outside a strategic castle which they had to take, with fire preventing them from reaching their enemies and tearing them apart. Khmar was far away, and known to be dying. The Princess Quenerain was close at hand, and she, tall, proud and beautiful, was a perfect victim.

That made two.

And Haveros made a third.

Stoning a man to death was unusual. But Haveros was known to have sinned with the princess before. Not everyone believed the story that Khmar had sent him to Estar: some thought him a genuine traitor. And the whole army was offended at a senior commander indulging himself in sexual pleasures while their comrades fought and died on the battlements of Castle Vaunting. Out of hate, superstition, jealousy, and, in some cases, a genuine desire for justice, they decided that he would be stoned to death with the women.

All things being equal, their commanders would have talked them out of it. However, all things were not equal. Chonjara clearly wanted to see Haveros dead. Chonjara remembered his father dying of a heart attack in the Enskandalon Square in Gendormargensis; before he expired, the old man had begged his son to come and help him. Thanks to the old combat rule invoked by Haveros, Chonjara had been unable to take a single step toward him. Chonjara wanted Haveros dead, and Chonjara's lobby was a powerful one.

Lord Alagrace saw only one way to save any of the three. Remembering how he had saved Haveros in Gendormargensis by getting a dralkosh to claim responsibility, he went and spoke to Yen Olass Ampadara:

'Admit your guilt. Admit that you're the one to blame. Say you bewitched the others. Say you dreamed their dreams for them. Say it's your fault.'

'But it's not,' said Yen Olass.

Unlike the dralkosh in Gendormargensis, Yen Olass had no child for Lord Alagrace to hold to ransom.

'I'm asking you to do this because I saved your life on the Yangrit Highway.'

'Saved my life!'

'You were a runaway slave, yet I spared you.'

'Tratz! I saved my life! In front of Khmar, I spoke for my life. Now you want me to save your life as well. That's not how it works. It's for you to save us, all of us, not for us to save you.'

'I'm not asking you to save me, I'm asking—'

'You want me to save Quenerain to stop Khmar skinning you alive. I want to save me! I want to live! I'm Yen Olass Ampadara, I have my own life, I'm me, I want to live. And Khmar will—'

'You must realise—'

'I must realise that I can't be there to see it, but that won't stop it happening. I hope he starts with your testicles.'

After a long and very distressing interview in Lord Alagrace's private sleeping tent—Yen Olass painted such a vivid picture of Khmar pulling his toenails out and biting his testicles off that Alagrace began to wonder if she really was a dralkosh —Yen Olass was taken back to the other prisoners.

And Lord Alagrace . . .

. . . did nothing.

Because it had already occurred to him that, since Chonjara had been able to secure a death sentence for Haveros, he might be able to do the same for Lord Alagrace, who was generally known to have had a long association with the oracle Yen Olass Ampadara.

*   *   *

The three prisoners were kept in a tent through the dying hours of the day and all through the night. They were not tied up, but there was no chance of escape: the tent was ringed with campfires and an ever-changing audience of men, talking, drinking, gambling. This time, there was no talk of rape, because now there was genuine fear mixed with the hatred; by the time the men had shared the true stories, the gossip and the rumours, there were few who believed the condemned women to be safe to touch.

For his part, Lord Alagrace became convinced that Yen Olass had used sorcery against him, because he woke in the night after enduring terrifying dreams of desexing and torture. He woke just in time to strangle a scream in his throat; for a few moments he was convinced that the Lord Emperor Khmar was actually in his tent.

Truth to tell, Yen Olass had done her very best to slip suggestions into his mind. She had succeeded in giving him nightmares, but had failed to compel him to action. When they had confronted each other, both had been very angry and, in their separate ways, very frightened; Lord Alagrace, all his energies mobilized for argument, had been a poor subject for skills of mind control which work best when the subject is relaxed, unsuspecting and concentrating on something else. Yen Olass, her skill rising briefly to genius, had planted suggestions which now conjured up the very shadow of the Lord Emperor Khmar in Lord Alagrace's tent. But Khmar was far, far away; Chonjara and the army were very close . . .

*   *   *

Morning came.

Signals came from the battlements: no food, running out of water, heavy casualties, our wounded are suffering.

Nothing could be done to help.

The mood of the army was grim, cold, hostile. The three condemned prisoners were hustled down to the Hollern River and pushed into the shallows just upstream of the bridge. Men lined both banks and the bridge itself. Those who had gambled for the privilege of casting the first stones chose their rocks.

Yen Olass Ampadara, her eyes red with crying, stood ankle-deep in the water. She looked around for Karahaj Nan Nulador, her only hope. She did not see him. And in any case, what could he have done? Nothing. She was wearing wool under her league rider's weather jacket and her mud-stained fur coat, but she was shivering. Why? Because she was tired, she was hungry—how ridiculous to be hungry at a time like this—and she was frightened.

They were really going to do it.

They were really going to throw stones at her and smash her face and smash her fingers and smash her and smash her till she fell down into the cold ugly water which was hungering into her boots, and they would carry on smashing her and smashing her till she was an ugly raggage of dead fur and naked bones gulleting away down the river to the cold claws of the sea.

She wanted someone to come and hold her and help her, but there was nobody. And Haveros and Quenerain both stood like statues, as cold and silent as stone. Both looked as if they were only waiting to die, they accepted it, how could that be?

The first man threw the first stone.

It hit Haveros on the side of the head. He grunted, and folded up. Dead? No. He steadied himself, managed to hold himself steady in a crouch, arse in the water, one hand thrusting down to seek for balance.

The second man threw the second stone.

It caught Quenerain a glancing blow on the side of the head. She grimaced slightly, turning her head to one side. Blood ran down her cheek. She was going to die like an aristocrat.

The third man threw the third stone.

It came flying through the air and hit Yen Olass on the shin. The pain was agonizing. She screamed. Snatching a rock from water, she hurled her strength against them.

She screamed:

'You smegma-eating arsefuckers!'

She threw another rock. Saw a man go down. Screamed:

'Goatsucking shiteaters!'

Everywhere men were muscling forward, picking up rocks. A shower of stones came flying through the air. Yen Olass dived. Hit the water and struggled for the depths. She was out of luck. The river here was at its widest and shallowest, the water scarcely waist-deep. Men stormed into the water. Yen Olass swam into a thicket of legs, spears and bamboo poles. She was grabbed, punched, slapped and forced back into the shallows.

Then the men drew back, so everyone could have a good view.

Yen Olass sat in the water, crying, sobbing, covering her face with her hands. She cried with the hopeless misery of a hurt and hunted creature with no refuge. The Princess Quenerain, looking down on this bedraggled creature, permitted herself the faintest of smiles.

Then a rock took her in the chest.

Quenerain gasped, sinking to her knees in the water. With open eyes—in the end, she had something of her father's undying courage—she faced the men. And saw them waver. Like a reflection in water.

Water, yes.

Quenerain sketched a picture in the water with her finger. She drew it very carefully, yet when she looked, there was nothing to be seen. Why? She smoothed the surface of the water with her hands and tried again. No picture. Puzzled, she looked around for a stick. Perhaps with a stick she could draw a better picture.

'Mother,' said Haveros.

He sat down in the water with his back against hers. She was his mother. She had been missing for so long: he was glad to have found her. He closed his eyes. For some reason, he felt very tired.

Yen Olass Ampadara watched Haveros and the Princess Quenerain. Why were they sitting in the water like that, back to back? Why was Haveros nodding off? Why was Quenerain drawing pictures in the water? Because they were human, of course, and human beings were notoriously unstable and unreasonable creatures.

Everywhere Yen Olass looked, there was proof of this. As far as she could see, the ground was swarming with human creatures, some eating mud, some eating their own fingers, some humping each other in the muck, some grasping at invisible insects, some trying to fly.

Looking further afield, to Castle Vaunting, Yen Olass saw what appeared to be human beings jumping from the battlements into the flames of the moat. Or were they being thrown? It did not matter: it did not concern her. Why not? Because she was an otter. That was why.

Yes.

For a moment she had suspected that she might be human herself, so it was with a feeling of immense relief that she realized she was really an otter. She walked deeper into the water, lay down in the cool of the river, and let the water take her. Floating downstream on her back, she smiled at the sky, and kicked her feet, but not very hard, because her legs hurt if she kicked hard.

Some distance downstream, Yen Olass pulled herself ashore and started looking for an otter-hole. When she found something suitable—a concavity under some tree-roots—she crawled into this shelter and huddled there in her fur.

For a while, Yen Olass lay in her otter-hole imagining the fish-smooth otter king who would romance her by the river-bank, and the little baby otters they would have together, and the excavations they would make to perfect their safe and secret otter-hole where nobody would find them not now and not ever, where nobody would ever find them or catch them or stone them to death.

Dreaming of the love her otter-king would teach her, Yen Olass fell asleep, and slept soundly.

CHAPTER
Nineteen

Yen Olass Ampadara woke in the early hours of night. She was cold, but the cold was not intolerable; wool, even when wet, tends to give warmth. She extracted herself from the hole she had been sleeping in, and scooped cold water from the river to appease the protest in her belly.

When she faced the river, the flow of the current was from left to right, meaning she was on the northern bank. Castle Vaunting, the ruins of Lorford and the Collosnon army were on the southern bank, somewhere upstream.

Yen Olass took off her boots and washed her feet and her foot bindings. Then she massaged her feet, wrung out the foot bindings, replaced them, then put on her boots again. Yen Olass had been around soldiers long enough to know that care of the feet is vital. When crotch and armpits are left unattended for a couple of weeks, and grow interesting growths of green fungus, that is unpleasant but not lethal; when feet go rotten, which can happen in a lot less than two weeks, an otherwise healthy person becomes a helpless casualty.

Low down in her gut, there was the beginning of a familiar and unwelcome cramping sensation. Mentally, she counted her calendar. Yes, her menses were due to begin. Swearing softly, Yen Olass hunted through the inner pockets of her weather jacket. Finding her box of volsh, she opened it, dipped her finger in the niddin-grease, and tasted it. Disgusting. She would have to starve for a little longer. In another pocket, she found her string of amber beads. Good for a bribe? No, there was no way for her to buy her way out of this mess. At last she found one of the pads she was looking for. It was soaking wet. She wrung it out: it would have to do.

Before padding herself, Yen Olass took off all her clothing, which meant taking off her boots again—if she had been under less strain, she would have organized herself better. She wrung out all her woolen clothing, knelt on her fur coat and did her best to force out any residual water, did the best she could with her weather jacket, then dressed again and put her boots back on. Already she felt warmer.

Now she considered the state of her body. The women of Monogail did not allow themselves to be disabled by their monthly flux; Yen Olass was more concerned with her bumps and bruises. She had been generously damaged, but all joints were in working order. Everything hurt, but she could still rely on her body to serve her faithfully. It was durable as a mule, strong, powerful, and well-fleshed to ward off starvation.

What now?

Madness had disabled the whole army. Yen Olass, knowing that she was not a dralkosh, knew the wizards in Castle Vaunting were to blame. Their power must be limited, because the spell no longer had effect—Yen Olass no longer believed herself to be an otter.

Remembering what had happened to the soldiers, Yen Olass knew they would now be ashamed and demoralized. They would be sleeping or drinking, or planning desertion. Now was the best time to attack the camp.

Yen Olass thought attack was her best option. She knew exactly what she needed: Hor-hor-lurulg-murg. The Melski male would be her salvation. By now, she knew colonies of Melski lived to the north, in the Penvash Peninsula. Surely they would take her in and shelter her. If not, she would take the mountain pass leading west from Lake Armansis to Larbster Bay on the shores of the Penvash Channel. There was said to be a small community of humans at Larbster Bay, and ships put in there to land travellers, to seek shelter from bad weather or to take on water.

Yen Olass followed the riverbank till she saw the army's campfires. Only a few fires: most people must be asleep. Or dead. The sullen hellfire glow from the moat of Castle Vaunting suggested that a senile sun was about to rise in the south. Yen

Olass was cautious now, facing danger. Yet she felt no fear: instead, she felt strong, bold and alert. Concentrating on shadow and sound, she no longer felt her injuries except when she bumped against a tree-stump or scraped against a bough.

She approached the bridge spanning the Hollern River. She halted, and waited. Watching. Listening. Looking for sentries. Listening for a cough, a snore, a whisper. The bridge appeared to be unguarded. Yen Olass remembered the voyage across the Pale, and how one of the soldiers (a scar-faced man with red whiskers, who had proclaimed that 'you have to kill a man to be a man') had lectured his squad on nightfighting, saying that, with even a trace of light, a silhouette against a skyline can betray movement at night to the skilled observer. ('So watch the curve of the hill and the tit at the top, and look for lice scuttling, boys.')

Crouching low, Yen Olass crawled to the bridge and began to slither across. Then a plank creaked. Under her? Behind her? She startled to her feet and sprinted, her boots hammering across the bridge. As she reached the other side, a man shouted at her from somewhere in the ruins of Lorford.

Yen Olass sprinted for a ruined wall, dropped down beside it, crawled along on hands and knees in its absolute shadow, then went to the ground. And waited. The man shouted again. She heard the swift squiff-squiff-squiff of blood as her heart pumped a pulse near her ear.

Nobody came hunting for her. But, now that she was in occupied territory, she felt smaller and less certain.

Picking herself up from the ground, she advanced on the unsuspecting army, moving in fits and starts, staying low and pausing often to look around. And listen. Soon she was passing tents, woodpiles, empty carts. She smelt latrines, woodsmoke, damp ashes—and food. Food! She drooled.

Yen Olass tried to estimate where the security section was. Sighting a camp fire which seemed to lie in the right direction, she set off toward it. When she drew near, she heard the men round the fire talking, but could not understand what they were saying. They were not talking in Ordhar, nor were they using Eparget. They had reverted to their own language, whatever that might be: this army had contingents from many regions of the empire.

All the guards from the security section seemed to have gathered round that fire. Doubtless they were talking murder or mutiny. Or desertion. Their voices were low, but angry. Going slowly so as not to make too much noise squelching through the mud, Yen Olass worked her way round to the back of the tents of the security section. Here, all was shadows and darkness.

Yen Olass eased a few tent pegs out of the mud, lifted the bottom of a tent and crawled inside. Into absolute darkness. She squatted there, waiting patiently for her eyes to become accustomed to the gloom. But after a while she concluded that there was no light at all to see by. Everything in the tent was very quiet. There was no sleep-murmur of dream voices, no sounds of bodies stirring in blankets, no snores, no creaking of joints, no whispering, no breathing. Yet the tent did not feel empty.

Yen Olass listened, screening out the noises of the outside world—faint guttural voices, occasional animal noises from a horse or an ox, the muted thunder of the flames still blazing in the castle moat. She listened, and she heard . . . moisture falling drip by drop. Each drip gathered itself in the darkness, meditating, then falling to plop into a pool of moisture. A leak in the tent? But it was not raining.

Suddenly Yen Olass was terrified. She lifted the bottom of the tent—and heard footsteps outside. Two men were walking through the mud. As they passed the tent, one said something to the other, and both laughed. Yen Olass crouched in the darkness. She looked over her shoulder, into the centre of the tent. But could see nothing but darkness within darkness.

When the two men were gone, Yen Olass slithered out, not caring how much mud she collected in the process. The night air was cool and good. For a while she stayed there in the shadow of the tent, gathering her courage. Then she heard snoring from a nearby tent. Her first thought was:

—So someone is alive.

Yen Olass stole through the night to the snoring tent, pulled out more tent pegs and slipped inside. Again she squatted down, waiting. This tent was full of the warmth of people and the little noises of people sleeping. But were they prisoners—or soldiers?

'Hello, Yen Olass,' said a deep voice.

Yen Olass felt the hairs stand up on the back of her neck. She knew that she had no occult powers of her own, but she was not prepared to disbelieve in the existence of occult powers—and it was a powerful shock to hear someone name her in the blind darkness. Her bounding heart was a rabbit, chasing away over the hills with a wolf at its tail.

'I know it's you,' said the voice. 'I can smell you.'

'You smell too,' retorted Yen Olass, which was not true.

There was a chuckle.

'Humans can't smell out the Melski,' said Hor-hor-hurulg-murg. 'Come here, Yen Olass. They've tied me up.'

Yen Olass crept through the darkness, wondering if she really did stink. On reflection, she presumed she probably did. Probably everyone in the Collosnon army was reeking of dirt and sweat, but humans who live in a communal stench seldom notice it. Indeed, when people live continuously in their own sweat, the smells they become particularly sensitive to are artificial scents, perfumes and soaps, which, in a combat zone, can sometime betray a newcomer at thirty paces or more.

'Can you really tell I'm me?' said Yen Olass. 'Or were you just guessing?'

She had not been taught the word for guessing, so she used the word for gambling instead. Hor-hor-hurulg-murg understood.

'I'm good at what I do,' said the Melski.

'That's not a proper answer,' said Yen Olass.

What she actually said, struggling with her limited vocabulary, was 'Your words are smoke', but again the Melski understood.

'It's what you should expect,' said Hor-hor-hurulg-murg. 'Tarish are known to be glunskoora.'

'What's tarish?' said Yen Olass, getting to work on the knots that secured him. 'What's glunskoora?'

She could not translate these two words from the Galish; they meant 'monster' and 'inscrutable'.

'Later,' said Hor-hor-hurulg-murg, for, like most people, he did not like having to explain his jokes.

The Melski had a very good idea of what most people thought of them, but, confident in the possession of their own river forests, their own language and their freedom, did not mind making the occasional joke at their own expense.

'Ah,' said Hor-hor-hurulg-murg, as Yen Olass undid the last knot binding his hands. 'That's good. I'll do the rest.'

'Me next,' said another voice, which Yen Olass recognized immediately. Draven.

'What are you doing here?' said Yen Olass.

'Lord Alagrace left late this afternoon. He was escorting some of our wounded back to Skua. He's going to draw on the reserves we've got waiting there. He wants some men behind him who haven't yet been tainted by mutiny.'

'And?'

'And what do you think?' said Draven. 'Come on, untie me.'

Yen Olass was not at all keen on the idea. She wanted to escape with her Melski friend. She did not at all fancy the company of a murderous and unprincipled pirate like Draven. Nominally, he was her slave, given to her by the Lord Emperor Khmar, but in a world of men that ruling had never meant anything, and once they were in the depths of Looming Forest it would mean even less.

'Where are you?' said Draven, impatiently.

'Here,' said Yen Olass, afraid he would start to shout if she refused him. 'But remember, I saved your life.'

'My life! Nobody's asking you to be a hero.'

'In Favanosin,' said Yen Olass, suspecting that Draven was being deliberately obtuse. 'I saved your life.'

'Did you?'

'In front of Khmar. You know I did.'

'So you saved my life. Come on!'

Yen Olass set to work, wondering what had happened. She supposed Chonjara's faction had taken the opportunity to put some of Lord Alagrace's supporters out of action while they had the chance.

'Were they going to—what were they going to do to you?'

'Cook us and eat us for all I know,' said Draven, echoing tough-talking words which had originally been the intellectual property of the Rovac warrior, Morgan Hearst. 'They're frightened. Confused. Men are always dangerous when they're like that. The sooner we get out of here the better.'

Yen Olass was aware by now that others were awake, and waiting. She would have to take them all. But once she had set Draven free, he helped, and soon there were plenty of hands to do the work.

'Yen Olass?' said a voice.

'Here,' said Yen Olass.

'Is it really you?' said Resbit.

'It's me.'

And Yen Olass, glad to have at least one female friend in this unreasonable world of men, took Resbit into her arms and hugged her. Breast to breast and cheek to cheek, they embraced each other, protecting each other, comforting each other. Yen Olass wanted to sit down and talk right then and there, and find out everything that had happened to Resbit, but there was no time. The escapers were already slipping out of the tent one by one, and Resbit and Yen Olass had to follow or be left behind.

'Where's Haveros?' said Draven, when they were outside.

'He's not with us,' said Yen Olass.

'I know that,' said Draven, sounding irritated. 'And keep your voice down!'

Which was unfair, since he was talking louder than she was.

'Why do you care, anyway?' said Yen Olass. 'What's he to you?'

'We need him. And the princess, if we can get her. Take them east, to Skua. Lord Alagrace will reward us.'

'I'd've thought you'd've wanted to run back to your pirate friends,' said Yen Olass.

'It's a long way from here to the Greater Teeth,' said Draven. 'Even for a creature good at running, which isn't me.'

'We'll have a better chance in the forest,' said Yen Olass. 'If we go east, they'll ride us down.'

'We'll take horses ourselves,' said Draven. 'Can't women think of anything?'

'The Lord Khmar—'

'The Lord Khmar can't help you now,' said Draven. 'Stay here. I'm going to look for Haveros and the princess.'

He slipped away into the night.

Yen Olass had been about to point out that the Lord Emperor Khmar had been a notable horse thief in his own right, in his younger days; from his youthful success, he had gained valuable experience which had saved his own armies from losing more animals than they had to. As a matter of policy, all horses were now corralled in the centre of the army at nightfall, wherever possible. On this campaign, the cavalry contingent was small, and all horses were safe in the centre; to liberate a horse would mean leading it through the tentlines.

'I can't ride,' said Resbit.

What a pair. A woman who couldn't ride, and a pirate—Yen Olass could her him blundering away through the night—who had no idea at all about how to move quietly in the dark.

'I can't ride either,' said Hor-hor-hurulg-murg. 'Even if I

could, no horse would consent to bear me. Who chooses the river?'

'I can't swim,' said Resbit.

'I wasn't suggesting it,' said Hor-hor-hurulg-murg. 'Do you choose to come north?'

'We do,' said Yen Olass.

There was a muttered consultation amongst the prisoners. Some of them, natives of Estar, were determined to try and slip away to find refuge in the south of the country, in the Barley Hills. Others thought it best to wait for Draven—he, after all, was a man, not a woman or a monster. In the end, only Yen Olass and Resbit accompanied Hor-hor-hurulg-murg through the darkness to the bridge, across the bridge to the far bank of the Hollern River, then along that bank, following the curve of the river, which soon saw them heading north toward Lake Armansis.

Yen Olass, in captivity, was very much a creature of daydreams and imaginings. But, following Hor-hor-hurulg-murg through the forest by night—in the dark, Melski could see better than humans—Yen Olass felt no need to indulge her dreams. Except that, toward morning, when they were all very tired, she did think just a little bit about how good a cooked breakfast would have been. It was more than a day since she had last eaten, and she was very hungry.

CHAPTER
Twenty

An otter woke in the forest. How had it got there? What was it doing there? Why did everything hurt so much? Why was the cold so vicious? Cold, hurt and dazed by a mix of fatigue and dreams, the otter rolled onto its hands and knees and lay there, suffering. A piteous mewling sound escaped it.

Bit by bit, it remembered.

'Oh shit,' said Yen Olass, remembering.

She opened her eyes, but shut them again. The light was vicious.

'Caltrops,' muttered Yen Olass.

But here in the forest, the light was not the blinding dazzle that glances off snow and ice. The fault was not with the light but with her eyes. They were dry and tired and she wanted to rub them, but saw her hands were filthy.

Yen Olass tried to sit up. On the third try she succeeded. She flexed her hands, trying to get some life into her fingers which, at the moment, were as clumsy as bear paws. Dirt stained the map-lines on the palms of her hands. What had her mother said? 'These are the tracks of the herds which roam the other country. Remember them, in the place beyond darkness.' Now what had she meant by that?

She rubbed her hands together vigorously then stuck them into her armpits. But there was no warmth there, only cold, cold, river-wet fur. Had they been through the river during the night? No. But they had marched endlessly, endlessly.

Yen Olass glanced up at the sky, which had cleared to a taunting virgin blue. It was early morning, and it was positively frosty. She closed her eyes again, then, opening them, looked at the others. Who were both asleep. The Melski was grunting and twitching in his dreams. Resbit was snoring ever so slightly, sleeping so sweetly that Yen Olass had an almost irresistible urge to give her just the tiniest poke in the ribs. Perched on a tree branch overhead, a bird poured out endless streams of exuberant song: joy joy joy!

'Shut up, bird,' said Yen Olass, the tone of her command suggesting that there would be dire consequences for disobedience.

The bird stopped singing, and started improvising a bizarre stream of squawks, sneezes and staccato clucking. Yen Olass leaned back against a tree and stared upwards, trying to see exactly where the bird was. Could she catch it? It flew away, giving her an easy answer to that. She squinched up her eyes, which were still protesting against the daylight. Was there anything at all to eat up there? Nuts, apples, onions? What time of year did apples get born? And did they get born as little apples, or were they something else first?

Up in the trees, Yen Olass saw a bird's nest. Spring meant eggs and baby birds. And that meant breakfast. She stood up. She was still groggy, either from sleep or the lack of it. She shook her head, which protested. She hobbled over to the bird nest tree. In spring, when visiting the hunting lodge at Brant-zyn, she had sometimes seen children scrambling into the trees to plunder nests for eggs. But she had never climbed a tree herself. Oh well, there's a first time for everything.

* * *

Resbit and Hor-hor-hurulg-murg jerked awake as something crashed into nearby undergrowth. Resbit looked around wildly then screamed.

'Yen Olass! Look out! There's something in the bushes!'

From the bushes came a stream of ferocious language. Resbit did not know what was being said, but she strongly suspected most of the foreign words being used were obscene. Yen Olass came blundering out of the undergrowth. She was scratched and bleeding.

'Don't laugh!' said Yen Olass.

'You're hurt! What happened?'

'Don't laugh,' repeated Yen Olass, as though it was very, very important.

But soon, Resbit was finding it very difficult to keep a straight face.

'Oh, Yen Olass! You thought a little branch like that would hold you? Surely not!'

Yen Olass, supposing that a tree was very much like a horse (if you fall off, you must get back on) was already looking for another nest. She found one, and was soon climbing for it, with both Resbit and Hor-hor-hurulg-murg shouting advice to her. Yen Olass, unable to translate from the Galish and climb at the same time, ignored them.

She was getting up quite high. From here, she could see the river, which was not far away. Clinging to a branch, another branch underfoot, she admired the view. On the far side of the river was a soldier who appeared to be admiring her.

'Yen Olass!'

'Shush!' hissed Yen Olass.

'What?' shouted Resbit. 'What was that?'

'Quiet, quiet!'

'What?' said Resbit. 'In case we scare the eggs away?'

She obviously found that very funny. Yen Olass tore off a small branch and threw it at her. What was Galish for soldiers?

'Enemy!' said Yen Olass. 'Over there!'

From the far side of the river, there was a shout.

'Yen Olass!' said Resbit urgently. 'Get down out of there! There's someone across the river!'

'Now you tell me,' muttered Yen Olass.

She began to climb down—slowly—finding, to her surprise, that it was much harder to climb down than to climb up. Now that was contrary to reason. The tree was the same tree whether she was going up or down. But she was finding it very difficult.

'Yen Olass—no, no, don't step there!'

Too late. There was a groan of tearing wood, a scream, a crash. And, from across the river, another scream. Harsh commands in Ordhar. The baying of a dog.

'Yen Olass,' said Resbit. 'What are they saying? What are they saying?'

Yen Olass did not translate the soldiers' Ordhar. Indeed, there was no need to. There was more screaming, and Resbit understood, and said, shocked:

'They're killing people over there.'

'Let's go,' said Hor-hor-hurulg-murg. 'Yen Olass, if you can't walk, I'll carry you.'

'Help me up,' said Yen Olass. 'I'm not a baby.'

And none of her bones were broken. But even so, every step cost her.

'Did they see you?' said Hor-hor-hurulg-murg.

'I don't know,' said Yen Olass.

The soldier who had looked in her direction might have missed her, as she had been well-hidden in the foliage.

'But they might have heard us,' said Yen Olass. 'Some of us were noisy enough.'

'Yes,' said Resbit, 'especially when we fell out of trees.'

Yen Olass grunted, said nothing.

*   *   *

The fugitives had no way to know if the soldiers on the far side of the river had been a patrol which had accidentally come upon some refugees, or whether their escape had been discovered during the night, leading to a deliberate manhunt through the forest. But they had to presume that, since there were soldiers on the far bank of the river, there were likely to be soldiers on their own bank of the river.

They pushed north till noon, then halted, because both Yen Olass and Resbit had absolutely had it. Hor-hor-hurulg-murg permitted them a little sleep, then woke them and made them march. They refused, but, when he threatened to go on alone and leave them, they dragged their weary bodies on for a few more leagues.

When evening came, and they halted, Yen Olass felt stuporous. She and Resbit laid themselves down then and there, and collapsed into absolute sleep.

Yen Olass had expected to sleep forever, but she woke in the night. A wind had got up, and the darkness was full of creaks and rustles, of sighs and moans, of little sounds and larger sounds which might have been animals or people or ghouls or ghosts. She felt the forest surrounding her, enclosing her, hemming her in.

'Yen Olass?'

'Yes?'

'Are you awake?'

'No. This is just a dream.'

'That's not kind, Yen Olass,' said Resbit.

'I can be kind,' said Yen Olass, 'if I try.'

'Then do try.'

They held each other close, and were comforted. They began to talk, and Yen Olass told Resbit about her plan to go west, across the mountains from Lake Armansis to Larbster Bay.

'But what will I do?' said Resbit.

'You'll come with me.'

'Oh no.'

'But you must. What would you do otherwise?'

'That's what I was asking.'

'You will come with me,' said Yen Olass firmly.

'No.'

Resbit was not to be persuaded. She made Yen Olass understand that the people at Larbster Bay were a degenerate clan of thieves, drunkards and slavers.

'They rape rats,' said Resbit.

'What?' said Yen Olass, not sure if she had heard right.

'Rats. Small. Four legs. Screeee! They rape them. At Larbster Bay.'

'Go to sleep,' said Yen Olass. 'You're dreaming already.'

'And when I wake, it'll be all over. Yes?'

'When you wake,' said Yen Olass, 'we'll hunt some eggs. First thing. Before we go anywhere.'

'You be careful hunting those eggs. Don't let them push you out of the tree again.'

'Let me tell you a little story,' said Yen Olass, 'about a young woman who fell asleep and rolled into a river.'

'Gamos!' said Resbit, giggling.

Yen Olass realized she had once again used the Galish word for a female horse instead of the Galish word for a human female. But she still didn't see why that was funny.

* * *

That day, as they marched north, they saw no sign of soldiers, so Hor-hor-hurulg-murg called a halt early in the afternoon. He caught fish in the river, and gave the women one each. Yen Olass found everything in her tinder box was damp, so she spread it out to dry; for the time being, they would have to eat the fish raw.

After the fish, the women climbed for eggs. Then they sat down to feast. Resbit started telling riddles, and Yen Olass tried to answer them. Their Melski guide helped them out with their language difficulties. Some of the riddles were easy enough, such as 'How do you sex an egg?' where the answer was simply 'By growing it into a chicken or rooster.' But one, which baffled Yen Olass, went as follows:

I was sired by a stallion.
I am furry as a rabbit.
I live in trees, unsuccessfully.

Yen Olass struggled with it for ages, then finally gave up. She demanded the answer.

'A gamos!' said Resbit. 'A gamos!'

And she rolled around on the ground, laughing.

'Now that wasn't fair,' said Yen Olass. 'It wasn't nice, either.'

But her protests just made Resbit laugh all the more.

When Resbit quieted down, Yen Olass heard something rustling in the undergrowth nearby. She stalked it and caught it, raked it out of the undergrowth with a branch, and displayed it for all to see.

'A veagle!' said Yen Olass, naming the hedgehog in Eparget.
'A crel!' said Resbit, naming it in her native Estral.
'The Galish call it a klude,' said Hor-hor-hurulg-murg.
'A klude,' said Yen Olass, committing the word to memory.

Resbit bent over the little klude and cooed to it, saying 'Skoon, skoon.' From the way she was saying it, Yen Olass guessed that 'skoon' meant 'cute', unless it meant something like 'Oh you sweet little beautiful thing you.'

'It's not skoon," said Yen Olass. 'It's food.'
'Don't be cruel,' said Resbit.
'I'm not cruel, I'm hungry.'

However in the end, even Yen Olass was not game to eat a hedgehog raw, and so the little klude escaped to live another day.

CHAPTER
Twenty-one

When the three fugitives were halfway to Lake Armansis, they ran into a Melski patrol. After some bloody clashes with the Collosnon army near Lorford, the Melski had withdrawn to the depths of the riverforest, where the odds would favour them. With a Melski to provide them with introductions, Yen Olass and Resbit were spared the indignities of interrogation. Otherwise, they might have found life rather unpleasant for a day or so, for the Melski were in an ugly mood.

Since the Melski ran all the raft convoys on the Hollern River, which was a part of the Salt Road, they were not naive and ignorant savages. They knew the conversations of travellers from all walks of life and from all the nations of Argan and the Ravlish Lands. They were well aware of the nature of empire, and knew they could only stay free by killing enough Collosnon soldiers to persuade the enemy to leave them alone. Defeat would be disastrous. The few humans living in Estar had never been much of a threat to the forest of the Penvash Peninsula, but Khmar's hordes could strip away the entire forest as they sought timber for firewood, houses and shipbuilding.

Melski living elsewhere in the continent of Argan, in isolated places such as the Rausch Valley in the high country east of Trest, sometimes were unsophisticated primitives, slow to see their danger until it was almost too late. But the inhabitants of Penvash had learnt the hard lessons of history from their ancestors. A hundred years previously, invaders had come from Sung, in the Ravlish Lands. They had crossed the mountain pass from Larbster Bay to Lake Armansis; even after four generations, the Melski were still bitter about that invasion. Now, remembering stories their grandfathers had told their fathers, they were preparing themselves for a new and possibly more terrible struggle.

When the fugitives met the patrol, Hor-hor-hurulg-murg conferred with its members, and caught up on the news. Shortly before the Collosnon army attacked Lorford, he had accompanied a flotilla of rafts taking a Galish trading convoy to Lake Armansis. He had left before the journey was completed, returning to the vicinity of Lorford with a patrol, which was how he came to be captured.

Now, he learnt that the Galish convoy had reached Lake Armansis, only to find that a southbound convoy had arrived there by way of Larbster Bay and the Razorwind Pass. The two convoys were camped by the lake while the southbound contingent debated whether to turn around and accompany their fellow traders to the Ravlish Lands.

'Soon we'll go north,' said Hor-hor-hurulg-murg, reporting to the women. 'Then you can join one of the convoys. For now, we wait. We've sent more patrols south. We want the latest news to take to the Galish.'

So they waited.

Yen Olass and Resbit made a small hut by staking the branches of a tree down to the ground, weaving in willow then slapping on mud and clay. They shared the Melski diet of fish, fish and fish; they gathered watercress and went bird-nesting. The Melski ate no red meat, and refused to kill the forest animals, but allowed Yen Olass to borrow a bow. Venturing into the forest, not knowing whether she was the hunter or the hunted—the presence of the Melski was no guarantee against soldiers—she sought out and killed a small deer. If well-fed, she might have thought it cute; hungry, the notion never occurred to her. Yen Olass and Resbit ate their fill, then hung up the rest to ripen, knowing that this would improve its flavour. When the Melski objected to the presence of dead meat, they moved it further away.

While they waited, Yen Olass tried to persuade Resbit to join a Galish convoy. That was surely safer than venturing over the mountains on their own. But Resbit still refused to consider a journey to Larbster Bay.

'We should stay by Lake Armansis,' said Resbit. 'With the Melski. They'd take us in. Hadn't you thought of that?'

'That's a ridiculous idea,' said Yen Olass.

Of course, it had once been her own idea. But a little time in the forest had swiftly changed her mind. The forest was wet, gloomy, oppressive, cold, alien and threatening, full of trees which hated her. She was made to live free in the open spaces, not to moulder away in the wilds of Penvash with the wooden giants nightly elbowing their way into her nightmares.

They argued about it while they waited for the Melski scouting parties to return with the latest news. But when the patrols came in, what they brought was not news but people. They had picked up a small party in Looming Forest: Draven, Haveros, the Princess Quenerain, a sea captain from the Harvest Plains by the name of Menjamin Naraham Occam, a soldier by the name of Saquarius who was a deserter from the Collosnon army, a young woman from Estar by the name of Jalamex, and two boy children of twelve or thirteen who identified themselves as Shant and Mation, both of Estar.

Haveros told the story.

After being released by Draven, Haveros and the Princess Quenerain had fled to the east on stolen horses (and here Haveros did not mind admitting that he was a horse thief every bit as good as his emperor) in the company of some other prisoners. They had been pursued by hard-riding cavalry. As the pursuit closed in, they had been forced to abandon their horses and flee north into Looming Forest.

Now Chonjara had a thousand troops in the forest, hunting them. There was no doubt that his men, thwarted by the failure of the assault on Castle Vaunting, were glad to have the chance of a hunt which promised a kill. One Melski patrol was already believed to have been wiped out by the invaders.

After a brief council of war, the Melski decided the humans should go north to join the Galish convoys, which would doubtless leave immediately for Larbster Bay rather than stay to face a thousand marauding soldiers. Hor-hor-hurulg-murg and three other Melski would take the humans to Lake Armansis, then go deeper into Penvash to alert the Melski nation (which was, in Melski terms, not exactly a nation but 'our arc of the circle', a phrase which Hor-hor-hurulg-murg did not translate, for it would have meant nothing to humans who stood outside the Cycle).

The other Melski would harass the enemy, pick off stragglers and try to kill or kidnap Chonjara. To find him, they would interrogate prisoners. Yen Olass taught the Melski one word of Ordhar: 'glot', meaning 'where'. In Ordhar, 'Glot Chonjara?' was a grammatically correct sentence meaning, 'Where is Chonjara?'; for the rest, the Melski would have to rely on sign language and pointed directions.

Haveros estimated that it would take eight days to cover the eighty leagues to Lake Armansis, their pace being dictated by their weakest member, the Princess Quenerain, who was suffering badly from blisters. Chonjara's men would gain on them during those eight days, and might even catch them. They set off as soon as possible and moved as fast as possible.

The only person who was not eager to get to Lake Armansis was Resbit. She almost seemed to think it would be better if Chonjara's soldiers caught them. She was, Yen Olass realised, truly terrified of making the journey over the Razorwind Pass to Larbster Bay.

'But why?' said Yen Olass, when they talked about it during a rest break.

'Because it's so far!' said Resbit, close to tears.

'It's not far at all,' said Yen Olass, thinking Resbit must have a very shaky grasp of their local geography.

'It's right out of Estar.'

'We're out of Estar now,' said Yen Olass. 'We're in Penvash.'

'We're still by the river,' said Resbit.

'It's always hard to leave a place,' said Yen Olass. 'I know. I've left many.'

And she thought of some of the places she had lived in, and the partings she had said.

'But I've never left Lorford in my life!' said Resbit.

'But you must have been to Trest,' said Yen Olass. 'Or north, or south, or down to the sea.'

'No, never,' said Resbit, starting to cry. 'No, never the sea. The sea eats people.'

And Yen Olass, holding her and comforting her, started to realise what very different lives they had led.

'I'm sorry,' said Resbit, sniffing. 'I should be brave.'

'You'll be brave once we eat well,' said Yen Olass. 'Nobody was ever brave on an empty stomach.'

She was sorry to see Resbit so badly upset. On the other hand, she was glad that the Melski had decided all the humans were to join the convoy, because that meant Resbit would be forced to go with her.

* * *

Each night, they were exhausted at the end of their march, and each night the Princess Quenerain, her feet steadily disintegrating, was close to collapse. Yet she did not complain: Yen Olass admired her for that. Each night, the princess slept in the arms of Haveros, her very dreams numb with exhaustion. Yen Olass curled up with Resbit, and Draven with Jalamex, to whom he seemed to have laid claim. The others slept as best they could; all of them usually woke before dawn, when the night was coldest.

On the morning of the fourth day, they found the swollen body of a man trapped in the roots of a tree by the riverside. From his clothing, he appeared to be Galish. Yen Olass, who had no fear of dead bodies—at least not by daylight—examined the corpse and tried to estimate how long it had been in the water. Quenerain came down to have a look, then turned away, feeling sick. The man had been hacked to death by a sword or an axe.

'Come away, Suggy,' said Haveros, drawing her away.

Hearing that pet name, Yen Olass remembered the princess whimpering with excitement in a room in Gendormargensis. It all came back to her. 'Suggy, you're so wet down there. So hot and wet.' 'That's because my little teni is crying for joy, Sonson.' Remembering, Yen Olass had to bite her hand to keep herself from laughing; if she remembered those scenes on her deathbed, she would die laughing.

'Come away, Yen Olass,' said Resbit, seeing she was in some distress.

'Son-son,' said the princess, 'I feel faint.'

Yen Olass collapsed to the ground, writhing.

'Yen Olass,' said Resbit. 'What's wrong? Speak to me, Yen Olass.'

'I'll live,' said Yen Olass, controlling herself with an immense effort of will.

She buried her head in her arms, her laughter sobbed out. And Resbit, thinking she was crying, comforted her as best she could. By the time Yen Olass had sobered up, Haveros, Draven and the sea captain Menjamin Occam were discussing the dead man with the Melski. It was a long, laboured conversation, with the polyglot Hor-hor-hurulg-murg bearing the brunt of the job of translation. The Galish did not fight amongst themselves; the Melski would not have attacked the Galish. So who or what was killing upriver?

'We have to go on,' said Draven.

Nobody disputed it. Leaving the body where it was—they could not spare the time or energy to dig a grave, and none of them wished to eat it—they continued north in a sombre mood.

That afternoon, a Melski raft came drifting down the river with a Melski body on board. Without a word, Hor-hor-hurulg-murg dived—and did not surface.

'Where's Hor-hor-hurulg-murg?' said Yen Olass to the three other Melski, using one of the few Melski words she had picked up. They signed her to be patient.

'Let's get under cover,' said Haveros, signing for them to withdraw into the trees.

But at that moment, Hor-hor-hurulg-murg surfaced near the bank, and started to clamber out of the water. Then he turned round, as if expecting someone to follow him. Seeing nobody, he plunged into the water again, reappearing shortly with a child-small Melski, which reluctantly allowed itself to be led ashore.

'He was under the raft,' said Hor-hor-hurulg-murg in Galish, after which he addressed the child in his own language.

He got no response.

'What happened?' said Haveros.

'Unknown,' said Hor-hor-hurulg-murg. 'But we know where the children usually shelter if trouble starts. I suppose the parents of this one were killed, so he took shelter.'

The child stood on the bank looking lost and frightened. Yen Olass advanced. He flinched.

'Dumadom!'

'Glum dumadom glum,' said Hor-hor-hurulg-murg sternly.

'Glum dumadom,' said Yen Olass emphatically, certain that she was not a whatever-it-was.

The Melski child squealed in panic and fled for the river. Draven blocked its path. It turned at bay and bared its teeth. Hor-hor-hurulg-murg laughed, and spoke again:

'Glum dumadom loglum.'

The child relaxed slightly.

'What's a dumadom?' said Yen Olass.

'Zardik,' said Hor-hor-hurlug-murg, using the Galish word.

'And what's that?'

'You know . . . fur, claws . . . like this.'

Hor-hor-hurulg-murg did a little pantomime, shambling on all fours, then lumbering on two legs. It was so funny that Yen Olass almost broke into hysterical laughter. She controlled herself, guessing that would be an irretrievable insult to Melski dignity.

'I think he means bear,' said Haveros.

'Oh, a bear,' said Yen Olass.

'You understand?' said Hor-hor-hurlug-murg. 'Good. So you know, glum starts no, but on its own it means maybe. Sometimes it even means yes. If you want one word that's always no, use loglum. Otherwise, glum glum, start and finish.'

Yen Olass committed that to memory as they set off again. The raft was now out of sight; floating downstream with a dead body on board, it would take a clear warning of danger to the Melski still in the south.

The little Melski managed to keep up the pace, but was exhausted when evening came. Yen Olass regarded it as a personal triumph when he allowed her to fold his small green body into the comfort of her furs. She taught the child her name, and discovered his, which was Wadu; this discovery delighted her, until Hor-hor-hurulg-murg advised that 'wadu' simply meant 'hungry'.

'Ask him his name then,' said Yen Olass.

Hor-hor-hurulg-murg tried, but failed. Little Melski were always cautious when talking to large Melski. This behaviour was instinctive, dating back to the Stone Days before the Merging had brought the wisdom of the Cycle. Back then, large Melski used to delight in eating little Melski.

'Try again,' said Yen Olass.

'He's too young to understand,' said Hor-hor-hurulg-murg;

this convenient formula excused him from having to explain
why it was really beneath the dignity of a Melski male to con-
verse with a child.

The child was a problem the next day, because it started lag-
ging behind. Toward the end of the day, Yen Olass was trudging
along with Wadu riding on her shoulders. That evening, as they
feasted on dead fish and (humans only) gently mouldering veni-
son, Yen Olass was concerned to find Wadu eating slugs; Hor-
hor-hurulg-murg, with a trace of weariness, explained that slugs
were the best possible thing for him.

Apart from this disconcerting eating habit, Wadu was in
many ways an ideal child. He was strong, sturdy, wore no
clothes, never caught a chill, and was never in any danger of
drowning in the river. Furthermore, he was awed into good
behaviour by the presence of so many adults. Yen Olass decided
that her first big project as a mother would be to get him to
speak. But what would happen when they got to Lake Armansis? Would she be allowed to take him west with her?

Her question was soon answered, because when they were
still one day short of the lake, they ran into a party of a dozen
Melski. Recognising one of the females, Wadu threw himself
forward with a scream of delight. He was picked up and comforted, and immediately started babbling away in his own language. The adults were so busy talking themselves that it was
some time before Yen Olass could get a translation.

'Among other things,' said Hor-hor-hurulg-murg, 'he says
you're a nice creature even if you are all covered in fur.'

The adult Melski brought the news from Lake Armansis.
About two hundred attackers from the west, probably Orfus
pirates from the Greater Teeth, had come over the Razorwind
Pass, wiping out the two Galish convoys camped on the western
shores of the lake. The pirates were now building a fort, as if
they meant to stay. Some Melski had been killed by the pirates;
this group had thought it safest to head south. Hor-hor-hurulg-
murg disabused them of that notion.

The dozen Melski joined the north-going fugitives and kept
pace with them to Lake Armansis. They camped near the lake,
planning to cross the river in the morning and skirt around the
eastern shores, picking up the river again at the northern end.

By morning, Draven had disappeared. The sea captain,
Occam, was also missing. Guessing that these two had headed
for the pirate camp, the party crossed the river—which meant a

hair-raising trip across a series of one-log bridges spanning the gaps between huge water-cleaving rocks—and started their journey round the eastern side of the lake. Haveros, who had more than half expected Draven to flee to the pirates, did not expect a pirate attack, doubting that men who had just looted two merchant convoys would mount an expedition to capture a tiny poverty-stricken group like their own.

The person most upset was the woman Jalamex, for Draven had abandoned her without so much as a goodbye.

CHAPTER
Twenty-two

With escape to the west cut off, Yen Olass would have liked to stay with the Melski, but she was a minority of one. The big, green animals made the others uneasy, and, as Haveros said, 'Once they start killing humans, there's no telling where they'll stop.' Even Resbit allowed herself to be persuaded by that argument. So, when the river forked north of Lake Armansis, the humans chose the westerly branch while the Melski took the easterly.

'Your way takes you into the Valley of Forgotten Dreams,' said Hor-hor-hurulg-murg. 'By tradition, for us it is a forbidden place. The first ten leagues are said to be safe. Beyond that— death.'

They thanked him. They only wanted a place to hide until pirates, soldiers and the wizards of Castle Vaunting had fought out their battles, and, with any luck, destroyed each other. The valley, with its rough-running river of rapids and waterfalls, its rugged banks and its evergreen forests (trees with leaves of a dark, dark green, so dark it was almost black—entirely unlike the deciduous growth of the south) should offer them refuge.

About five leagues up the valley, they came to a place with a little flat land on either side of the river, which surged past, deep and narrow, then foamed into wide and shallow rapids.

'This will do,' said Haveros. 'We won't find anywhere better.'

Yen Olass, who refused to live in a nameless place, called it Nightcáps, which sounded a good name for a wild place in the back of beyond. With Haveros supervising them, they built lean-to shelters, sharpened sticks and dug latrines, hauled rotten logs out of the forest and broke them up for firewood, made bird snares and fish traps, and booby-trapped animal tracks with pits and deadfalls. Then they tore apart the local vegetation, sampling leaves, fern shoots, bark, pith, vines, pulped roots and fungus growths.

After ten days, they had settled in properly, and were beginning to think of curing hides and making extra clothing. But all such plans ended when three exhausted pirates came stumbling into Nightcaps, bringing the news that Chonjara and his men were close behind them.

The pirates were their old friend Draven, a vicious little man called Toyd, and a man named Mellicks who was short-sighted and forever squinting to try and make sure of his footing. After hearing a brief account of how Chonjara's men had attacked the pirates at Lake Armansis, and were patrolling the forest to cut off retreat to the west, Haveros ordered everyone to break camp and move out.

Yen Olass and Resbit were most reluctant to go. They had worked hard on their lean-to, sealing off every draught and leak. Though Resbit's pregnancy was in its early stages, they had been talking baby clothes. Yen Olass had been designing a trap to kill bush rats for a supply of small, soft, furry skins; as Yen Olass knew next to nothing about making clothes, Resbit had promised to show her how it was done. And now they had to leave everything and run.

Just before they pulled out, Haveros disabled all the snares, deadfalls and pits. None was placed where it might catch any of Chonjara's men, and his hunting ethic did not allow him to kill for no reason, or, worse, to leave disabled animals to die slowly in the forest.

Haveros forced the pace up the river. They had fed reasonably well over the past few days, and carried food for three days. All blisters from their earlier marches had healed, except in the case of the Princess Quenerain, who still had trouble with her feet. She was reluctant to march, and begged Haveros to try and negotiate with Chonjara.

'We both know his arguments,' said Haveros, and lightly touched a small scar on her face where a stone had hit her.

This logic did not convince Quenerain, who argued with Haveros for hours at the end of the first march; argument ended when he lost his temper and hit her, and she sobbed herself to sleep.

Haveros put his trust in speed. He was not inclined to slink away into the hills and hide. They could only survive in this forest if they were free to fish the river, tear down the vegetation, set hunting traps, and range widely to hunt. They could not do this if they were hulkering in the hills, trying to make themselves invisible. So they would run north, until their food ran out. And then? Then they would establish themselves on some height overlooking the river, and, once Chonjara's men went marching past, Haveros and his party would double back, make for Lake Armansis, follow the river south, the try and slip away to the east, to Skua.

To Haveros, it was all a bit of a game, even though he was playing with his own life. His people, who were not skilled woodsmen, left trail-signs Chonjara's men would be able to follow easily. Haveros supplemented these by breaking the occasional branch now and then. He wanted to lead Chonjara as far into the Penvash Peninsula as possible, knowing that ever day deeper would stretch Chonjara's supply lines and increase the likelihood of Chonjara finding his retreat south cut off by the Melski when he got back to Lake Armansis. If the Princess Quenerain had not been so distressed and distressing, Haveros would actually have started to enjoy himself.

* * *

When they camped at the end of their first march north, Draven —a professional opportunist—tried for Jalamex. But she had taken refuge in the shelter of a fallen log, together with Haveros and Quenerain. She refused to respond to Draven's whispers, and, when he raised his voice, he woke Haveros, who treated him to the full force of that rich, magnificent, eloquent obscenity known only to mule drivers, professional soldiers and low-class whores.

Haveros, his oratory tapering off toward the end, addressed Draven rather more mildly than he had been, saying:

'So drag your cock back to its slime-pit, you ignorant sack of arseholes.'

And Draven, awed by his fury, complied.

As Draven retreated, the Princess Quenerain mocked him; she used some words which were quite obscene. She had her own small gift for languages; she knew Ordhar, and had learnt enough Galish to make herself objectionable. Haveros shut her up: swearing was a man's prerogative.

CHAPTER
Twenty-three

Early the next day, it began to rain. As they marched, steep banks forced them into the river, where they waded knee-deep; few things are more disgusting than soaking wet boots just after breakfast, but nobody complained.

Further on, the river widened, though the banks were still high; they splashed through shallow water and across stones and shingle. The way ahead was blocked by two shoulders of rock, each ten times the height of a man. These shoulders flanked a narrow gorge where water thrashed over boulders. In places, the gorge was scarcely wide enough for swordplay.

The gorge ran for only thirty horse-lengths, but it was a formidable obstacle. They were soaked by the time they had clawed upstream against the battering water. The river widened again; on the eastern side, a stream descended steeply between high V-shaped banks.

They rested briefly, then Haveros urged them on again. The banks drew in after a few more horse-lengths, and steepened, forcing them to wade through water.

Through wavering water pocked by rain, Yen Olass saw a blurred yet gleaming fist of green. She plunged her arm into the water and seized it. Her catch was a perfect sphere of stone, heavy, yet transparent. Multicoloured stars shone within its misty green: solitary luminaries, constellations and entire galaxies.

She was still admiring her find when she realized everyone else had frozen. A wark was coming down the river. The big, lumbering bear advanced with a leisured, measured gait, as if it owned the world—which, as far as they were concerned, was fair enough, as they were hardly going to dispute ownership.

Carefully, Haveros stooped down and picked up a rock. The bear paused, and turned this way and that, as if sniffing the air. With a sudden jerk of his body, Haveros threw the rock. It sailed overhead to land with a splash, upstream of the bear. The animal wheeled. Draven and Haveros waded to the sides of the river and hauled themselves out, clinging onto trees. Yen Olass tucked her stone globe into one of the inner pockets of her weather jacket.

The wark turned back downstream. Everyone still in the river broke and ran for the trees. The banks were almost sheer, but terrain yielded to desperation. Confused by the sudden flurry of noise, the bear peered downstream. Like all animals of its kind, it was short-sighted. And unpredictable. As it hesitated, the men drew weapons and backed up against trees. The bear proceeded, coming downstream through the hissing rain.

Yen Olass picked up a stick. If the wark came too close, she would wallop it over the nose. Then it would either retreat or tear her apart. She should have been terrified, but instead she was fascinated. She had never seen such a huge animal so close up. She watched as it went by, almost close enough to touch. She imagined riding on it, clutching great handfuls of fur.

When the bear had gone past, Yen Olass slid down the bank and waded into the river, careless of the cold water, and watched the bear disappearing downstream toward the gorge. Her eyes were wide with excitement.

'You like bears, do you?' said Haveros.

Yen Olass, to her consternation, blushed. She was ashamed that he knew she was entranced by a big, furry animal; she was much too old for that.

'Maybe,' said Yen Olass.

'Then remember this,' said Haveros. 'Bears don't necessarily like you.'

Yen Olass bowed her head slightly, accepting his rebuke. As a child of the wastelands of Monogail, she knew how to accept a warning intended to help her survive. This was true wilderness: unmapped, uninhabited and unforgiving. Survival demanded unrelenting concentration. Nevertheless, Yen Olass was glad she had seen the bear.

And glad that she had her star-filled stone. She was convinced it was very rare and very valuable. She had never seen anything like it. They would not be travelling up the river forever; in the Ravlish Lands or some other civilized territory, the globe would surely be worth a fortune.

A little further upstream, the travellers found a strange construction by the riverside: a flat-topped mushroom made of the same star-burning stone. They all gathered round it. Yen Olass touched it gingerly; it was cold, and twice her height. She picked up a rock and started hammering it, trying to break some off. She was convinced that now was her chance to get really, really rich. But the mushroom refused to chip, break or shatter.

'Having fun?' said the deserter Saquarius.

'Shut up,' said Haveros, who did not like deserters on principle. 'Or I'll have fun with your face.'

Saquarius turned on him.

'I bet on the ugly one,' said the pirate Toyd.

'Which one's that?' said Draven.

They laughed. The two Estar boys, Shant and Mation, sniggered in sympathy, not because they were amused but because they wanted to take on themselves something of the glory of the rough-striding pirates. Haveros and Saquarius turned on them.

'Soldiers against pirates?' said Yen Olass. 'Chonjara would love this.'

'He'd place his bets at random,' said Quenerain. 'It'd be all the same to him.'

Shant made a joke in his native Estral, and Mation laughed. Haveros, who had enough Estral to know the comment was obscene, cuffed him round the head.

'Enough of this,' said Draven. 'Let's have a look at this thing. Up you go, Yen Olass.'

'I can't!' said Yen Olass. 'It's much too high.'

But Haveros and Draven boosted her up, making a rising step out of their linked hands. Yen Olass clambered onto the top, which was slippery and solid. And somewhat curved. She wondered if it was a stone phallus, the relic of some ancient fertility rite. It glistened in the streaming rain.

'What can you see?' said Draven.

'Nothing much,' said Yen Olass. 'There's not much of a

view. Except . . . if you really want to know, you're losing your hair.'

Draven clapped his hand to his head, then withdrew it, looking partly angry, partly sheepish. Yen Olass laughed.

'Stop clowning around,' said Haveros. 'Can you get inside?'

'No,' said Yen Olass.

'Can you get it inside yourself?' said Quenerain.

'Who knows?' said Yen Olass. 'What's your expert opinion?'

'You'd have more of a chance with that thing than you would with a man,' said the princess. 'You'd have to pay a man to do as much as rape you.'

'I don't know about that,' said Yen Olass, looking down on her. 'I had to fight off half the army once. Not like you, spreading your legs and—'

'That's enough, both of you,' said Haveros, sharply.

'Did you hear the way she spoke to me?' said Quenerain. 'The ugly little strumpet ought to have her scalp ripped off.'

'Any more trouble and I'll batter the pair of you,' said Haveros.

He was the leader. He was ashamed that he had dishonoured his leadership by almost coming to blows with Saquarius, embarrassed that two women had used their diplomacy to prevent the fight, and annoyed that those same two women should now start arguing with each other for no reason at all. Quenerain was his lover, but he was in no mood to grant her special favours, even so. The combination of shame, embarrassment and irritation made him fierce.

'Let's horse horse,' said Haveros, in Eparget. Then, this pungent saying being entirely untranslatable, he said in Galish: 'Get going.' Then, in Estral, pointing the two boys up the river: 'Go!' Then, to Yen Olass: 'Get yourself down from there.'

'How?' said Yen Olass.

'Jump,' said Draven. 'We can pick up the pieces.'

Yen Olass snorted. She grabbed hold of an overhead branch.

'Careful,' said Resbit.

'Tree,' said Yen Olass. 'Drop me in the dirt and you'll get yourself ringbarked.'

She had just learnt about ringbarking in the last few days, from the soldier Saquarius, of all people.

She swung herself down, hand over hand, sprays of raindrops shaking loose as the branch lurched beneath her weight. Then she dropped the last little bit, and brushed a few fragments of bark from her hands.

'Onward,' said Haveros.

And on they went. They were so wet by now that they hardly noticed when the rain eased. Just before they halted to rest at mid-morning, the rain stopped, but the sky was still encumbered by everlast cloud. They had no food to spare for a snack; instead, they squatted amidst the trees, resting in silence.

Yen Olass watched Jalamex kneading water from Quenerain's hair. The princess liked to have people waiting on her, and had more or less managed to coerce Jalamex into being her servant. She had tried to get Yen Olass to do things for her, too— 'Grease my boots, serf'—but had failed. Yen Olass took the attitude that here they were all equal, fugitives struggling to preserve their lives. So she had refused the princess—but saw no need for Quenerain to be rude to her. Surely Quenerain could have tried to make friends. At times, Yen Olass had almost liked her.

Quenerain saw Yen Olass watching her, and gave her a look which meant 'One day I'll have you underfoot.' Yen Olass put her little finger to her tongue, which in Gendormargensis was the ultimate gesture of contempt; the princess looked away, pretending she had not seen.

At that moment, Yen Olass felt very homesick. She remembered Gendormargensis and her room in tooth 44, Moon Stallion Strait. She remembered her cat Lefrey. She had been so comfortable there. But that was long ago and far away. Now she was here, in the evergreen forest north of Lake Armansis, squatting on a soggy mass of decaying leaves which, in time, would mulch down to earth. No sound but the talk of the river and the drip-drop-thrup of water filtering down through leaves. That's another thing about trees: when the sky stops raining, the trees don't.

'Yen Olass,' said Resbit.

Yen Olass started. She had been drifting away, allowing her own thoughts to take her away from the world, bearing her away like a river.

'What is it?' said Yen Olass.

Resbit had a snail on her hand. Very delicate, it eased its tiny speck-black eyes out to the limits of their tubes. Fascinating.

Yen Olass watched as it began to migrate across cold wet female skin.

It didn't get very far.

Yen Olass reached out, pinched the snail between thumb and finger, cracked its shell, picked away the pieces then bit the snail in half. She chewed it with determination rather than enjoyment, giving the remaining half to Resbit, who accepted this love offering with a smile.

Then they sat together in the forest, shoulder to shoulder. Yen Olass let her head lean against Resbit. She closed her eyes. She wondered about the Rovac warrior, Elkor Alish, who had coupled with Resbit. By day or by night? Had he tasted her? Had he touched her . . . there? Or there?

That was strange to think about. A man and a woman. Yet it happened. Thousands and thousands of times. Entire tribes and nations peopled that way. And for every moment of sword-slaughtering glory, nine months of myth and darkness, years learning to crawl, to walk, to talk . . .

Did men ever think about that when they hacked each other with swords, making themselves heroes? Somehow, Yen Olass doubted it. She wondered what it was like to be a man. She found it hard to imagine. Men had no sense of proportion.

Yen Olass remembered Lonth Denesk and Tonaganuk killing each other in the Enskandalon Square in Gendormargensis. Two old men hacking each other to death with axes when they should have been at home keeping themselves warm under featherdown quilts. With cats. And bread. Spread with honey from honeycombs—very thick honey with bits of wax in it which you could chew.

Men were always fighting, and for what purpose?

'Yick,' said Resbit.

'A spider?' said Yen Olass, who was not afraid of them, but did not favour them.

But it was not a spider, but a dung-drab caterpillar which had fallen from the trees onto Resbit's knee. Yen Olass wondered if caterpillars were edible, and decided not. She had squished a few in her time, finding them green or yellow inside. This caterpillar, unaware that it was in danger of immediate demolition, was elongating and contracting, sliding its body forward. Yen Olass intercepted it with a stick; it climbed aboard, and she lofted it into the air then set it down on the ground.

There.

She had known the caterpillar would climb aboard the stick. She knew how to manipulate it, but that took her no closer to understanding what it was like to be a caterpillar. Similarly with men. As an oracle, she had learnt how to teach reason to men who were proud, vain, arrogant and unreasonable, but she had never understood why men were the way they were. She knew a man hates to take advice from a woman. That was why the Sisterhood had developed the apparatus of Casting Board and Indicators—so that an oracle would appear to be only a mouth-piece for the apparatus, rather than a voice in her own right. But why did men hate women to be their equals?

Yen Olass knew she could be much more interesting as a person in her own right than as a slave, a thing, an object. Yet she knew most men would prefer her as a slave. She understood that the drive for power and mastery was responsible. Yet she could not understand what made power so attractive.

Maybe it was . . .

'Time to move,' said Haveros.

'Must we?' said Quenerain.

That complaint did not deserve an answer, and did not get one. They set off again, with Yen Olass still thinking about her problem.

Maybe fear was the answer. Maybe men struggled for power because they were afraid. Afraid of losing. Afraid of being con-quered. Afraid of other men. But then, what about the Lord Emperor Khmar? He was a man. And it was hard to believe he had ever been afraid of anything. He was not afraid of death. Was not even afraid of the sickness that was killing him.

Yen Olass was still thinking when she was distracted by a vaporous sun which briefly emerged between the clouds, shin-ing down briefly on the abrupt geography of jagged pinnacles and sheer-faced bluffs they were now traversing. Then the clouds closed in again.

They began to encounter strange trees with shining green bark and variegated leaves of orange and grey. Yen Olass, standing knee-deep in the river, plucked an overhanging twig. Yellow sap came out, reminding her of caterpillar guts; there was a sharp, bitter smell which clung to her hands. The strange trees clustered together in their own encampments by the river;

the rest of the forest was the same monotonous evergreen as ever.

While she was still wondering about the trees—did they ever bear fruit, and, if so, could you eat it?—a rivercastle came in sight. Haveros called a halt, and signed them into the trees. They perched precariously on ground too steep to walk on. They waited. Watching. Listening.

The river was piped through the castle, spilling out through culverts on the downstream side. The castle was a low, squat building with one open doorway facing downriver. It seemed to be made of polished grass-green jade. It showed no sign of wear, but the low-lying roof, which was flat, was littered with dead leaves and branches.

'It's empty,' said Draven to Haveros, in Ordhar; Yen Olass saw the suspicious looks his fellow pirates gave him when he used this language which they could not understand.

'All right then,' said Haveros. 'Let's move in.'

The others had soon decided the castle was abandoned, but Haveros—a good hunter, and a dangerous quarry—had allowed himself plenty of time to make his mind up. The pirate Mellicks, eager to see if there was any loot, pushed on ahead. Haveros let him go, happy enough to see someone else brave the way into what might well be a potential deathtrap.

Mellicks had scrambled up to the doorway and disappeared through it by the time the others drew near.

'Stay back,' said Haveros quietly, advancing. 'What's inside, Mellicks?'

There was no answer. Peering inside, Haveros saw a low-roofed chamber. Up close, he could see the castle rock was filled with stars, just like the phallic mushrooms they had encountered earlier in the day. The glow of multicoloured starlight flooded the chamber, where Mellicks stood, looking round disconsolately.

'Nothing,' said Mellicks, giving a belated answer to the question Haveros had asked.

'We can go in then,' said Haveros.

That was all there was to the castle—this one vast room above the river, with the one doorway leading into it. And, in the centre of the room, horse-length oval strips of metal spreading out from a grey metal disk.

'What's that?' said Draven.

Haveros tried to pick up one of the strips of metal. It refused to budge by so much as a shadow-width. There were strange characters graved on the metal: the smoothflowing cursive characters of a language of abstractions created without reference to birth, death, flesh, bones, blood, buildings, cities, war, horses, ploughing, barley, rice, tin, gold, sunlight, coal, flowers, grass, trees.

The strange writing reminded Yen Olass of the characters written on the ceramic map she had stolen from the War Archives complex, Karling Drask, to satisfy the scholarly lusts of the text-master Eldegen Terzanagel. That writing, she knew, had been in the High Speech of wizards. Was this the same? She tried to picture the map and the writing that had been on it. The general outlines came to her—and the shape of some of the pieces that had been missing after the map got damaged—but beyond that, nothing.

'We could stay here,' said Quenerain, looking around.

'Where will the servants' quarters be?' said Yen Olass.

'Right by where the whores are quartered,' said Quenerain, stabbing her finger in Resbit's direction.

Toyd saw where she was pointing, and looked at Resbit significantly. Resbit shrank into shelter behind Yen Olass, who did her I-killed-my-first-man-at-the-age-of-twelve routine; Toyd, who had never heard it before, was suitably impressed. Then Haveros shut them all up: he had had enough.

'We can't stay here,' said Haveros. 'Chonjara won't be far behind.'

'You don't really think that,' said Quenerain. 'Otherwise you'd be driving us on much faster.'

'You're none of you fit to go much faster,' said Haveros. 'In any case, Chonjara can't travel too quickly. He'll be held up a long time at that gorge, putting scouts on top of those rocks to find out if we're waiting up here.'

'Why?'

'In case we drop stones on his head.'

'And why didn't we?'

'Because it's just the thing he'd expect me to do.'

'And instead . . .'

'We're going up the river, then we'll double back and slip past him. Of course, he expects me to do that, too. There's lots of things he expects me to do. Split out party in half and try for east and west. Leave a rearguard to try and hold him up. Wait myself, to try for his head when he camps at night. He's right, too. I might try any of those things. Whatever I do, I won't disappoint him.'

Yen Olass was disgusted at this kind of talk. She knew Chonjara as a violent, hot-headed man capable of immense amounts of rage and hate. If he was a dog, you would put him down and think yourself well rid of him. Yet here was Haveros, speaking of his enemy as if there was some special understanding between them. Almost as if they were friends.

'Who says he's chasing you?' said Yen Olass. 'He might only be after the pirates. He might have turned round and gone back home.'

'He came up the Hollern River hunting me,' said Haveros. 'And it's me he's after now. He knows I'm here. The Melski never caught him, so we can guarantee he caught some Melski. He'll have found out where we went. He's good.'

Haveros seemed positively proud of his enemy.

'A pity we don't have more people on our side,' said Mellicks, trying to shift the grey disk at the centre of the oval strips, in case it was a trapdoor to a treasure dungeon.

'We've got Lord Alagrace on our side,' said Haveros. 'When he gets back from Skua, he'll bring Chonjara to heel. You can't go whoring through the forest with a thousand men, not to settle a personal feud—not when you've got a siege to fight. With any luck, Alagrace will take his head.'

'From what I've heard,' said Mellicks, 'your Lord Alagrace doesn't sound like the world's greatest gift to leadership.'

'He'll get reinforcements from Skua who haven't been tainted by mutiny,' said Haveros, watching Mellicks kicking the grey disk in disgust. 'Officers, too. By now, Chonjara's people will be finding out the fun's over. Not many women up in this neck of the woods—unless you fancy a Melski bitch.'

'It's been known,' said Mellicks, sagely.

He stepped onto the grey metal disk, and the oval horse-length metal strips folded up into a flower-bud, trapping him before he could scream.

CHAPTER
Twenty-four

'Mellicks!' shouted Toyd.

Draven swore, Haveros drew his sword and Quenerain screamed. Everyone crowded round the metal bud. Except for Yen Olass, who fled to the doorway, terrified, thinking that any moment the stars would go out and some drop-door or sliding stone would block all chance of escape.

To her relief, she reached the open air safely. She squatted down just outside the doorway, while the others thumped on the steel bud, hacked at it, tried to pry the metal petals open, and shouted words of hope and encouragement in case Mellicks could hear them. Then, slowly, they gave up, and drifted outside: Resbit first, then Jalamex, the boys Shant and Mation, the deserter Saquarius, then the pirates Toyd and Draven.

Only Haveros, with Quenerain kneeling at his feet, remained to watch the steel bud.

'We're not going to get him out,' said Draven. 'We'll have to leave him.'

'Leave all of them, that's what I think,' said Toyd. 'We can travel faster on our own.'

'We'll do better with Haveros.'

'What? Mucking through the jungle till we fiddle our way through to his darling Lord Alagrace? What kind of law will they give us then? A close shave with the knife, that's my bet.'

'Haveros guarantees our safety,' said Draven.

'Ay, so you say.'

'I've lived with these people.'

'Yes, when your shipmates died. How did that happen?'

'As I've told you,' said Draven.

'Ay. As you've told. As I've heard. Wait till we get to the Greater Teeth. You'll be telling some more then.'

184

'The truth makes the best story,' said Draven. 'That's why I'm sticking to it.'

Yen Olass, listening, wondered exactly what Draven had told his comrades. She remembered the interview with Khmar: one pirate dying at the hands of the Lord Emperor himself, a second killed by bodyguards, then a third knifed by Draven.

Toyd seemed in a mood to start a quarrel. And no wonder. They were all hungry, on edge and short-tempered. Tramping up this river on the shortest of all possible rations, with pursuit behind and no certain prospect of escape, they were not the happiest of travelling companions.

But before Toyd and Draven could fray each other's tempers further, Haveros called them all inside.

The bud was beginning to open.

None of them would have been surprised if a dead man had been inside. Instead, there stood Mellicks. He blinked, then yawned. The central disk he was standing on glowed bright yellow. As the metal petals folded flat against the floor, the disk turned grey again. Mellicks stepped clear.

'What happened?' said Haveros.

'A . . . call it a dream,' said Mellicks. 'But . . .'

'But what?'

'I can see. As clearly as anything!'

The pirate was positively radiant. Joyful. Since Orfus pirates were not by nature the happiest bunch of people you could hope to meet, Haveros was suspicious.

'What do you mean, you can see?'

'You. Her. Everything. Polished. Sharp. I've always . . . I've always wanted to see properly.'

'What is this?' said Draven. 'Miracle magic?'

'I suppose you could call it that,' said Mellicks.

'A wish machine!' said Quenerain. 'You could wish for—'

'Your eyes are yellow,' said Haveros abruptly.

'Mine?' said the princess.

'Mellicks! Your eyes are yellow.'

'Are they?' said Mellicks.

They were.

Everyone stared at these bright yellow eyes. They were as yellow and glossy as buttercups.

'What of it?' said Mellicks. 'I can see. The voices told me.'

'Voices?' said Haveros.

'Try it for yourself,' said Mellicks, a little truculent now, because he did not like the way the others were reacting to his excellent eyes.

Haveros persisted.

'What kind of voices?'

'Faint,' said Mellicks. 'And very far away.'

'How did you understand them? You've got no truchman's skills yourself.'

'They spoke as I speak,' said Mellicks. 'If you want to know more, ask them yourself.'

'I wouldn't go near anything so dangerous,' said Draven.

'I'm alive,' said Mellicks.

'Yes,' said Draven. 'And the shark doesn't always bite the first time.'

'I don't think it's a shark,' said Quenerain, touching Haveros lightly on the shoulder. 'I think it's here to grant . . . what we desire. You're not afraid, are you, dear?'

'No,' said Haveros. 'I'm not.'

And, deciding suddenly, he laid down his sword and stepped onto the grey metal disk. The bud closed around him; when the petals eventually opened again, he stood there holding a sword, and smiling. He had what he had wanted for a long time; a blade of the fabled firelight steel from the distant southern island kingdom of Stokos.

'Your face!' said the Princess Quenerain.

'What about it?' said Haveros, stepping forward.

A yellow stain, like a birthmark, sprawled down one side of his face, but he could not see it. He listened impassively as they told him about it.

'I'll live,' said Haveros.

And while the others were still wondering over the sword and the yellow stain, Yen Olass Ampadara, who knew exactly what she wanted, stepped onto the grey metal disk.

'Yen Olass!' shouted Haveros.

But it was too late.

The metal petals closed up. Yen Olass was enfolded in darkness, and there, in a dark space filled with stars, she listened to the voices.

—What are you doing with a piece of ourselves?

'What piece?' said Yen Olass.

—That.

With the word, the voices made her understand.

'I found it in the river,' said Yen Olass.

—In the change.

'I want . . .'

—You want to stay.

'No.'

Something unpleasant started to happen. The darkness hardened and started to squeeze Yen Olass. The voices started to nag down into her brain, stirring up dead memories better left to coagulate down in the lower sump. The memories sharpened into events. Hands grappled and clawed. The needle stabbed. Yen Olass screamed.

'No!'

—You want to stay.

'No!'

—You want to stay.

A crushing pressure. A tongue flushed with saliva, forced against her face. Beef wrenched home, ripping her membrane. The needle stabbed home, and the old woman laughed. Chonjara! His boot slammed home, the Casting Board broke apart, the ivory Indicators scattered. The knife. Her mother's breast. A stone smashed into her skin.

Yen Olass screamed:

'You smegma-eating arsefuckers!'

Silence.

Floating stars.

Yen Olass floated. All pressure was gone. She sensed the voices. They were cringing, appalled at the strength of her anger.

'Do what I say,' said Yen Olass. 'Or you'll be sorry.'

—Join us. Stay.

'Do what I say!'

The voices closed around. Deferential, this time. Lightly, they roused her flesh. Worked her wish. She trembled. Accepted her change with a sigh. Delighted, she waited for her release from the metal bud. She saw the petals start to open.

Then, at the last possible moment, the voices hurt her. Lacerating pain ripped at her fingernails. She screamed as the bud opened. Looked down at her hands. And saw ten grey scabs. Her fingernails were gone.

She screamed again.

And did not stop until Resbit was holding her.

'What is it?' said Resbit. 'What is it, Yen Olass? What did they do to you? Yen Olass?'

Someone touched her hands.

'Claws,' said Haveros.

Tentatively, blinking away tears, Yen Olass looked at her hands. Held them close to her face. There was something there. Hard and sharp. Then grey scabs. Thick metal-slab fingernails, tapering to sharp chisels.

'You'll be all right, Yen Olass,' said Resbit, comforting her. 'You'll be all right.'

Yen Olass nuzzled her face into Resbit's comfort, and allowed herself to be calmed.

'Did they try to hold you?' said Haveros.

'They hurt me,' said Yen Olass. 'They tried to make me stay. They wanted . . . they wanted to eat me. I think. Take me all. Make me them.'

'Did you wish . . . ?'

'Not for this!' exclaimed Yen Olass. 'They did this. They hurt me.'

'That's enough then,' said Haveros. 'Whatever the thing is, it's waking up. It's getting stronger. We can't risk it again—it's trying to eat people.'

'You've got what you want,' said Toyd. 'Why should the rest of us be scared off? Because the girl got scared in the dark? Because she's grown a little cold steel? I can spare a bit of my beauty—I want to eat.'

And before they could stop him, he jumped onto the grey metal disk, and the metal petals closed around him.

He was inside for a long time.

When Toyd was released, he tottered forward. His mouth opened. He tried to speak, to scream. No sound came. He fell face-first and landed heavily. His skull broke open with a soft plop, collapsed gently into liquid and began to ooze across the floor. He was definitely, undeniably dead. Draven stepped forward and nudged at a growth that pushed out from his ribs. It was an embryo.

'Is this what you wished for?' said Draven.

As a pirate, he knew his anatomy, having cut up a few pregnant women in his time—though more for sport than to satisfy a habit of inquiry.

'No!' said Yen Olass.

She most certainly had not wished for a child. Though perhaps the idea of a child had been at the back of her mind, and perhaps the alien voices had stolen that idea from her.

'So what did you wish for?' said Draven.

'I can't tell you.'

'Why not?'

'I can't tell you!'

'You killed him,' said Draven.

'I didn't do anything to him,' said Yen Olass.

'She's pregnant!' said Quenerain in a shrill voice.

'Pregnant!' said Yen Olass. 'What would I do with a child here? In the wilderness?'

She knew that, sometimes, she yearned for a child. On the other hand, there were other times when she was thoroughly glad that she had no children to burden her. And it was absurd to think that she would wish to be pregnant at a time like this, when they were running for their lives in the forest.

'Yen Olass,' said Haveros. 'If you'd really wanted . . .'

'It'll be born with yellow eyes,' said Quenerain viciously. 'And people will stone it to death.'

'They will not!' said Yen Olass.

'You see?' said Quenerain. 'She admits it! She admits it! She's pregnant. Made pregnant by wishing herself.'

'Unnatural bitch,' said Saquarius.

Yen Olass saw they were convinced she had got herself with child without first allowing herself to be dominated by a man: and they hated her for it.

'Still,' said Draven, kicking the dead body. 'He was warned. He had it coming to him.'

And Yen Olass saw that Draven was glad that Toyd was dead. Those questions about how Draven had survived the wrath of the Collosnon Empire had clearly worried him, as well they might.

'Come on,' said Haveros. 'There's nothing else for us here. Let's leave.'

And so they departed from that place, and went on up the river, leaving the castle to its mystery.

Yen Olass, for her part, carried a mystery within her. Was she pregnant, or was she not?

She sincerely hoped she was not.

CHAPTER
Twenty-five

Upriver from the castle, they encountered more of the strange starstone mushrooms growing in bunches of two or three. Further north, they found an ominous array of holes in the riverbank. These, big enough for a man to walk inside without bending, snorted steam and scalding water intermittently. There were seventeen of them.

Haveros had no idea what this phenomenon might portend. But it suggested danger. Although this was only their second day of travel, he was unwilling to go any further north. He decided they would backtrack half a league then head east up a small stream. Then they would turn south, ultimately hoping to find refuge with Lord Alagrace. With any luck, Chonjara would be killed by the voices of the wishing machine at the castle, or else he would press on north and be destroyed by whatever dangers waited there.

Following this plan, they hastened through the last hours of the day. When there was still a little daylight left, they halted, for they had found a cave. It was not a warm, snug refuge, or a plunging chasm mining the depths of darkness, or a luminous palace of quartz crystals and glowworms—instead, it was a meagre hollowness, a wide mouth gaping open to the sky, more of an armpit than a womb. There were a few spiderwebs toward the back but no secret places.

The stream they were following ran by outside the cave-mouth. Rain was falling again, coming down in a persistent drizzle from a darkening sky. They gathered wood, which was all damp and waterlogged. For kindling, they stripped the bark from a resinous tree, then Draven lit a fire. Yen Olass watched him, fascinated by his patience as he worked with tinder and flint. He had never struck her as a patient man, but, coaxing a flame to life, he revealed resources of infinite tenderness.

190

Men could be so kind when they chose, lavishing love and care on infant fires, cherished weapons, a loyal pair of boots or a bit of soup they were nourishing with gentle heat. So why did they have to be so cruel to Yen Olass? Nobody in this group had said the word yet, but she knew what they were thinking: dral-kosh.

As yet, there was no proof that she was with child: even if she was pregnant, it would be months yet before the thought sleeping in her womb grew large enough to swell her belly. So, for the moment, her companions could not be certain that she had really got herself with child. But what if she was pregnant? What would happen once there was undeniable proof?

Sitting back from the firelight, Yen Olass watched the fatigued faces of her companions, finding nothing there to comfort her. Later, after the fire had died down, she lay in the darkness, staring at the stars burning within the stone globe she had recovered from the river. She remembered the way the voices had hurt her just before she escaped from the bud.

What if there was a child, and the voices had hurt it? What if she gave birth to something with a liquid head or steel hands? Something dead? Or something . . . otherwise changed. Mad, maybe. Born without ears. Without eyes. Without bones.

Very quietly, Yen Olass began to cry. Resbit was already asleep, snoring very lightly; there was nobody to comfort her.

That night, Yen Olass dreamt of her homelands, dreamt of Monogail. In the moments just before waking, she was certain she had returned to those northern reindeer lands; waking, she knew otherwise.

*   *   *

When Yen Olass woke, everyone else was still asleep. The rain had ceased; mist obscured the stream. The grey morning light revealed trees bulking out of the mist. It was quiet, but for the low-voiced chatter of water talking to stone as the stream ran west toward the river.

Yen Olass slipped outside and went to use the little toilet which had been excavated near the cave the previous evening. It was brimming over. There is nothing in the world more squalid and depressing than an overflowing shitpit; Yen Olass crept into the bushes and dug her own little cat-scraping.

Granted such privacy, she examined herself carefully, looking for the changes she had wished for inside the metal bud. To control their virgins, the Sisterhood mutilated them. By abusing its members, the Sisterhood demonstrated a concern for discipline which conformed its subservience to the Collosnon Empire and the empire's need for order and obedience at all costs.

Yen Olass still remembered how she had fought. Someone had smashed her in the face, making her nose bleed. She remembered the taste of blood in the back of her throat. She remembered the grin of a razorblade sadist, the pain as a blade cut away her clitoris. She remembered the monstrous agony she had endured as flensing steel thinned the flesh of her lower lips. She had screamed and screamed and screamed. They had laughed at her. And the old woman with the needle had sewn up her vagina with strong cords which prevented it from opening far enough to accept a man.

Now, the cords were gone, with not so much as a scar to show where they had once been; the full flesh of her lower lips had been restored, and the most sensitive part of her anatomy had renewed itself. Yen Olass was both pleased and frightened. Pleased, because the mutilation of her body—an obscenity unknown in Monogail, though common in many other human cultures—had always shamed and disgusted her. Frightened, because she knew the power of the empire, and knew that she had set herself up against that power by claiming her body for her own purposes.

Creeping out of the bushes, she allowed herself a smile. She was Yen Olass Ampadara, pleased to be her own person making her own choices. Washing her hands in the stream, scouring them with a little gravel, she found a spot of rust on one of her fingernails. She was alarmed, but did not allow this to destroy her growing sense of triumph. She would treat her fingernails with boot grease, making sure they did not rust through. It was a small price to pay for the rebirth of her body.

*   *   *

That morning, the men went hunting while the women gathered snails and dug for worms. The mighty hunters returned toward noon with two frogs, a newt and a nest of baby birds. These, together with watercress and assorted invertebrate protein, made a meal which, though interesting, was less than entirely satisfying.

After lunch, the men set off again, returning much later with a bear. They had surprised it in a clearing. It had fled for the safety of a tree, which they had cut down. The bear had been killed in the fall.

This creature was not a wark, but a brown bear the same size as Yen Olass. The two boys, Shant and Mation, boasted outrageously about how they had chased the bear, and how funny it had looked falling from the sky. Yen Olass was glad when Draven, irritated by this prattle, cuffed them roughly and told them to shut up. She felt sorry for the bear: but she helped skin it all the same. It had been gutted already.

While the bear was being skinned, the men talked about two strange creatures they had seen, fox-fur animals which seemed to walk on two feet before dropping down on all fours and hastening away into the undergrowth. They wondered aloud if these were any good to eat.

This talk ended when the bear was skinned and a bright fire was blazing. Without waiting for the fire to die down to red coals, everyone hacked off chunks of bear meat, stuck these on pointed sticks and jostled each other as they contended for cooking space.

Draven was ready to eat his meat rare, but Yen Olass cautioned him against it:

'Bears are like pigs. They carry lots of diseases. You have to cook the meat properly.'

'What do you know about bears?' said Draven.

'There are more bears in Tameran than there are on the Greater Teeth,' said Yen Olass.

That was true, as far as it went.

In the end, Draven, grumbling, cooked his meat thoroughly.

Bear was not as appetizing as pork, but they all ate with a will, then cooked more meat to eat cold later. Their hunger was now appeased, and they all felt stronger and more confident.

They were ready to march.

*   *   *

That evening, Yen Olass examined the lightweight coat of rabbit skin which she had bought so long ago in Gendormargensis.

War had not been kind to it. She needed to replace it urgently, but how? Draven had already snaffled the bear skin. Fortunately her league rider's weather jacket, made to stand the punishing routines of military life, was lasting well. So were her boots.

She greased her boots—and then her fingernails.

CHAPTER <u>*Twenty-six*</u>

Lord Alagrace was weary. He knew the truth: he was too old for campaigning. In particular, he was too old to go tramping for league after league through wet, damp forest in pursuit of mutinous officers. He said as much.

'This is going to be the death of me,' said Lord Alagrace. 'Given the choice, I'd rather have died in Gendormargensis—not in some nameless place like this.'

'It isn't a nameless place,' said Yen Olass. 'It's called Nightcaps.'

'Who told you that?'

'Oh, everyone knows it,' said Yen Olass vaguely.

'I asked you a question,' said Lord Alagrace, displeased by her offhand manner. 'Who told you that?'

'A dragon. A little one. His name was Tiz. He was—'

'That's enough,' said Lord Alagrace, with a sigh.

He knew he should really have her taken out and whipped to bring her into line, but he lacked the energy to be sufficiently outraged at her misbehaviour. Besides, he still thought it might be possible to use her as an oracle, and if he expected others to accept Yen Olass as an oracle then it was important to refrain from having her beaten like a common slave.

'Anyway,' said Yen Olass, 'you're not going to die. Not yet, not on a beautiful day like this. What's this? Wine? Here, drink some. Go on. It'll make you feel better. Where did you get it?'

'The same place as we got those furs you're wearing,' said Lord Alagrace. 'It's loot from the pirate camp.'

He accepted the wine Yen Olass poured for him, and watched her exploring the rest of his headquarters tent. It was tiny compared to the tent he had at the siege site at Lorford, but it had still taken four men to carry it through the forest.

'You could have found me better furs than these,' said Yen Olass. 'They smell!'

'Don't worry,' said Lord Alagrace. 'Nobody's going to notice.'

'They might, you know. When we kiss.'

Lord Alagrace took this in silence. Yen Olass was bright, flushed, ebullient and irrepressible. Through all the years in which they had been associated, he had never seen her in a mood like this. In an adolescent girl with a handsome young lover, he would have attributed this mood to sexual excitement; in a mature oracle, it was hard to explain.

'Have you been drinking?' said Lord Alagrace.

Yen Olass made a formal bow and arranged herself at his feet. She looked up at him, her face demure.

'Your oracle awaits instructions,' said Yen Olass, in a cool, formal voice.

Lord Alagrace suspected that this formality contained its own subtle form of mockery. Somehow, while being chased through the wilderness, Yen Olass had gained a new pride and confidence; her growing ego-strength disturbed and unsettled him. In Gendormargensis, she had obeyed him in all things, and her every obeisance had been sincere.

'First,' said Lord Alagrace, 'I have to know the truth. Are you pregnant?'

'How would I get pregnant?'

'Haveros says you were taken by force by a metal flower.'

'Is that how it happens?' said Yen Olass innocently. 'With a flower? I always thought—'

'This is a serious question!'

'The only person who ever said I was pregnant was the Princess Quenerain,' said Yen Olass. 'Are you going to believe a hysterical woman like that? Of course, there's the children's story about Alakin Malakin who got taken by the lily god, but that's—'

'Don't be impertinent,' said Lord Alagrace.

Yen Olass bowed her head.

'I am your oracle. I exist only to serve.'

Lord Alagrace could not see her face, but he was half-convinced that she was smiling. A small sound escaped her: unless he was mistaken, she was just barely suppressing an attack of the giggles. It seemed that she no longer took him seriously. Perhaps she was in such high spirits because, after days of fear and danger, she thought she had reached a place of refuge.

'Do you think you're safe?' said Lord Alagrace.

Yen Olass looked up.

'But of course, my lord. I was frightened when your patrols caught us in the forest—but only because I thought they were Chonjara's men.'

'They are.'

'They are?'

'They are—or might be. I've tried to order them south. They won't go. They're waiting for Chonjara to return. They want us to face each other. Then they'll decide.'

'They'll choose their own leader?'

'It seems so.'

'There's a simple cure for that,' said Yen Olass. 'Find the ringleaders then kill them. Do it by night. Haveros will help you. If it comes to that, I'll cut throats myself.'

'If it was that easy, I'd have done it,' said Lord Alagrace. 'I came from Skua with a hundred hand-picked men. I thought that would give me enough steel to put down any mutiny. Chonjara's made a bad mistake, withdrawing hundreds of men from the siege to go whoring through the forest after a few fugitives—or so I thought.'

'But?'

'I find him popular,' said Lord Alagrace. 'Though he runs from the true battle men think him a great battle commander. Why should that be?'

'The greatest power in Argan is the wizards',' said Yen Olass. 'Already hundreds of men have died fighting against them. Your duty demands that you take Castle Vaunting for the Lord Emperor Khmar, even if the siege costs you half the army. You've never wavered in your duty. Isn't it natural for men to see, in you, their death?'

'But they talk of me as—as a . . .'

'They talk of you as a coward. As a weakling. Of course they do. Men want to think themselves brave. So they pretend that they're heroes, running through the forest, killing a few Melski, crossing swords with the occasional pirate, hunting a handful of fugitives. They pretend the warlord who leads them is the greatest commander since time began. Isn't that natural?'

'But the hundred men I brought from Skua,' said Lord Alagrace. 'They know better. I chose—'

'You chose your best, then found them no different from the others. Why be so surprised? Here, everything's changed. In Tameran, you could have summoned up a squadron of executioners from Gendormargensis. Here . . .'

'They all have to face imperial justice sooner or later.'

'Do they? If the wizards can't be defeated, then best to give up now. Tell the army you'll lead all volunteers down the Salt Road to take up service in one of the warmland kingdoms. Or offer them a journey west, into the Ravlish Lands. Maybe that's what they're waiting for.'

'Are you tempting me?'

'The real question,' said Yen Olass, 'is different. Are you tempting them? What have you got to offer them? A death outside the walls of Castle Vaunting? The enemy commands fire, and madness. Can we stand against weapons like those?'

'Nobody's asking you to stand against anything,' said Lord Alagrace.

'My fate is linked with yours,' said Yen Olass. 'You've got two choices. Promise your men some honey-tongue future. Or else abandon your command—and run.'

'I won't do either,' said Lord Alagrace. 'I'll stay here and meet Chonjara.'

'And die.'

'If that's the way it has to be, then . . .'

'I don't want to die!' said Yen Olass.

'Do you think the world turns on what you want or don't want?' said Lord Alagrace. 'Do you think imperial policy shapes itself according to the whims of an insignificant upstart female slave? Do you think—'

Yen Olass got up and walked toward the door of the tent.

'Yen Olass!' said Lord Alagrace sharply.

She did not stop, and she did not look back. She walked out into the sunlight. Lord Alagrace did not follow, and did not call for guards to bring her back. He had thought of winning some victory over Chonjara by using Yen Olass, in her role as oracle, to manipulate the sentiments of his soldiers. Now he realised that was impossible. Things had gone too far for that.

He would have to face down Chonjara, or die in the attempt. Which meant that he would probably die. Facing his death, he felt no terror: rather, a sensation of relief. Knowing that he would soon be gone, he turned to the last task awaiting him, which was the composition of his grace notes, which is to say, his death song.

According to the traditions of the High Houses of Sharla, this composition should by rights have been carved on his tomb. Since he was going to die in the wilderness, he would be denied a tomb. Never mind. He would write out his grace notes in a fair hand on a piece of wood, and arrange for the words to be burnt with his body on a funeral pyre. Chonjara would not deny him that much.

Over the next few days, while working on his grace notes, Lord Alagrace set aside time to practise with his sword. He did not want to disgrace himself in combat, and so made the effort necessary to perfect his long-standing mastery of technique and timing. He knew Chonjara's daring, skill and reckless strength would overwhelm him: nevertheless, the fight would not be easy for the conqueror. Perhaps Chonjara would carry away a few scars from the battle.

Practising, meditating, dreaming and waiting, Lord Alagrace found the words for his grace notes:

> All this I yield:
> Earth and sky.
> My bones lean down to join my shadow.
> Breathing out to join the greater air,
> I let my heart withdraw its labour,
> And fix my eyes on horizons far receding.

With the words done, Lord Alagrace had a piece of timber prepared, and inscribed the words on the same in letters large enough for his ageing eyesight to read.

Now he was ready. But still Chonjara did not return. Meanwhile, patrols were bringing back increasing evidence of Melski activity in the area. For the Melski, destroying the intruders obviously took precedence over the traditions which should have prevented them from entering the Valley of Forgotten Dreams. When two patrols failed to return, Lord Alagrace sent out no further scouting parties. He began to be aware that his position was somewhat tenuous.

At Nightcaps, there were a mere two hundred men—not very many considering the strength the Melski nation could muster. Chonjara was known to have another two hundred men with him, somewhere upstream, in the north. Another seven hundred or so men were back at Lake Armansis, camping where the pirates had once built their fort. The rest of the army was still maintaining the siege of Castle Vaunting—unless it had been destroyed by wizards in the interim.

Lord Alagrace called the men together and suggested that they withdraw to Lake Armansis, pointing out the danger the Melski posed. The response of the meeting was that reinforcements should be called up from Lake Armansis, and they should all then push north in an effort to find Chonjara, who might possibly have been taken prisoner by the Melski.

Lord Alagrace pointed out that any group taking a message south would have to be strong to survive the Melski danger, which was steadily increasing. By splitting their forces they would be increasing the danger of attack. The meeting finally decided that they would all wait at Nightcaps for another five days, then go south as a body to get reinforcements for a drive up the Valley of Forgotten Dreams.

*   *   *

The pirate Draven was in no hurry to go anywhere. He was comfortable where he was. The woman Jalamex had yielded to him once again, and he trusted that no harm would come to him while he was under the command of Lord Alagrace.

However, the pirate Mellicks did not share such trust, and did not think the five-day wait at Nightcaps would be wise. Confident of his ability to find his way downriver by night—his new eyes gave him amazing night vision—he slipped away by himself one evening. Nobody troubled themselves much over his disappearance.

Mellicks never made it south to Lake Armansis. He evaded one Collosnon party that was heading north, but later blundered into another—and found himself answering to a very formidable interrogator indeed.

CHAPTER
Twenty-seven

Two men were fighting.

Bored by dull days spent camped by the river, other men gathered round to urge them on, to shout, to cheer and lay bets on the outcome. Disturbed by the noise, Lord Alagrace came out of his tent, and saw immediately what was happening.

His first thought was of Yen Olass Ampadara. Guessing that she would escape if given the chance, he had assigned men to keep watch over her by day and by night. She might be no good to him as an oracle, but she might have her value if the army renewed its call for the death of a dralkosh . . .

Looking around, at first Lord Alagrace could not see Yen Olass anywhere. Then he caught sight of her. She was right in the middle of the crowd, shouting and laughing—and making a bet with someone.

Lord Alagrace pushed his way into the crowd and stood over the two bruised and bloody men, who were now wrestling on the ground, each seeking a stranglehold.

'Cut!' bellowed Lord Alagrace.

The two men took no notice.

'You!' said Lord Alagrace, pointing. 'And you! Pull them apart!'

For this task, he had nominated two of the most sober and disciplined of the common soldiers. This was one of the tricks of command he had learnt over the years. Even in an unruly mob, there are usually a few who will obey, and when these accept commands the others will often follow.

The two fighters were dragged apart, panting and bleeding. They were not seriously damaged. The crowd did not disperse: they were interested to see what would happen how.

'Since you've got so much spare energy to burn,' said Lord Alagrace. 'There's an experiment I want to carry out.'

He pointed south. There, the narrow, swift-running surge of the river widened to a shallow flurry of foam as it leapt between boulders.

'Down there,' said Lord Alagrace, 'in the middle of those raids, there's a female stone about so big. Her name is Gwenalyn. Go and get her for me. Now! Come on, come on, move yourselves! You should be back by now!'

The two men raced away, dodging round the occasional tree as they sprinted down the riverbank. They waded out into the rapids, slipped, fell, went over, recovered themselves, got hold of a stone 'about so big', manhandled it toward the shore, dropped it, plunged into the water to recover it, then laboured it back to the campsite.

Panting, shuddering, dripping wet, they dropped the stone down in front of their audience. By now, everyone else was taking their ease, some squatting down, others sitting on boulders or tree stumps.

Lord Alagrace got to his feet, stepped forward and nudged the stone with the toe of his boot.

'This isn't Gwenalyn!' said Lord Alagrace. 'This is Nagala. Don't you know the difference between a girl stone and a boy stone?'

'So what's the difference?' said the more reckless of the two miscreants.

'If you don't know the difference between a boy and a girl by now, it's a bit late for me to be teaching you,' said Lord Alagrace. 'All I can say is, it must make for some interesting nights.'

This quip raised lazy laughter from his audience. Lord Alagrace sent his two fighters back to the rapids to get him the girl stone Gwenalyn. When they came back, lugging the stone along between them, they were clearly exhausted.

'That's Gwenalyn all right,' said Lord Alagrace, stroking the stone, a fond smile on his face. 'Isn't she smooth and silky? And only eleven years old! Well, boys, I had a really interesting experiment in mind, but you both look too shagged out to help me with it. So put these children back in the river where they came from. No, you don't have to go back to the rapids—just put them in there, they'll make their own way home. Not like that! You're grown men, you can lift a child without any help, surely.'

The stones went back into the river, the spectators dispersed, and the two exhausted men went to dry themselves off in front of a fire. Lord Alagrace was left to ponder the deficiencies of his own leadership. Even though his troops refused to withdraw from Nightcaps, they had not thrown up their own leader to replace him; the responsibilities of day-to-day management were still his. However, he had spent his time in his tent, producing variant versions of his death song, and dreaming back to days gone by. Waiting for his death.

But perhaps he was not going to die, at least not this year. Perhaps Chonjara was irretrievably lost in the depths of Penvash. Perhaps he was dead—and if so, it was unlikely anyone else would challenge Lord Alagrace for control of the army.

Lord Alagrace knew he should get a grip on his people now, and restore discipline. They should work hard, building a stockade to defend against the Melski. They should have daily weapons drill—Haveros could organize that. Regulations concerning the use of Ordhar should be enforced: it was not good to allow the men to natter away to each other in their barbarous foreign tongues. Maybe Draven's woman should be taken away from him and given to the men for their amusement—that would raise morale. The pirate could always be disposed of if he was foolish enough to resist. That woman Resbit, she could be shared around too.

Entering the area set aside for latrines, Lord Alagrace saw there was work to be done here, too: the men should be set to work digging some decent pits, and soon, otherwise they would be wading ankle-deep in sewage.

Squatting over a stinking hole, Lord Alagrace endeavoured to excrete some of the weight lumping inside him, but failed. He was profoundly constipated, and had been for three days now. He tried again, but his bowels were still reluctant to move. He exerted himself. He felt a small pain, dull and localized, down in the lower left quadrant of his gut. Guessing he would rupture himself if he forced the issue, he gave up for the time being. He was getting old, yes. Old man with grey pubic hair. Everything slowing down, seizing up, becoming unwilling and recalcitrant. His spine resented the disciplines of gravity; his bones complained of the weather; he grew tired easily. Lord Alagrace was still meditating on this when he heard voices raised:

'They're coming!'

'Who?'

'Chonjara!'

Lord Alagrace stepped out of the latrine area, forcing himself to adopt an easy, confident stride. He saw Yen Olass idling south along the riverbank, with Resbit beside her.

'Yen Olass,' said Lord Alagrace, pitching his voice to carry. 'Here! Heel!'

Yen Olass obeyed, reluctantly; Resbit came with her. Looking at her, Lord Alagrace knew he had not been the only one to think Chonjara might well be dead.

Turning to face the north, he watched for the approach of Chonjara and his men. Before long, they came in sight, escorted by sentries who had been guarding the campsite perimeter. There were six of them. Lord Alagrace went forward to greet them. They were all battered, filthy, stinking and tired. They moved like sleepwalkers: they were in the last stages of exhaustion.

'Where are the others?' said Lord Alagrace.

'There are no others,' said a haggard man, who, with a shock, Lord Alagrace recognised as Chonjara. 'There're all dead. We're the only ones to survive.'

And he sagged forward, and fainted. Now was the moment to seize the initiative: to strike. With Chonjara dead—

But before Lord Alagrace could pull out his sword and do the obvious, men crowded round, and Chonjara was carried away to the safety of a lean-to. One of the remaining five hobbled away after him. His height betrayed the identity of this scarecrow figure: Karahaj Nan Nulador, General Chonjara's bodyguard.

'What happened?' said Lord Alagrace, confronting the last four.

'Later,' said Yen Olass, pulling at his sleeve. 'They're in no state to talk yet. Let's take them to your tent: I'll get them food.'

And Lord Alagrace, recognizing that all his authority was gone or soon to go with the return of Chonjara, allowed himself to be instructed by this slave girl, and did as she said.

*   *   *

For two days Chonjara and his men rested, feeding on fish, rice and barley meal cakes. They related confused stories of a ruined city of starfire stone, a monster that attacked only by night, men lured into tunnels and eaten alive, a pit-trap filled with burning fluid which ate away the flesh from the bones.

On the third day, thirty men from the south struggled into Nightcaps with their own tale of terror. They had set out from Lake Armansis, a hundred strong, but they had been ambushed by the Melski.

To get timber out of rugged country, foresters sometimes use a trip-dam. This is a wooden dam rigged so it will collapse when a few vital supports are pulled away. Water piles up behind it, logs are floated in the water, then, when the dam is tripped, a wave of water carries the logs down some stream bed which usually would lack sufficient water in which to float a good-sized branch. The Melski had attacked the soldiers by unleashing such a wave of wood and water against them.

The men had come from Lake Armansis to discover the reason for the lack of communication. Couriers and patrols had been sent earlier, but had disappeared without trace, so they had decided to come in strength.

At Lake Armansis itself, the Collosnon forces were in disarray. Some two or three hundred soldiers had gone downriver to Lorford, intending to place themselves under the command of whoever now ruled the siege forces. Others had slipped away in small groups, deserting for destinations unknown. Fifty or sixty adventurers had set off to cross the Razorwind Pass and raid whatever settlement or community they might find at Larbster Bay. The remainder were quarrelling and fighting amongst themselves, forming factions on the basis of their native language groups. Melski patrols were known to be in the area, and were blamed for the disappearance of several men who had gone hunting and had never been seen again.

Lord Alagrace was deeply ashamed to hear that his army was disintegrating. He saw that the dispute between himself and Chonjara must be settled quickly, otherwise there would be nothing left for the victor to control. Demoralised troops reaching Lorford from Lake Armansis would undermine the morale of the siege forces surrounding Castle Vaunting; men would think Chonjara and Lord Alagrace both dead; the entire army would mutiny, desert, or go over to the enemy.

Lord Alagrace knew that a duel was now inevitable and desirable. To bring order to this shambles, a man would need prestige: success in single combat would give the victor that. And a death would be valuable because the loser could be blamed for all that had gone wrong. This would comfort the soldiers, for men hate to live in an unexplained universe. Lord Alagrace was ready to fight: and to die.

Discarding all chances of gaining the upper hand by conspiracy, diplomacy or an appeal for all to respect the authority vested in him by the Lord Emperor Khmar, Lord Alagrace presented Chonjara with a formal written challenge, duly witnessed by five warriors. Lord Alagrace could have called out his enemy with a few well-chosen words, but he liked the formal elegance of his written challenge. In conflict, he had always favoured words as his weapons; now that he had chosen to resort to force instead, he saw no need to adopt the manners of a street fighter.

For half a day the camp waited, while Chonjara composed his reply. When it was ready, Karahaj Nan Nulador took the part of a herald, and, in a battleground voice, announced to all the world his master's reply:

'These are the words of Chonjara, son of Tonaganuk, horse-lord of the northern birthtribes, commanding men under the authority of the Lord Emperor Khmar, who gives his favour to the strongest.

'I have received what claims to be a challenge. It is said to be issued by a man named Alagrace, who pretends to be commander of the Collosnon forces in Argan. I know of no such commander; I do not recognise any such challenge.

'As all men know, we have in this camp a senile old caretaker by the name of Alagrace. He arranges rosters of men to bring in firewood and empty the fish traps. He sees that the rice gets cooked and that the rats are kept from the barley sacks. Such is the extent of his authority. If anyone has issued a challenge in the name of this senile old man, the joke is not appreciated.

'Only two men can command a claim to lead the army. One is myself. The other is Volaine Persaga Haveros, lately employed as a spy in the imperial province of Estar. To Volaine Persaga Haveros, I issue my challenge. I will meet him here and now, blade against blade, in a fight which must end with the death of one of us if it does not end with the death of both.'

Haveros accepted.

Hearing the challenge and acceptance, Lord Alagrace knew he was finished as a commander. Even when he knew what he had to do—get a grip on his men, get his people working, share out the women and assert himself as a commander—he had hesitated. And now it was too late.

As Chonjara and Haveros prepared themselves for combat, Lord Alagrace advanced on Chonjara, thinking to force him to a fight. But Karahaj Nan Nulador took him from behind, mastering him first with a stranglehold and then with a wristlock.

Disarmed, and put under guard along with Draven, Yen Olass

Ampadara, Resbit, Jalamex and the Princess Quenerain—Chonjara had thought of everything—Lord Alagrace wept bitter tears of shame and frustration. And wondered if he really was going senile.

CHAPTER
Twenty-eight

The two men met by the river within a semicircle of spectators. Even the men directed to guard Lord Alagrace and the others had come to watch, bringing their prisoners with them.

Chonjara and Haveros, lightly clad, wearing no armour, drew their swords and faced each other. They carried no shields. The two men glowered at each other and began to circle, slowly, moving their feet deliberately. Haveros struck: Chonjara parried.

As the sharp sound of steel clashing against steel died away, Lord Alagrace assessed what he had seen. Haveros had attacked first. The big, ugly man, mutilated by the loss of one ear, had moved in with aggressive confidence. There had been a lot of strength in that blow. And yet . . .

Chonjara struck: Haveros parried.

And now Lord Alagrace knew what he was seeing. Every move Haveros made lacked the final perfection of the swordmaster's grace and ease. His movements were faintly slurred; his reactions lagged slightly. Chonjara and Haveros were well-matched, but Haveros had abused his body with alcohol for too many years, and was now paying the price.

Lord Alagrace knew the odds favoured Chonjara. How many others knew? Even among experts, few were skilled enough to analyse the nuances which led Lord Alagrace to his conclusions. Perhaps even Haveros did not yet know that he was a dead man. A dead man? Combat lies in the province of uncertainty: a slip or a moment's misjudgment might still cost Chonjara his life.

The two warlords clashed again, then broke apart and circled slowly. Each was intent on the other. Regarding each other boldly, their eyes never wavered. Both had dreamed of this fight often enough in the past. Their concentration did not admit even the faintest tremor of fear. Committed to combat, they regretted nothing. Both had dedicated their lives to battle, and this was their apotheosis, the consummation of their dedications.

They clashed again. Steel slashed aside steel. Light shivered and splintered as blades chimed. For a few moments, as perfection matched perfection, they achieved the harmony of a dance of ecstasy. Then Haveros began to falter, and the illusion of beauty collapsed. Striving to murder him, Chonjara hacked and stabbed, and Haveros parried and faltered. Haveros was forced back toward the river. Aware of his peril, he exerted himself manfully. As he was forced to the edge of the riverbank, he mastered all his strength into a headlopping blow. Chonjara parried.

His sword shattered.

Haveros screamed in exultation. Chonjara stabbed with the wreckage of his sword. Haveros knocked away the stub of metal and slashed home to Chonjara's ribs.

Then the riverbank gave way.

Haveros fell backwards with a cry. Chonjara snatched up a stone. Haveros hit the water, went under, surfaced, fighting for balance. The stone took him smack in the middle of the forehead. He went down, his sword discarded to the depths of the river. Grappling air, Haveros made one last attempt to stand upright, but the river snatched him, bearing him away in its salmon-fast shouldering currents.

Chonjara ran along beside the river, panting as he sprinted for the rapids. The white water slammed Haveros against a boulder, then grounded him on a reef of shale. He started to struggle upright. Chonjara floundered into the water, slipping and sliding as he braced his way through the churning shallows. Haveros, weaponless, reached down into the water. Chonjara flung up his hands and warded off a stone.

The two men closed the distance and grappled with each other. They went down and fought in the water, gouging, biting, struggling for a stranglehold. They slipped into deeper water, and went under. As they broke apart, Chonjara grabbed a rock. Surfacing, he smashed Haveros. Who mouthed air and fell backwards. Chonjara hefted his rock and smashed again.

Embracing Haveros, accepting his limp weight, Chonjara

lugged his enemy to the shore, hulking the body over rocks and through the greeding white waters. Chonjara, flushed, gasping, soaking wet, blood streaming from the swordslash which had ripped across his ribs, bellowed for a rope. Haveros, stone-slugged, unconscious, damaged and dying, lay there on the ground, fungus-soft outgrowths of bloodswollen flesh massing on his forehead. He vomited up a thin yellow slurry. His breath fluttered strands of vomit at his mouth. He was scarcely breathing.

'Rope!' screamed Chonjara.

Why was there no rope? And who let that woman—

'Get her out of here!' shouted Chonjara.

Someone dragged away the Princess Quenerain, who was screaming, her fingers gripped home to her face.

Yen Olass Ampadara knelt down beside Haveros. She tried to clear the vomit from his mouth, but his teeth clenched together, locking hard and fast.

'Volaine,' said Yen Olass firmly, using the name his mother would have used. 'Open your mouth. I'm trying to help you.'

His teeth stayed locked together. He vomited again. One of his teeth was missing. Yen Olass sucked the vomit out through the hole, sucked and spat, sucked and spat. There was not much, but what there was might still choke him. Then he would die a real drinking man's death: drowning in his own vomit.

'Volaine,' said Yen Olass again. 'Open your mouth.'

She scarcely tasted the vomit, but wiped away a little which had clung to her lips. She wondered if she should use a stone to smash away his teeth. No: the idea was grotesque. And the violence of a stone jolting into his head would damage his brain, which had taken too much of a pounding already. If he vomited enough to start to choke, surely his teeth would loosen as lack of air sapped his strength. Then she could try and clear his mouth and throat.

'Volaine, can you hear me?'

Somewhere in the background, Chonjara was screaming for rope. Yen Olass pulled back one of the injured man's eyelids. The blank black disc of a pupil stared out at her, numb to the daylight. She let the eyelid sink back into position.

Yen Olass was sweating feverishly, trembling as her heart sprinted, yet her voice was cool and commanding. Her ruling intelligence maintained its poise and managed even a degree of detachment.

'Volaine, stay with us,' said Yen Olass, knowing that hearing is often the last sense to go. 'We're trying to help you.'

Kneeling there in the mud, she found the time to note that goosebumps were standing out on his body. She was surprised that flesh so badly damaged could manifest such a quotidian symptom. She was vaguely aware of others clustering round; vaguely, she wondered why nobody tried to help her. Haveros moved. His arm curled up toward the shoulder, hand warping outward in a gesture strong but spastic. A bad sign.

'Volaine—'

Yen Olass was pushed to one side. Looking up from the mud, she saw Chonjara glowering above her. Someone dragged her away to safety: Resbit. Working rapidly, Chonjara knotted a rope round the neck of the fallen man. He had the end thrown over an overhanging branch. Four men hauled on the rope, dragging Haveros toward the sky.

'Kick, you bastard!' shouted Chonjara. 'Kick!'

But Haveros hung there limply.

He was dead.

Chonjara, realizing he had been cheated of the chance of imposing one last torture on his enemy, screamed with rage. He smashed his fists into the inert flesh, spitting, shouting, swearing. Snatching a knife from the belt of the nearest man, he hacked into the body and ripped the belly open. As the wet, slithering mass of glistening intestines collapsed outward into the daylight, Chonjara laughed. His mirth came in spasms.

Shocked, Yen Olass looked away.

Tried not to hear.

Haveros was dead and disembowelled. But Chonjara was not finished yet. Slicing away ropes of hanging gut, he cut into his enemy's flesh. Tore away the last clothing. Exposed his enemy's sex, and bunched the balls and the slack cock in his hand, intending to—

'No,' said Lord Alagrace, pulling him away.

'What are you doing here?' yelled Chonjara.

He pushed Lord Alagrace aside, and turned back to—

'No,' said Lord Alagrace, restraining him.

Chonjara turned on him, grabbed him by the throat.

'You senile old fuck, I'll—'

He gave a shrill whinny of pain as Lord Alagrace drove his knee home. As Chonjara went down, bent over his agony, concentrating on mastering his pain, he saw the faces of the soldiers. Silent. Restrained. Some . . . appalled?

'What did you think we were doing?' said Chonjara, forcing the words out, each syllable hissing with pain. 'Dancing?'

Nobody replied.

'Cut him down,' said Lord Alagrace. 'You—clutch up those men and go and cut some timber. We've got a funeral to make ready.'

The men he gave his orders to hesitated. Some were not sure whether they wanted Chonjara as their commander, thinking he might be mad. But none had much confidence in Alagrace.

'They're not sure whether to obey you, old woman Alagrace,' said Chonjara, managing something like a grin. 'I don't think they will. Seize him!'

There was a fight then, as some men made to grab Lord Alagrace, and others resisted them. Yen Olass nudged Resbit, who nodded, and they began to slink away to the south. After a moment, Draven followed them, with Jalamex in tow. Then, as the brawl escalated, the Princess Quenerain followed, tagging along behind.

Karahaj Nan Nulador, standing apart from the fight, saw them go, but said nothing. It was Shant and Mation, the boys from Estar, who raised the alarm, shouting one of the few words of Ordhar they had managed to pick up:

'Look! Look!'

The soldier Saquarius was the first to turn and see what was happening. The Princess Quenerain was just disappearing into the undergrowth to the south.

'Our women!' roared Saquarius. 'Our women are escaping!'

The brawl broke apart, and the men, in a mob, went roaring down the riverbank, yahooing in high excitement. Chonjara, Alagrace, Karahaj Nan Nulador and a few bruised and bleeding soldiers stayed behind.

'Pax,' said Lord Alagrace, offering.

'You're finished,' said Chonjara. 'And you know it. I've no need for a truce.'

Lord Alagrace bowed his head.

'I will conform to your commands,' he said, surrendering.

CHAPTER
Twenty-nine

The escapers were caught, dragged back to camp, roughed up a little, and tied up to improvised torture posts. A big bonfire was lit. Chonjara had an extra ration broken out and shared around. Some of the soldiers produced a little wine or hard liquor which had been stored away in the bottom of their packs. A festive atmosphere prevailed.

Yen Olass and Resbit had been tied up near each other. They did not yet know whether they were going to be raped or torn to pieces or beaten to death or what.

'Whatever they do,' said Yen Olass, 'Scream loudly.'

'Yes?' said Resbit.

'Men get angry if they think they can't hurt you.'

'Don't worry, Yen Olass, I'll scream.'

Yen Olass watched some men gambling. For fun? For wine? For food? Or for the privilege of being the first to do something to her body? She heard Resbit sniff. Hot tears started out from her own eyes.

Someone was climbing out of the river.

Yen Olass blinked tears out of her eyes and tried to focus. It was only Karahaj Nan Nulador. He was carrying a sword. Chonjara had sent his bodyguard into the river to find the sword Haveros had dropped, and now Nan Nulador had succeeded. From the way he walked, Yen Olass could tell he was exhausted. The water was cold, and he had been in it a long time.

She watched the men, wondering what they would do to her first. She resolved to submit, to obey, and to give them the satisfaction of hearing her scream. Anything else would only make it harder on all of them—including Resbit.

'Hello, beautiful woman,' said a voice behind her.

A man's voice.

A man's hand touched her cheek.

'Tash on-steh!' said Yen Olass, spitting out the obscenity then trying to bite the hand.

So much for her good resolutions.

The man laughed, then sliced away the strips of fibrous bark which a frugal soldier had used instead of rope to tie her to the torture post. Free, she found no strength in her hands to fight with, no strength in her feet to run with. No strength, at first, to stand with. But the man caught her and held her, then said:

'Cut my daughter free.'

A warrior moved to obey. Yen Olass saw that both his cheeks had been cut away, and this helped her remember him: she had seen him last in Favanosin.

The men of the camp now looked up from their gambling, their eating, their drinking, their jokes, their laughing, and studied the small party of strangers which had slipped out of the forest, reaching the prisoners before anyone was aware of their presence.

Silence settled over the gathering. Then one man advanced to greet the newcomers. Yen Olass, her strength recovering now that bonds no longer restricted her circulation, released herself from the arms of the Lord Emperor Khmar and went to help Resbit. Khmar stood alone, watching the man who approached —a strange figure, his hair shaved off, his body stripped to the waist and smeared with charcoal.

The man halted, and made reverence.

'Greetings, my lord.'

'And to you, greetings, sal Pentalon Sorvolosa dan Alagrace nal Swedek quen Larsh,' said Khmar, freighting every word with sarcasm. 'How do you account for your appearance? Are the High Houses of Sharla once more setting a new trend in fashion for the empire?'

'My lord,' said Lord Alagrace, 'we've been having some . . . some . . .'

He faltered.

'Some fun, perhaps?' said Khmar, muscling forward. 'And my daughter was part of this fun? Alagrace, the Red Emperor does not take pleasure in seeing the flesh of his flesh tied to a torture post.'

'Times . . . times have been difficult.'

'So I understand. Chonjara! Get yourself out here! Now!'

Reluctantly, Chonjara came forward to greet his emperor.

'I left Lake Armansis with fifty men,' said Khmar. 'As you see,

I'm here with ten. The green animals are formidable. Three of my survivors are wounded. Have them seen to. Put out perimeter guards. Get your men to work. Rocks and tree trunks. A wall round this place by nightfall. And you—you'll meet my justice later.'

'My lord,' said Chonjara.

And Chonjara and Lord Alagrace withdrew, and began to shout orders, to make sure that the emperor's bidding was done.

'You should have them roasted alive,' said the Princess Quenerain, rubbing her wrists, where angry red marks showed where bindings had bitten into her flesh.

'And you?' said Khmar, looking at her, his eyes, glittering beneath his heavyweight brows.

'I . . .'

'You don't know what to say,' said Khmar. 'And neither do I.'

He spat.

'Yen Olass, as Khmar's Sisterhood in the South, tell me: how should I shape my anger?'

'Their nightmares will serve your silence,' said Yen Olass.

Khmar grunted.

'Has your slave been obedient?'

For a moment, Yen Olass did not understand. Then she remembered. On the day they first met, Khmar had given her the pirate Draven as her slave.

'He has served a woman too long,' said Yen Olass.

'Then he can come west with us.'

'West?'

'We have ships at a place called Larbster. I've been with my son in the Ravlish Lands. His idea. We've been talking ports. The people there will give us ports. It will help us win Argan. Alagrace should have suggested it.'

Resbit, speaking in Galish, asked Yen Olass who the strange man was. Yen Olass tried to shush her, but it was no good.

'Who is the young one?' said Khmar.

'A woman of Estar,' said Yen Olass.

'Tell her who I am.'

Yen Olass told Resbit that the squat, ugly, bowlegged man with the filed teeth was the Lord Emperor Khmar, absolute ruler of Tameran.

'Does he want me?' said Resbit timidly.

'What does she say?' said Khmar.'

'She wants to know if . . .'

'If I want her? Yen Olass, I want to rest.'

Yen Olass was alarmed to hear Khmar speak like this. He had come out of the forest to save her, like the prince in a hero-song, but ever since then his behaviour had left a lot to desire. He should have lashed Lord Alagrace with his scathing tongue until his victim was grovelling belly-down in the dust, begging for mercy. He should have eaten Chonjara alive. He should have lopped off heads and flayed men alive. His fury should be so intense that he should still be breathing fire. Instead . . .

She saw he was tired. Profoundly tired. He could imitate the strength and the anger of the man he had once been, but the truth was that his life was failing. He was too sick to be marching through the wilderness, battling with the Melski and disciplining unruly commanders.

Yen Olass organised Khmar into the tent Lord Alagrace had brought up from Lake Armansis. She had boughs cut to make a bed, and had blankets confiscated so the emperor could sleep warm. Soon Khmar was slumbering, with his daughter Quener-ain keeping watch at his side, and his bodyguards taking turns to rest and stand guard, talking to each other quietly in Eparget.

Yen Olass talked to the man who had suffered the loss of his cheeks. He told her about their journey to the Ravlish Lands, then about how they had stopped at Larbster Bay, and what they had found there, prompting Khmar to march inland. He told her about their arrival at Lake Armansis, and the fearful discipline Khmar had meted out to the soldiers he found there in arms against each other. She heard of the march north, and how they had captured the pirate Mellicks, learning much by interrogating him.

'What happened to him?' said Yen Olass.

'Khmar sent him south.'

'He was lucky to be left alive.'

'He had offered Khmar life. He said there was a machine here in the north which grants wishes.'

For 'machine' he used the formula 'steel-which-lives', speaking of this ancient evil with distaste tinged with fear.

'Khmar believed him?' said Yen Olass.

'He had yellow eyes. He said he got them by wishing. Khmar chose to believe him.'

'What he said is both true and false,' said Yen Olass. 'There is a machine. It can grant wishes. But lately, it's taken to killing. I don't suppose he told Khmar that.'

'Oh, but he did.'

'And Khmar?'

'He chooses to seek out the machine regardless. Our emperor . . .'

'He's dying,' said Yen Olass, speaking the truth even though it might be treason to do so.

'Well,' said the man without cheeks, 'let's just say, even Khmar is not immortal.'

'But he's not dead yet,' said a voice.

And, turning, they saw Khmar watching them from his bed of blankets and branches. Yen Olass wondered how long he had been listening for. The Princess Quenerain whispered something to her father.

'No,' said Khmar. 'Let her stay. Now get me Alagrace and Chonjara.'

*   *   *

That evening, there was a funeral for Volaine Persaga Haveros. As the flames caught hold of the funeral pyre, Lord Alagrace and General Chonjara each cut off one of their ears and threw these offerings onto the blaze. Since Haveros had been killed in a fair fight, Khmar saw no reason to punish anyone for his death; instead, he was disciplining Alagrace and Chonjara for the way they had failed him as army commanders.

Both Khmar's victims were amazed to find that the Lord Emperor was going to let them escape with the loss of an ear apiece. They had expected, at the least, to have their feet burnt off and then to be buried alive.

That night, Khmar dismissed everyone from his tent. Everyone but Yen Olass Ampadara. In the morning, Resbit asked Yen Olass what had happened.

'We shared an apple,' said Yen Olass. 'And he gave me one all for myself. But I saved it for you.'

And she gave Resbit the extra apple.

'Will you be empress?' said Resbit.

'That,' said Yen Olass, 'remains to be seen.'

She worried about what would happen when Khmar reached the wishing machine in the north. Surely it would kill him. Or keep him. She was glad when he decided to stay and rest for another day.

They shared another apple that night, but she knew his strength was failing. He said he lacked the appetite for another march: should he have himself carried? She told him to rest. To wrestle with the wishing machine, one had to be strong, aggressive and fighting fit. If he was not ready to fight, then . . .

'Then here is where I dismount,' said Khmar. 'I never thought to live forever. I have had a good life.'

They talked together, their voices murmuring late into the night. He told her of his first wife, who died in childbirth, and of his second wife, who eloped with the fair-haired stranger from across the seas, and of his third wife, who met the fate which must not be told to strangers.

The next night, they shared one last apple.

'You will bear a son for me,' said Khmar. 'He will be emperor. A real man and a real emperor. Not like Celadric.'

'You have other sons already,' said Yen Olass.

'Chonjara will stand between you and them until my son is old enough to stand at the head of his own army,' said Khmar. 'Tomorrow, I will instruct him.'

But his voice was grey in the dark. There was no fire left, only ashes. When he slept, Yen Olass called his bodyguards into the tent, and they kept the final watch together, so that there would be witnesses to the death.

Khmar died that night, and Yen Olass said a parting for him. The bodyguards gave her permission to stay or go, as she chose. She chose to leave. The most powerful man left in the camp was Chonjara, her enemy, the one whom she had defeated in combat in front of the army at Lorford, and who had almost succeeded in having her stoned to death as a dralkosh. If Khmar had lived long enough to instruct Chonjara to protect her, he might have obeyed. But as things were, it was best for her to flee.

Under cover of darkness, she roused Resbit. Draven, Lord Alagrace and Jalamex were sleeping in the same lean-to, so they woke as well. Yen Olass explained. Shortly, they were on their way upstream, with sufficient stolen packs, food, clothing, weapons and blankets to guarantee them a good chance of survival in the wilderness.

Yen Olass felt no guilt whatsoever at leaving the Princess Quenerain behind. When Yen Olass had stopped playing at being Yarglat of the Yarglat, and had met Lord Alagrace on the road to Favanosin, the Princess Quenerain had been all for having her put to death immediately—and Yen Olass found it very hard to forgive people who had tried to have her killed.

CHAPTER
Thirty

They chose the river rather than the forest because navigating through a forest at night is a difficult undertaking; with the need for speed, and the promise of pursuit, it becomes nightmarish. They could not go through the forest without leaving footprints and breaking branches; blundering round in the dark they would inevitably be noisy; they might run into a hostile Melski patrol, or walk round in circles, and they would certainly leave a clear trail for the pursuit to follow.

By taking the river they at least had a chance.

They could not go swiftly under cover of darkness, for the footing was uncertain. All of them were periodically dunked in the water when they slipped off rocks, bruising themselves in the process. They did not speak to each other; the only sound was the occasional splash and the murmur of water talking to water.

After hours of slow and painful progress, greyfaced dawn allowed them to see their surroundings and assess how far they had come. Lord Alagrace, who had not marched along this route before, was under the impression they had done very well, but the others knew better.

'We'll have to move faster,' said Draven.

Lord Alagrace yawned, tasting the cool clean early-morning air.

'Eat first,' said Lord Alagrace.

They were all ready to eat, though what they really wanted to do was sleep.

A brief rest, a bite to eat, and they were off again. But Jalamex and Resbit could not push themselves along at speed. They were afraid of the pursuit which they knew would have started by now, but they were also bone-weary after their night's exertions. Rests were needed frequently, and the rests grew longer. Even so, both Jalamex and Resbit stumbled and fell as the day dragged on.

Lord Alagrace himself was feeling the distance. His left hip ached; the blood sang in his ears. Pausing while Resbit negotiated a difficult section of rock, he closed his eyes. His head nodded down, and he was instantly asleep. He swayed on his feet, woke, blinked, and shook his head. He was too old for this, and he knew it.

Late in the afternoon, they heard a shout behind them. Looking back, they saw a soldier by the riverbank, whooping with triumph. He must be the lead scout for the pursuit: the main body must be close behind him. Mobilized by fear, the five fugitives pressed ahead with speed. Ahead they saw shallows where the water rippled across stones and banks of shingle. Beyond that were two shoulders of rock, each ten times the height of a man, between which water cascaded through a narrow gorge.

When they had first come up the river, they had got here by tramping for one day and a bit of the following morning. This time, exhausting themselves by contending with the river by night, they had not done as well: it had taken them half a night and the better part of a day to get this far.

'We're finished,' said Lord Alagrace, surveying the obstacle ahead.

'We can get through,' said Yen Olass, 'then lose them. Maybe. Come on.'

'I'm not going to give up now,' said Draven. 'Come on, Jalamex.'

Draven led the way, and the others followed. Just before he entered the gorge, Lord Alagrace paused and looked back. He wiped sweat from his forehead then scanned the river. Already twenty men were in sight. And they were closing the distance.

Lord Alagrace turned and followed the others, but, when they had gone a little further, he halted. Draven looked back.

'Go on,' said Lord Alagrace, raising his voice above the buffeting water.

'Giving up?' yelled Draven, with a hint of a jeer in his shout.

Lord Alagrace drew his sword.

'I'll hold them,' he shouted.

'Your life,' called Draven.

'I know.'

'Luck, then,' said Draven.

And with the briefest of bows he continued his retreat, hustling the women along with him.

It was cold in the gorge. A fine, cold spray filled the air. Lord Alagrace coughed. His flesh was aching where he had sliced away his left ear as an offering for the funeral pyre. Looking up, he saw the walls on either side rising almost sheer to the sky. Here the gorge was kinked: any man attacking him would have to come round a sharp corner, seeking footing on smooth boulders drowned in the river-rush. Lord Alagrace had dry footing on larger rocks clear of the current, and room enough to swing his sword.

Lord Alagrace waited, leaning back against one wall of the gorge, for he was weary. He watched intently. His hearing would give him no advance warning: the rumble-roar of the river, jolting through this white-water chute, tumbled echoes from the walls. Beneath the boulders, the water was deeper than a man was tall.

The first man edged round the corner. Lord Alagrace styled his sword in the traditional position known as Waiting Hawk. Seeing him, the soldier started, slipped, and fell. The avalanche of water rolled his body under, forced it into a hollow where the river undercut the cliff, and held it there for drowning.

Lord Alagrace waited, trembling.

Two men peered round the corner. They conferred together. Then the boldest started forward, closing the distance. Lord Alagrace made the feint, slash and legsweep known as Shadow Avoiding Rain. His opponent moved to meet the feint, narrowly parried the slash, then went down as the legsweep hooked his balance out from underneath him. Embroiled in the water, he was swept away.

They came on, then, the heroes, one after another. Hacked, stabbed and gashed, they fell away, and the river took their bodies. Lord Alagrace, panting harshly, gasping, sweating, bleeding, took his death-count to nine, and snarled with satisfaction.

He waited for his tenth victim.

Suddenly, a wasp stung his shoulder, burned deep, seared home, driving him backwards. If it had not been for the cliff at his back, he would have fallen. He reached up, clutched the shaft of the arrow which had driven into his shoulder, and broke it off short, so it would not impede his movement.

Looking up, he saw the archer high up on the opposite side of the gorge, perched precariously on minimal footing. It must have taken some delicate climbing to get up there: and supreme skill to shoot from that position. As Lord Alagrace watched, the archer nocked another arrow and began to draw back the bowstring. There was no escape.

Lord Alagrace raised his sword in salute.

The arrow slammed home.

Lord Alagrace fell as if hit by lightning, his senses numbed by a shock which outmastered pain. Swamped by the river, he tried to rise, but could not find his hands. He found himself wedged between two rocks. Sheets of glass rushed over him: the glass was water. With rising terror, he gasped for light, but swallowed water. Pain monstered within his skull.

Then suddenly—easing away without warning—fear and pain were gone. And, for just a moment, Lord Alagrace experienced an access of grace, sufficient to allow him to recall just this:

'. . . and fix my eyes on horizons far receding.'

Then darkness filled his eyes, and he died.

*   *   *

Beyond the gorge, the river widened, and a stream flowing in from the east joined its waters. Further upstream, it narrowed again. A little more tramping, and they came to the first mushroom phallus of star-burning stone. Here they halted: they could not go much further.

Draven took a length of rope out of his pack, and began to make knots.

'What's that for?' said Jalamax.

'A trap,' said Draven.

He did not elaborate. Yen Olass was not interested: she doubted that anything could save them now. Even if they split up and ran in different directions, they were too tired to go far. And Chonjara had brought enough men upriver to slit his people into four different hunting parties. Besides, Yen Olass doubted that Resbit could survive on her own. And Jalamex would not go much further unless forced by Draven.

Yen Olass let her head sink down on her knees. She was far too weary to indulge in luxuries like despair: instead, she promptly went to sleep. She was jerked awake as her arms were wrenched backwards. She tried to resist, but it was impossible. She tried to turn and bite. Draven slapped her.

'Any more of that and I'll kick your head in.'

Yen Olass hissed.

'Hiss away,' said Draven. 'It won't do you any good. Resbit, come here.'

'Run!' shouted Yen Olass.

Resbit hesitated. Draven picked up a stone.

'Come here,' said Draven, 'or I'll batter you.'

Resbit surrendered herself. Draven tied her up, so that Resbit and Yen Olass were knotted together, back to back.

'A present for Chonjara,' said Draven. 'I hope it makes him happy.'

Then he set off upstream, with Jalamex at his side.

'I saved your life!' shouted Yen Olass.

Draven turned.

'Did you hear me? I saved your life!'

'Well now's your chance to save it a second time,' shouted Draven.

And laughed, and went on his way.

'You worthless bastard!' screamed Yen Olass.

Then she swore at him, using the very worst words she knew. Unfortunately, these were all in Eparget, and Draven was unlikely to understand them. Besides, he was soon out of earshot.

Hissing and swearing, Yen Olass tested her bonds. She tried to work her fingers free, to find some slack in the rope, to get into a position where she could scrape the rope against a stone. But it was hopeless. Draven, a pirate for most of his life, was skilled at binding people so they would be helpless while they waited to be raped, killed, tortured or traded. As Yen Olass struggled, she only succeeded in tightening the rope.

Finally she gave up.

Resbit was crying.

Yen Olass tried to comfort her, but had little success. They were both tired, cold and hungry. And soon Yen Olass was crying herself. Eventually, night came, and she slept, dreaming restlessly, jerked awake from time to time when her head lolled sideways.

Toward morning, she woke from dreams of talking water to find herself cold. The cold was accompanied by cramps in her arms and legs. And, what was more . . . surrendering to the inevitable, she relaxed her control over her bladder, flooding her things with hot urine which would soon become cold and uncomfortable. A faint stink of urine eased itself into the night air then faded. Resbit moaned faintly in her sleep.

'Ule,' said an owl.

'Shut up, owl,' said Yen Olass.

Out in the night, a stick broke.

Yen Olass stopped breathing.

Was something out there? No, surely not. The stick must have broken on its own. Sleepwalking, no doubt. Yen Olass suppressed a hysterical giggle. She found that effort of discipline difficult. She was cold, she was still tired, her arms in particular were hurting her as the muscles cramped, she was humiliated by her predicament and entirely at the mercy of anything that wanted to come along and eat her. She thought of warks. And of those strange fox-fur creatures which had been seen in the forest. And of wolves. Were there any wolves in Penvash?

Maybe she was going to find out.

The hard way.

Yen Olass listened. No more breaking sticks. But the rustling river would conceal the sound of any soft cut-throat approach. Listening to the river, Yen Olass realized she was thirsty.

Something touched the back of her head.

Yen Olass started.

'Yoh!' said Resbit, waking from sleep.

It was the back of her head which had touched Yen Olass.

'Hush,' said Yen Olass.

'Yen Olass, is that you?'

'No,' said Yen Olass, hissing. 'No, you groggy sluggin of smats, its Lork the Starhunter with his pack of fifty gropters. Now be quiet.'

'What's smats? An . . . oh. My arms. Yen Olass, can't you . . . no, I suppose you can't. Oh. I wish I could . . . Yen Olass, what was that? What is it? There's something out there! Yen Olass, what is it?'

'Who knows? But with the racket you're making, you're asking for a personal introduction. Now shut up!'

Hearing the vicious hiss of anger as Yen Olass spoke, Resbit was quiet. For a while, no untoward sounds intruded. Then, out in the night . . . the clear, unmistakable sound of teeth graunching into bones.

Resbit panicked.

'Yen Olass, Yen Olass—

'Resbit, shut up! There's a great galumphing mother of an arse-eating carnivore out there. You're just asking—'

'I'm sorry.'

'Don't by sorry, be silent!'

Resbit was.

So were the teeth.

They had finished eating.

But they were still hungry.

Out in the night, the monster began to move. Smashing through twigs and leaves with an ominous deliberation, it advanced toward them. It sounded huge. They could hear a kind of groping snuffling snorting, suggesting some vast half-blind squashed-nose face. Mouthing toward them.

Yen Olass hissed softly. The monster was coming straight toward her. She drew her knees up to her chest, protecting her belly and her breasts.

The monster was almost upon them.

'Gaaa!' shouted Yen Olass.

Kicking out with all the force she could muster.

Hitting nothing.

She drew back her feet for another try—then thought better of it, and let her legs slump down. Spikes stabbed into her skin. She screamed. Her gut-wrenching cry of terror razored through the night. Resbit screamed in sympathy.

Then—

Silence.

Then . . .

'Shit,' said Yen Olass in disgust.

'What?'

'It's a hedgehog,' said Yen Olass, her voice rising as her anger mounted. 'A hedgehog. A shit-spawned arse-faced pig-buggered spit-licking dog of a snot-sticking hedgehog. I'll kill the bastard!'

'I don't think you've got much chance of catching it.'

'I've got him already. I've got the spavined little pervert between my legs. I'll kill him! I'll bite his balls off!'

Resbit laughed.

'What's so funny?' said Yen Olass. 'What's so arse-ripping funny, huh? Share the secret.'

'Bite his balls off. Oh, Yen Olass?'

And Resbit went off in a fit of giggles.

'I will,' said Yen Olass, not relenting in the slightest.

'You can't hold him there all night.'

'All right, it's . . . it's soft enough. I can dig in with my heels, yes, like . . . yes. I can dig a hole and bury him alive. The little bastard won't climb out with me sleeping on top of him.'

'Yen Olass, you wouldn't!'

'I've started digging.'

'It'll run away.'

'He's not going anywhere. He's scared shitless. The ratshit little quirk is huddled into a ball, that's what.'

'Yen Olass . . . it might be a girl.'

'What? What's that?'

'It might be a girl.'

'No, it's a man.'

'How can you tell?'

'Of course it's a man. Raping around in the night without any clothes on. Crawling straight for my—'

'Oh, come on, Yen Olass. It's probably a mother hedgehog. A mother hedgehog with little baby hedgehogs back at her house, all little ones with white spines, really cute and soft, waiting for her to come back with lots of yums.'

'Hedgehogs don't have houses.'

'They do. They build houses so they can be all warm and cosy when they have their babies.'

'Hedgehogs don't have babies. They lay eggs.'

'They do too, and the men eat them half the time, so this one should get put down.'

'It's a she,' said Resbit, positively.

'How do you know?'

'I know.'

'All right then,' said Yen Olass, 'we'll wait till it's daylight. Then we'll see.'

Silence.

Then a giggle.

'What is it now?'

'How do you sex a hedgehog?' said Resbit.

'With something sharp, I suspect,' said Yen Olass grimly.

Silence. Then:

'It's probably got fleas,' said Resbit.

'What?'

'You know. Fleas. They probably think you're very nice and warm. You are nice and warm, Yen Olass. If I was a flea, I'd . . . I'd find a warm place.'

Out in the night, there was a piercing shriek.

'What was that?' said Resbit, in alarm.

'An owl,' said Yen Olass wearily.

'Oh . . . I wonder what it was doing . . .'

'Hunting,' said Yen Olass.

'Yes. Fleas, probably. Big ones with twenty legs and sharp biting things. Have they started to migrate yet?'

'Shut up.'

'I think there's one right now, crawling up your . . .'

Yen Olass thunked Resbit a couple of times with the back of her head. Resbit giggled, then was quiet. They sat there back to back. Yen Olass . . . began to itch. Surely it was imagination.

'Shit,' said Yen Olass, softly.

She spread her legs.

For a while, nothing happened. Then there was a snort, a tentative scrabble of feet. Then suddenly the hedgehog was blundering away through the night, making a staggering amount of noise in the darkness, which amplifies every fearsome sound stalking beneath the stars.

Resbit started to giggle again. Surrendering her anger, Yen Olass joined her. Soon, they sobered up. They eased themselves, this way and that, trying to soothe out the tensions in the muscles of their arms. Staggering a little, they braced against each other and forced themselves into a standing position. They took a few clumsy double-backed steps, kicked their feet, moved their hips, stretched their spines, and found sufficient freedom to work their arms a little.

Then they sat down again.

And now, warmed a little by their exercise, and weakened by the fatigue that follows episodes of absolute terror, they found themselves drifting off to sleep again. Yen Olass, who had thought herself condemned to wakefulness for the rest of the night, was so surprised at this that she almost became wide awake again. However, conjuring up a soothing image . . . a bed with a cat sleeping on it . . . she eased herself into the territory of dreams.

CHAPTER
Thirty-one

Daylight.

Bright and harsh.

The sun was well up.

What had awakened them?

The answer, in a word: Chonjara.

He stood by the riverbank, surveying them in silence. Then he blinked, and looked around, scanning the trees. With curt, emphatic gestures, he pointed men into the trees. Swiftly, they swept forward, weapons at the ready, attacking the forest in battle formation. But there was no ambush, no lurking party of pirates or Melski. The men regrouped. All this in silence, without a word having been spoken: Chonjara was an efficient commander.

With the sweep completed, Chonjara pointed a man at the two captives. The man laid a knife against Resbit's throat.

'No, stupid,' said Chonjara. 'Cut them loose.'

With the rope cut away, the two women started to ease the crinks out of their bodies.

'Been enjoying yourselves?' said Chonjara.

'We had a busy night,' said Yen Olass. 'Seducing hedgehogs.'

'But Draven.'

'Gone north. You'll catch him.'

'I would if I wanted him.'

'Of course you want him, he's—'

'He's not important,' said Chonjara.

Lord Alagrace was dead. And now, Chonjara held Yen Olass prisoner: he had a dralkosh he could produce for the satisfaction of the army once he got back to Lorford.

'What took you so long?' said Yen Olass. 'We've been waiting here all night.'

Chonjara did not answer, but turned away. In fact, he had spent all the night in a defensive position just south of the narrow gorge. He knew there were Melski in this area, so he had declined to push on in failing light. That decision might have allowed Draven to escape with Jalamex, but Chonjara did not regret it. He gave orders for his men to begin the march south. They would make for Lake Armansis with all possible speed.

'Hey,' said Yen Olass, 'what about breakfast?'

'We've eaten already,' said Chonjara.

'In the name of the Lord Emperor Khmar,' said Yen Olass, 'I charge you to see to my rations. I carry within me the child of the Red Emperor, the heir to the throne of Tameran.'

Chonjara snorted, and set off downstream. Resbit and Yen Olass followed, on empty stomachs.

As his people began the march downriver, Chonjara reviewed the events of the last few days. He had lost an ear, but he was not unhappy. He had avenged his father's death by killing Haveros. Lord Alagrace was dead, leaving him with absolute control of the army. The Lord Emperor Khmar was dead; the future offered power and glory to those prepared to seize it.

And Chonjara was ready to seize whatever was going.

When they reached the gorge, Chonjara called a halt, to give his men a breather. He sent scouts ahead to climb to the heights of the gorge, to make sure no Melski were waiting there in ambush. He was at least half-hoping to clash with the Melski. Cutting their way through some of that green muck would sharpen up his men and test their mettle.

Resting, Chonjara looked across the river. On the far side, on his left, a stream flowing from out of the east spilled its water into the river. It was a small stream; across the width of the river he could scarcely hear the low murmur of diplomacy as the water negotiated its way over the last few rocks. But something about it had attracted his attention. What?

Listening intently, he heard . . . a rumbling. Like . . . almost like distant thunder. But thunder fades and dies away. This, on the other hand . . .

Chonjara stared at the stream with widening eyes. His perceptions heightened to the intensity of terror. He saw the patterns of leaves and stones, water and light. He was trembling. A small flushet of water giggled down the stream.

And Chonjara found his voice, and screamed:

'Get out of the river!'

His men, hearing the approaching thunder, realized what it meant—and fled. They clawed for the safety of the banks.

Chonjara bounded into the trees. Someone was already ahead of him, but slipped and fell. Yen Olass. Chonjara hauled her to her feet and whacked her on the buttocks:

'Run!'

Yen Olass panted upwards, scrambling up the bank with Resbit in front of her. Chonjara outflanked them both and fought for height, hauling himself up handhold by handhold. A young sapling bent and broke beneath his weight. In a frenzy, he scrabbled for a little more height.

The onslaught of thunder was almost upon them.

Chonjara turned, bracing himself against a tree. Yen Olass and Resbit were on the slope below him, climbing. He looked through the undergrowth and glimpsed a wall of water and rearing logs plunging forward. Then the vision disintegrated as the avalanche slammed into the river and spray filled the air.

The waters boiled up, a slurry of floodwater, timber and churning sunlight. Chonjara saw Yen Olass swallowed by the rising flood. Resbit grabbed her by the hair—then the water took her. Whirlpool waters flooded upward. Chonjara gasped air, then a shock of cold water swamped him. He fought toward the rising surface.

A tree grabbed him.

Trapped underwater, Chonjara flailed and kicked till he broke free. He struck out for the surface. He jolted out into the sunlight and gasped for air. He heard shouts and screams. Melski were attacking, crashing down the steep banks. Chonjara spat water, and swore.

He was floating in a swirling pool of dirty water. The surface was swarming with sticks, leaves and the bobbing heads of dozens of survivors. Here and there were drifting logs. Looking downstream, Chonjara saw other logs locked in a helpless jam in the entrance to the gorge. The water level was beginning to sink swiftly.

'Downstream!' shouted Chonjara. 'Downstream!'

He saw some Melski leaping into the water. As he struck out for the logjam, a man in front of him vanished under the water. Blood belched to the surface. His men were being dragged down and butchered in the depths. Something grabbed Chonjara's heel. He kicked out, hard, and was released.

Burdened by boots and clothing, Chonjara made it to the logjam. Someone helped haul him up onto the logs.

'You!' said Yen Olass, a born survivor.

'Kill him,' said Resbit.

Neither woman had any weapons.

Rocks splintered around them. The Melski had possession of the heights overlooking the gorge: they were hurling down rocks.

'Run!' said Chonjara.

The women fled, bumping down the far side of the logs. Chonjara followed. Men died ahead of them and behind them. There was no hope for the wounded. The rapidly sinking water level exposed the boulders they needed as stepping stones, and they leapt from stone to stone, running so fast they were almost flying.

They regrouped beyond the gorge, where the river flowed over beds of stone and shingle. Chonajra made a quick head-count. Only thirty of his men had survived. He saw movement downstream: more Melski were coming out of the trees, barring the way downriver.

'This way!' shouted Chonjara, plunging into the forest.

He led his men into the forest, heading west. Then he halted. The soldier behind him was Saquarius, a strong capable man, even if not entirely trustworthy.

'Take the lead,' said Chonjara. 'Force the pace.'

Saquarius nodded, and strode ahead. Chonjara stood where he was, urging his men forward. He saw Yen Olass and Resbit were being hustled along with the column; he noted the men who had taken the two women in charge. All of his men had weapons of some kind, though some had lost their swords and just had knives or tomahawks which had been secured to their belts.

At the end of the column were a few stragglers. Chonjara gave them the rough edge of his tongue. He went last, urging them on in front of him. He could still hear distant sounds of fighting. Some of his men were trapped and dying, struggling out of the gorge disabled by wounds, falling victim to the Melski. Good. It would give the survivors a little time.

When the column entered ground which Chonjara thought suitable, he pushed forward and took control of his men. They struggled up a steep gully, and Chonjara directed them into position. He kept Yen Olass and Resbit with him, warning them:

'One sound, and you're dead.'

With his men in position, he looked back down the gully, and saw a body lying there, moaning. Who was it? Nassos.

'Nassos!' said Chonjara. 'Get your arse up here!'

Nassos did not move. Saquarius plunged down the slope, hauled him to his feet and dragged him up to the position. Chonjara gave Nassos a kick as he went past. The useless little prick wasn't hurt, he was just giving up.

Now Chonjara's men lay in ambush. Shortly, a dozen Melski came in sight. They were eager and panting; they were the boldest and most reckless of the enemy.

With a ferocious scream, Chonjara lauched himself forward. His men joined him. Crashing down the slope, they over-whelmed the Melski. A brief butchery, and it was all over. Flushed, excited, the men grabbed the weapons from the dead Melski. One of Chonjara's men had died in the fight. Not Nassos—a pity, that.

'Come on,' said Chonjara.

He noted the swagger in the stride of his men as they set off up the slope. The ambush had cost them very little time. They had bloodied the enemy, and had transformed themselves from a retreating rabble to a coherent fighting force.

They got back to their ambush position. Chonjara looked around.

'Yen Olass!' he bellowed.

The fight had made an appalling racket, so there was no call for silence now.

'Resbit!'

No answer.

Chonjara looked around. The dense undergrowth could have hid an infantry company and a couple of squadrons of cavalry. The ground was trampled by men moving into position and then launching themselves into the attack; the two women could have faded into that undergrowth at any of fifty different points.

Given 'time, he would have swept the forest for them, and doubtless he would have caught them. However, to survive, he needed to set off with all possible speed. Now.

'Bring up the rear,' said Chonjara to Saquarius. 'The man who lags is dead.'

Then Chonjara led them west with all possible speed. His men smashed through the forest, leaving a trail of blind man could have followed walking backwards. When they were deep in the forest, Chonjara halted the column. They backtracked two hundred paces, then turned sideways and melted through he forest, stepping carefully so as to leave no tracks behind them.

The column reformed, and this time set off south. The

Melski would be delayed for some time while they cast around in the forest to pick up the trail again.

Chonjara hoped the Melski had not attacked and over-whelmed the men he had left at Nightcaps: the ones who were slow, fat, sick or otherwise unfit for a breakneck pursuit mission. Karahaj Nan Nulador, who had begged off from this hunt, pleading diarrhoea, had been left in charge. A poor choice: Nan Nulador was not command material. But this campaign did not seem to be throwing up many competent leaders.

Why not?

Because they were all demoralized. In Tameran, there had always been an inevitable logic to their conquests. Their victims had always lived in territory physically continuous with the empire, so ... they were absorbed as a matter of course. Here, in this land of myth and legend beyond the Pale, that logic no longer operated.

So what was the answer?

Courage, that was the answer. And ruthlessness. Be strong. Be confident. And give the men victories. The crisis demanded the leadership of a true fighting man, a warlord who knew how to be brutal when the occasion demanded it. Chonjara knew he was that man.

*　　　*　　　*

The Melski, lacking practice in the arts of warfare, and suffering also from the lack of any true warlords, failed in the final phase of their attack: the pursuit of the defeated enemy. As all commanders know, this is one of the most demanding phases of warfare. The troops are tired; they have risked their lives; some of their friends are dead or wounded; they have routed the enemy, so surely no more can be demanded from them. In this respect, the Melski were no different from human beings.

The pursuit was disorganized. The most eager hunters were cut down by Chonjara's men in the ambush. Discovering the dead bodies, those who came after them held back, uncertain as to how many soldiers opposed them. There was a considerable delay before Hor-hor-hurulg-murg arrived on the scene with another fifty Melski, and led the way forward.

Reaching the site where Chonjara's men had lain in ambush, he stopped, and sniffed the air. His sense of smell was not good enough for him to track humans through the forest like a dog, but he was certain there was someone close at hand. Two people, in fact. both women.

Hor-hor-hurulg-murg looked up into the trees.

'Come down, Bear-Fond-Of-Climbing.'

Accepting her new name, Yen Olass climbed down out of the trees, with Resbit following behind her.

CHAPTER
Thirty-two

The men were gone.

All of them.

A series of forced marches had taken Chonjara's troops south to rejoin the siege at Lorford. The stragglers and deserters left in his wake had quit the forest, some urged on by Melski patrols following closely behind. A few, trying to establish themselves in Penvash, had been hunted down and killed. Last to leave were Draven and Jalamex, who came downstream from the Valley of Forgotten Dreams, tired, haggard and footsore. Reaching Lake Armansis, they camped for a week by the lakeside, recuperating. Then they set off for the Razorwind Pass, their progress monitored by discreet and subtle Melski scouts.

Of all the invaders, only Yen Olass and Resbit remained. The Melski turned them loose at Lake Armansis, on a beach near the site of the pirate fort. They were free to stay or go, as they pleased. Hor-hor-hurulg-murg assured them of at least two days warning if intruders came their way.

'The campsite is that way,' he said, pointing into the forest. 'Close. I can smell it. What's there is yours, if you want it.'

'Aren't you coming?' said Yen Olass.

'No,' said Hor-hor-hurulg-murg. 'There was fighting. There are dead bodies.'

'I understand,' said Yen Olass, who knew by now the horror the Melski had of dead, rotting meat.

'Goodbye then, Bear-Fond-Of-Climbing.'

'Where are you going?' said Yen Olass.

'South,' said Hor-hor-hurulg-murg. 'If we have to fight again, we will. Otherwise, we wait. Maybe we sign a treaty— for what that's worth. But whatever happens, we'll be going north in the winter. If you're still here, you can winter with me and mine, if you wish.'

'Thank you,' said Yen Olass.

'Till then.'

'Yes,' said Yen Olass, 'till then.'

Yen Olass and Hor-hor-hurulg-murg bowed to each other, then the Melski set off down the beach. They did not look back.

Yen Olass and Resbit were left alone. Silently, they turned to each other, and hugged each other close and tight. They were all alone now. They had to take care of each other.

'Be brave,' said Yen Olass. 'It may be ugly.'

'I'll be brave,' said Resbit.

And they broke their embrace and slipped into the forest, following a well-defined track. Spring was easing toward summer, and the day was warm; a flutterby lofted through the sun-dappled treeshade, and somewhere a bird sang with a warbling luladula-teru.

'Stop,' said Yen Olass.

She grabbed Resbit.

'What?'

'Look.'

'What? I don't see anything. What is it? A ghost?'

'The ground.'

There was something wrong with the ground. Yen Olass hauled a big stick out of the undergrowth and poked the ground. It gave way. Earth pattered into a pit. Jabbing at the earth, Yen Olass broke open the rest of the crust covering a circular hole. At the bottom of the pit were seven sharpened stakes.

'A bear trap,' said Resbit.

'No,' said Yen Olass. 'A Resbit trap. If Chonjara camped here, then I'm sure he was busy before he left. So watch yourself.'

Moving cautiously now, scanning ground, trail and trees, the two women advanced. In this uninhabited place, there was something delicious about the faint sense of risk and menace. Yen Olass found herself hot and sweating. She felt strong and dangerous. The outlines of things sharpened, and the air tasted good.

Up ahead was a clearing. A big clearing. Stark sunlight showed the burnt-out remains of a stockade, a few dozen lean-to shelters, six or seven large pits, a big heap of kindling, a logpile and the beginnings of a wall of earth. Orfus pirates had stayed here after attacking and destroying two Galish convoys. Later, Collosnon soldiers had camped here after defeating the pirates.

'Where are all the bodies?' said Resbit.

'There,' said Yen Olass, pointing.

On the far side of the clearing, five corpses hung from a makeshift gallows, victims of military discipline.

'Is that all?' said Resbit.

She had braced herself for the most extravagant of ghoulish sights: heaps of skulls, dismembered bodies, stacks of fleshrot oozing worms and maggots, arms and legs spiked at random onto stakes and tree branches. The five men so quietly dangling could not compete with her imaginings. Resbit was a little disappointed.

'That's all,' said Yen Olass, leading the way out into the clearing.

The ground was dry and dusty. A rat skulked away as they investigated the lean-to buildings. Put up in a hurry as temporary shelters, they were just about ready to collapse. Yen Olass pushed at a support pole, making a whole building fold up with a clatter of falling timber, sending up a cloud of dust.

'Yen Olass!'

'What?'

'We could have slept in that.'

'I'm not sleeping here. Lice and bedbugs. And scabies. Anyway, there's plenty more buildings. You got a fright, that's all.'

'All right, I got a fright.'

'I won't do it again,' said Yen Olass.

And they hugged each other again.

Then, hand in hand, they explored the rest of the campsite. Nothing much remained. There was certainly no food. So what would they eat? Fish, birds, watercress, snails, worms, frogs, and ants. They would manage. They could probably hunt down the occasional deer, too. But what about later, when Resbit got large and heavy? Could Yen Olass hunt for both of them? And what if she got large and heavy herself? (She was beginning to suspect that she too was pregnant.) Would they have to throw themselves on the mercy of the Melski? They could if they had to, but Yen Olass wanted to be independent for once. She wanted to live her own life, not be a charity guest in someone else's household.

Pausing by the burnt-out stockade, Yen Olass rubbed her hand over one of the posts. Fire had eaten deeply into the wood, eating black charcoal gulches deep into the timber. It was warm to the touch; her hand came away black from the charcoal. She reached out to dab Resbit's cheeks with this make-up, but Resbit ducked away. Yen Olass chased her, then:

'Look out!' screamed Yen Olass.

Resbit froze, then looked around wildly. Earth, sky, stockade.

'What?' said Resbit, frightened. 'What is it?'

'The ground. Look.'

Now Resbit saw it. A pattern of cracks leading in to a faintly depressed centre.

'Another Resbit trap, I bet,' said Yen Olass.

She fetched a heavy stick so she could break open the ground and reveal the pit beneath. But the ground refused to break.

'There's nothing there,' said Resbit.

'There is too,' said Yen Olass. 'Don't do that!'

But, disregarding this injunction, Resbit advanced until she was standing in the shallow depression. She stamped down hard.

'It's a trap!' shouted Yen Olass. 'You'll fall through!'

Resbit danced up and down, doing a war whoop. Then she stopped, looking up at the sky. High overhead was a bird— probably a hawk.

'Look, Yen Olass. A bird. In a bird-trap. It's caught there. Oh, and I can see a funny kind of net in the forest. There's a spider stuck in the middle. A spider trap. Oh, and look at all those leaves. They're stuck to the trees. They can't get away. They're trapped. Yen Olass, what can we do to help them? Oh help, Yen Olass, help me, I'm stuck on this brown stuff, I'm trying to jump, I can't get free.'

And Resbit jumped up and down on the earth, whooping again. Yen Olass lost her temper and heaved the stick at her. Resbit rolled out of the way and collapsed on the ground, panting and laughing.

'There's something down there,' said Yen Olass, grimly.

'Yes,' said Resbit slyly. 'Probably a gamos.'

'You'll see,' said Yen Olass.

She hunted round for a sharp stick to dig with, then squatted down in the centre of the depression and started stabbing the earth viciously.

'There's nothing down there,' said Resbit. 'You're imagining it.'

Yen Olass did not reply, but hacked away at the earth.

'Oh come on. Don't be like that. Can't I have a little fun now and then? Don't sulk, Yen Olass.'

'I'm not sulking, I'm digging.'

'And really enjoying yourself, I'm sure. Lots of fun. If you strike gold, give me a call.'

And so saying, Resbit wandered off, pausing now and then to scratch patterns in the dust with the toe of her boot.

'Where are you going?'

'I'll be on the beach if you want me.'

'Come and help me dig.'

'I'm going to dig my own hole. In the lake. I'll dig down into the water so I can find some fish. I bet I find something before you do, Yen Olass.'

But before going down to the lake, Resbit had to go and have a good look at the five bodies swinging from the gallows. Flies buzzed away as she approached. She looked at them for some time, glutting her curiosity. They were really dead. Once they had been up and about, walking the world on their hind legs, eating fish and sticking their things into dogs and women, and now they were entirely finished with all that. Their faces were opening, revealing the bones. It was hard to say what they had looked like.

With one shy, hesitant hand, Resbit reached out and gave one of the men a tiny push, shoving at one of his boots. He swung from the gallows. The rope holding him creaked faintly; Resbit stepped back, in case the rope broke and dropped the man down into her arms.

She shuddered.

She had seen enough.

Yen Olass was still grubbing in the earth, grunting and swearing. She did have a temper when she was roused. Vaguely, Resbit remembered her Rovac warrior, Elkor Alish. He used to have a temper, and had showed it on the rare occasions when she had dared to cross him. She remembered his cold fury, and the way he had bruised her face once, knocking her backwards so that she ended up on the floor. Yet, other times he had been kind. It was his child she was carrying, and she did not regret it.

Slowly, Resbit made her way down to the beach, avoiding the pit in the middle of the track. The Melski were already a long way down the beach, tiny figures diminishing in the distance. Resbit took off her boots. Her socks stank. They were going into holes. If she could get material, she would make footbindings like those Yen Olass used. But there was not much chance of that.

Resbit wiggled her toes. They felt happy to be out in the warm sunshine. It was a good day for naked toes. And naked bodies, maybe. Slowly, Resbit stripped off her clothes. She stood there naked on the beach, with the freefalling sunlight caressing her skin. Lightly, she touched her nipples, her breasts, her stomach, her flanks. Thinking of her child shaping within her darkness, she smiled. She looked out across the lake, out across a shimmering immensity of water.

She felt incredibly free without her clothes. And without... without fear. It was a new and delightful sensation to be able to act without being constrained by conventions which specified slander, calumny and rape as the punishment for so many acts of selfhood which a woman might wish to undertake.

Resbit walked down to the water's edge. The beach was made of small stones and the shells of fresh-water shellfish. The most recent shells were a pale blue; the older ones were bleached white, and had sometimes splintered to a crackle. Resbit waded out into the lake until the water infiltrated the fuzz of fur at her crotch. Half water, half sky, she stood there, suddenly exhilarated. She felt as if all the trials of her life were justified by this one perfect moment. And she thought:

—It is enough.

Gathering a breath into her lungs, she dived. Limpid shadows floated below her as the impetus of her body was damped down by the water. Finally she hung motionless, gazing down at the underwater world below her.

First lifting her head to take in air, she swum downward, then turned a slow, lazy somersault underwater. She blew out air, watched it globe into bubbles, then chased them to the surface. She was a perfectly fluid, fluent animal, free from the constraints of gravity.

Her hair misted in front of her face. Which reminded her of when she had last washed it—about half a year ago. Standing in the shallows, she rubbed her hair vigorously, scratching at her scalp. Then she attended to the rest of her body. The water round about her grew dark with a spreading stain; she felt immensely invigorated and refreshed.

She lay down in the water and floated on her back, kicking gently with her feet. She propelled herself round in huge, leisurely circles till she grew tired, and made her way to the shore. There she spread her coat on the beach and laid her body down on that battered luxury, and went to sleep.

Resbit was awakened when someone kissed her buttocks. Opening her eyes, she craned her neck and saw it was Yen Olass. Who now came and sat down by her head. Resbit propped her chin on her hands, her elbows braced against her coat, and studied Yen Olass, liking the strength she saw there. Having cleaned her own body rigorously, she was aware that Yen Olass stank of sweat, grease, earth, blood, rancid fat and earwax. She did not find this unduly offensive, but even so:

'You need a bath,' said Resbit lazily.

'Later,' said Yen Olass. 'When we've finished digging.'

'We? Dearest heart, if you want to grub away with the beetles, that's your business, not mine.'

Yen Olass flicked something into the air. It flickered into the sunlight then fell with a plop just in front of Resbit. It was a golden coin.

'You told me to call you if I struck gold.'

Resbit reached out for the coin and bit at it. The metal refused to yield to her teeth.

'Yen Olass, this isn't gold. It's flash of some sort, that's all.'

'Flash?'

'Pretty metal. Besides, what're you going to spend it on?'

'Don't be like that. Come and help me dig.'

'Yen Olass, I'm all clean.'

Saying that was a mistake, for the next moment Yen Olass was dumping handfuls of stone and shell onto Resbit's back, then following it with grit she found deeper down. Resbit surrendered, dived into the lake briefly to clean her body, then followed Yen Olass back to the clearing. She walked naked, her bare feet leaving damp prints in the earth, and picking up a brown coating. By the time she reached the clearing, she was beginning to dry out; she unrolled the clothes she had been carrying, and put them on, feeling how coarse and dirty they felt. Everything would have to be washed.

Yen Olass, working with furious energy, had excavated a considerable hole. Looking down into it, Resbit saw the mouth of a leather bag. It was full of coins. She admitted to a little bit of rising excitement, but:

'I still don't see what we can spend the money on.'

'Goose,' said Yen Olass, 'I don't want money. Think some. The pirates didn't drag treasure all the way over the Razorwind Pass just to bury it here. They found it here. They took it from the Galish. So . . . this is just the beginning.'

Yen Olass was right. By evening, they had uncovered enough to know that the pirates had buried a considerable amount of Galish loot. There were tools, weapons, bolts of cloth, jars of olive oil, sacks of rice, plates of keflo shell and leather bottles full of wine.

Resbit and Yen Olass got drunk that night, celebrating. The next day, they were far too sick to do any digging, but they guessed their cornucopia held everything they needed. A few more days of excavation proved this supposition correct. Yen Olass thought this just as well, for she grew more and more certain that she was pregnant.

'You will bear Khmar's son,' said Resbit, with a hint of something close to reverence in her voice. 'The son of an emperor!'

'Khmar belonged to a different world,' said Yen Olass firmly. 'I will bear the child of my own body. A child born to Penvash —to a land without emperors and kings.'

CHAPTER
Thirty-three

Resbit and Yen Olass built a house by the lakeside. They put up a woodshed and a storehouse. They designed and built traps for rats, not to secure skins for making clothes, but to protect their store of food. They were rich, and did not hesitate to deny their wealth to the bushrats of Penvash.

The days eased out into a long, leisurely rhythm, unlike anything they had ever before experienced. Rising with the dawn chorus of forest birds, they hauled in longlines from the lake, then gutted and scaled fresh fish which they cooked for breakfast.

With breakfast over, they tidied the house, checked the rat traps, disposed of any vermin, then made the rounds of the bird snares, pits and deadfalls which they had built in the forest. On these long, cool walks through the early morning forest, they were silent, feeling no need to speak.

Later in the morning, they worked on House Two. Unlike their present shack of sticks and branches, this was to be a proper log house with a fireplace and chimney, so they could winter over by the lake without suffering undue hardship.

In the afternoon, when the forest was suffused with lazy heat, they went swimming, and afterwards generally slept for an hour or two on the beach. Each evening, they massaged each other with a little warm olive oil, and made love to each other tenderly, teaching each other their own pleasures.

When they caught a sow and a piglet in one of their traps, they killed the sow but kept the piglet; Resbit planned to teach it how to hunt truffles. By the time the full heat of summer was upon them, House Two was finished, and they moved into it, leaving House One to the pig, who now carried the name Pelaki; however, Pelaki, by now thoroughly socialized, refused to be excluded from their company, so House One became the exclusive preserve of spiders and woodlice.

With housebuilding over, the days were slow, lazy, idle. They studied their own bodies, observing the changes. Flesh slowly thickening, casting a heavier shadow. A leisured, inescapable uneasiness surfaced in dreams which sometimes became nightmares. They were both aware, though they did not speak of it, that they were very much on their own, with nobody to help them if anything went wrong. And so many things can go wrong.

Then Yen Olass had a nightmare. First she was trapped in the darkness, with jaws locked tight around her. She knew where she was: inside the metal flower in the strange castle in the Valley of Forgotten Dreams. Voices spoke. Silken light smoked from her hands. Knots of time unravelled. She plucked a flower from an underwater branch, inserting it into her womb.

And then—

'Don't be scared,' said Lefrey.

But the voices hurt her. Lacerating pain struck through her pelvis. Fetid breath grinned down at her, crushing her body beneath groping weight. She saw a Collosnon soldier, a ceramic amulet gleaming at his throat, hacking away her mother's breasts. The voices swore, ripped away her fingernails.

Then General Chonjara was pulling her child out. His fingers were made of splintered wood. The child was jammed. He tugged. It ripped its way out. Its head was a wedge of steel. A spear blade. Slashed open, she stared aghast at the white gash—

wounded flesh into which blood suddenly welled, and suddenly—

The pain struck home.

Waking with a scream which startled Pelaki and shocked Resbit into instant wakefulness, Yen Olass started to cry. She sobbed helplessly while Resbit comforted her. She was convinced that the dream was a warning. She was convinced that the child in her womb was damaged. A monster. Or a dead thing, swelling there like a fungus. A bag of blood.

Resbit held her and kissed her, soothed her and stroked her. Pelaki snuffled into her armpit. And, eventually, her fears eased by this comfort, Yen Olass slept again.

But now the two women did talk, sharing their fears and pooling what knowledge they had. Yen Olass found Resbit knew much more than she did. Yen Olass had always distanced herself from women things, hating the life of the Woman Sanctuary which stank of servitude, and, in some secret part of her heart, despising herself for being a woman—and, in a much less secret part of her heart, despising the sewn and mutilated body which had marked her as a slave. She had never cared to follow gossip about distant concerns such as pregnancy and childbirth. But Resbit was well versed in both subjects.

There were more nightmares after that, but, talking through her fears with Resbit, Yen Olass found the courage to face them, even if she could not entirely subdue them. She could not forget how the metal flower had killed the pirate Toyd, turning him loose with his skull ready to melt into liquid and a sick wet embryonic growth forcing out from between his ribs in a vicious parody of pregnancy.

Resbit, for her part, had her own worries, though these were less severe. She wished she had the help of an experienced midwife who would know how to cope if the baby was born buttocks-first, or if the cord started to strangle the baby as it was born, or if the afterbirth failed to follow the child, or if she started to bleed afterwards . . . she had heard that eating the afterbirth would, in an emergency, help stop bleeding, but she did not know if that was true. Besides, she had seen two births, and was of the opinion that an afterbirth was hardly the most attractive thing in the world, and surely only marginally edible.

In fact, in an emergency, eating a chunk of the raw afterbirth will tend to stop bleeding; many animals eat the afterbirth as a matter of course, gaining the benefit of its food value and the chemical intelligence it carries. But Resbit had no way to confirm this. So she discussed it with Yen Olass, and they argued it out.

'It's not meant to be eaten,' said Yen Olass. 'It's meant to be kept all in one piece so people can look at it. That's very important. Even I know that.'

'That's only so the wise woman can look at it to see that it's all come out,' said Resbit. 'If you get a piece left stuck inside, you can die. But there won't be any wise woman here.'

They decided that, in the absence of anyone to tell them otherwise, they would eat the afterbirth if they found themselves bleeding to death, on the principle that if they were going to die anyway it could hardly do any harm.

'And otherwise,' said Yen Olass, scratching Pelaki behind the ear, 'our best friend here can have it.'

'No!' said Resbit, truly shocked. 'That's a barbarous thing to say.'

'Then I'm a barbarian,' said Yen Olass complacently.

'Well you feed the pig as you see fit,' said Resbit, 'but it's not getting part of me to eat.'

Yen Olass laughed at her dismay, then kissed Pelaki on the snout. She, for her part, had no intention of disappointing the pig.

Talking over the details of the two births Resbit had seen, the two women prepared themselves for their own deliveries. Resbit by now was five months gone; she could feel her child kicking inside her body. Her rate of weight-gain was increasing. Her breasts had enlarged, and were tender; the colour of her nipples and areola deepened. A streak of pigmentation appeared, running from her navel to her crotch; it widened to a fat, dark band. She did not know if that was normal or not.

Yen Olass, with some sixty days to go before she reached the same stage, followed these changes with interest. As an oracle, living amongst virginal women, soldiers and administrators, she had scarcely ever seen a pregnant woman, not even in the crowded streets. Yet, in Gendormargensis alone, there must have been thousands of pregnant women. Otherwise, where would all the children have come from? But they had all been hidden away somewhere . . . doubtless confined to their homes while their mothers and daughters performed whatever tasks demanded a venture out into the markets and thoroughfares.

The summer heat reached its blistering peak. The air became febrile with biting insects. Retreat to the lake became a necessity; they wallowed in the water for hours, and were thankful for the evenings when the bloated sun finally sank behind the hills in the west. Ringed by hills, Lake Armansis was sheltered from the sea winds which, in the south, invaded Estar, sometimes bringing cold and rain even at the height of summer.

Sometimes, as Resbit floated in the lake, Yen Olass watched Resbit's child kicking within her belly. And, as autumn drew near, that same child took to kicking her during the night, when she was curled up with Resbit.

The approach of autumn brought also the approach of the last stages of Resbit's pregnancy. That autumn, her wrists and ankles swelled. There was little room left in her body for her bladder; with its diminished capacity, she had to urinate frequently. She draped her body with loose clothing worked up from cloth and wool which had once belonged to the Galish. She experienced moments of triumph, times of anxiety and one or two moments of terror and outright horror. Yen Olass supported her without fail through all these vicissitudes.

As Resbit entered the last stages of her pregnancy, her vaginal tissues softened in preparation for the advent of her child. She found an ooze of colostrum on her nipples; her vaginal lubrication increased; membranes swelled in her nose. Heavy and swollen, she waddled down to the lake each day to swim in its steadily cooling waters. Then, toward the end, she started to feel more comfortable; she found she had more energy to spare. But Yen Olass, growing increasingly nervous about Resbit's health, insisted that she take life easy and get plenty of rest.

Then it happened.

Yen Olass was woken one cool autumn night by a piercing squeal.

'What've you done to Pelaki?' said Yen Olass, jolted out of dreams by that ear-splitting sound.

'Pelaki got clouted on the nose,' said Resbit, her voice shaky. 'Too curious, that's the trouble. Yen Olass, the pains have started.'

'All right,' said Yen Olass.

She raked over the ashes of the fires, found some hot coals and started a small blaze. Pelaki crouched in a corner, obviously frightened.

'Put the pig out,' said Resbit.

'If that's what you want,' said Yen Olass.

After a short scuffle, she muscled Pelaki out into the night, closed the door, and barred it against intruders. Then she settled down to wait with Resbit.

The shifting firelight splayed vague shadows through the room, shadows which danced and lilted as the flames leapt and sheltered. Here they were warm and safe, sheltered by strong walls; the firelight illuminated a familiar array of weapons, traps, fishing lines, blankets, furs, pots, bottles, boots, shell necklaces, and other items of utility and decoration.

In this safe and comforting place, Resbit sat with her back resting against the wall. Yen Olass bundled together some furs and slipped them behind her back to cushion it, then arranged more padding to go under her knees. There have in certain times and certain places arisen human cultures in which women were compelled to go through labour and delivery lying flat on their backs: however, such a bizarre notion never for a moment occurred to Yen Olass or Resbit, and if it had they would have noted that the birth canal points upward, whereas babies, like apples, fall downward.

Yen Olass leaned against the wall herself, and closed her eyes. The contractions at the moment were slow and widely spaced; Resbit was quietly talking about the name her lover, Elkor Alish, had wanted for any son that was ever born to him. The name was Elkordansk Talshnek Branador, which in the language of the Rovac warriors meant Elkorson Scalpslicer the Swordwielder. Yen Olass did not argue, though on previous occasions she had said—and loudly—that she thought that was a hideous name. She wondered what Resbit would do if the child was a girl.

'I wonder if he often thinks of me,' said Resbit.

'Who?'

'Elkor, of course.'

'Probably,' said Yen Olass, yawning, and hoping Pelaki was not suffering too much out in the night all on his own.

'I wonder where he is,' said Resbit.

'Out there, of course.'

'Yes, but where?'

'Somewhere in the forest, all on his own,' said Yen Olass, meaning the pig.

'No,' said Resbit. 'He'll be in a banquet hall somewhere. Drinking up large with a thousand roistering heroes.'

Yen Olass bit her, very gently.

'That's nice,' said Resbit.

Yen Olass resisted the temptation to bite harder. This talk of

Elkor Alish was making her jealous. She had no doubt—though she had never confronted Resbit with her theory—that to the Rovac warrior Resbit had been just an amusement to while away his idle moments. Yen Olass, with vast experience of soldiers and their ways, knew how they used and abused women.

'He used to tell me how he loved me,' said Resbit.

'Did he?' said Yen Olass.

'He said I had the most beautiful body he'd ever seen.'

'You do have a nice body,' said Yen Olass.

But there was a catch in her voice as she said it. She remembered the slave women who used to be brought in to entertain Lord Alagrace from time to time in his quarters in Karling Drask in Gendormargensis. Sometimes, encountering Yen Olass, one of those women would engage her in gossip which pretended to be casual, but which was in fact calculated to gouge out information about Lord Alagrace.

In this way, Yen Olass had learnt how Lord Alagrace, with his subtle and generous language, had managed to convince even these most experienced professionals that they were valued, that they were honoured, that they were, indeed, surely on the verge of becoming a permanent part of his entourage. Yen Olass remembered some of the reports which had come to her. 'He said nobody had ever done that for him before.' 'He said I made him feel young.' 'He said he would remember our night together forever...'

Yen Olass kissed Resbit, and hoped she would never be confronted with Elkor Alish, who, by this time, surely had some other woman with him.

'Hold my hand, Yen Olass.'

Resbit reached out, and Yen Olass took her hand. Again Yen Olass yawned. She wondered about Lord Alagrace. She presumed that he must have died in the gorge, fighting against Chonjara's soldiers; doubtless she would have heard the full story if she had not managed to escape so quickly. She wondered what Lord Alagrace had thought of as he died. Had he thought of any of those gentle women, so vulnerable to his lies? Doubtless they had told him their own lies, had counterfeited pleasure and mimicked orgasm to boost his ego, had stroked his aging body and whispered that they loved him . . .

But that was the way of it . . . for their own safety, the powerless must pretend to enjoy their slavery, hiding resentment, conjuring up a false enthusiasm to conceal a weary apathy, bowing and kowtowing and practising deferential manners of speech lest they be thought uppity. The deceptions of slavery were not pleasant, but captive women did not choose their own condition . . .

Vaguely, Yen Olass wondered why the bed was not soaking wet. The waters broke . . . when? At the start, she had thought. But obviously she was wrong. Or not yet right . . . or . . .

Or the fire was . . . floating . . .

Floating gently on waves of fatigue, Yen Olass slipped off to sleep.

*　　　*　　　*

Elkordansk Talshnek Branador was born at dawn with a caul over his face. Yen Olass broke the sac immediately, slicing it open with the tip of one of her steel fingernails, and her hands received Branador into the world. She had opened a single shutter to provide light enough to work by.

'It's a boy,' said Yen Olass.

'Of course it is,' said Resbit.

Branador drew his first breath. Yen Olass waited for a wailing cry. But there was none. She lifted Branador onto his mother's abdomen, and saw, by the dim light, Resbit smiling in something like glory.

'Are you tired?' said Yen Olass, wondering at the enthusiasm she saw in that face.

'Not now,' said Resbit.

Yen Olass touched the silvery blue umbilical cord, and started as she felt it pulsing. Despite all their rehearsals, she was confused as to what she should do now. Tie it off straight away? Or leave it?

'Can you get me some more water?'

'The cord . . .'

'That can wait.'

Yen Olass fetched more water, and Resbit drank it down. Yen Olass felt her own child kick in her womb. More than once, she had been kicked awake by the strong, aggressive, lusty life now perfecting its vigour within her body.

'He looks just like Elkor,' said Resbit, scanning the face of her child.

'That's nice,' said Yen Olass, without much enthusiasm.

Yen Olass, feeling exhausted, recalled the events of that night. She had slept only for a small part of it. The rest had been spent stoking the fire, cooking a little rice for Resbit, finding a bowl big enough to use as a chamber pot when Resbit was too scared to step out into the night to void her bladder, comforting Resbit when she was in pain, massaging her back . . . then gently supporting El-kordansk Branador as he passed through the gate between the world of fishes and the world of men.

The afterbirth emerged into the world, looking like something from an offal shop. Yen Olass let it be. She touched the child, gently, curious to find him so warm, so slippery, so quiet.

The bed was an unholy mess, soaked with amniotic fluid which had been trapped until the caul was broken. There was also a moderate amount of blood, though not enough to scare Yen Olass, who had seen enough battlefield butchery to know a little goes a long way. However, no excrement had been pushed out along with the baby, which was hardly surprising considering that Resbit had been cleaned out by diarrhoea during the two days before her labour began.

Yen Olass made up a new bed for Resbit. By the time she was finished, the umbilical cord had stopped pulsing, and was cool and limp. Yen Olass tied it off securely in two places with lengths of string, then cut between them. Then she helped Resbit and her child move to the new bed.

'What would you like now?' said Yen Olass.

But Resbit needed nothing from her. Resbit was cradling El-kordansk in her arms, and he was feeding. For the moment, he was all she had eyes for.

*   *   *

While Resbit fed her son for the first time, Yen Olass decided to clean up properly.

Opening the door, Yen Olass was assaulted by Pelaki, who was overjoyed to see her. Pigs are as affectionate and as intelligent as dogs, only more so. Yen Olass scratched Pelaki behind the ears, then betrayed him by dragging him away and shutting him up in House One; she was very tired, and did not think she could cope if Resbit got traumatized by the vigorous attack of an energetic young pig.

The lake was pale in the early morning light; the sun was still burning away a little mist. Yen Olass threw all the soiled bedding into the lake, and washed it, then hung it up to dry on a rope spread between the trees. Then she started to fetch in more wood for House Two.

On her return from her second trip to the woodpile, she was startled by a silent apparition standing between her and the door to House Two. It was a gnarled green monster with gill slits, a massive neck, skin that was hard and almost chitinous, a knotted complexity of tendons, muscles and raised ridges at the groin. Caught out in the open, at the limits of her strength, bleary with fatigue, Yen Olass started and dropped the wood the was carrying.

'P'tosh,' said the monster. 'P'tosh, and the cat went miaow.'

Remembering, Yen Olass blushed.

'P'tosh, Hor-hor-hurulg-murg,' said Yen Olass.

'There is blood on your face. Are you hurt?'

'No, it's a . . .'

Yen Olass knew no Galish word for 'blush', and so invented one, 'mara-lalisk', meaning 'blood-smile'. This conveyed nothing to Hor-hor-hurulg-murg.

'There is blood on your face,' he said. 'Has there been a killing?'

Doubtless he saw her fatigue. And saw the bedding hanging up, slowly dripping water—obviously some kind of cleansing had taken place. Yen Olass wet one of her fingers and rubbed her face.

'The other side,' said Hor-hor-hurulg-murg.

He indicated on his own face. Yen Olass scraped a little dried blood from her cheek.

'A little goes a long way,' said Yen Olass. 'This is not from a death, but from a birth.'

'How is your child, then?'

'Not mine. Mine isn't for . . . for sixty days or so.'

'Resbit's child, then.'

'Resbit's child is fine. Come in. I shouldn't keep you standing out here. Come in, there's smoked fish. Do you like smoked fish?'

Hor-hor-hurulg-murg hesitated, not wanting to intrude on a mother with her newborn, which was an offence against Melski custom, and not wanting to refuse hospitality, which was an equally serious offence.

'Let's go and pull the longlines first then,' said Yen Olass, thinking that maybe the Melski did not eat smoked fish.

The job was soon done. With fresh fish cleaned and gutted, they went into House Two. Resbit and her man-child were asleep in each other's arms. Yen Olass cooked fish, moving very slowly, for she was very tired; Hor-hor-hurulg-murg wanted to help, but custom made that impossible.

'Thank you for your hospitality,' said the Melski, when they had eaten. 'I must go now, I have others to meet. My people are scouting west. But I will return soon, then we will talk.'

'We will be pleased to talk with you,' said Yen Olass, too far gone to care what they might talk about.

They bowed, and parted. And Yen Olass, feeling absolutely ragged, curled up beside Resbit. And slept, like the dead.

*   *   *

Elsewhere, inside House One, a pig by the name of Pelaki snoozed in a comfortable glow of contentment. Between washing the bedding and fetching the firewood, Yen Olass had found time to open the door to House One and throw in the afterbirth, and this little short pig had greatly enjoyed that bit of long pig. Doubtless revenge had something to do with it.

CHAPTER
Thirty-four

In the days that followed, the two women learnt what had happened in the south. The army laying siege to Castle Vaunting had been destroyed by madness. Leaving madness guarding the castle, the garrison had marched away to the east. There were rumours to say that they had conquered more Collosnon troops at the High Castle in Trest by another application of madness. After that, their movements were not known. They had disappeared.

'But where could they have gone?' said Yen Olass.

'Who knows?' said Hor-hor-hurulg-murg. 'As it is, the land around Lorford now lies waste. There will be nobody there to trade with the Galish convoys when they start to arrive next year.'

'If they start to arrive,' said Yen Olass, knowing full well that no Galish convoys had reached Lake Armansis all through the summer and autumn.

"They will,' said Hor-hor-hurulg-murg. 'Rumours of war will have frightened them, but this trade route is too valuable to be abandoned forever.'

'What about the Collosnon?' said Resbit. 'Won't they come back?'

'The soldiers, those who survived, all withdrew to Skua on the coast of Trest. We think most have gone back to Tameran, leaving only a garrison at Skua.'

'But Skua's only a fishing village,' said Resbit, remembering the talk of people who had been there. 'What can they want with that?'

'It's important so they can go home and say they conquered part of Argan,' said Yen Olass. 'That's much better than going home defeated.'

Having outlined the situation, the Melski got down to business. They wanted to build a trading post here by Lake Armansis. When the Galish convoys came through, the Melski wanted Yen Olass and Resbit to help them as translators, and, more importantly, as ears and eyes.

'As interpolators,' said Yen Olass, using an Eparget word which nobody else understood.

'What are interpolators?' said Hor-hor-hurulg-murg.

'People who help with big things and little, as needed,' said Yen Olass, practising her diplomacy.

Yen Olass had no objection to being a Melski spy. What she did not know was that the trading post was just one part of a far-ranging plan. The Melski, believing that their troubles had only started, were determined to establish a small human colony at Lake Armansis to provide them with a permanent pool of agents, spies, assassins and diplomats. Even if Yen Olass had known this, she would still have accepted it.

When Resbit and Yen Olass had first set up house by the shores of Lake Armansis, their freedom had been exhilarating. Nevertheless, even during the most idyllic moments of summer, they had always been aware how vulnerable they were to sickness or injury—or any strangers who managed to infiltrate the forest without being stopped by the Melski.

Now, with winter approaching, their need to belong to a community was becoming more and more obvious. One child already meant a lot of work. Two children would prove a heavy burden, even if they were granted unlimited supplies; as it was, sooner or later—toward the end of winter or the beginning of spring—their stores of food would run out, and they would have to forage to eat.

A way of life which had seemed delightful in the good weather, when they had plenty of looted food stashed away, now seemed increasingly impractical and, indeed, dangerous. They were glad to see the Melski establishing themselves in the area. If they had to be members of a community, the company of Melski was preferable to that of humans, for Melski males would never dream of interfering in the private arrangements of two human females, whereas to any man the two women would represent at least a temptation, if not an outright challenge.

Winter came.

The Melski lived in mud-daubed huts while they worked on permanent buildings for the trading post. Yen Olass and Resbit had felled the logs for House Two in the spring, when the wood is full of sap and moisture; the Melski explained that this would encourage rot and warping. The Melski felled their own logs in the cold weather, when the trees were scarcely alive, and the wood was dry with its food value at a minimum.

'A dead tree is a dead tree,' said Yen Olass, convinced that it made no difference; House Two was certainly showing no signs of falling apart.

While the work of tree-felling was still going on, Yen Olass gave birth to her child. Her labour was very different from Resbit's. Early on, her waters burst with an audible gush which startled her, since she had never heard that such a thing was possible. She thought this might signal a swift labour, but her child was not born for a day and a night.

Long before the end of her labour, she was screaming with pain, exhaustion and utter frustration. Then the head of her child began to emerge, and, as she panted, it slithered out in a spectacular sprint to the open air.

Yen Olass felt an overwhelming sense of relief. It was out! Her labour was over!

Her child started bawling.

'A girl,' said Resbit.

'Let me see her,' said Yen Olass.

Finding herself, after all that pain and all those long hours of exhaustion, animated by an intense curiosity. The child was

heavy and wet and slippery. She looked very much like Yen
Olass, except that her eyes were a startling gold.

'Bring me a burning stick,' said Yen Olass.

'A what?'

'A burning stick!' commanded Yen Olass.

Resbit hesitated, then obeyed.

'You're not going to hurt her, are you?' said Resbit.

'No,' said Yen Olass, without much conviction.

If the child was blind, she was going to strangle it. She
watched the child's eyes as she waved a burning brand in front
of its face. The eyes did not follow the movement of the flame.
Yen Olass handed the stick back to Resbit, who tossed it into
the fire. The child screamed senselessly.

'What are you going to call her?' said Resbit.

'It's going to be buried without a name,' said Yen Olass, her
throat choking up.

'What are you talking about?'

'It's blind!'

'Yen Olass, they don't see properly when they're born. Now
you just lie back. You should feed her. Look, she's got a chin
just like the emperor!'

Yen Olass looked, but could see no resemblance at all. This was
not Khmar's child. This was some kind of demon spawn conjured
into her body by the wishing machine which had hurt her.

'It's just as well she doesn't have the emperor's eyebrows,' said
Resbit, prattling on. 'You wouldn't want to wish that on a girl!
Now I've got to feed my little hero. Put the child to your breast,
Yen Olass. What's her name? What're you going to call her?'

'I'll think about it,' said Yen Olass.

*   *   *

For the first few days, Yen Olass was intensely suspicious of
her child, expecting it to turn into a frog or an old woman or
something equally hideous.

But the female infant proved to be vigorously human. She was a
lusty, aggressive child, bawling for food and attention, savaging
the breast when she was given suck, and, though at first she spent
much of her time asleep, still managing to disrupt the nights with
her demands. And she was so messy! Pissing and shitting and
dribbling and snorting snot and burping up milk.

On the tenth day, Yen Olass decided her child had shown enough humanity to deserve a human name.

'I'm going to call her Monogail,' said Yen Olass.

'I still like Valadeen better,' said Resbit.

'No, she's going to be Monogail, because she's a true child of my homeland.'

And Yen Olass hugged her child, her very own skinned rabbit which she herself had brought into the world.

Slowly, she began to learn to take pleasure in her child. As she grew to be at ease with her infant, breastfeeding itself became pleasurable, bringing her, at times, secret swollen pleasures reminiscent of the sexual gratification of the flesh; wondering, with a little bit of guilt, if she was abnormal, she kept silent about this, being far too shy to discuss it with Resbit.

Sometimes, snuggling down in the warmth of her bed, she felt infinitely contented, thinking herself, for a moment, all-nourishing earth mother, fulfilled by producing, bringing forth, nourishing and mothering.

However, even though her rapport with her child was steadily developing, these earth mother moods did not last. Children were just too much hard work for anyone to be starry-eyed about them for long.

Fortunately the Melski females, appreciating that help might be welcome, and doubtless curious about the raising of human babies, came in and helped out with the household tasks. Yen Olass could not imagine how women coped when they had a newborn baby plus one or more young children plus a house to run and a man to feed, and clothes to make and shopping to do, and maybe an aged parent to look after as well.

The weather closed in. Forced to stay home and look after Monogail, Yen Olass was not free to go on long tramps through the winter forest. She found herself increasingly trapped inside House Two. It was dark; the fire smoked; the wind discovered chinks in their amateurish walls, and came whistling in. The fire smoked; the one room filled with smoke and the smells of cooking and damp mildewed clothing. Two women, two babies and a pig: at times, when there were two voices crying, two shouting and one squealing, it was utter chaos.

Yen Olass felt trapped.

Though at times she felt she really loved Monogail, at other times she wished the steel flower had given her a pig instead— a pig already cooked, with an apple in its mouth. Then at least everyone would have got one good meal out there in the wilderness of the Valley of Forgotten Dreams.

More and more, she appreciated the presence of the Melski. They were great talkers, when they loosened up. From perfecting her command of Galish, Yen Olass went on to learn the language of the Melski, a complicated tongue with seven different levels of formality and eighty-three variations of the word 'you'. Yen Olass had an acute, disciplined brain, a lifetime of language-learning behind her, a desire to communicate, and long dark hours in which she could revise her lessons. She made good progress.

Resbit, on the other hand, made no effort to learn the native language of the Melski. Speaking Estral and the Galish Trading Tongue, she thought of herself as highly cultivated already. In many ways, Resbit thought of the Melski as animals. Instead of studying, Resbit spent hours talking to the babies. She loved them without reservation. she was in her element. Love with Yen Olass had been a game: this was life.

Yen Olass, unable to share this enthusiasm, resigned herself to captivity, and waited for the spring.

*   *   *

Working between spells of bad weather, the Melski had finished the trading post by the time spring came. It stood on the lakeside half a league to the south of House One: a stockaded establishment complete with lodging house, warehouse, a corral for any animals that travellers brought with them, and a wharf leading out into the lake. Yen Olass and Resbit were suitably impressed.

'For people who never work with wood,' said Yen Olass, 'you've done very well.'

'What do you think our rafts are made of?' said Hor-hor-hurulg-murg.

He was, to say the least, offended. Yen Olass apologized, but it was a whole day before relations between them were back to normal. Yen Olass understood this as proof that the Melski accepted her as one of their own. She was no longer an outsider, for whom excuses can be made; she was one of the people, and should know better than to condescend to a full-grown Melski male.

That spring, Yen Olass was free to roam the forests again, with Monogail slung papoose-style on her back. When it was warm enough to venture into the water, the Melski taught the women how to find shellfish beds where they could dive for fresh-water clams. They refurbished their old traps, and made new ones, kept a lookout for any deer unwary enough to venture near House Two, and fished. Birds mated and nested; Resbit and Yen Olass stole eggs for their babies.

Yen Olass found her spirits revived as the weather warmed. Her child was more lovable when she was squaddling on the beach instead of lying in a dark smoke-filled room bawling her eyes out. Yen Olass began to make plans for her. Monogail would be a translator, and a trader. She would raise scores of pigs and teach slaves how to hunt with them. She would hold the truffle-trading monopoly for all of Penvash . . .

Yen Olass did not speak of these plans, but Resbit boasted shamelessly about what her son would do when he grew up.

'Branador's going to be a hero,' she said, teasing his little thing. 'With this sword, among others. Maybe he'll marry Monogail. Would you like that, Yen Olass? You can be his mother-in-law.'

'He'll have to be tough to stand up to me,' said Yen Olass.

Resbit smiled fondly.

'I mean it,' said Yen Olass, and she did.

No man was going to bully her daughter, or turn her into a household slave. She was certain of that.

*   *   *

Toward the end of spring, the Melski told the women that four travellers had passed through Estar earlier in the year—the Rovac warrior Morgan Hearst and companions named Blackwood, Miphon and Ohio, who were, respectively, a woodsman, a wizard and a pirate. They had come from Trest, and were heading south, hunting Elkor Alish, who was said to have command of a world-destroying power known as the death-stone.

The rest of the story was fragmentary and confused. There had been a battle between soldiers and Melski in a valley far to the east of Trest; a fight against an evil wizard; a journey down an underground river; a mutiny; an epic struggle with a dragon; treachery and murder; a storm at sea; a battle with the Collosnon navy. Somewhere in all this hero-play, Morgan Hearst had lost a hand. Yen Olass thought it served him right: if he hadn't gone swaggering through the world cutting people's heads off, he would never have come to grief. She still remembered his outburst when he had come to parley with the siege forces outside Castle Vaunting:

'Elkor Alish has said nothing about his whore!'

Resbit, who had never been told of these words, was thrilled to learn that Elkor Alish was still alive. And maybe on the way to becoming a world-conqueror. The more distant he grew in her life and memories, the more she idealized him. By now she believed that their commercial fornications had been True Love; that Elkor thought of her always; that when he ruled the world, he would send agents north and south, east and west, in search of her.

Yen Olass, long-time observer of the cynical sexual politics of an imperial city, could only wonder at this naivety. Though Yen Olass had never entirely lost the ability to play like a child, there was nothing childish about her appreciation of power, sex and the manipulation of one human being by another. But she did not try to disillusion Resbit. She doubted that they would ever again hear of Elkor Alish, or for that matter any other Rovac warrior.

But in the autumn came the news that Elkor Alish, after many battles, conquests and subsequent defeats, was in Estar with an army of Rovac warriors, seeking to hold it against vaguely defined monsters from the south, known as the Swarms. Then winter cut off further news; when spring came, they learnt that Elkor Alish was dead, killed in a fight with Morgan Hearst, who now ruled Estar, sharing his power and responsibilities with the woodsman Blackwood and the wizard Miphon.

Hearing of Elkor's death, Resbit wept, and for a week could not be comforted. But Yen Olass, while displaying her sympathies, was secretly glad that this man-nonsense was at an end: and that there was no chance of the hero of Resbit's daydreams stealing her away to some distant palace of opal and amethyst, there to live out her days as a helpless prisoner of lust.

Intermittently, more news came from Estar. For a while, Estar seemed to flourish. Then Resbit and Yen Olass head news of a three-way power struggle between its rulers, Blackwood, Miphon and Hearst. Rumour came to them saying Blackwood and Miphon, making an alliance, had removed themselves and their followers to Sung, in the Ravlish Lands, taking with them certain implements of power.

When intelligence next reached Lake Armansis, the two women learnt that Morgan Hearst was now undisputed ruler of Estar, a Rovac army supporting his rule.

CHAPTER
Thirty-five

In the spring of the year Celadric 4, when Monogail was three years old and a bit, the Rovac came north to Lake Armansis. There were three hundred of them, the ragged remnant of a rearguard which had fought the Collosnon forces while covering the retreat of the Rovac armies down the Hollern River to ships waiting to take them to the Lesser Teeth.

The rearguard reached Lake Armansis, unopposed by the Melski, who had granted them safe conduct, knowing their real quarrel would be with the Collosnon thousands following on behind.

After the death of his father, the Lord Emperor Khmar, the cool and elegant Celadric had contemplated murdering his brothers, but had finally decided to let them kill each other. So he had appointed them joint commanders of an army of invasion, believing such shared responsibility would lead to murder.

Eager to win power and glory, the brothers had come south. Meddon, the seasoned warrior, slaughterhouse comrades at his side. Exedrist, a lame-brained semi-invalid dominated by those two notorious generals, Chonjara and Saquarius. York, the brawler, the thug, travelling with his personal bodyguard of axeblade executioners, torturers and professional rapists. The stage was set for a vicious three-way power struggle.

But, to begin with, the brothers fought the enemy rather than each other.

At the time of the invasion, Rovac seapower had been concentrated on the western coast, contending with the Orfus pirates of the Greater Teeth. Most Rovac landpower had been in the south of Estar, commanding the hills and mountains against the monsters of the Swarms now trying to force a way into Estar.

With the enemy thus dispersed, the Collosnon had struck, and conquered. The survivors of the Rovac rearguard now at

Armansis planned to turn west to cross the Razorwind Pass to Larbster Bay, hoping to be picked up by their own sea patrols. The long-standing ancestral dream of Rovac, which was to conquer all of Argan, was at an end.

The Melski still maintained their trading post at Lake Armansis, even though the invasion of the Swarms had halted the passage of the Galish convoys, which were now denied a road south to the rich markets of the Harvest Plains and the Rice Empire. Those great powers, in turn, had ceased to be. So the trading post waited, in case conditions changed, though nobody could see how that was possible. By now the Swarms were no longer shadows and rumours, but were known by name. Worst were the Neversh, the flying double-spike monsters.

Outnumbered and just barely tolerated by the Melski, the Rovac were constrained to respect the trading post and the nearby human community (still only four-strong). Even so, a small group of them got drunk and made trouble. First they murdered Pelaki. They slashed the pig's throat, strung their victim up by the heels to bleed to death, then cooked and ate the meat. After this outrageous act of terrorism, they decided to start on the women; by the time Morgan Hearst arrived on the scene, Yen Olass had disabled three of his braves, and the heroes had retreated so they could plan how best to burn down House Two.

Hearst restored discipline, then interviewed the two women. The Melski had told him only that they were under Melski protection. Hearst could not think why two women with young children would be living with the Melski, so he was entirely prepared for them to be lepers or lunatics, or worse.

To his great surprise, he found he recognised one of them. He had long ago forgotten her name, but still remembered her face. She had been Alish's bedpartner during the days long ago, when a prince by the name of Meryl Comedo had ruled Estar, and Hearst and Alish had fought side by side in the same battles.

'What brings you here?' said Resbit, who knew Hearst well, having seen him often enough around Lorford.

'I'm here to apologize for the behaviour of my men,' said Hearst, studying the two shy children who hid in the shadows, and the formidable black-haired woman who stood to one side, leaning on an axe and watching him intently.

'We don't need apologies,' said the black-haired woman. 'All we need is to be left alone.'

'Who are you?' said Hearst, surprised at her hostility.

'She's Yen Olass,' said Resbit. 'I'm Resbit.'

'I know you are,' said Hearst, doing her the courtesy of pretending he had remembered her name. 'I've seen you in Lorford in the . . . in the old days . . .'

'When Elkor Alish was still alive.'

'Yes. You've heard . . . ?'

'The deeds of Hastsword Hearst are famous,' said Resbit, with a touch of bitterness. 'Even here.'

'I'm sorry,' said Hearst. 'Still, that's in the past. As for the future, you're under my protection.'

'What future is that?' said Yen Olass.

Again Hearst was surprised.

'I thought you were free to leave,' he said. 'The Melski told me they weren't holding you here in slavery.'

'We're free to do as we wish,' said Yen Olass. 'So get out.'

Hearst hesitated. He had killed Elkor Alish—but that was a tragedy, caused by a misunderstanding. Resbit was his last link with a man who had been his valued comrade for many years, who . . .

'What are you waiting for?' said Yen Olass.

'I mean you no harm,' said Hearst. 'Is there anything you need? For yourselves? For your children? Are they twins, the little ones?'

The children, still shy as mice, were half-hidden in the shadows. Both of them had black hair. Resbit was a brunette, so it was not surprising that Hearst thought they both belonged to Yen Olass, who, after, seemed more likely to be the mother because of her protective attitude to her territory . . . and who certainly had good, wide, child-bearing thighs.

'Of course they're not twins,' said Resbit. 'The girl is hers. Elkordansk is mine.'

'Elkordansk?'

'That's the name he chose,' said Resbit, 'before he went away.'

'I see,' said Hearst.

'He does see,' said Yen Olass. 'He's killed the man, now he's going to kill the child.'

'There'll be no killing here,' said Hearst. 'Alish was my friend once. And this . . .'

Hearst looked around the interior of House Two. Blackened by more than three years of smoking fires, it looked small and dark and dirty.

'. . . this is no place for his son.'

'We've done our best,' said Resbit.

'Yes,' said Hearst, 'but on the Lesser Teeth you could have a proper house. Not a hovel like this. Besides, the boy needs companions. How old is he? He must be . . . at least three years old by now.'

'At least that,' said Resbit, beaming.

Yen Olass stepped forward, and wiped her hand over Hearst's mouth.

'Look,' she said, holding up her hand. 'See? Blood. This is a warrior: a monster who eats people.'

There was no blood on her hand.

'Yen Olass,' said Resbit. 'Don't be silly.'

'What kind of hospitality is this?' said Hearst, rubbing his mouth.

'You're not our guest,' said Yen Olass. 'You're an invader.'

'Yes,' said Hearst, with his temper starting to rise. 'An invader. And why? Because there's an army at my heels. Do you think you can go on living here in dreamland? Sit down, and listen!'

He shoved Yen Olass, hard, intending that she should go down to the floor. But Yen Olass was heavier than he had thought. She went back half a step, recovered her balance and slugged him, smashing her fist into his solar plexus with all the force she could muster. The next moment she was clutching her hand in silent agony, struggling to keep from crying out.

'Chain mail,' said Hearst, patting his green-brown linen jacket. 'I'm a creature with three skins—wool, steel and linen.'

'Why,' said Yen Olass, mastering her pain, 'are you wearing armour here?'

'In case of attack.'

'The Melski would tell you if there was any danger.'

'The Melski might be the danger,' said Hearst. 'Besides that, there's irrational women to cope with.'

'Irrational!' said Yen Olass.

And she swore at him.

'She is rather, isn't she?' said Hearst to Resbit.

And Yen Olass saw with dismay that Resbit did not contradict him, but just bowed her head slightly.

'Bring the child out into the light,' said Hearst. 'I want to get a good look at him.'

'Come on, 'Dansk,' said Resbit, enticing her child toward the door. 'Come outside with your mam.'

'What's his name?' said Hearst. 'Wasn't it Elkordansk?'

'Yes, but we call him 'Dansk for short,' said Resbit.

'You musn't do that,' said Hearst, leading the way out into the sunlight. 'It doesn't mean anything.'

'But Elkor said—he told me it meant son. Elkordansk. Son of Elkor. Your friend.'

'My friend,' said Hearst. 'Yes. But 'Dansk is for putting on the end of words. It doesn't mean anything by itself.'

'So what's the word for son?'

'The word for son is gada,' said Hearst. 'Elkordansk, na gada Elkor. Elkordansk, son of Elkor.'

'Shouldn't it be Elkordansk gada na Elkor?'

'No,' said Hearst. 'Na is a word meaning . . . meaning . . . this item which I have just brought to your attention is. That's the best way I can translate it. I don't suppose our Elkordansk has a single word of his father's language to his credit.'

'I didn't know any to teach him,' said Resbit.

'So what does he speak? The Galish Trading Tongue?'

'That most of all. A little Estral—I speak to him sometimes . . . in my own language. Then he speaks with the Melski. He plays with their children. But at the moment . . . sometimes when he's speaking it's all three languages jumbled up together.'

And she laughed.

Hearst smiled, then gestured at their surroundings.

'In a few days, this is going to be swarming with Collosnon soldiers. What were you going to do? You can't stay.'

'We were going to run north. With the Melski. They'd give us shelter.'

'I'm sure they would,' said Hearst, looking at Elkordansk. 'But the boy . . . he's meant for better things than living off fish with the green things. You say he speaks? He's very quiet.'

'He's shy, that's all,' said Resbit.

She picked him up, and held him. She was proud of him: her strong young son who, she was sure, was destined for great things.

'Come,' said Hearst. 'Let's go to the camp. There are other men who knew Alish. They will be pleased to see his son. We . . . we none of us wanted his death. It was . . .'

'A thing between men,' said Resbit.

'Yes,' said Hearst. 'A thing between men.'

'This man wants to take you west,' said Yen Olass. 'By way of Larbster Bay.'

'I'm not afraid to travel,' said Resbit. 'I'm not a child, you know.'

She had entirely forgotten her earlier fears of moving away from her homeland—or perhaps, over the years, she had just grown out of them.

'Let's go,' said Hearst.

And they set off for the camp together.

Monogail wanted to go with them, but Yen Olass held her back.

'Come into the house, Monogail. No, you can't go with them. No. Because I say so!'

In the house, it was dark and quiet, but for Monogail, who complained bitterly at being shut up inside. Yen Olass shut her up by giving her some smoked fish to chew. She sat on the bed, looking around at the interior of House Two. Was it really such a terrible place? It was a house of their own. It had sheltered them for years: them and their love.

What love? Resbit had left without protest. So how could there have been love? Didn't love mean loyalty? After all these years together, Resbit had yielded to a man without any protest at all. Of course, she had her son to think of. But is a son more than a lover? Resbit was too young: too innocent. She had never been a slave. She had never had bits cut out of her. She had never been kept like an animal, humiliated by . . . she had no idea of all the terrible things that could happen. Would happen.

They were safe here. Had been safe for years. To the north were the highest mountains of Penvash. Places no army could ever conquer. They could be safe there. With each other. Surely. It wasn't too late. Was it?

But Yen Olass knew it was too late. Far too late. A hero had come for Resbit—a brutal skullknuckle slaughterer with one swordgrip hand and a razor-sharp slicing hook glinting at his other wrist. He had promised Resbit a future, and she had already accepted—that was clear enough, no denying it now—and her time with Yen Olass was . . .

A silly thing, which was over now.

A charade. A game.

Something that had happened, oh, long ago, in another world, altogether different from this one . . .

Yen Olass remembered Resbit lying face down on her coat on the beach, her naked body warmed by the sun. She remembered bending over and kissing Resbit on the buttocks, lightly, gently, with such . . . tenderness. They had been so good to each other. So tender. So happy. And now . . .

Now, fists clenched, eyes clenched, Yen Olass wept, her chest heaving as the hot wet tears squeezed out of her eyes.

'Mam?' said Monogail, patting her on the back. 'Mam?'

'Oh Monogail, Monogail, Monogail.'

Her voice was fat and blubbery, distorted by her misery. She held Monogail in her arms, acknowledging the question she had tried to pretend she would never have to face:

—Monogail, Monogail, what will become of you?

*   *   *

Yen Olass Ampadara sat on the end of the wharf at the Melski trading post, watching her girlchild Monogail swimming in the waters of Lake Armansis in the company of a dozen Melski children. Monogail had been able to swim before she could walk; in the water, she was as confident as an otter.

Yen Olass watched two Melski children, on a floating log. They were playing 'walking stones', where you fold your arms and walk straight into the other person, shouting 'walking stones'. The winner is the one left standing on the log, though usually both go overboard. Yen Olass knew she could surive amongst the Melski, but she had to think of Monogail. What kind of life would it be for the child, when Yen Olass died and Monogail, grown to maturity, was the only human in a tribe of Melski? Yet what kind of life would it be where they were going?

Sitting beside Yen Olass on the wharf was a battered leather pack holding all that she would be able to carry away from this lakeside life. There was food, blankets, spare clothing for herself and Monogail, a trifling amount of Galish gold, a sharp knife, two leather water bottles, a tinderbox, a small cooking pot, a string of amber beads, a stone globe filled with stars—and that was about it. Not much to carry away from a life.

She had thrown her best cast-iron skillet into the lake. Now she regretted getting rid of it, and thought about asking one of the Melski to dive for it. She resisted the temptation. As it was, she was going to have a struggle to pack everything she was taking over the Razorwind Pass. If she took the skillet, she would have to throw out some food—and Monogail hated to be hungry.

Morgan Hearst had offered help, but Yen Olass resolutely refused to accept it. Every man she had ever relied on had betrayed her. Khmar, who should have made her empress, had died in her arms instead. Lord Alagrace had committed suicide by indulging in futile last-stand heroics. Draven had tied her up and had left her for Chonjara. From now on, Yen Olass was not going to make any futile alliances with men.

She felt very much alone.

She looked along the lakeside, wondering if they had done it yet. Yes. Half a league away, smoke was rising. House Two was burning, so that nothing would be left for the Collosnon marauders. Yen Olass closed her eyes, feeling the sharp prick of tears. Poor House Two. They had been so happy there, at least for a while.

Yen Olass wept, quietly.

She remembered . . . the first step Monogail ever took, and the triumph on the child's face. The first word Monogail ever spoke: 'Mam'. A lot had been forgiven on the strength of that one word: Yen Olass, failing to adore her baby, nevertheless liked her child more and more as she grew. Now House Two was burning, and with it were burning so many bright hopes . . .

Yen Olass thought of her own people, slaughtered or enslaved by the Yarglat, their homeland laid waste. At least she was still alive. And where there was life, there was hope: or so it was said.

*   *   *

Monogail made no protest when told they were going away. She was too young to understand what it meant.

Yen Olass had said her goodbyes to the lake, to the ruins of House Two and to her tears. Now she said her parting words to Hor-hor-hurulg-murg:

'Till we meet again,' said the Melski gravely. 'Though that will not be in this lifetime.'

Hearing his voice, she realized he was afraid. This time, the Collosnon were coming north in force. Perhaps even the depths of Penvash would not prove a sufficient refuge in the face of such strength—and the Melski had nowhere else to run to.

Yen Olass bowed.

'Be strong,' she said.

And you, Bear-Fond-Of-Climbing,' said Hor-hor-hurulg-murg.

And he in his turn bowed, and they turned away from each other, and went their own ways.

CHAPTER
Thirty-six

'Bears!' said Yen Olass.

Monogail threw herself flat in the sand dunes. She hugged the ground for a little while, then lifted her head to look around.

'Down!' said Yen Olass. 'The bears are very close. I can see them. Big ones. The kind that eat Monogails.'

'But you're not down, mam,' said Monogail.

'Today I'm a bear too,' said Yen Olass, 'so I'm safe.'

A little while later, Monogail lifted her head again.

'Maybe the bears are gone now,' said Monogail hopefully.

'No!' said Yen Olass. 'They still want to eat you.'

'Maybe they've eaten a seagull instead.'

'All right,' said Yen Olass, relenting. 'They've eaten a seagull.'

'Ya!' screamed Monogail. 'Seagulls!'

And she went bounding over the sand dunes and down to the beach, giving war whoops and bird screeches. Yen Olass followed sedately, with Quelaquix padding along behind her.

The tide was in, so Yen Olass could not work. Nevertheless, as she walked along the beach she kept her eyes open. She did not feel like lugging great loads of driftwood and seaweed down the beach, but, where she found these valuables—the wood bleached by long days in the ocean currents, the seaweed hulking in great blackening masses—she piled them up above the high tide mark so she could retrieve them later.

Monogail, at the age of five, was spared from work. Not

because she was too young to work—elsewhere, children of her age laboured daily to help their families—but because Yen Olass did not choose to impose such obligations upon her daughter. As Yen Olass walked along the beach, with her lyre-cat Quelaquix at her heels, Monogail ran ahead of them, chasing seagulls.

The walk was almost at an end. They were drawing near Skyhaven, their home, a small stone cottage crouching in amongst sand dunes which were stabilized by marram grass and wind-gnarled saltwater pines.

'Come along, Monogail,' said Yen Olass.

But Monogail went larking down the beach after the sunwhite windscrawn gulls, which went wheeling into the air, filling the sky with their lonely scree-scraw of disaffection.

'Monogail!'

Yen Olass watched as her daughter kicked round in a big circle then started to return, skidding now and then and wheeling into mock falls from which she always recovered, grinning broadly.

'Clean yourself up,' said Yen Olass, 'and go inside.'

Monogail did another circle.

'Come on!' said Yen Olass, clapping her hands. 'Let's horse horse!'

'Let's bear bear,' said Monogail, sprinting for the door.

'Brush the sand off before you go inside!' shouted Yen Olass.

'Let's cat cat!' screamed Monogail, still running. 'Let's gull gull.'

Quelaquix followed, but Yen Olass paused for a moment, and stood looking out to sea. Low, grey cloud concealed the further distances of the ocean. Somewhere out there, almost lost in the cloud, she thought she saw a sail. Was it friendly or hostile? It hardly mattered, either way. There was no need to fear pirates here: for three leagues out from the coast, the sea was a maze of shawls and sandbanks, lethal to any ship foolish enough to venture inshore.

Yen Olass fetched the wooden bucket from the woodshed, where driftwood was heaped up high, then she went to the well. This was protected by three weatherbeaten boards. Yen Olass removed one of them and laid it aside. A little sand fell into the water and lay floating on the surface. She reached down—the well was only elbow-deep—and stirred the water so the sand sank to the bottom.

When Yen Olass stirred the water, she did so very gently, not wanting to disturb the inhabitants. One was Monogail's pet fish Straff, a fingerlength freshwater kelling. The other, sitting on top of a rock which poked out of the water, was a yellow har-bucker dune frog. Her name—or his, with a frog that small it was hard to tell—was Alamanda. Early in life she had lost a leg to a seagull or a cripple beetle. Finding her under a lenis bush at the edge of the sward pond, Monogail had insisted on keeping her, and Yen Olass had been unable to resist.

Despite these indulgences, Yen Olass had at various times refused house room to a big hairy mottle spider, a rabbit snake, a baby rat and a stink lizard. Fortunately, baby sharks, flatfish, stingrays and jellyfish could not live away from the sea, other-wise Yen Olass would have had other battles on her hands. The last time they had visited Uncle Hearst, he had come into Bren-nan Harbour on a boat with a dead lynch shark on board; when it was cut open, there had been a dozen live and viable baby sharks inside, almost ready to be born.

Observed intensely by Alamanda, Yen Olass dipped a cup into the well and filled the bucket bit by bit. Straff settled on the bottom, waiting till this procedure was over.

Yen Olass filled the cup one last time, and drank from it. The cold water hurt her mouth, reminding her of the trip she had made to Vinyard the day before, where old Martha had pulled two of her teeth. The pain reminded Yen Olass that in a few more years she would be forty.

She was no longer tempted to pretend she was young. She was definitely middle-aged, and very definitely settled; it seemed that she was destined to grow old here on Carawell, the largest island of the Lesser Teeth, that minor archipelago lying west of Lorp, south of the Ravlish Lands and a little more than a hundred leagues north of the Greater Teeth.

Well, as a place to grow old in, Carawell, otherwise known as Mainland, did have its advantages. Grey, windy and wet, it was nevertheless spared the hardships of snow and ice, thanks to the moderating influence of the surrounding sea. The island communi-ties were small, stable and friendly, and the islands were at peace; the Orfus pirates, who had once seemed to have positively impe-rial ambitions, had reverted to their old habits of casual raiding, for their present leader, Bluewater Draven (not to be confused with Draven the leper or Battleaxe Draven or the late and unla-mented Draven the Womanrider) was a pirate of the old school.

Lying within easy reach of Lorp, the Lesser Teeth traded fish and shark liver oil for wool, mutton and boatbuilding timber; with easy access to the Ravlish Lands, they traded amber and ambergris for knives, fishhooks, nails and soapstone, for Tamarian honey, Dulloway beer and the occasional cask of Renaven wine. Amongst themselves, they traded boats and land, the titles to land being based on traditional family holdings. When Yen Olass had come to Carawell, she had purchased title to Skyhaven from old Gezeldux, paying with her gold, her amber beads and her stone globe filled with stars.

Yen Olass lived free of rates and taxes, for there was no government in the Lesser Teeth. The people were poor, but they were free—they maintained their lives and their dignity without making any compromises whatsoever with any throne, kingdom, power or outer authority.

This is not to say they had built themselves a paradise, for they had not; like people everywhere, they still yielded on occasion to their lesser nature, and, apart from this, living as they did where they did meant that many came to grief while fishing or sailing, so there was an uncommonly high number of widows and orphaned children on the islands.

It also needs to be said that anyone planning to live on the Lesser Teeth would have to get used to the idea of living mainly on fish. Or shellfish.

In the case of the household at Skyhaven, shellfish was the staple which kept life and limb together. However, Yen Olass also gathered edible seaweeds, speared flounder during nightstalks in the shallows with spear and burning brand, raised chickens, and, nourishing the sandy soil with dead seaweed and chicken manure, was endeavouring to grow vegetables—an enterprise best described as optimistic.

Taking her first bucket of water to the vegetable patch, which was currently lying fallow as everything had died, she poured the water into the soil. She theorized that the vegetables had died because the substratum of seaweed buried down below had failed to rot down into fertile earth.

All over Carawell, seaweed was widely touted as the best of all possible fertilizers, but the greater part of this batch had been buried underground for rather more than a year without showing any inclination to convert itself to anything other than seaweed. On her last grip to Brennan—when she had bought a coat of coney-fur for Monogail, and had bested old Gezeldux first at wrist-wrestling and then in a drinking match—she had been led to understand that a liberal application of fresh water, repeated some two or three hundred times, would produce amazing results.

She was now on day seventy-six of her watering schedule, but, digging down to inspect the seaweed, she found the sample she uncovered was still a slightly resilient mass of lubbery fronds, stout stalks and durable bobbles. Not for the first time, Yen Olass wondered if she had been had.

With this depressing thought in mind, she stopped at one bucket, and went inside, to find that Monogail had tracked sand all through the house.

'Monogail!'

The problem with sand is its high mobility—upwards, downwards and sideways. Among other things, it gets in clothes, hair, food and the bed. Living on a beach, Yen Olass was in some respects in a state of seige, with sand the constant and unrelenting enemy.

'Monogail, come here!'

Monogail came. Yen Olass gripped her by the shoulder and looked at her. Hard. Monogail grinned a big toothy grin. She had a scratch on her cheek where Quelaquix must have tagged her, probably after getting his tail pulled, or after getting chosen as the target in a one-on-one game of whales and boats. There were tiny, tiny beads of blood oozing from the scratch.

'What did you do?'

'I didn't touch him!'

'Then don't do it again. Do you hear me?'

'Yes, mam.'

'Otherwise you'll get your eyes torn out. And then what will you do?'

Monogail had no answer to that.

'Mam, is it teatime yet?'

'Almost,' said Yen Olass. 'We need two eggs. You can go and get us some eggs.'

'And say hello to Straff.'

'Yes, and say hello to Straff.'

'And Alamanda.'

'Yes, and Alamanda.'

'And feed her an egg.'

'No!'

'Not really, though. Just an onzy one.'

'Fifty onzy ones, if you like. Go along now—it'll be dark soon.'

'Not for ages.'

'But I have to have light to cook with.'

'Cook with light? You don't cook with light, mam.'

'You're so quick you'll step on yourself. Now go outside. And check the chiz trap while you're at it.'

'If there's a chiz—'

'You can't have it because it'll eat the chickens. Besides, it'll be dead.'

'Like my father,' said Monogail.

'Yes, like your father.'

'Did he fall in a trap?'

'No,' said Yen Olass. 'He got old.'

'Very very very old?'

'No,' said Yen Olass. 'A little bit old but a very much sick. Now off you go, mam's got to sweep up this sand. And don't bring any back when you—'

But Monogail was gone, running out of the door. Yen Olass sighed. Were all children so curious, so energetic, so full of questions? She swept up the sand, wondering if there really might be a chiz in the trap. She had never seen this curious weasel-like animal, and would have thought it a mythical invention—the islanders were good at inventions—if she had not at times seen its delicate tracks in the sand. Usually the morning after a raid on the hen coop.

Monogail came back with three eggs and a ghost which, she said, had been caught in the chiz trap; Monogail talked earnestly with the ghost while Yen Olass cooked their evening meal. Then, when they sat down to eat, Yen Olass had to shift one place to make room for the ghost.

'Hadn't you better introduce us?' said Yen Olass. 'That's polite, you know.'

'Even among pirates?'

'Especially among pirates,' said Yen Olass firmly.

'Can we be pirates, mam?'

'No.'

'Why not?'

'Because.'

'But why?'

'Because first you have to cut off your nose.'

'Really?'

'Yes, really.'

'Doubt it,' said Monogail.

'All right, doubt it then,' said Yen Olass. 'So who's your ghost? Tell us her name.'

'It isn't a she, it's a he.'

'Why?' said Yen Olass.

'Because,' said Monogail.

'Because what?'

'Because that's how, that's why. His name's Vex. He's a ghost because he got killed. He's a dragon, that's what. Uncle Hearst killed him.'

'Now that's a story,' said Yen Olass.

'No it isn't!' said Monogail. 'Uncle Hearst told me. He killed lots and lots and lots of dragons. That's why.'

'Dragons don't exist,' said Yen Olass. 'Uncle Hearst tells lots of stories, most of them aren't true.'

'This dragon—'

'When Uncle Hearst—'

'You're not listening!' said Monogail impatiently. 'You have to listen. Now? All right. Vex was a good dragon. He had two wings. He had sharp teeth. Like this. Gnaaar! Teeth to bite you with.'

'Eat your egg,' said Yen Olass absently.

'All right,' said Monogail, killing the egg then mutilating it. 'Gnaar! Dragons. Biting.'

Vaguely, Yen Olass wondered how long they would have to share the house with the ghost of a dragon. Chewing a stalk of sendigraz, she wondered, equally vaguely, if dragons really did exist. Raging through the skies and burning things. Long ago, in a different life, Resbit claimed to have seen one, but Yen Olass doubted it. One dragon, burning . . . yes . . . burning, that was a thought . . .

All that seaweed . . .

She had plenty of driftwood, cached in the dunes up and down the beach . . .

Dig up the topsoil, so called, and expose the seaweed. Then a big, big fire. Burning for two days, if necessary. Or three. A mountainous pyre. A real volcano . . . a firemountain, like the ones Uncle Hearst talked about. More stories, yes . . .

After such a fire, what wisdom?

After such a fire, wood ash, and what was better, the ashes of all that slightly resilient seaweed, which of late had taken to writhing in her dreams. Pour fresh water on it! What was that going to do? If anything, the water seemed to be nourishing it, keeping it in tone, so to speak. She could imagine them laughing about it in Hagi's Bar in Brennan. Well, she'd show them. Ashes this year, vegetables next. She'd get the better of them.

Yen Olass recalled her first days on Carawell, when she'd been renovating Skyhaven. Strangers had dropped by, and, after watching her work for some time—in the beginning, their studied silence had unnerved her—they had ventured to introduce themselves and to assist with a little tactful advice, advice which was always given in that dry, sage, wisdom-of-generations manner which they had brought to such perfection.

Which was how Yen Olass had come to dig forty-seven earthing holes to protect against crawling lightning, to rig up a net over her door at night to entangle any invasive land octopuses, and to crowd the roof with sharpened finials to ward against garret hawks. All these fortifications had long since disappeared, but on every trip to Brennan, someone was always sure to remind her about them—old Gezeldux would always rise to the occasion, even if nobody else did.

'Mam?'

'What?' said Yen Olass.

'Mam, Quelaquix wants to go out.'

'Then you get up and let him out.'

'I can't.'

'Why not?'

'Can't you see? Vex is sitting on my lap.'

Why did I ask? thought Yen Olass.

'Sitting is all right,' said Yen Olass. 'But rumpaging isn't. Especially not in bed.'

'What's rumpaging?'

'What dragons do that they shouldn't.'

'But dragons don't exist,' said Monogail. 'Mam said so.'

'Did she now?' said Yen Olass, skilled by now at extricating herself from these predicaments without getting too deeply entangled in advanced metaphysics. 'Maybe that's so, but cats do exist, so I've got to let Quelaquix out.'

'To go hunting.'

'Yes,' said Yen Olass. 'Hunting a chiz.'

The cat was eager, alert, poised for a big adventure in the dark. That suggested it would be a fine night, and probably a good day tomorrow. If it was going to rain during the night, Quelaquix became an altogether different animal: a profoundly recumbent heap of fur sagging over the floor in a prime spot enjoying the full benefit of the fire.

Yen Olass opened the door, and Quelaquix slipped outside. Looking out into the starlight, Yen Olass saw a dark figure standing watching. She reached up to the lintel and fetched down a gollock, a thick-bladed machete nicely weighted for demolishing a man's face. Sliding outside, she closed the door behind her, slipped sideways and lost herself in amongst the saltwater pines. There she went to ground.

Hiding in the shelter of the trees, she closed her eyes to adjust her vision to the darkness, and listened. Opening her eyes again, she saw the figure moving through the night. Soundlessly. Whoever he was, he must have seen her break for the trees, and now he was coming after her. Stealing a glance over her shoulder, Yen Olass waited. She was ready.

'Yen Olass,' said the man.

Spitting out the breath she had been holding, Yen Olass got to her feet and stalked out of hiding.

'You bastard!' she said. 'You whoredog rat-rapist, how long have you been skulking around in the dark?'

'Give you a fright, did I?' said Morgan Hearst.

'Fright!' said Yen Olass, inserting the gollock between his legs. 'I'll give you fright! How would you like to sing soprano?'

'Not today, thanks,' said Hearst, reaching down to remove the cold steel. 'Anyway, you've got the blunt edge uppermost.'

'For sure,' said Yen Olass. 'I wouldn't want to hurt a pathetic old cripple unless I had to. What've you been doing out here?'

'Practising,' said Hearst. 'I have to stay sharp.'

'For what? Is it true what they say—that your last trip to Sung was to kill a man?'

'My lips are sealed,' said Hearst. 'I'm a professional. Remember?'

'Okay, professional, how did I do?'

'You did well,' said Hearst. 'A regular nightfighter. But I still think you should build a back door.'

'Come and stay for a few days with a few of your braves,' said Yen Olass. 'You could get it done in no time.'

The door opened, and a small figure stood in the doorway illuminated by the glow of firelight.

'Mam!'

'It's all right, Monogail.'

'What're you doing, mam?'

'I'm chasing a chiz.'

'Oh, really? Have you caught it? Can I help?'

'Go back inside,' said Yen Olass. 'It's cold out here.'

But Monogail came racing out into the night. Shouting.

'Gnaar! Dragons! Ah! What? Uncle Hearst!'

'How's my darling?' said Hearst, scooping Monogail into his arms and giving her a kiss.

'Put her down, you lecherous old monster,' said Yen Olass. 'Now come inside—but don't sit on the dragon.'

'Dragon?'

'Not a dragon, mam,' said Monogail. 'A ghost. His name's Vex. He was a dragon once, but now he's dead. You killed him, Uncle Hearst. Killed him dead.'

'Did I?' said Hearst. 'Which one was that? Tell me about it.'

With Monogail clutching his hand and chattering excitedly, he led the way inside.

*   *   *

Morning.

Yen Olass woke, and yawned. The door was ajar. Quelaquix had come in while she was asleep, and was now curled up on top of Monogail. Yen Olass couldn't imagine how her child could sleep with that great lump of a cat on top of her.

Careful not to disturb child or cat, Yen Olass got out of bed and opened the shutters, and looked out to sea. The tide was in, with a brisk wind sending waves surging up the beach.

Going outside, Yen Olass found Hearst practising with his sword. She watched, till his shadow-fighting brought him wheeling round to face her.

'You left the door open,' said Yen Olass sharply. 'Were you born in a tent?'

'No,' said Hearst cheerfully. 'I was born under a boat. What's the problem, anyway? Afraid of land octopuses?'

He sheathed his sword and came to the door, grinning. He looked strong and healthy.

'What's for breakfast? Vegetables? How's the seaweed growing?'

'It needs nourishment,' said Yen Olass. 'How would you like to be manure? Come on, let's go to the fish-garth.'

As they walked inland, Yen Olass wondered whether to ask Hearst about his business. He was too much a man of affairs to have come here for pleasure. Although most of the Rovac had left the Lesser Teeth two years ago, abandoning all dreams of power in Argan, Hearst remained the leader of a hundred warriors who had chosen to stay in Brennan. With these fighting men and five ships at his disposal, he was rapidly becoming a rich man, daring his vessels past the Orfus pirates to trade for steel in the island of Stokos. He was now building a warehouse, and a big residence for himself made from imported cedar.

The night before, they had talked about Resbit, about the exploits of young Elkordansk, and about Aardun's first birthday. Aardun, son of Resbit and Morgan Hearst, was their second child; the first, the ill-fated Nesh Enelorf, had died of colic a few days after birth. With gossip over, it was time to talk seriously, though Yen Olass could not imagine what Hearst might want.

Inland, amidst the hath grass and the gallows trees, the sward pond lay in the centre of a piece of marshy ground. With a hand net, Yen Olass fished a dozen kellings out of the confines of the fish-garth, and placed them in a string carry. Hearst, hungry, snatched another from the water, and ate it raw. His hand hovered, posed to snatch one more.

'Hey!' said Yen Olass. 'Ease up!'

'Breaking into next week's rations, am I?'

'Something like that,' said Yen Olass.

'Now that's what I call poverty,' said Hearst. 'How would you like to earn some money?'

'This is a proposition? If you want my body . . . a hundred crowns to you. And ten more for not telling Resbit.'

'And Monogail?'

'For five crowns you can have her. And her pet dragon. But seriously . . .'

'Yes,' said Hearst. 'Seriously . . . who or what is the Silent One?'

'The what?'

'The Silent One. Of the Sisterhood.'

'Oh . . .'

Yen Olass got to her feet. With a dozen dripping quick-kicking fish in her string carry, she set off toward Skyhaven, with Hearst walking along beside her. When they came in sight of the house, they saw Monogail running over the sand, pulling along a piece of twiner vine. Quelaquix was chasing it. They settled down in the shelter of a saltwater pine and watched.

'She's a very vigorous child,' said Hearst.

'Yes,' said Yen Olass. 'And a virgin.'

'A virgin?'

'Don't sound so surprised!'

'Sorry,' said Hearst. 'It's an odd thing to say, that's all. You don't really think I . . .'

'You might want her when she's older,' said Yen Olass. 'But I spoke of virginity because you asked about the Silent One. She's a virgin. She's head of the Sisterhood. Head of all the oracles. And an oracle is . . . well, a storyteller, if anything. Sometimes an oracle shows people the hidden side of themselves. Sometimes she shows . . . possibilities.'

'Possibilities?'

'An oracle sometimes describes a possible future. She shows the consequences of actions.'

'For what purpose?'

'To discipline the lives of men.'

'She sounds like the kind of person I could live without,' said Hearst.

'You could,' said Yen Olass. 'You can. You do. But the Collosnon Empire needs this . . . this secular priesthood. If you had a week to spare, I could teach you why. But I don't know that I could feed a big hungry man like you for that long. Come on, let's go inside.'

Yen Olass cooked breakfast, and they ate together. Unlike the Yarglat, the Rovac saw nothing odd in sharing a meal with a woman.

When breakfast was over, Yen Olass bullied Hearst into helping her bring some driftwood back from the piles cached along the beach. While they were about this labour, Hearst reviewed, aloud, what he knew about Yen Olass. He had heard some of her life from her own lips, and had got much of the rest from Resbit. He knew the outlines of her life reasonably well. He knew of the three apples she had shared with the Lord Emperor Khmar.

'Do I know what I know?' said Hearst, when he had finished his story. 'Or have I been fed a fantasy?'

'It's true enough,' said Yen Olass, vaguely, watching the falling tide.

Soon the flats would be exposed, and it would be time for her to begin her day's work.

'Then I've got a proposition for you,' said Hearst.

'A hundred crowns then,' said Yen Olass. 'I told you that before. Kisses are extra.'

'No,' said Hearst. 'This is not a game. Listen: I want you to be the Silent One.'

'Too late for that,' said Yen Olass. 'I've lost my virginity long ago.'

'Let me explain,' said Hearst.

'You want your own Sisterhood in Brennan?' said Yen Olass. 'You're crazy. Why don't you have your own Rite of Purification as well? We could make ceramic tiles, just like all the Collosnon soldiers wear, paint them with spiders and—'

'Yen Olass.'

'All right,' said Yen Olass. 'Tell me what you really want.'

And she listened as he talked. When he had finished, she gave her answer:

'No.'

When Hearst tried to argue, she elaborated:

'This time, you really are crazy. It'll never work. And I'm not going to have any part of it. There are much easier ways to die much closer to home.'

And a little later, she watched him set off for Brennan, limping a little from the wound he had taken in the battle of Razorwind Pass. He was a professional hero, and would be until he died. He had other battles ahead of him—storms to fight, dragons to kill, kingdoms to win, fortunes to gain and world-conquering powers to subdue. But she was a woman with a five-year-old child to raise, and so could not venture her life in such frivolity.

CHAPTER
Thirty-seven

Living by the sea, Yen Olass had to take special care to prevent her fingernails rusting away. She painted them with imported lacquer and wore gloves when she was working out on the flats.

Shortly after Morgan Hearst had departed, she was following the receding tide out over the flats. She was armed with a probing spike, a digging stick and a swatching knife; on her back she carried a pack.

As always, there was a certain excitement in discovering what the sea had left behind it. Sometimes, in water channels gouged between sandbanks, there were big fish which she could hunt down, using the probing spike as a spear. Sometimes, after a hard blow from the west, there would be scallops lying exposed on the sand, although usually three or four days of constant storm was needed to force the scallops that far shorewards.

Today, scanning each new wave-shaped vein of shell-shatter, Yen Olass was glad to be able to dedicate herself to her work, and forget Hearst's hero-talk, so heavily larded with disturbing names from the distant past: Celadric, Meddon, York, Draven, and, most surprising of all, Eldegen Terzanagel . . .

Hunking over a big sclop of dark sea-smelling seaweed, Yen Olass found its roots clutching a lump of coal. She knifed away the seaweed and put the coal, knobbled with big pink carbuncular barnacles, into her pack. Rooting itself in the seabed, seaweed often clung to interesting things which were then brought to the flats when storm turbulence uprooted them. Once, in the winter just gone, Yen Olass had even found a glass bottle knotted in the clutches of a mass of seaweed; it was hidden away in her sand scully while she waited for an opportune time to market it.

When she had first come to Carawell, she had been frightened by these tidal flats, so different from the modest littoral zones she had seen at Favanosin and Skua. Now, after two years, she thought of this as an essentially friendly environment arranged very much for her own wellbeing and comfort— storms to recruit scallops for her kitchen, seaweed to mine the depths of the sea for her, ocean currents to bring in an endlessly renewing supply of driftwood all year round.

The further she got from the shore, the more life there was on the flats. There were holes in the sand, in which lurked funny little creatures like centipedes; swimming over the flats in the warm days of summer, she had sometimes seen them venture briefly from their holes. She saw the feeding holes of wedges and tullies; hard-shelled sand snails wormed their way across the sandflats in places where a thin slick of water still persisted; little sea anemones grew on dead shells, as did the convoluted white loops of odd little worms which, when submerged, would extend multicoloured fans—finer than eyelashes and brighter than peacocks—out into the water around them.

Yen Olass squatted down and dug enough wedges for lunch and dinner. There was an endless supply of these small shell-fish; they were a little bit tasteless, but it took very little time to gather enough for a meal. She also picked up two horse mussels and threw them into the pack. Twice the size of her hand, these oversized shellfish were too rubbery for her taste, but Quela-quix would eat them if they were chopped up fine. (And if not, then not—the lyre-cat knew exactly what he liked, and would turn up his nose at anything not prepared according to his taste.)

With this task done, Yen Olass walked out across beds of black-green seagrass to the edge of the sea, now rapidly retreat-ing toward low-water mark, habitat of whittle-crabs, snerd oc-topuses, claw-claws and luxuriant orange starfish. Out in the water lay a low, dark shape. A whale? She had heard a lot of Carawell talk about stranded whales, and she dearly wanted one of these beasts for herself—a fortune in flesh, bone, oil, am-bergris and scrimshaw teeth. Although, to be realistic, if she found one she would probably have to share it with the people at Vinyard, or lose most of it to the next tide.

Drawing near to the stranded alien, Yen Olass was disappointed to see it was not a whale but a tree. Something moved in one of the few remaining broken-off branches. It slipped down on the far side, as if it had seen her. What was it? Closing the distance, Yen Olass circled round the tree, probing spike poised to strike in case she found herself hunting something edible.

There was nothing to be seen.

Yen Olass wrinkled her nose and walked right round the tree. Twice. There was something odd here. She scrambled up onto the tree, which was bare-backed, all bark and leaves having been stripped away long ago. There was no hiding place here for anything even half the size of a kitten.

Yen Olass surveyed her world. The flats stretched away to the sea and the shore; she could make out Skyhaven in amongst the dunes and the saltwater pines, although anyone not knowing where and what to look for might easily have missed the distant cottage. A gull slid through the sky overhead, silently. There was a little wind, just enough to flay a little spume from the backs of the waves guggling at the sea's edge.

Yen Olass sneezed, three times, loudly. Then wiped her nose. She sat astride the tree as if riding a grenderstrander, and kicked its flanks with her heels.

'Come on, tree. Where's your rider? Give!'

But the tree maintained an obdurate silence.

Yen Olass got to her feet and walked the length of the tree, bending down now and then to inspect marks gouged into the wood. Some were recent. And they sure weren't made by seagulls. She took another look at her surroundings. There were three places to hide: in the tree itself, under the tree, or under the sand.

Yen Olass rapped at the tree with her digging stick. Thunk thunk. It sounded solid. Could something have dug its way under the tree? It looked like it was firmly bedded in the sand . . . unlikely. She took another look at the sand, considering the nuances of shape and texture. She paid special care to the sand beneath the hair-thick slices of water still easing off the flats. That was the natural place for any fugitive to bury itself, knowing the water would soon confuse the marks of its retreat underground.

After long and careful scrutiny, Yen Olass identified five sinister low-slung humps in the sand. Each almost imperceptibly raised disc was about the length of her arm. Whatever they were, they had gone to ground, each a horse-length apart from the next. Yen Olass found she was frightened.

But they had run away from her. Which meant they must be more frightened than she was. And they were small compared to her—whatever they were. Crocodiles? No, crocodiles were thin and lean, like little dragons without wings. Anyway, they were friendly, good-natured beasts, content to live in their own rivers in unimaginably distant warm-weather lands, maybe eating the occasional incautious explorer now and then, but otherwise largely content to live and let live. Unlike . . .

Unlike the Swarms, for instance.

Despite herself, Yen Olass recalled tales Morgan Hearst had told her of the onslaught of the Swarms. Pushing north, destroying civilisations as they went, they had been defeated in a battle at the southern border of Estar. Mountains had been positioned across the Salt Road, blocking the advance of the Swarms. But now, according to Hearst, the Swarms were building their own coast road, a slick grey highway outflanking the coastal mountains guarding Estar. He claimed to have seen it as he sailed close inshore on one of his trips to or from the distant island of Stokos.

He had also told her about the monsters that tried to venture north over the mountains . . . or to come by sea.

Yen Olass counted her enemies. All five were still there. Creatures of the Swarms? No, the idea was ridiculous. The

Swarms were huge. Much bigger than people. And they lived above water, not under it.

As Yen Olass was thinking this, there was a 'shlock' as a red tube burst free from the sand. It was about as long and as fat as her thumb; it looked like an obscene little prick sticking out of the flats, waiting to be reaped, but she supposed it was probably a breathing tube. Shortly, there were five breathing tubes protruding into the air.

So these creatures could not live underwater.

Whatever they were, they had to count as invaders. Living on the tree for days on end, they were doubtless weak, with little fight left in them. But once let them get to shore, and they would rest up, and feed, and grow stronger. And maybe . . . yes, maybe they would breed.

Yen Olass thought about running to Vinyard to get help. Then she remembered the mobile, slippery form which had slipped down out of sight as she approached the tree. Once she left, these things would move. By the time she got to Vinyard, they would have hidden themselves in the hinterland. And, ten crowns to half a pickle, nobody in Vinyard would believe her if she came bearing a tale of monsters from the sea. They would think she was seeking revenge for all she had endured in the way of mythical land octopuses and crawling lightning.

Yen Olass took off her pack and hung it on one of the tree branches. She took out the lump of coal and smashed it. She threw one small piece onto each of the concealed aliens. Then she gathered up her weapons and jumped down to the sand. As she landed, the red breathing tubes retracted smartly, but the pieces of glittering black coal marked each of her enemies.

'Gah!' shouted Yen Olass, driving her probing spike into the back of the nearest alien.

The sand heaved up. She whacked it with her digging stick. It subsided. Yen Olass stamped down on the sand and pulled out her probing spike. It was stained with green.

A sucking sound behind her gave warning.

Yen Olass wheeled. She saw a lump of coal sliding away as a creature heaved itself up from the sand. As it leered up into the daylight, she saw eight legs, vicious underslung claws, a clutch of groping feelers and a dozen nameless lugs of green and yellow flesh. She speared it with her probing spike. The creature flailed. She tried to withdraw her weapon. The claws gnashed at the steel. It was stuck. So she pushed instead, trying to drive it right through the creature.

Something grabbed at her boot.

Yen Olass screamed. At her feet, an armlength disc of faded rainbow colours. It was encroaching on her boot. Green slime oozed from its back: this was the one she had wounded. She kicked at it, releasing herself.

She lost her hold on her probing spike, and the alien she was spiking fell on her weapon. Now the steel was trapped under the creature's weight. Now she could only see its shell, instead of the fearsome apparatus underneath the shell.

The alien which had grabbed her boot had another go. Yen Olass kicked it away, then jumped on it with both feet. Its shell broke with a sick crack.

With a sucking sound, the remaining three enemies scabbed out of the sand. Briefly, she saw their undershell apparatus as they climbed up from their hides. Then, legs and jaws hidden under their shells, they scuttled toward her.

Yen Olass threw her digging stick at the nearest and took to the tree. The aliens followed. Wood ripped and tore as they gouged for holds in the tree trunk. Yen Olass unhooked her pack and hurled it with all her strength. One of the enemy went down.

And now?

One of the aliens swung itself up onto the broad top of the tree trunk. It scuttled towards her. One was still climbing up. Yen Olass jumped, hitting the climbing alien with her feet together. The impact smashed her enemy loose from the tree. They landed in the sand together.

Yen Olass looked up.

The creature left on top of the tree stared down after her. Moving too fast, it lost its grip and tumbled down. When it landed, Yen Olass slashed it. Her swatching knife tore into its shell. Then she jumped backwards as the creature rushed her.

Running swiftly on its low-slung legs, it slammed into her at knee-height. Yen Olass was knocked backwards. The next moment, the creature was greeding at her stomach. She slammed her strength upwards, feeding it steel. Her swatching knife ripped into something soft.

She heaved at the weight above her and rolled the alien onto its back. It lay there, apparatus kicking. Yen Olass screamed, and hacked into it with her knife. She killed it, killed it, killed it, shouting, spitting, slashing, swearing.

A noise behind her.

Yen Olass wheeled to find one wounded alien dragging itself toward her. She sprang forward on the attack, jumped on its back and gashed its shell open. It started to gyrate and buck, trying to throw her off. Anchoring herself with her knife, Yen Olass hung on for dear life. Every time the creature paused for a moment, she whipped the knife out and slammed it into a new spot.

When it stopped moving once and for all, she gouged a deep channel in its shell until it was just about cut in half. Then she went to work on the others to make sure they were dead for real and forever. She counted the corpses. One, two, three, four, five. She counted them again, to make sure.

Her stomach was hurting. As if it was burning. Shedding her clothes, she found the alien which had crawled over her had ripped right through her weather jacket and a woolen singlet. There were half a dozen shallow scratches on her belly. Green gunk from the body of the dying monster had reached her wounds. That might be partly to blame for the pain.

Yen Olass shovelled away sand in the centre of one of the thin slicks of water still streaming off the flats—the water would still be draining away even when the tide returned. Water spilled into the hole she dug, and she washed her wounds, cleansing them vigorously. That hurt, but she thought it best to have them clean.

The wounds bled a little; she decided to leave them open, to bleed freely into the air. Blood would carry away the last contamination. Blood was clean, unlike that filthy green monster slime. She did not want to put on her contaminated clothing, but, even in its torn and tattered state, it was too valuable to throw away. Though her weather jacket was not going to be any good for anything other than patching. It had survived all the adventures of six years and more—and now it was ruined, just like that! How was she going to replace it? Still, it had saved her life—she could not complain too much.

Yen Olass looked out to sea. The Skowshan Rocks were uncovered by now. If she went out there, she could pick some sendigraz. Out there, too, were the dark mud sands concealing the remains of an ancient forest which had branched strong and tall many thousands of years in the past, when the sea was land. It was out there that she did her work, prospecting for amber, sometimes picking up the occasional lump uncovered by the sea, and otherwise testing the sand with her probing spike till she struck something which felt promising enough to dig for.

Her probing spike.

It was still under the corpse of one of her enemies. Yen Olass recovered it, and shouldered her pack. She was starting to cool down now; it was time to start moving. No work today, that was for certain. Back to Skyhaven. What she needed was a warm fire, a cup of mulled wine and then . . . then maybe straight to bed.

She counted the corpses one last time, then set off. When she had gone a dozen paces, she turned and looked back, in case any were moving. She saw a gull alight on one dead body; it stood there, its knees bent back at an impossible angle. Where one gull discovers carrion, soon there will be a hundred. But when Yen Olass looked back a little later, the one gull had flown away, and no new birds had arrived to replace it. The aliens had been tested, tasted and found wanting. That, to Yen Olass, was proof that she had just killed five creatures of the Swarms. Baby ones, no doubt. She was glad they were dead.

The weight of her pack comforted her as she hiked on. She paused to gather a couple more horse mussels and dig some more wedges; she felt it might be a good idea to spend the next day in bed. At the moment, she felt strong and victorious, but she could expect a wave of exhaustion and a backwash of fear to take her under sooner or later.

CHAPTER
Thirty-eight

Arriving at Skyhaven, Yen Olass dumped her pack down by the door, which had been left ajar.

'Monogail!' said Olass. 'I'm home!'

She went inside. The briefest glance showed her everything was in order; her home was so much a part of herself that the slightest disturbance would have sounded an alarm note in her brain.

Automatically, she reached up and touched the gollock concealed above the door lintel. It was still there. Tonight she would be glad that her cottage had strong stone walls and a strong wooden door; she would be glad of the comfort of heavy steel honed to a razor edge.

'Monogail!'

Quelaquix was absent. There was nothing surprising about that. Yen Olass was back early; usually she did not return until the rising tide drove her in from the flats. The cat knew that, and timed his returns to coincide with the arrival of fresh food; that cat had all the angles figured out.

Yen Olass examined her wounds. They had stopped bleeding and were crusting over; in a few days there would be nothing left to show for them. She pulled on a fresh woollen singlet and a linen jacket. She still mourned for her weather jacket, ripped apart by some stinking arseblind monster.

Finding some hot coals in the ashes, Yen Olass got a fire going; she was glad she did not have to sit down and work with tinder and flint, because she was a bit shaky. She emptied out her pack, and piled all the shellfish into her one and only bucket. With a layer of fresh water over them, they would stay fresh until evening and still be alive tomorrow; she had learnt long ago that shellfish die quickly, and are dangerous if eaten once they are dead.

She went outside to draw water.

Removing one of the boards that covered the well, she thought that Monogail should really do this job. It was time for the child to start doing a bit more round the house. But she was probably down at the sward pond, hunting frogs or watching Quelaquix stalking birds. Let her have her childhood, then . . . she might have precious little else in life.

Without looking or thinking, Yen Olass dipped a hand into the water. She drank from her cupped hand, surprised to find she was thirsty. The water was cool, and tasted good.

Looking into the well, she saw . . .

Five golden discs, shimmering as the water settled . . .

For a moment, gripped by a shock of occult dread, Yen Olass thought that some witchery had translated the corpses of the five dead aliens and placed them, as discs of hostile energy, at the bottom of her well.

Then the water settled, and she saw the discs for what they were. Gold crowns, from Sung, adorned with the familiar profile of Skan Askander. Again she thought of the five alien corpses lying dead on the sand. Five gold pieces. One for each dead alien. Magic?

Then she remembered her joke with Morgan Hearst:

—And Monogail?

—For five crowns you can have her. And her pet dragon.

She looked down into the water again. Counted the coins. Pulled them out, dripping wet. Their weight almost convinced her. She looked for the familiar denizens of the well; shaken by her encounter with the five monsters, she had forgotten about them till now. They were gone. The frog Alamanda and the fish Straff—both gone.

Yen Olass stood up.

She looked around. What about her chickens? Usually they were scratching around within sight of the cottage; they never went far. Had they been shut up in the hen coop? She checked. No. Nothing. A chiz, then? Had a chiz been raiding? She checked her chiz trap, and found a twist of paper in the strangling noose she had rigged up with such skill and care.

Opening the paper, Yen Olass found words in Galish orthography, inscribed with a bold, clear hand:

'One chiz. Success at last. Yours, Vexbane.'

It had to be a message from Morgan Hearst. And he dared to joke! Yen Olass strode inside and seized her gollock. A world-destroying anger boiled inside her. Blood burned in her cheeks. The world rolled under her feet; her every movement was gifted with effortless power, as if she were riding a stallion. Buoyed up by her wrath, she was ready for a killing.

Swiftly she secured the house, closing the shutters and wedging the door shut so no stormwind would burst it open. She wondered what to do with the five gold crowns. Take them into Brennan and throw them in Hearst's face? No. The rat-rapist could give her another five by way of apology. If there was anything left of him by the time she was finished.

She thought of going back inside to hide the coins behind the loose stone in the floor of the fireplace. But then, if any stranger made free with her house while she was away, a fire lit to cook or to warm the house would melt the gold. She could always cache them in her sand scully hidden away in the dunes; they would be safe enough there, along with her store of amber dug from the flats and ambergris scavenged from the shoreline. But she didn't want to take the time to dig down to the scully then camouflage it again.

Yen Olass hid the coins in the bottom of the well under half a finger of sand. They'd be safe enough there. She hefted her gollock and set off for Brennan.

The party waiting in ambush caught her when she was striding through the little wood beyond the sward pond. They disarmed her easily, laughing at her threats and curses, and escorted her the rest of the way to Brennan.

*   *   *

In a house in Brennan, Yen Olass found Monogail tucked up in a warm bed and sleeping soundly, with Quelaquix bulked down beside her. In a big earthenware dish, a paradise of rocks and weed and water, Straff and Alamanda were similarly settled for the night.

When Yen Olass had been given the opportunity to check her sleeping child, she was led to a large room where Morgan Hearst reclined on a couch, waiting for her. Half a dozen men were seated on chairs or lounging against the walls: Yen Olass recognised the text-master, Eldegen Terzanagel. How long was it since she had seen him last? Six years? Or seven? She was tired, and could not work it out.

Hearst stood up. The couch had belonged to a merchant who had owned the house before him, and it did not really suit him; there would be no couches in the house of cedar which he was now building for himself.

'Yen Olass,' he said. 'What a pleasure to see you. What brings you here?'

'A matter of blood money,' said Yen Olass. 'You owe me five crowns for five chickens. Pay now, if you value your life.'

She would have been reassured if Hearst had laughed, but he did not. Instead, he smiled, a little sadly.

'Yen Olass,' said Hearst. 'We're committed. We can't go back now. We need you.'

Yen Olass understood that he meant what he said. He would do whatever he had to to ensure her compliance. If forced to it, he would threaten to torture her child. If she resisted, he might well carry out that threat. He was playing for high stakes: control of the western coast of Argan. In that game, a child—even a child like Monogail, sole product of Yen Olass's loins—was expendable.

Now it was all too much for her. She had endured a terrible day—the fight with the monsters, the loss of her child, the ambush on the path to Brennan, and now this ultimatum. Unable to stand it any longer, Yen Olass broke down and wept.

'Take her away,' said Hearst, a little wearily. 'We can talk tomorrow.'

Someone came out from behind an embroidered screen.

'Yen Olass.'

It was Resbit.

Still sobbing bitterly, Yen Olass allowed herself to be led away. Resbit took her to a small bedroom and settled her down for the night. Yen Olass thought Resbit was going to stay, but instead she bestowed a chaste kiss on the forehead of her long-ago lover, and withdrew.

Yen Olass was left to weep alone.

*   *   *

After a while, Yen Olass calmed herself, and began to take stock of the situation. She did not appear to be locked in. Perhaps she could escape. Perhaps she could escape with Monogail, stealing a boat and sailing to Sung. That would be difficult, because she had never learnt to sail. But she refused to give up without a fight.

Shortly, Yen Olass left her room, and went exploring. She found the house positively infested with guards, all of them armed and awake. A few, Collosnon deserters, mocked her with a Collosnon soldier's salute. One still wore the hateful ceramic tile which was issued as part of the Rite of Purification, but which, to Yen Olass, was always associated with the destruction of her homeland.

She found her way to the kitchen, where she found two men sitting at a table, gnawing on hunks of bread and drinking some kind of hot brew.

'Hello, Yen Olass,' said one of them, winking at her.

She said nothing, but began to rummage around, looking for things to loot and plunder. She found plenty.

'Don't you recognize me?' said the man she had ignored.

'Should I?' said Yen Olass.

'The name's Occam,' said the man. 'We escaped from Estar together.'

'Oh,' said Yen Olass. 'I remember. You were a sailor.'

'A sea captain.'

'Captain, then. What're you doing here?'

'That's a long story. Sit down and I'll tell you all about it.'

Yen Olass sat down, and pulled his mug toward her. She sniffed it.

'What's this?' said Yen Olass.

'Coffee,' said Occam.

'And what's that?'

'Expensive.'

Yen Olass sipped it.

'Bitter,' she said, and got up.

'Aren't you going to stay?' said Occam.

'Not if that's all you've got to drink,' said Yen Olass.

And she completed her looting by abstracting what was left of his bread from his plate, vanishing from the kitchen while Occam's companion was still spluttering with laughter.

Yen Olass gnawed on the bread as she made her way to Monogail's room. With so many guards around, she could not escape, but she could certainly sleep with her child. Though Monogail had celebrated her first lustrum, she had yet to spend a night away from her mother, and Yen Olass, for her part, did not think she could bear to spend this night alone.

Monogail woke when Yen Olass slipped into bed.

'Is that you, mam?'

'That's right.'

'Uncle Hearst said you were coming. I waited for ages, but you didn't come. So I went to sleep.'

'Well, I'm here now,' said Yen Olass. 'So you can sleep now.'

And sleep they did.

CHAPTER
Thirty-nine

Yen Olass woke to find morning sunlight streaming through a window of white waxed paper. Somewhere, someone was drilling troops, shouting harsh commands in Ordhar.

'Why's the man shouting, mam?' said Monogail.

'Because he's warped,' said Yen Olass. 'Come on, let's go to the kitchen.'

In the kitchen, chefs and kitchen hands were bustling round making breakfast for Hearst and all his braves. Yen Olass saw two plates heaped high with steamed vegetables, rice and gaplax. She snaffled them.

'Hey,' shouted a man. 'That's reserved for Morgan Hearst and Watashi!'

'I know,' said Yen Olass. 'I was sent to get them. Come on, Monogail.'

And she exited from the kitchen bearing her trophies. They found their way to a courtyard, which was empty but for an old man painting oval ceramic tiles according to the Collosnon military fashion. They sat down to eat, using their fingers. The man drilling troops was still bellowing at the top of his lungs, as if hoping to be heard 'in backwater Lorp', as the local expression had it.

Yen Olass and Monogail were still eating when a shadow blocked out the light. Looking up, Yen Olass saw a big, big man, a hulking brute with ox-yoke shoulders and sheep-strangling hands.

'Why!' she said, with pleasure. 'Nan Nulador!'

Nan Nulador nodded gravely.

'So this is the child,' he said.

'Yes,' said Yen Olass. 'The last child of the Lord Emperor Khmar. She's got his chin.'

'I cannot speak for the Lord Emperor Khmar,' said Nan Nulador solemnly.

'Nobody's asking you to,' said Yen Olass, supposing he was making a clumsy joke of some kind. 'What're you doing here? I thought Chonjara was in Celadric's dungeons.'

'He is,' said Nan Nulador. 'He released me from my oath of loyalty. I took service with the prince. So I ended up on the Greater Teeth. We—'

'I know the story,' said Yen Olass.

'We got to meet some of the pirates,' said Nan Nulador. 'One of them was Mellicks.'

'Yes?' said Yen Olass.

'Does that name mean anything to you?'

'No,' said Yen Olass. 'Here, do you want some gaplax? It's very good. They cooked it especially for me. Take some.'

'No,' said Nan Nulador. 'This Mellicks—he had yellow eyes. He got them from a wishing machine.'

'Oh, him,' said Yen Olass. 'I'd forgotten about him.'

'He said you got your child from the same machine,' said Nan Nulador. 'Now I see your child. It has yellow eyes.'

Monogail munched gaplax, and stared at Nan Nulador, too shy to speak or ask questions.

'Mellicks must've been drunk,' said Yen Olass. 'You were at Nightcaps yourself. You know the child is Khmar's.'

Nan Nulador picked up her hand. She twisted it away, cutting him with one of her fingernails. He stared at the bright flash of blood burning out of his flesh.

'Claws,' he said 'What else changed when you made your pact with the powers of death? What else did you ask for?'

There was an ugly expression on his face.

Yen Olass got to her feet.

'Hearst!' she roared.

A guard looked into the courtyard.

'Get me Hearst!' ordered Yen Olass. 'Now!'

Very shortly, Nan Nulador was being dragged away by a squad of guards, shouting and struggling. Yen Olass was more than a little relieved to see the last of him.

'What's that thing he said, mam?' asked Monogail.

'Eat your gaplax,' said Yen Olass.

'But what's a dralkosh, mam?'

'A bad word.'

'Like tit?'

'Yes.'

'And bum?'

'Yes.'

'And burdok malor skida dik?' said Monogail innocently.

'That's enough!' said Yen Olass sharply.

She was a little shocked. Honestly! Where did they learn these things?

'Eat your gaplax, then go and find Elkordansk,' said Yen Olass, 'and play somewhere quietly.'

*　　*　　*

Hearst was in a bad mood when he met Yen Olass. She had stolen his gaplax, she had quarrelled with one of his allies, and her child had led Elkordansk on a raiding mission into his wine cellar, damaging, among other things, a year's supply of coffee.

'Don't worry about it," said Yen Olass. 'That coffee stuff's vomit-making. I tasted it last night. It stinks. You're better off without it. Anyway, once you're master of Argan you'll have no trouble replacing it. As for the gaplax—I want the same again tomorrow.'

'It's not good manners to make demands like that,' said Hearst. 'A guest has obligations, you know.'

'I'm the Silent One now. The Silent One always gets gaplax for breakfast. That's the tradition. Now, as for Nan Nulador—'

'Yes, Nan Nulador. That very valuable warrior—'

'Is harmless as long as nobody puts ideas into his head. But now someone's managed to do just that, and there's so little competition that it's running his brain for him. He thinks I'm a...'

'A dralkosh?'

'Yes,' said Yen Olass, relieved that she did not have to explain.

'So what is a dralkosh?'

'I thought you knew.'

'I'd never heard the word until today. Monogail said Nan Nulador had used it. She asked what it meant.'

'So what did you tell her?'

'I told her she had other things to worry about. Yen Olass, did you know these two children broached my only cask of Carvel Squen? What's more, they were drinking it!'

'A little wine is good for the digestion. Now listen—I'm going to tell you about the Yarglat and the dralkosh.'

She told him all about it, then said:

'I'm surprised you didn't know that to begin with.'

'Yen Olass,' said Hearst, 'I know bits and pieces of twenty different languages and fifty different cultures, but I can't know everything.'

'Well, you should learn some more about the Yarglat, and fast,' said Yen Olass. 'Before you have to deal with them face to face. Now I've got something else to tell you about.'

'Before you start,' said Hearst, 'how are we going to punish the children?'

'If they've drunk as much as you seem to think they have,'

said Yen Olass, 'their hangovers will be punishment enough. Now listen. This is important.'

And she told him of the five monsters she had killed on the flats. Hearst identified them as keflos.

'Baby ones,' said Hearst.

'Baby ones? Blood's grief, what do the parents look like?'

'Well,' said Hearst. 'The adults—'

'No,' said Yen Olass, cutting him off, 'I don't want to know. I just don't want to know.'

'Don't be afraid of them,' said Hearst. 'They can be killed— you've found that out for yourself. When I rule the west coast of Argan—'

'If you rule the west coast of Argan.'

'When I rule the west coast of Argan,' said Hearst, his voice rolling on, 'we'll wipe them out. Eliminate them.'

Yen Olass knew he would never be able to eliminate her nightmares.

*   *   *

That evening, Yen Olass visited Nan Nulador in the dungeon adjacent to the wine cellar. She assured him that he would be released once she and Hearst returned from their dangerous mission—and would also be set free if they died on that mission. Nan Nulador just swore at her.

She knew what his problem was. He had trusted her, and had benefited greatly from that trust. She had saved his wife, and thus had given him a son. So now, finding that she was a dralkosh, he was faced with an enormous disaster. Since Yen Olass —a dralkosh!—had comforted him when he wondered if he should put his wife to death, that meant his wife must be a dralkosh too. And his son? The child of a dralkosh . . .

Yen Olass gave up in the end, and left him. She looked in on the wine cellar, and located Hearst's precious cask of Carvel Squen, which was still nine parts full. She summoned two soldiers and pointed them at it.

'Morgan Hearst has commanded you to take that cask of wine and share it amongst your comrades. So take it—then come back and take this one as well.'

They were good soldiers—the best. They obeyed without question.

*   *   *

Morgan Hearst was woken in the middle of the night when a brawl broke out amongst his roistering soldiers. He was enraged to find his men all drunk, and his fury was not mollified when they toasted him when he appeared on the scene. And his anger when he found Yen Olass had escaped would not bear description.

By dawn, scouting parties were spreading out all over Cara- well, searching for the missing woman and her child. But it was not until noon that Hearst got his first news of the fugitives. A fishing smack was reported wrecked on the Dungon Banks, two leagues offshore.

Hearst mounted a rescue mission, taking a longboat crewed by experienced sailors out to the Dungon Banks. He found the boat wrecked beyond repair. Yen Olass was sitting on deck fil- ing her nails, which, though they were steel, still grew, and needed to be kept in order. Monogail was playing on an ex- posed sandbank, making sand castles.

Hearst saw at a glance that the fishing smack would be im- possible to salvage. In the interests of public relations—the islanders could make very dangerous enemies—he would have to pay the owner full compensation.

'You,' said Hearst to Yen Olass, as he took her aboard, 'are staying under close arrest until we leave.'

'And when is that?' said Yen Olass.

'As soon as possible!' said Hearst. 'Before you organize my head onto a platter or something.'

'I've thought about it,' said Yen Olass. 'It wouldn't be im- possible.'

He hoped she was only joking.

CHAPTER
Forty

On a ship in the harbour of Brennan on the island of Carawell in the archipelago known as the Lesser Teeth, the oracle Yen Olass Ampadara said goodbye to her child Monogail, who was given over to the care of a young Rovac warrior by the name of Altol Stokpol. The warrior was scarcely twenty years old, and to Yen Olass he looked like a boy. His wife was even younger; Yen Olass had briefed her successfully on the care of frogs and fish, but had found it difficult to convey the niceties of the feeding, grooming and sleeping habits of the ghosts of long-departed dragons. Yen Olass could only hope that Monogail would be all right.

The ship slipped out of the harbour that evening, and sailed south by night. Very shortly—in three or four days at the most —they would be landing at Iglis. Yen Olass would once more find herself under the jurisdiction of the Collosnon Empire. She remembered precisely what that empire had done to her. She suffered nightmares in which the coarse breath of men oppressed her, in which a knife cut away her flesh, in which a needle stabbed at her privacy—and, waking from those nightmares, she knew them as memories.

The ship they sailed on was a big-bellied merchantman. There was a stateroom in the stern, which was reserved for Yen Olass, so she could prepare herself in the little time which was available to them. The day after they left Brennan, the warrior Watashi came to the stateroom and found Yen Olass dressed in white silk, her face veiled. She was positioning Indicators on a Casting Board, muttering to herself as she did so; a copy of the Book of the Sisterhood lay open beside her.

As the door swung open on its leather hinges, Yen Olass looked up. She drew herself up to her full height, and demanded, in a clear and penetrating voice:

'Who is it who intrudes upon the Silent One?'

'What?' said Watashi, who did not understand, because Yen Olass had addressed him in Eparget, the ruling language of the far-distant city of Gendormargensis.

Yen Olass rephrased the question in the Galish Trading Tongue.

'You know who I am,' said Watashi easily.

'I know you as a barbarian from beyond the Pale,' said Yen Olass, still practising the grand manner of the Silent One.

The Silent One is silent only in that she does not give readings; otherwise, her voice is a formidable weapon. Apart from the need for practice, Yen Olass was genuinely curious to know who Watashi was. They had been introduced, but in the confusion of plotting, scheming, arguments, child-care arrangements, briefings and conspiracies, Yen Olass had entirely forgotten who he was.

'I am Watashi,' said Watashi, matching her own grand manner. 'Son of Farfalla the kingmaker, ruler of the Harvest Plains. In my own right, I am master of the island of Stokos, which is mine by right of conquest. I am a companion of the quest-hero Morgan Hastsword Hearst, dragonbane; I have fought by his side, matching my sword against his enemies.'

'Then hear me, Watashi, son of Farfalla. Know that you stand in the presence of the Silent One of the Sisterhood; make reverence accordingly.'

Watashi laughed.

'For a slave girl, you've got quite a way with the language,' he said.

'Whom are you addressing?' said Yen Olass, in a voice that would have frosted dragon-flame at fifty paces.

'The slave I see before me,' said Watashi, who did not appreciate his danger.

'An oracle is a pivot,' said Yen Olass. 'The turning point of the destinies of lives and nations.'

'Pivot?' said Watashi, querying the Eparget word she had used for want of any equivalent in Galish. 'What kind of sex toy is that?'

'One that castrates the unwary,' said Yen Olass.

'Then perhaps I should have worn my armour,' said Watashi, amused by the way in which Hearst's slave girl felt so free to contend with him.

'You are not amusing me,' said Yen Olass.

'It is not my function to amuse you,' said Watashi, now annoyed at her pretensions.

Reaching out, he lifted the veil from her face. He kissed her, pressing his lips against hers, grappling with her when she resisted. This was a mistake, as he soon found out. However, by the time he recovered consciousness, Yen Olass was ready to forgive him; she poured him a cup of wine, and, now that he had learnt a measure of respect, they talked as equals.

For hours, as the ship sailed south, Yen Olass quizzed Watashi about his recent history. She had heard one story from Morgan Hearst, but she wanted to know whether she had been told the truth. Watashi confirmed the outline of the tale she had been told, and filled in some of the details for her.

Alarmed by the incursions of the Swarms, the Lord Emperor Celadric had ordered his brothers to secure the western coast of Argan. Knowing this task was beyond their combined military strength, Meddon and York had dragged their heels. Urged on by his military advisors Chonjara and Saquarius, the lame-brained Exedrist had declared his brothers traitors, and had attempted to have them executed. Saquarius had bungled the job, which had cost him his life—his had been a brief and inglorious career, from deserter to fighting soldier to general to the gallows—and in the subsequent brief civil war in Trest and Estar, Exedrist had been killed and Chonjara imprisoned.

Celadric, investigating, had discovered that the Swarms were stronger than his advisors had previously let him know. Realising that Meddon and York were right in refusing to commit their forces against the full strength of the Swarms, Celadric had sought allies, travelling south in force to Stokos. There, as a seasoned and skillful diplomat bearing gifts and peace treaties, he had been welcomed; the Swarms had been making local incursions across the seat to Stokos, and Watashi was ready to commit himself to a joint operation to recover the west of Argan.

To celebrate the new alliance, Celadric planned to remove the heads of his two dangerous brothers, and place Watashi in command of all forces in Argan. The armies of the Collosnon Empire, drawn from many foreign parts and united only by their common knowledge of the command language Ordhar, would have no difficulty in accepting a stranger as commander.

Celadric and Watashi had travelled north from Stokos on the same ship, bound for Estar. However, a storm had scattered their convoy, leaving them without an escort; the pirates of the

Greater Teeth had fallen upon their single ship and had taken them prisoner.

Draven, lord of the Greater Teeth, had sent word to Meddon and York in Estar. If they wanted to see Celadric alive, they would have to hand over a ransom—gold, silver, warm wool and a woman. The woman was the Princess Quenerain, previously a mistress to the General Chonjara.

Before a reply could come from Estar, Celadric had suborned some of Draven's men with promises of power and money. With that help, the prisoner had broken out of their holding cells; they had fought their way to the pirate harbour; under the command of Watashi, the survivors had escaped to sea.

'But Celadric . . .'

'He died?'

'I don't know. I hope not. We were separated when it was sword to sword. After that, I didn't see him any more.'

'What about the Silent One?'

'Everglen Tamara? She got herself killed. An arrow. Through the back and out through the front. You won't be seeing her any more, I'm afraid.'

'I never knew her, at least not on a personal basis,' said Yen Olass.

The words she used for 'personal basis' were the Galish words 'ken shen lokday', literally 'bargain-making level'.

Watashi continued with his story.

With pirate vessels in hot pursuit, the escapers had run north, thinking to lose the enemy in amongst the shoals and shallows of the Lesser Teeth. They had succeeded in doing previously that. They had also succeeded in wrecking their ship on a sandbar. Once ashore, they were swiftly rounded up by men under the command of Morgan Hearst.

Now Hearst was risking his life—and theirs—in an attempt to finesse control of the west of Argan. Their party, ostensibly led by Watashi, was going to land at Iglis and claim the ransom for Celadric, stating that the Lord Emperor was now held prisoner on the Lesser Teeth.

Once in possession of the ransom, Hearst intended to barter with Draven for Celadric's life. And once in possession of the emperor, he intended to negotiate an agreement with that worthy which would give him, Morgan Hearst, title to at least the west of Argan—preferably all of it—and command of all the imperial forces on Argan.

The plan was, to put it mildly, hair-raising. So many things could go wrong. What if Meddon and York decided that they would prefer their brother Celadric dead? What if Draven attempted to take the ransom by man force rather than exchange? What if Celadric subsequently reneged on any arrangements made under duress, and made it his business to eliminate Morgan Hearst and his entourage? What if Watashi . . . well, there was a simple way to find out about Watashi.

'Don't you feel cheated?' said Yen Olass. 'Hearst is trying to take what was going to be yours—command of the west.'

Watashi grinned, denied nothing.

'I've sworn an oath to support him until he gets Celadric in his power,' said Watashi. 'After that, there'll be plenty of time later for a trial of strength.'

When their interview was at an end, Yen Olass sent Watashi away with orders to fetch Eldegen Terzanagel. The text-master entered the stateroom looking old—Yen Olass had a hazy notion that he was now a bit over sixty-five—and weatherbeaten. And rather ill. Yen Olass realized he was feeling seasick. She had been too busy to pay much attention to the motion of the ship, but she realized they were lubbering through the waves in a way which might well disconcert those with weak stomachs.

'Sit,' said Yen Olass curtly.

She felt a little thrill of power as Terzanagel sat. She remembered those years long ago, when she had been brought to Gendormargensis in chains and he had purchased her at auction. And had then tried to rape her. She had resisted, biting him— she wondered if he still had the scars. While he tried to think what to do with her, she had been kept locked up in a pitch-black cellar with only rats for company. In those hours of terror and darkness, she had sworn that she would kill him, slowly, if he ever came into her power.

Now she had the opportunity. Terzanagel, was expendable; she was sure Morgan Hearst would not object if she wanted to have the old man skinned alive. She could do the job herself, with a small, sharp knife. She could castrate him first . . .

'It's been a long time,' said Terzangagel, speaking in Eparget.

Hearing that familiar voice once more, hearing that familiar language, Yen Olass suffered unexpected pangs of homesickness. Terzanagel was her one and only link to so much which had once been dear to her. It all came back to her with a rush:

her room in tooth 44 in Moon Stallion Strait, her humble little corner table in the Canoozerie, her balcony seat in the Hall of Heavenly Music, her horse Snut, her cat Lefrey, her dreamquilt and her seven-stringed klon.

'It has been a long time,' said Yen Olass.

Tears started at her eyes as, with a shock, she realised how often and how totally she had been displaced, suffering the loss of an entire way of life. She had been a child in her homeland of Monogail, a slave in Gendormargensis, a translator with an imperial army of invasion, a refugee in Penvash, a pioneer by Lake Armansis, an amber hunter in the Lesser Teeth—and now she was launched on her most dangerous venture yet, impersonating the Silent One of the Sisterhood.

Her veil hid her tears.

She wondered if Terzanagel was a potential traitor. No. He had broken imperial law by leaving the continent of Tameran, without permission; for that breach of law, his fellow text-masters would arrange his death no matter what pardons he obtained from any other quarter. Terzanagel had placed himself outside the protection of imperial law; he was committed to their own cause.

'I never thought to see you again,' said Terzanagel.

'Or me you,' said Yen Olass. 'Tell me, what happened to Nuana Nanalako. Tell me all about it. Leave nothing out.'

So Eldegen Terzanagel told the story of how he and Nuana had left Tameran, departing from Port Domax on a voyage south which was supposed to take them, eventually, to the Stepping Stone Islands, where he had planned to complete his researches into the life and works of that greatest of all poets of antiquity, Saba Yavendar.

He spun her a lurid tale of piracy, shipwreck, mountan treks, dragons, nomad tribes, imprisonment, escape, capture, torture and slavery. Having lived through so many incredible events herself, Yen Olass could hardly doubt him. Terzanagel had last seen Nuana in Havanar a Asral, a seaport on the island of Asral in the Ocean of Cambria, east of the Inner Waters. She had been sold to a ship owner; he had been sold to a visiting wizard, who, delighted at his command of the High Speech of wizards, had employed him as a scribe.

When the Swarms breached the defences of the Great Dyke, Drangsturm, and started their invasion of the lands to the north, the wizards had retreated from the castles they had occupied near Drangsturm. In the company of his master, Eldegen Ter-zanagel had fled to the Harvest Plains; on the journey, his master had died of cholera. After many vicissitides, Terzanagel had finished up on Stokos in the court of Lord Watashi, working as a scribe and translator.

'And now,' said Terzanagel, winding up his long and weary tale, 'they want me on this adventure as a pair of eyes and ears. And you . . . if I may be so bold as to ask?'

'The same,' said Yen Olass. 'This interview is now termi-nated.'

It was fear which made her conclude their meeting so abruptly. She disliked talking about what she had to do. As the Silent One, she could review the readings of every oracle she could have brought before her. Now that Trest and Estar were established provinces of the empire, they had their usual complement of oracles. Few of these would have seen the Silent One in years, and none would have been personally acquainted with her—but any one of these intelligent young women might discover a mistake which would betray Yen Olass as an imposter.

And then?

Yen Olass could only imagine the kind of punishment which might befall a slave who impersonated the Silent One. If she got off lightly, they might let rats eat her breasts, then take her out and burn her alive. On the other hand, if they decided to be vindictive . . .

Pushing such thoughts out of her mind, she turned her atten-tion once more to the Indicators, the Casting Board and the Book of the Sisterhood, struggling to master delicacies of tech-nique and interpretation which had once been second nature to her. It had indeed been a long time.

*   *   *

That evening, Yen Olass slept alone for the second night in succession. She found it hard to get to sleep in her lonely bed. She yearned for Monogail. That, indeed, was part of the reason why she had filled her day with so much talk and work—it helped take her mind off the pain of separation.

CHAPTER
Forty-one

After sailing some distance south, the good ship Ebonair turned east, on a course designed to take it to Iglis. Before getting there, they were intercepted. A sleek patrol boat overhauled them and challenged them. The Ebonair hove to and was boarded. The swaggering Collosnon intruders came to order promptly when Yen Olass emerged from her stateroom in the guise of the Silent One of the Sisterhood, and, carrying off her role with an enviable degree of panache, called on them to obey her and do her bidding, in the name of the emperor.

Soon the patrol vessel was on its way to Iglis to announce their imminent arrival; the Ebonair, rolling like a drunken pig in the heavy sea, trudged along in its wake, and had soon lost sight of the white-winged envoy.

Yen Olass, thrilled with the ease at which she had handled this first encounter, began to toy with fantasies. What if Celadric was dead? What then? Would it be possible for her to continue this pretence and play her role for real? If Hearst's quest proved impossible, and the Rovac warrior returned to the Lesser Teeth empty-handed, could Yen Olass Ampadara step into the shoes of the Silent One and live out her days in state and power in Gendormargensis?

The thought of her child Monogail recalled her to her senses. She had her own home to go back to, as soon as this madcap adventure was over—and the sooner, the better. Now that her moments of madness were over, she coldly calculated her chances of surviving an extended stay in the Collosnon Empire, and found them worse than slim. In Trest and Estar, uncouth garrison provinces far removed from the imperial court, no doubt she could hold her own. But if she ever reached Gendormargensis, she would encounter people who, at the least, would know the Silent One by her voice.

Then what about Meddon? And York? There was a slim chance that one of those formidable killers would remember the true voice of the Silent One. Or, alternatively, the voice from behind the veil might remind York of the oracle he had seen give a reading in Gendormargensis on the day that Lonth Denesk and Tonaganuk fought to the death. Or, considering that so many people passed through Gendormargensis at one time or another, it was possible that—

Yen Olass realized she was not doing herself any good at all by trying to calculate the odds against success. She consoled herself with the thought that Hearst and Watashi were not fools; neither of them would put their heads inside a dragon's mouth unless there was at least a sporting chance that they would be able to withdraw before the jaws closed.

Once more, Yen Olass turned her attention to the Indicators, the Casting Board and the Book.

*   *   *

Arriving off Iglis, the Ebonair was delayed by plague. Warning flags cautioned them against going ashore; a hoarse-voiced signaller calling from the deck of a pilot cutter warned them that the surrounding countryside was in the grip of cholera. Watashi, speaking as the nominal leader of their party, stressed that their need was urgent; the reply was that orders banning all movement had been issued from Garabatoon, and could not be countermanded by Watashi, even though he claimed to speak in the name of the emperor.

For three days they were anchored off Iglis. The text-master Eldegen Terzanagel treated them to a sepulchral rendition of the tale of the cholera epidemic which had claimed his master when he had been slave to a wizard; Morgan Hearst lamented the absence of his friend of many adventures, the healer Miphon, now in exile in Sung.

Then they received landing permission. They could not enter Iglis, or take their ship up the Hollern River to Garabatoon, but they could come ashore on a deserted part of the coast, the transport would be arranged from there. Their route would take them through the countryside without bringing them into contact with any of the plague-stricken communities.

This outcome had its attractions, at least for Yen Olass, as it spared her the danger of being identified as an imposter. On the other hand, these rigorous quarantine measures made it impossible for her to gather intelligence, which was her main task on this mission; she could not meet any oracles resident in Iglis to review their readings and to find out what the current concerns of the community were.

When they landed, they were met by men with horses and ox-carts. They travelled with all possible speed toward Garabatoon, the town the Collosnon Empire had built on the site of Lorford. At nightfall, Yen Olass conferred with Hearst, Watashi and Eldegen Terzanagel. They agreed that if she felt they were under suspicion, she should feign sickness. Once they were immersed in the formal protocol which would attend their arrival in Garabatoon, it might be difficult for Yen Olass to meet with the others, but news that she had fallen sick would travel fast, warning them that they should abandon their mission and flee.

Which left Yen Olass with at least one unanswered question: under such circumstances, how would she escape? When Hearst failed to come up with any satisfactory answer, she forced him to commit himself to several formidable oaths, guaranteeing that in the event of her death he would dedicate himself to Monogail and Monogail's future.

*   *   *

On a day of wind and sunlight, the convoy entered Garabatoon. They were led by Watashi, who was playing himself; he was accompanied by Yen Olass, posing as the Silent One of the Sisterhood: Morgan Hearst and Eldegen Terzanagel, dressed in formal grey robes, were travelling as courtiers from Watashi's court. With them were twenty-six men. Some, Collosnon deserters who had been in the employ of Morgan Hearst for years, were passing themselves off as soldiers from Celadric's entourage; the others were dressed as what they actually were, soldiers and sailors from Stokos.

They were met on the outskirts of Garabatoon and were told that a reception had been prepared for them. Messengers, breaking plague quarantine, had brought news of their impending arrival some days previously. After the reception, there would be a formal banquet; to celebrate their arrival, and to celebrate the fact that the plague had not spread to Garabatoon, there would be a river festival the next day.

Yen Olass welcomed this news. Thanks to the festivities, no

serious business would be discussed for at least two days. In that time, she should be able to interrogate at least some oracles, and learn whether anyone suspected Watashi of deceit. Naturally, Meddon and York would hesitate before handing over a substantial ransom to a stranger; if Yen Olass could achieve a good rapport with the oracles, and convince them that she, the Silent One, vouched for Watashi's good intentions, then anyone who consulted an oracle for guidance would probably get a reading indicating that it was best to hand over the ransom.

With growing confidence, Yen Olass thought of the days ahead, and began to delight in the subtle challenge awaiting her. And quite apart from that, she was excited by the thought of a river festival. She hadn't seen one for years—for more than half a decade, in fact. She'd always loved river festivals, with their boating duels, horse-crossings, swimming races, archery contests, drums, trumpets, drinking, dancing and gambling.

For at least two days, she would be the Silent One, which was almost as good as being empress. Maybe better. She wondered what she would get to eat that night. She supposed she could have whatever she wanted: she started thinking up lists of things to order. Would they have grapes? No, much too early in the year. What a pity. But someone could surely come up with a gaplax or two, if she really insisted. And insist she would.

She should try and get hold of some nice clothes, too, so she could take a present back to Resbit. Something in silk. And some furs for Monogail, for the winter. And a new jacket. But how would the Silent One justify asking for children's clothes and a heavyweight jacket? She would have to ask Watashi to put it all on the list of things required as a ransom.

Perhaps she should ask for a horse, too. Or at least a pony. But there was no decent pasture on the Lesser Teeth. So she would need some turf as well, maybe half a shipload. Or was that being too extravagant? No. They were ransoming off the Lord Emperor of Tameran, the great Celadric. The higher their demands, the more credibility they would gain. If their demands were too modest, their hosts might begin to suspect that the emperor was actually dead.

That was logical. She decided to inform Watashi of this exquisite logic as soon as possible, and put in an order for a couple of horses, a shipload of turf, a case of the best silk, a wardrobe of leather clothes with fleece linings, a complete set of four-season furs in a child's size and an adult's size, a mirror, a dreamquilt, and a female lyre-cat to mate with Quelaquix. And some talking birds with bright feathers, if available.

Why not?

Opportunities like this only came once in a lifetime; it was best to make the most of them. Besides, she had given years of good service to the empire, as an oracle, and she had never been paid for any of her work, except when Lord Alagrace had tipped her; she was rightfully entitled to what she was asking for.

Feeling more relaxed and cheerful than she had for days, Yen Olass began to look forward to the reception which was awaiting them.

*   *   *

Castle Vaunting was no more; the great fortress built by wizards had been destroyed. Hearst claimed the damage had been done by a walking mountain. Yen Olass knew that was ridiculous—nevertheless, something had smashed the castle.

The moat which had once been filled with fire had been buried for the most part, but the fire now forced its way up through pits, craters, and chasms which gashed Melross Hill at random. Scattered masonry, tottering fragments of walls and the stumps of ruined towers littered the landscape. The rains had washed away part of the hillside, making high-rising ruins out of some of the castle's dungeons. In places, the skull-bald rock of the hill itself poked through to the open air, revealing the dark mouths of caves and tunnels.

This glorified rubbish dump was known as the castle scrag. Perched on the edge of the castle scrag was Castle Celadric, named to the greater glory of the reigning emperor. Compared to the ruins of the wizard fortress, it looked like a toy. A beautiful toy, because it had been built for height; Yen Olass counted thirty fluted spires. She knew that they had been built for a grim purpose: to be used as platforms for archers to shoot at the Neversh when those monsters made their incursions. In the town itself, other spires echoed those of the castle. To the south, the monsters of the Swarms commanded the lands, and worked steadily at the causeway designed to give them access to Estar. Once Hearst had got the ransom, taken it to the Lesser Teeth, negotiated with Draven to redeem Celadric's life and had negotiated with Celadric for control of the west of Argan, then the real battles would be only beginning.

Remembering the five baby keflos she had killed on the flats near her home on Carawell, Yen Olass shuddered. She was glad that only men would be condemned to those epic battles of the future; with her part done, she would be able to go home and forget about such world-redeeming heroics. She had never yet seen one of the Neversh, and trusted that she never would.

Castle Celadric, commanding Melross Hill, was built out of stone, but the town of Garabatoon, down by the river, was built of logs. To the north, the forest had been felled, and the land brought under cultivation; the tallest vegetation was now hedges of sprite bamboo. Yen Olass wondered what had happened to the Melski—then turned her attention to other things, because they were approaching Garabatoon's High Hall, where the reception was to be held.

Entering the high-gabled wooden hall, she found it was everything she could have desired. In contrast to the rather stark garrison town outside, the interior of the hall was lavishly decorated. Tapestries hung on the walls, and the entire ceiling was ablaze with flowers, cunningly entwined in fishing nets.

At the far end of the hall, a chair was set up on a dais, like a throne. With a lordly confidence, Watashi strode forward and assumed the chair. Servants scurried forward, and, bowing and scraping, explained his error in tense whispers. Yen Olass already knew what he had done wrong. The chair was for the most senior guest present; the Silent One, as a member of Celadric's entourage, outranked any uitlander overlord like Watashi. Looking decidedly miffed, Watashi quit the chair for a lesser seat on one side of the hall. Yen Olass, a slight smile hidden behind her veil, stepped forward and seated herself in the place of honour.

She studied the other members of their party. Morgan Hearst and Eldegen Terzanagel, their grey robes flowing, their heads cowled, their hands—and Hearst's hook—hidden in their capacious sleeves as they walked forward with their arms folded, both looked like venerable scholars. And, indeed, they seemed to be absorbed in some deep and scholarly argument, almost oblivious to their surroundings. Yen Olass thought they were playing their roles perfectly. In fact, they were not playing at all—speaking to each other in the High Speech of wizards, they had become absorbed in a low-voiced but vigorous argument concerning the aetiology of the Swarms, and of the Skull of the Deep South which controlled those monsters.

When all the guests were seated, a minor functionary approached. He regretted that Lord Meddon and Lord York were delayed; they were reviewing urgent despatches from the southern borders, giving details of an incursion by the Swarms. In the meantime, would Yen Olass deal with two urgent matters of discipline?

She said she would.

Trumpets blared, and guards led in a young, pale, frightened woman. A herald advanced with a sheaf of papers.

He bowed.

'This is the evidence against the accused. Do you wish to have it read in public?'

'I will examine it with the eye's silence,' said Yen Olass, glad that she had reviewed the section on Trial Proceedings in the Book of the Sisterhood.

The herald advanced, knelt before her and yielded up the papers. Yen Olass began to read, swiftly.

The Silent One dealt with delinquent oracles and with people who tried to suborn the Sisterhood for their own purposes. The woman now in front of Yen Olass was an oracle who was said to be delinquent. In this kind of trial, there was no bill of particulars; the accused had no right to know the nature of the charges being brought against her; evidence could be presented in writing, without the accused ever knowing who was bringing such evidence against her, or, indeed, what that evidence was.

In this case, it was mostly rumour, gossip, hearsay, and, quite possibly, outright fabrication. On the principle that where there's smoke there's fire, Yen Olass assumed that the girl before her had certainly done something wrong. But what? She might have stolen a kiss on the sly with the baker's boy, or she might have whored her body through half the army. Yen Olass knew that the maintenance of good order and discipline required the administration of immediate punishment; at the same time, she had to endeavour to protect the mystique of the Sisterhood.

In a penetrating voice, Yen Olass proclaimed her judgment:

'You have dared altogether too much. You will restrict yourself to your quarters until you have completed a suitable period of penance. Now, out of my sight!'

Weeping bitterly, the girl withdrew. Yen Olass spoke to the herald, directing him to deliver any and all additional or supplementary copies of the evidence to her quarters by nightfall. She had not yet been assigned quarters, but did not trouble herself about that—she would most certainly have a suitable suite of rooms before dayfail, or know the reason why.

Already she knew what she would have to do. She would have to interrogate the girl in private, and find out exactly what had happened. Then, if the offence was minor, penance could be fixed at two or three days of solitary confinement; if there was some major scandal, Yen Olass would have to root it out, and might have to send some people back to Gendormargensis for execution.

She did not find the challenge formidable. Instead, she found it quite delicious. In the past, faint rumours of amazing scandals had reached Gendormargensis from the provinces—members of the Sisterhood involved in prostitution, or money-lending, or gambling, or opium rings. If there was a real full-blown scandal here in Garabatoon, Yen Olass would find it exquisitely interesting to poke and probe and get to the bottom of it.

Her investigation would also allow her to interrogate oracles in depth about the politics of Garabatoon and the intentions of its leaders.

Serendipity, she thought.

(To be precise, what she actually thought was 'dara ta kara', an idiomatic phrase from her homeland of Monogail, meaning 'apples from heaven'; as there were no apples in the northern wastelands, this indicates that within the last four or five thousand years, the people of her racial stock had lived in warmer lands further to the south.)

While Yen Olass was cogitating, a squad of armoured guards led in the second prisoner. At first she did not look at the prisoner, but rested her eyes on the four guards, who were armoured, not with the simple cuirass and openfaced helmet standard in the armies of the Collosnon Empire, but with a gilded panoply of full body armour, the crowning glory of which was jewelled and visored helmets decorated with flowery plumes of green and gold and blue. She had once had a plumed helmet herself—but it had not been as pretty as these, and she had soon lost it.

She turned her attention to the prisoner, and was surprised to see it was the Ondrask of Noth. He stood there before her in his stinking animal skins; as always, he was loaded down with feathers, beads, skulls and assorted other talismans. There was a faint smile playing across his face.

'What is this prisoner accused of?' said Yen Olass.

'An act of impropriety in relation to an oracle,' said the herald.

This was a serious charge, yet the Ondrask seemed amused

by the proceedings. Yen Olass was annoyed. He was in the presence of the Silent One; he should comport himself accordingly. Perhaps there was something wrong with him. Perhaps he was slightly touched.

'What is the nature of this act of impropriety?' said Yen Olass.

The herald did not answer. He seemed embarrassed. He looked at the papers relating to the case, coughed, then looked away.

'Well?' said Yen Olass.

The herald hesitated.

'If it's too obscene to say in public,' said Yen Olass, 'then give me the papers and I will examine them with the eye's silence.'

'No need,' said the Ondrask of Noth boldly. 'I will demonstrate.'

'You will do no such thing!' said Yen Olass, outraged.

The Ondrask of Noth cackled madly. He dropped down on all fours and came bounding toward her. He mounted the dais, reached her throne, and began to lick her hands. Yen Olass swatted him, and shouted:

'Guards!'

The four guards in gold-gleaming armour removed their visored helmets and stood revealed as the Lord Emperor Celadric, his brothers Meddon and York, and the pirate chief Draven. The Ondrask tore away Yen Olass's veil.

'Welcome, Yen Olass,' said Celadric. 'Welcome to Garabatoon.'

'But . . . but you're in the Greater Teeth!' said Yen Olass.

Draven laughed.

Meddon wheeled to face the seats where Yen Olass's followers were waiting, undecided as to whether everything was entirely lost.

'Seize them!' shouted Meddon, pointing.

The reaction was instantaneous.

Morgan Hearst threw aside his grey robes, revealing arms and armour. Left-handed, he drew his sword with a scream of defiance

'Ahyak Rovac!'

And Watashi was drawing his own blade to fight beside him. They leapt forward—and went down as lead-weighted nets plummeted from the ceiling. An entire section of flower-upholding nets had been dropped at Meddon's shout. Men swarmed forward to overpower and disarm their captives before they could cut themselves free of the nets.

Yen Olass got to her feet. But before she could try to escape, the Ondrask of Noth grabbed her. His arm came throttling round her throat and jerked her backwards. He pressed his body against her. She felt his urgency.

'Let her go,' said York. 'She's not for you.'

'What?' said the Ondrask.

At his exclamation of outrage, Yen Olass smelt the stench of his breath adding itself to the stink of his body.

'She's mine,' said York. 'I claim her.'

'What would you want her for?' said the Ondrask. 'You've got women—'

'She would amuse me for a night,' said York. 'After that . . . the armies are waiting.'

Yen Olass felt the Ondrask's grip slacken. She was able to breathe more easily. Her breathing was quick, frantic, shallow, shocked. She felt her skip-quick heart rabbiting for the horizon.

'My lord,' said the Ondrask, appealing to the emperor.

Celadric smiled, and shook his head.

'But you promised!' shouted the Ondrask. 'Your word! Are you going to deny . . .'

His voice trailed away. Celadric was waiting. Waiting and watching. For what? Yen Olass, familiar with the politics of the Collosnon Empire, understood exactly what Celadric was waiting for. He was waiting for the Ondrask to say something unpardonable. Once that happened, he would find himself negotiating with the sharp edge of an axe. Celadric, with his new ideas for a sanitary, streamlined empire, was ready to do away with the religion of Noth with its sweat and its dirt, its dances and horse sacrifices, its shamans and dream-saying. The Ondrask of Noth understood too; he said no more.

Celadric spoke to the silence:

'Do you expect your emperor to be your pimp?'

'My lord,' said the Ondrask, 'the woman is old and ugly. I thought your brother might care . . . might care for an opportunity to review his declaration.'

The Ondrask was stumbling. He was finding it difficult to find suitable words. This was not surprising: his life was in the balance. Unlike Yen Olass, he was not used to confronting people who wanted to kill him.

Celadric cocked his head at York.

'Well?'

'Old earth ploughs easily,' said York.

This brought a laugh from the assembly. Yen Olass was unfamiliar with this agricultural idiom, as it had entered the language and had become popular while she had been living on the Lesser Teeth. Nevertheless, it conjured up images—earth, horse, plough, sun, sweat, fluid, blood. She remembered something which she had entirely forgotten about in the excitement of reaching Garabatoon

'I have my months,' said Yen Olass.

Her penetrating voice was heard by everyone. Someone stifled a giggle; someone else failed to stifle a hearty guffaw. York did not look disconcerted, not even for a moment. A slow smile spread across his face, then he spoke:

'Messy but nice.'

Celadric frowned; he found his brother rather too crude and earthy for his taste.

'You,' said Celadric curtly, pointing at the Ondrask. 'As a favour to compensate you for the loss of the slut, I dedicate a human being for you to sacrifice tomorrow, instead of a horse. The human being is Morgan Hearst.'

The Ondrask's face fell. This offer, ostensibly a special honour, was an insult to his religion. In war, captive horses were more valuable than captive men; to kill a prisoner was nothing, an empty gesture, but to slaughter a horse demanded a real commitment to the values of religion.

'As my lord wishes,' said the Ondrask, and bowed.

Like many other people faced with the alternative of immediate death, the Ondrask chose to eat the shit that was set before him. Yen Olass knew just what it tasted like. To her surprise, she felt a momentary pang of sympathy for him. It passed swiftly, for she had other things to think about.

CHAPTER
Forty-two

By tradition, the Yarglat did not eat with their womenfolk. It was true that, during the reign of the Witchlord, the dralkosh Bao Gahai used to dine with Onosh Gulkan on a regular basis—but she had been an exceptional woman in more ways than one.

Since Celadric came to power, however, the tradition had been declining. Celadric had deliberately held a series of banquets to which men and women were invited. Some important Yarglat generals who had refused to attend those banquets had subsequently been demoted, exiled or assassinated.

Over the generations in which the Yarglat had ruled the Collosnon Empire, the old traditions had been reinforced by wave after wave of immigrants coming south from the homelands of the horse tribes. But, under Celadric's rule, nomads coming south no longer received a warm welcome. He was breaking down the last vestiges of tribal culture, deliberately fostering a cosmopolitan atmosphere.

By breaking the old patterns, Celadric hoped to destroy the power and prestige of the high caste Yarglat warlords, ending their independence and subjecting them to the full discipline of imperial law. He wanted to put an end to the disastrous feuding and duelling of past generations. Breaking the old tribal monopoly on power would also allow him to recruit talent from elsewhere in the empire.

Remembering the fearsome lesson of the Blood Purge, talent had been reluctant to let itself be recruited. But now, at last, Celadric was starting to have some success. In a few more years, he would no longer be in the ridiculous situation of trying to run an empire with only a handful of competent bureaucrats; over the next few decades, he hoped to be able to start tackling the empire's larger problems, such as dredging the Yolantarath River to avoid the annual spring floods.

On the day on which Yen Olass Ampadara was captured, Celadric held one of his famous mixed banquets. In part, he was pursuing his policy of cultural change. But, quite apart from that, he wanted to celebrate. And he certainly had plenty to celebrate.

While Celadric's brothers had debated about whether to raise the ransom Draven had been demanding, Celadric had negotiated his own release. Tomorrow morning, his sister Quenerain —the source of so much unpalatable scandal—would be married off to Draven. And a solemn treaty would be signed, thanks to which the Greater Teeth would become a part of the Collosnon Empire, administered by Draven.

Celadric knew that the times had favoured him. With the reduced trade in the Central Ocean, the pirates had fallen on hard times of late. After the treaty was signed, the Greater Teeth would be used as a base for operations against the Swarms, and Celadric had been able to offer hefty payments in the form of rents for military bases and harbour dues. To put it simply, he had bought out the pirates. Nevertheless, the fact remained: he had conquered the Greater Teeth, which had successfully resisted some of the world's most formidable military minds.

He was in a good mood.

The only thing that irritated him was his concubine, Yerzerdayla. She had asked him to release the captive oracle, Yen Olass Ampadara. Over the years they had spent together, her cool judgment and her carefully calculated advice had served him well. But lately. . .

More and more, over the last year or so, Yerzerdayla had been making little requests of him. Spare this man. Free this woman. Restrain the torturers. Let the hostage go. Sometimes, she didn't really seem to appreciate how difficult it was to rule the empire. Given a perfect world, of course he would have been the perfect ruler. He was not given to gratuitous cruelty, like his father, Khmar. But the world was not perfect. And, in an imperfect world, it was sometimes necessary to be a little bit ruthless in order to expedite the efficient administration of the empire.

Once, quite recently, Yerzerdayla had embarrassed Celadric badly by making one of her requests for mercy during the course of a banquet. He had refused—but, doing so, had put himself in quite a bad light. To avoid any similar scenes at this evening's entertainment, he ordered Yerzerdayla to confine herself to her chambers until the morning.

He wanted to enjoy himself.

CHAPTER
Forty-three

At the banquet that evening in Castle Celadric, Yen Olass sat in a place of honour, on York's right; from time to time he thumped his fist on the table and shouted out, calling for special treats and titbits to be brought forth for her. Serving maids scurried to obey.

York spoke to her with elaborate courtesy, addressing her as 'my Lady Ampadara', 'my beloved honey-sweet', 'light of my life', 'consort of the seventh moon' and 'star of stars, joy of the summer heavens'.

When a low-ranking warrior down the far end of the banqueting table cried out that she was a dralkosh, York got to his feet, stalked the warrior (he tried to run, but guards barred his exit), slashed his face, smashed his jaw, bit off his nose, cut off his ear, broke his neck, opened his throat, then rammed the wreckage with a roasting spit. (His father, the late Khmar, would undoubtedly have approved.)

Such little courtesies were the honours properly due to a royal consort, and a naive young girl might have thought her luck was changing. But Yen Olass was not fooled for a moment. York had spoken clearly enough in front of the assembly earlier in the day. Her fate was to be raped by royalty then handed over to the army to be raped to rubble and then, in all probability, smashed with rocks in a muddy field, with her remains being left to rot in the open until the scavengers came to dog down their hunger.

For a moment, she played the game. She returned York's compliments, she got him to compel the kitchens to yield up a gaplax (grapes unfortunately proved unobtainable—indeed, she

was informed that none grew in Estar) and she applauded her
hero when he defended her honour by junking the man foul
enough to call her a dralkosh. (Her applause was genuine; she
had no sympathy whatsoever for anyone ready to call her by
that obscene name.)

While Yen Olass played this cruel game, she kept her wits
about her. She ate well, but did not gorge herself, and she
watered her wine heavily. Toward the end of the banquet, she
excused herself so she could go to the toilet. As she left the
room, two brawny serving maids fell in beside her; they
escorted her to the stink pits and stayed with her until she returned to the banquet. Yen Olass was not disappointed: she had
not expected escape to be that easy.

Shortly after she returned to the banquet, heralds shouted for
silence, guards ejected those drunks too intoxicated to know
when to shut up, and Celadric rose to speak.

'It is late,' said Celadric.

An incautious warrior groaned, and he, too, was ejected
without ceremony. But many at the banquet table would have
shared his sentiments. When the Lord Emperor Celadric indulged himself, he did so only very mildly, for he was something of a kill-joy; in his father's day, on a night like this the
whole court would have partied until dawn, with at least one
warrior drinking himself to death, but it was almost certain that
Celadric was now going to tell everyone to go to bed.

'It is late,' said Celadric, emphasizing the point. 'And we'll
all be up early tomorrow, for the river festival. So, very shortly,
we'll all be going to sleep.'

There was another groan, but this time the guards failed to
detect the culprit.

'Good sleep makes for good health,' said Celadric.

The truth was that he did not like drunks roistering through
his castle late at night, fighting, shouting, swearing and vomiting over the floor. And he certainly saw nothing heroic in those
drinking men who liked to compete in drinking matches until at
least one of their number was dead.

'But first,' said Celadric, 'we have a presentation to make to
a very important person.'

York shifted restlessly. He hated speeches.

'Darling,' said Yen Olass. 'Shall we depart?'

'Wait,' said York.

'We have a very important guest here tonight,' said Celadric, 'an ambassador from that formidable power in the world of events, the Lesser Teeth.'

There was idle laughter around the banqueting table. Just as Yen Olass realized whom he was talking about, his eyes met hers, and he smiled.

'Yen Olass Ampadara,' he said. 'You ordered gaplax tonight. Did you enjoy it?'

He sounded very, very pleased with himself.

'Yes,' said Yen Olass. 'Was it poisoned?'

'I hope not,' said Celadric. 'The chef was told it was for the emperor himself.'

There was more lazy laughter.

'I understand you choose to spend tonight with my brother York,' said Celadric.

'I will strive to be worthy of such a noble warrior,' said Yen Olass.

'A bit of the old striving, eh?' said the pirate chief, Draven. 'Nothing like it for rousing the appetite.'

That was one of the least witty comments of the evening, but it raised a laugh all the same. Celadric frowned; he did not like being interrupted.

'So speaks a master of the strategy of striving,' said Yen Olass. 'And a master of the strategy of survival.'

She was reminding him how he had survived in Penvash: by tying her up and leaving her for Chonjara. She looked at him steadily, and he dropped his eyes. She was surprised. She had not thought him capable of shame.

'Striving and survival apart,' said Celadric, annoyed at all this cross-talk, 'we're pleased that you've enjoyed our hospitality so much, Yen Olass. And now, especially in your honour, I'm pleased to announce that we're putting on a special breakfast for you tomorrow. We're going to cook you something very special to eat.'

Celadric smiled, spinning out the silence. From round the table, eager eyes watched Yen Olass. With rising horror, Yen Olass wondered what dish he was going to name. Her breasts? Her ears? Her eyes? Her fingers?

'Bring in the pig!' said Celadric.

Four men entered, accompanied by a huge black-masked executioner. The men were carrying a big cage shrouded by a triple-ply solskin horse blanket. The executioner swept cups and plates onto the floor, clearing away the litter of the banquet with the flat edge of his falchion. Still holding his sword, the executioner stepped to one side, and the men put the cage down on the table. The heavy horse blanket muffled the noise of whatever animal was inside it.

'Do you like pork, Yen Olass?' said Celadric.

It had to be a trick question. Something monstrous must be in that cage. A baby keflo, perhaps? Yen Olass did not know whether to answer yes or no. If she said 'yes', she might be offered something poisonous. If she said 'no', then Celadric might get the thing in the cage to eat her. Thinking on her feet, she found an answer of sorts:

'I shared lunch with your father once. I'd be happy to share breakfast with you.'

'My pleasure,' said Celadric.

Then he nodded to the executioner, who whipped off his black mask, revealing himself as—

'Nan Nulador!' said Yen Olass.

The horseblanket was whipped away and the thing in the cage screamed:

'Mam!'

'Monogail!' screamed Yen Olass.

She slashed the first guard who tried to grab her, laying his face open with five steel-tipped fingernails. But York grabbed her from behind, twisted her arm up behind her back and forced it almost to the breaking point. Monogail was wailing.

'You can't do this!' said Yen Olass, gasping, her eyes watering with pain. 'Not to a child. It's too cruel.'

'A child dralkosh,' said Nan Nulador, his voice heavy as death. 'An abomination.'

'Butcher it,' said Celadric curtly.

'No!' screamed Yen Olass.

And she went on screaming as Monogail was dragged out of the cage. The handlers grabbed her hands and feet and held her flat to the table.

'Don't do it,' said Yen Olass, begging now. 'Don't hurt her. Don't do it. I'll do anything, you know. Your father—'

'Do it,' said Celadric.

'She's your half-sister!' shouted Yen Olass. 'Your own flesh and blood!'

'A monster or a bastard,' said Celadric. 'Either way, I don't care. Do it! Now!'

Nan Nulador raised the falchion. And Yen Olass dropped her voice and said, in a special tone:

'Nan Nulador...'

The big man faltered.

'Sleep,' said Yen Olass.

He swayed on his feet. He staggered. Then righted himself, and shook his head, clearing his mind.

'Sleep,' said Yen Olass.

But this time, the word had no effect at all. Nan Nulador raised his sword. The weight of the falchion was all in the big swell of steel down toward the tip, so the mass of the blade was concentrated on the point where it would slice through Monogails' neck.

Nan Nulador chopped down.

And jolted sideways, felled by a single blow. The Ondrask had smashed him with a battle hammer. The falchion went flying, and clattered to the floor. Monogail screamed senselessly.

'Bear witness!' shouted the Ondrash hoarsely. 'Bear witness! The emperor executed me because I tried to stop him eating a child. Bear witness! Tell it in Gendormargensis!'

The Ondrask gasped for breath, and was about to shout again, but Celadric cut in on him:

'Silence! Not another word! What's this about eating? Don't you know a joke when you hear one? We were just ridding the world of a dralkosh, that's all. Once it's dead, we can turf it down to the flames, for all I care.'

'Give it to me,' said the Ondrask. 'I'll take care of it.'

Celadric looked at the Ondrask of Noth. He smiled. Then his voice went silky smooth, and he addressed the Ondrask by name:

'Losh Negis, children are for women. Do you want the child? This can be arranged. But we'd have to make you a woman first. All it takes is a little work with a sharp blade. Is that what you want?'

The Ondrask was silent.

'You see?' said Celadric. 'You thought you were a hero. But you're not, really. You were ready to die—but anyone can die. People do it all the time. They manage even if they haven't practised. What's difficult is living. And, as I've shown you, when it comes to living, you're no hero. Tell that in Gendormargensis, if you wish. Losh Negis made his choices.'

The Ondrask bowed his head. His attempt to shame Celadric into letting the child live had failed. Celadric had made him look like a fool. And, in some people's minds, a bit of a coward as well. Though what man in his right mind would choose to be made into a woman?

'You only want to kill the child because your father thwarted you when you wanted to kill me,' said Yen Olass, trying to see if Nan Nulador was dead or unconscious or what.

'Really?' said Celadric, raising an eyebrow. 'The emperor is not so pretty. We wish to destroy the . . . the pig only because it is a dralkosh.'

'She's a perfectly ordinary child,' said Yen Olass steadily, 'and you know it.'

But she knew she could not win this argument.

'I don't choose to bandy words with a slave girl,' said Celadric. 'The child is a monster, and everyone here knows it. The eyes are yellow. Look!'

He lifted Monogail's head by the hair. She wailed, and Yen Olass struggled, trying to break free. York put more tension on her arm, and she hissed with the pain.

'Give me a knife,' said Celadric, holding out his hand, 'And I'll do it myself.'

Someone slapped a knife into his hand.

'No,' said a voice.

And Yerzerdayla stepped into the room, entering by way of one of the service doors.

'Yen Olass is right,' said Yerzerdayla. 'You must not kill the child. To do so would be a gratuitous murder.'

Celadric straightened up. He was sorely annoyed.

'The oracle betrayed the empire. She should feel the weight of the empire's punishment.'

'Then burn her alive,' said Yerzerdayla, who could not reasonably plead for mercy for a traitor. 'But spare the child. Or does your hold on the empire depend on your ability to murder children?'

'If you're so concerned about the child then you can have it,' said Celadric.

'Thank you,' said Yerzerdayla, with a small bow.

'Providing, that is,' said Celadric, 'that you can find a man prepared to support you and the child thereafter. A man who will guarantee to protect the empire from the child if it should prove to be a dralkosh.'

And he looked around the banqueting hall.

'Well? Which man speaks for the woman and the child? Not

you, Losh Negis! You're not a man! You're half way to being a woman already! Throw him out of here!'

The Ondrask was hustled out of the hall.

'You're not being fair,' said Yen Olass. 'You don't want to give your father's child a chance to survive.'

And, with the word 'survive,' she shot a glance at Draven. The pirate looked away.

'This child doesn't have a father,' said Celadric savagely.

He was really worked up now. He had meant to have the child hauled in and casually butchered so Yen Olass would feel the weight of imperial discipline. Instead, this terrible woman had managed to entangle him in a crazy debate which he should cut off—now!—by killing the pig.

'And even if it was my father's bastard,' continued Celadric, 'There's nobody here to speak for it. Nobody wants a dralkosh spawned by a bitch who's a dralkosh herself.'

Lightly, Yerzerdayla reached out and plucked the knife from Celadric's hand.

'Give me that!' said Celadric.

The emperor and his concubine confronted each other.

'You take great risks,' said Celadric, his voice very cold.

There was a sigh from Draven, and the pirate rose to his feet, slowly, reluctantly.

'Peace,' said Draven. 'We come here to sign a peace. It would be a bad omen to have a killing the night before a peace treaty. I will stand as father for the child.'

Celadric turned on him.

'Why,' said Celadric, 'are you doing this?'

There was death in his voice.

'A debt of honour,' said Draven, reluctantly. 'As your father's son, I'm sure you understand the meaning of honour.'

Celadric took a deep breath. He could have Draven killed here and now. For opposing the emperor like this, the pirate deserved to be killed. But if Draven died, there would be no marriage between the pirate and the Princess Quenerain, and no peace treaty—and the pirates of the Greater Teeth would choose another leader, and go back to their old habits of raiding and plundering.

'Take the child then,' said Celadric. 'And the woman. And get out of my sight!'

The last words were said in a snarl.

Silently, Draven motioned to the four handlers holding Monogail down, and they released her. Yerzerdayla tossed the knife she was holding into a soup tureen, and gathered Monogail into her arms. Screaming for her mother, Monogail was carried from the room as Yerzerdayla exited in Draven's wake.

'The night is ended,' said Celadric, meaning that the entertainments were over. 'Everyone get out!'

York released Yen Olass.

'Well, my dearest heart,' said York. 'Shall we retire to our nuptial bed?'

Yen Olass wanted to faint, to weep, to sleep. Instead, she mustered up a smile.

'The night's pleasure is all mine,' she said.

Yerzerdayla had done what she could. The rest was up to her.

CHAPTER
Forty-four

The castle was in darkness, except where flaming brands burnt here and there in the flagstone corridors. As York led Yen Olass to his own suite of rooms, a slave went in front bearing a lantern. In the bedroom, the slave smoothed the feather mattress and turned down the feather duvet. Then York dismissed her, and she departed. Yen Olass was alone in the suite with Celadric's brother.

Yen Olass put all thought of Monogail out of her mind. Yerzerdayla had risked her life to save Monogail, and Draven had chanced his; with such protection, the child would survive the night. Now Yen Olass had to concentrate on the task at hand. She had to contend with York. She felt very tired. Exhausted, in fact. But she did not allow herself to collapse.

'That was fun tonight,' said York.

'Yes,' said Yen Olass.

She considered attacking him. If he had been drunk and helpless, she would have killed him without hesitation. But he had drunk little. He was a strong, ugly, battle-hardened thug. Furthermore, he had insulted his brother by wearing chain mail to the banquet, and he was still clad in this armour. He was also carrying weapons.

York yawned.

He was weary; he was well-fed. Perhaps, given the chance, he would prefer to make love to her rather than to rape her. All evening, until Monogail's entrance had interrupted the party, they had played the game of love, and, to a certain extent, people become what they pretend to be. Yen Olass knew something of the arts of seduction—she had studied the Princess Quenerain often enough—and now she decided to romance her warlord. With a little luck, she would make him hers.

She would make him her ally.

Yen Olass, letting the slightest husk of desire steal into her voice, said to her warlord:

'I intend to enjoy this night together.'

Then she softened her lips for a kiss, and yielded up her mouth to his. But he did not respond. His lips were hard and dry, almost leathery; beyond them, his teeth barred the way into his mouth. He took her by the throat and pushed her face away from his. Then he scooped her up and threw her onto the bed. She was a solidly built woman, but he tossed her onto the bed as if she had been a child. As she landed, her head cracked into the wooden bedstead. She lay there shocked and dazed.

'Dralkosh,' said York.

Yen Olass felt stunned. How could he reject her like that? So absolutely? So completely? For a moment, she had been prepared to offer him her tenderness, the full cooperation of her body, and her unstinting assistance in every intimacy that he might desire. But he had pushed her away and then he had thrown her on the bed like a sack of potatoes.

York drew a knife and threw it.

The blade slammed into the bedstead by her left ear. Yen Olass started as the heavy-bladed weapon buried itself in the wood. She did not turn to look at it, but she could see it out of the corner of her eye.

'To cut you open,' said York.

Yen Olass did not understand. Did he think she was still a sewn-up woman? Surely he must know she had slept with his father? If he had never heard the gossip, he must have learnt as much from the argument in the banqueting hall. Yen Olass tried to speak, and found she could not. She cleared her throat noisily, and regained her voice.

'I'm not a virgin,' said Yen Olass.

'Θh?' said York. 'If you want a true confession . . . neither am I.'

York did not seem particularly interested. He started to un-buckle his swordbelt.

'I . . . I know how to please a man,' said Yen Olass.

York raised an eyebrow.

'Both of us?'

'It would please me as well,' said Yen Olass. 'You have . . . you have a very beautiful body.'

'When I spoke of us,' said York, 'I didn't mean you and me. I meant me and my friend.'

And he gestured at something near Yen Olass's head.

At first, through a deliberate act of will, Yen Olass prevented herself from understanding. But then his meaning forced itself upon her. His friend was his knife. He was determined to cut her. At the beginning or at the end? She was going to find out very shortly.

She watched as York discarded armour and clothing, drop-ping each item carelessly. She watched with helpless fascina-tion. Her head still hurt where it had hit the wooden bedstead. She had felt his strength then. If she fought, he would break her as a bully boy breaks a kitten. And if she surrendered, he would break her anyway. She felt paralysed with fear.

What weapons did she have? Her steel finger nails, which were no match for a knife. And her voice.

Yen Olass used her voice.

'I killed my first man at the age of twelve,' said Yen Olass.

All her skill and training went into the threat. Undertones of menace rumbled in her voice. Her tones were the tones of truth, making her threat a statement of absolute, irrefutable fact. By rights, York should have blanched, flinched and faltered. But he did nothing of the sort. Instead, he laughed.

'Maybe so, little Yenolass,' said York. 'But it didn't make you a man.'

'My name is Yen Olass,' said Yen Olass, emphasizing the way her name broke into two words.

Her name was the last dignity left to her.

'A slave owns nothing in its own right,' said York. 'Not even a name. Tonight, I'll call you Skak.'

He took off the last piece of his clothing, and stood before her, naked. She could not keep herself from looking. His cock was flaccid, a dead weight hanging limply. That was the final insult. He had rejected her love: now he was not even lusting after her body. Yet he was going to rape her all the same.

Yen Olass still did not look at the knife, but she thought about it all the same.

'What's your name?' said York, working his flesh.

Yen Olass held silence.

'Your name!'

His shout hit her like a battering ram. She flinched, as if she had been struck. Then, reluctantly, she named herself:

'Skak.'

And, speaking the word, naming herself with the crude Yarglat term for the female part, she finally accepted her destiny, which, she saw now, was the true and inevitable destiny of a woman—to humble herself before the power of a man, and to be broken by a man. York stood before her, naked, his male strength now rising erect. Now, gazing on his raw masculine might, she said.

'Skak. That's what I am.'

Defeated, she closed her eyes. Though she was lying down, she felt dizzy with fatigue. The moment she closed her eyes, she seemed to be falling. She felt as if the world was collapsing, as if her body was disintegrating.

'Open your eyes,' said York.

He wanted her to watch. To see.

With a dull, helpless obedience, Yen Olass complied. Then, unbidden, she began to slide out of her clothes. York laid himself down beside her. His worm sagged, as if starting to lose interest, so he played with himself, keeping his flesh alert while she stripped. Finally, all that remained to dispose of was one small item.

Yen Olass removed the blood-rag guarding her quim, and held the ghastly item between thumb and finger, momentarily uncertain as to what to do with it.

'That's one thing I won't have to worry about tomorrow night,' said York.

'Tomorrow?'

'When I take Monogail.'

Yen Olass was no longer sleepy. Her body burnt as if her veins had been filled with scalding water. Suddenly alert, as tense as a beast of prey about to strike, she stared at the man lying beside her and said:

'I don't think you'll have her. First, she's too young. Second, she's under protection.'

'Oh, don't worry your head about that,' said York cheerfully. 'I've had them that young before. They rip, of course, but there's no helping that. As for her protection, so called . . .'

He laughed.

Then yawned, closing his eyes for a moment.

Yen Olass stuffed the blood-rag into his mouth.

As he gagged, she snatched the knife and stabbed him. He tried to sit up. She punched him in the throat. His eyes rolled up and he collapsed backwards. Yen Olass wrenched the knife out. Holding it with both hands, she plunged it into his heart. Then lugged it out and struck again. And again. And again.

'For Monogail!' said Yen Olass, slamming home the knife one more time.

Then she grunted, strengthened her grip on the knife, and twisted, turning the blade in the body.

'For my mother!'

She was hot, burning, sweating. With one hand she pushed down on the dead man's body, and with the other she hauled out the knife. Her frenzy was passing, and she began to realise exactly what she had done. She felt no horror at this murder. Instead, it gave her a profound sense of satisfaction. She licked the blood from the blade. Slowly. Tenderly.

'Dara ko cha,' said Yen Olass, using a phrase from her homeland which meant 'The apple bites back.'

She had bitten back with a vengeance.

But was York really dead? He looked dead enough. She had seen battlefield corpses which looked prettier. Nevertheless, it was best to make certain.

Carefully, Yen Olass aimed the knife at a well-chosen spot and jabbed it in. There was no response. She smiled, as happy as a cat with cream.

'Darling,' she said, and kissed the dead man.

But she did not kiss him on the lips, which were stained with her blood and his. Instead, she kissed him on the throat. Then, remembering how the Lord Emperor Khmar had once demolished a man in her presence, she gave York a love-bite. Then she went to work.

When she was entirely finished, Yen Olass looked as if she had just climbed out of a bath of blood. Searching the suite, leaving bloody footprints on the floor, she found plenty of spare linen. She washed her body in wine, there being no water available; she finished up clean but reeking of alcohol. Never mind. She dressed herself in wool and leathers which had belonged to York. She wore no armour, because she would be moving through the castle by stealth.

Yen Olass took the knife which had already served her so well. There was going to be a lot more killing in the castle tonight. She was going to free Hearst, Watashi and the others, even if she had to kill a dozen guards and sentries to do so. Once she had liberated her manforce, they would be tasked with the job of liberating Monogail and Yerzerdayla. Then they would kill out the castle, taking their victims while they slept. By dawn, the floors would be knee-deep in blood, and Yen Olass and her companions would be far away on stolen horses or a stolen ship. If they had to ride, Monogail would sit on her horse. Once she had recovered her child, nothing would separate them, not ever again.

Yen Olass opened the heavy wooden door which guarded York's suite, and slipped out into the hallway, closing the door behind her. By the light of a guttering torch, she saw a sentry sitting in the hallway, his head nodding down to his chest.

Yen Olass held her breath.

Was he asleep?

She hoped so.

She crept forward, moving stealthily, knife in hand so she would be ready to strike if the sentry woke and grappled with her.

'No need to mouse along like that,' said a deep, heavy voice. 'He's dead. I've killed him already.'

Yen Olass started.

A shadow advanced out of the shadows. To her horror, she saw it was Nan Nulador. This time, he was armed with a double-bladed battle-axe.

'I was going to give the happy couple a little more time to finish their business and get to sleep,' said Nan Nulador. 'You've saved me a long wait.'

'Nan Nulador,' said Yen Olass, dropping her voice down, using a special tone. 'Sleep.'

Nan Nulador continued to advance. Her voice no longer had any effect on him at all. Suddenly, he leapt forward on the attack, the axe sweeping toward her.

Yen Olass screamed at him.

Her scream killed him.

He fell face first, chopped down dead.

Yen Olass started at his dead body in amazement—then saw the shaft of the arrow sticking out of his back.

'Drop the knife,' said the archer, advancing out of the shadows.

By the light of the guttering torch, Yen Olass saw that the archer was a Yarglat. She had never seen him before. He had already nocked another arrow.

'Drop the knife!'

Yen Olass threw it with all her force. It winged wide, and went clattering into the darkness.

'You need practice,' said the Yarglat dryly, drawing the bow. 'But I don't. Any more tricks and I'll kill you without blinking. Understand?'

Yen Olass nodded.

'Good,' said the Yarglat. 'Now come with me.'

CHAPTER
Forty-five

The castle was asleep, and Morgan Hearst was ready to move. His cell was pitch black, as the torch they had left with him had long since expired. But by now he knew this prison intimately. He had tested the door for weaknesses, finding none. Climbing up onto the heavy lintel above the door, he had probed the stonework. Again he had been disappointed. But the floor and the walls had yielded up interesting secrets.

Now, moving in the dark, he removed the loose flagstone and took out the items he had earlier discovered beneath it. There was a length of rope, a knife and a half a horseshoe, which had been ground down at one end to make a kind of chisel. Hearst explored the wall, once more finding the lose stone. Using the horseshoe chisel, he levered it out, exposing a steel tunnel descending from unknown heights. It was wet, but it was not a sewer; it smelt dank, but was not unclean.

Hearst had feared to leave earlier in the night, thinking that the turnkey might come and check on him, and raise the alarm. But there had been no checks, so he doubted that anyone would come for him before dawn. Now he would escape. And if escape proved impossible, then he would kill himself to deny his enemies the pleasure of sacrificing him.

Silently, Hearst eased himself into the tunnel. It was a tight squeeze to get through the hole made by removing a block of stone, but once in the tunnel he had room enough to go on all fours or to waddle. He went downward, hoping the tunnel would exit somewhere near the base of the castle. Once he was clear of the castle, there would be no holding him.

As he worked his way down the tunnel, it started to get steeper. He went cautiously through the dark, wary in case he encountered a drop-hole. He was reminded of the time when he had retreated through darkened tunnels exiting from a dragon's lair on the mountain of Maf; these memories of times past were unwelcome, and he suppressed them.

As the tunnel got steeper, it became drier. And warm. Then hot. Then Hearst saw a flicker of fire up ahead. He paused, unable to keep himself from recalling past encounters with dragons. Was it possible that his Collosnon enemies were holding such a monster in their dungeons? It was unlikely, but not impossible.

Hearst doubted that he could tackle a dragon with a bit of rope, a knife and an improvised chisel. Yet he crept forward. The flames grew brighter. He could see his own hands now; he could see the stone blocks the tunnel was made from. He saw a drop of his own sweat fall to make a small damp patch on the hot dry stone. It faded rapidly.

A little further, and Hearst found himself on the edge of a chasm, looking down into a pit of seething fire. There was no dragon to contend with: but this inferno was impassable. The chasm was a remnant of the fire dyke which had once moated the ancient stronghold of wizards, Castle Vaunting.

Hearst studied his surroundings carefully. He leaned out and peered to right and to left. There was no escape from this end of the tunnel. Still, if escape ultimately proved impossible, he had an easy way out . . .

So he thought for a moment. Then his old fear of heights claimed him, and he withdrew from the edge of the chasm, shuddering. If in the end he was forced to suicide to escape being sacrificed, then he would not jump into that pit. Instead, he would slash his carotids, allowing him to bleed to death swiftly without excessive pain.

But it was not yet time for that.

Hearst turned round and followed the tunnel upward. Soon it grew too dark for him to see, but his questing, testing fingertips found the hole marking the place where he had removed a block of stone from his cell wall. He paused, resting. Not for the first time, he wondered about the prisoner who had actually chipped away the mortar to loosen that stone, and who had secreted rope, knife and chisel under a loose flagstone. Had that prisoner been taken away and executed just before escaping? Or had the prisoner perhaps fallen ill, escape again being prevented by death?

What Hearst was trying to avoid was the thought that maybe there was no escape via this tunnel.

After a short rest, he continued on up the tunnel. Again it grew steeper. Finally it became vertical. He worked his way upward, bracing his back against one wall of the shaft and his knees against the opposite wall, using hand, hook, forearms and elbows in his struggle.

He was halted at length by a metal grating. He pushed it with his head. It refused to shift. Bracing himself with back and knees, jamming himself in the shaft so he could not slip and fall, he heaved upwards, using head, hand and forearm. Sweating and straining, he managed to lift the metal grate. He pushed it aside. It made a hideous sound as it scraped over stone.

Swiftly, Hearst hauled himself up and sat on the edge of the shaft. He snapped his fingers and listened for echoes. Something was deadening the sound. He was in a room of indeterminate size, possibly a room clad with soft furnishings.

Moving round in the dark, Hearst found bundles of linen. Then a clothes horse. Behind that, a fireplace. He raked through the ashes with his knife, uncovering a few dying embers. He found a woodbox to one side of the fireplace, trimmed shavings from a log to use as kindling, and before long had a fire going.

By the firelight, he saw that he was in a laundry. He had guessed as much already. Some poor unfortunates must have the job of carting water up from the river; once dirty, it was tipped away down the shaft, riding the tunnel down to the fire chasm. In Garabatoon, faced with the threat of the Swarms, a lot of effort had gone into putting as many people and services as possible behind the protection of stone walls.

Hearst looked for the door leading out of the laundry. To his surprise, it was barred from the outside. He could not shift it. It was a massive, hulking door made out of baulks of timber. Even with an axe, he would have been some time smashing a way through it; without an axe, any such effort would be futile. The weakest point of a door is often its hinges, but in this case the hinges were on the far side.

The windows were narrow slits which would not even admit his head. Looking out, he saw a dark night sky and darker countryside. He hunted all through the laundry, but found only one way of escape—up the chimney. Heat fanned his face as he leaned over the fire. He peered up the dubious black shaft then withdrew, and sat down to think.

He was very comfortable there by the fire. The blue flames talked to the red and the gold, murmuring quietly. Occasional sparks ascended. Some were wafted on upwards, while others clung to the blackened walls of the chimney, glowed momentarily then died, adding their own weight to the thick coating of soot.

Hearst was tired; he was more than ready for sleep. Could he hide in the laundry and escape when the workers came? No. He would either be caught sleeping, or else he would die fighting his way out of castle. To survive, he had to escape from Castle Celadric tonight, and get away under cover of darkness. He got to his feet.

Hearst sorted out three hooded cloaks and donned all three. Once he escaped, he would discard them, since travelling the countryside covered in soot would draw unnecessary attention to him—to put it mildly. He drew dirty water from a tub which had not yet been emptied down the disposal chute. The fire hissed and spluttered when he threw on the water. The flames died, but he used more water to kill the fire entirely, not wanting any smoke in the chimney while he was climbing it.

Belatedly, he realised it might be a good idea to protect his hand—best to take good care of it, as he only had the one. Working in the dark, he tore cloth into strips and bandaged it. Then he started up the chimney, which was warm, though he had not had the fire burning for long; with three cloaks over his other clothing, he was soon uncomfortably hot.

He climbed past a junction where another chimney joined the one he was ascending. He forced his way on upward, and then, to his dismay, found that the chimney narrowed to a chokepoint too small for him to get through. Looking up, he saw a span of stars. His hand reached up, counted one, two, three bricks, then found an open space which he supposed was the roof. He made a tentative effort to chip away at the mortar holding the bricks, then abandoned it. Speed was essential. He might be half the night removing the bricks—and even then, having gained the roof, he might find no easy way to exit from it.

He decided to climb back to where the chimney branched. If he could not find an escape route, he could always return to attack the bricks barring him from the roof. He descended carefully, reached the junction, and followed the unexplored shaft.

He found it strangely clean—there seemed to be no soot in it at all. As it went down, it began to widen. Soon it was almost too wide for him to brace his back against one side and his knees against the other. Hearst found himself getting nervous, fearing a fall. If it got much wider, he would have to give up and climb back again.

Then he found a wooden ladder pegged into the side of the shaft. He accepted its assistance gratefully, and climbed down it. All around him, the shaft opened out. He wondered what on earth could be below. He paused, linking his right arm through the ladder, and scraped the soot out of his nose. Now he could smell something curiously foul—a compound stench of wet and rot, of bad meat and maggots, of stinking potatoes, of sewage. He peered downwards into the darkness, but found himself unable to see anything.

He had rested long enough. He climbed on down. Suddenly, without a moment's notice, the ladder tore free from the wall. Hearst fell. Falling, he shrieked. His scream of terror echoed from the walls. Then he smashed home into—

He was buried in it.

He forced his head out, spat, breathed, gagged, then forced himself to breathe again. He had fallen into a pit filled with everything he had been smelling earlier. He spat repeatedly, fighting nausea. He dared not open his eyes. His clothes, his face, his hair—everything was covered in evil-smelling slime. He was neck-deep in the stuff.

Hearst struggled to the wall. It curved overhead. Working his way right round the pit, he found it the same all the way round. It was as if he stood in the bottom of an hourglass. It was impossible to climb that curving wall. There was only one way out: a slimy round pipe set in the wall at neck height.

Hearst struggled into the pipe and began to crawl. It was

narrow, and it stank. After a long, hard struggle the smell got worse, as it was joined by the stink of something scorching. The pipe was getting warm; he guessed it emptied into another fire chasm.

He felt his way carefully, stopping when the heat grew intense. The muck coating his eyelids had dried by now; he flaked away the crust and opened his eyes. As he expected, he saw firelight reflecting from the walls ahead. So this was the end! He was going to die in a sewer. He was, he realized, already very thirsty. How long would he last? A day? Two days? Maybe longer.

Unless there was a way past the fire.

He crawled forward, and found himself confronted by a man-wide chasm. It went down a long, long way, widening as it went; below was a veritable lake of fire. On the other side of the chasm was a rock ledge, one horse-length wide, studded with stone bollards. In the rock wall behind the ledge there was a door, revealed by the glowering, shadowy light of hellfire.

Hearst, crouched in the sewer pipe, could not jump across the chasm, even though it was only man-wide. However, he still had the length of rope he had found under the loose flagstone in his prison cell. He could make a noose and throw it so it landed on one of the stone bollards. Then he could swing across the chasm, open the door and—

And what if the door refused to open?

Hearst declined to think about that. Swiftly, he made a lasso out of his bit of rope. On the third try, he managed to drop it over the nearest bollard. He hauled on the rope to tighten the noose. The bollard toppled over and fell into the chasm. As it fell, the rope snapped taut and was wrenched from his hand. He gave a small, involuntary cry—and then was ashamed of himself for doing so.

Hearst backed into the sewer, until he was in the cooler sections, away from the fire. By means of long and involved contortions, he managed to strip off the three cloaks he wore over his other clothing. He cut the cloaks into strips and tied the strips into ropes. Each cloak made a rope long enough to bridge the chasm even after he had fashioned a loop at one end.

He was ready to try again.

He was very tired now. His body was weary from crawling, scrambling and climbing, and from the shock of his plunge into the pit. He was starting to suffer occasional muscle cramps. He crawled back to the fire chasm and tried again.

The first time he threw a rope, the loop at the end dropped

neatly over a bollard. He pulled on it. The bollard did not move. But would it hold firm when it supported his full weight? For that matter, would the rope hold? He would soon find out. He wrapped the end of the rope round his right forearm, careful to keep it clear of his razor-sharp hook. He gripped the rope in his hand, pulled it taut then advanced.

As he hauled himself out of the pipe, a blast of heat flushed his face, neck and belly. When he was out of the pipe as far as his navel, he felt his body starting to sag in the middle. He paused, winding the slack of the rope round his right forearm. He wriggled forward. Soon the rope was taking half his weight, with his feet supporting the rest. He was now suspended over the fire chasm; he felt as if he was cooking. The far side was just out of reach.

His toes worked their way to the edge of the sewer. He lifted one foot, and explored the edge of the sewer with his boot. Then he kicked off, jerking his knees in to his chest.

He swung across the chasm. Knees tucked in to his chest, he slammed into the far side. His feet took the brunt of the impact. There was a ripping sound: his cloth rope was tearing. Desperately he reached up with his left hand, took the full weight of his body in that hand, wound in the slack with his right forearm, then repeated the process.

His hand slammed home on level rock. He had gained a purchase on the top! In a few seconds, he had hauled himself up onto the rock ledge. He rolled away from the heat and lay panting. His body was wringing wet with sweat; his mouth was a desert. Slowly, he gathered his strength and got to his knees. He stood up. He felt the blood swoon from his head; dizzy, he collapsed to his knees. He crawled to the door, one horse-length from the chasm.

He rested by the door for a while, then, when he had recovered somewhat, he got up and inspected it. There was no handle on the inside. He tried to lever it open, and failed. The hinges were on the far side. When he threw his weight against it, it did not even creak. It was a solid door. He would have to cut a hole in it. Either that, or die.

He decided to work in the middle, cutting a hole he could reach through to lift whatever bar secured the door. Of course, if the door was bolted shut, the bolt would be to one side, out of reach. With that happy thought, he set to work with knife, hook and chisel.

Morgan Hearst had by now entirely lost track of time. He worked methodically, without thought, pausing only when his arms cramped, and he had to straighten them to ease the muscle spasms. He was very tired now; as he worked, he had occasional hallucinatory dreams for two or three breaths at a time.

At last he managed to make a small hole which he could poke his chisel through. Peering through the hole, he made out the dim outlines of a small, bare room. Or was it a section of a corridor? He could see very little of it. But what he could see was a slit window admitting grey dawnlight.

He had run out of darkness.

Hearst worked harder. Every time he stopped to look at his steadily widening hole, the light on the far side was brighter. Eventually, brilliant daylight was streaming in through the slit window. Panting, sweating, swearing occasionally—silently, for it hurt his throat to speak—he hacked, gouged, jabbed and scraped, splintering the wood and ripping it away.

The first time he tried to force his hand through the hole, it got stuck. Splinters jagged into it as he wrenched it back. He attacked the door in a vicious frenzy, expending the last of his energy. When he halted, gasping, the hole was large enough. He reached through and groped around, searching for a bar which he could lift to open the door.

Someone grabbed his hand.

Hearst hauled with all his strength, trying to retrieve his hand. It was impossible. He swore aloud. His voice was a croak. He swore again. He had been caught in a trap. After all that effort, he had been caught. His rage overmastered him. He slammed his head against the door in frustration.

The door began to open.

As the door opened, Hearst was dragged into the daylight. Then his hand was released, suddenly. He fell backwards onto the floor. He lay there, exhausted, half-blinded by the light. A small group of people gathered round and stared down at him. His vision blurred then focused. He recognised the Lord Emperor Celadric, dressed in lightweight silks; the emperor's brother, Meddon, wearing chain mail and bearing weapons; the Ondrask of Noth, in his ceremonial regalia; the pirate chief Draven, and, standing beside him and looking very pale, the Princess Quenerain.

'You took longer than I expected,' said Celadric.

'Yes,' said Meddon. 'Still, you're lucky to have made it. Half our prisoners die in the attempt.'

Hearst managed a few words in a wretched, rusty voice.

'Am I free then?'

'Oh no,' said Meddon, laughing. 'Not that lucky. The Ondrask has sharpened a knife for you.'

'Any last requests?' said Celadric.

'You can have my woman, if you like,' said Draven.

The Princess Quenerain flinched.

'Water,' said Hearst.

'The prisoner is to be denied all water,' said Celadric, then turned and walked away.

'If it's any consolation,' said Meddon, 'you're going to be executed today. That's part of the deal with our friend Draven. He doesn't want the general escaping then coming looking for his woman.'

'Watashi?' croaked Hearst.

'He goes into the stocks in the market place at noon,' said Meddon, 'along with your other friends. They'll be stoned to death by the mob.'

And Meddon smiled, produced a wilted flower and dropped it on Hearst's chest. This was a subtle insult, reminding him of how easily he had been taken the day before. Then Meddon too turned and walked away.

Hearst jerked his hook up to his throat, intending to slash his carotids then and there. But the Ondrask stepped on his right arm before he could do himself any injury. The Ondrask gave a curt order in a language Hearst could not understand.

And guards seized hold of the Rovac warrior Morgan Hearst, and carried him away.

CHAPTER
Forty-six

Garabatoon was crowded for the river festival. Just upstream of the bridge, a clutter of rafts and small boats jammed the Hollern River. Then there was a long stretch of river which had been left clear for boat races, river crossing competitions and so forth. Then, further upstream, there were three rafts.

The three rafts lying upstream from Garabatoon all belonged to the Ondrask of Noth. One was a floating funeral pyre, on which sacrifices would be carried out. Another was the Ondrask's personal residence. The third housed the Ondrask's retainers, who numbered about two dozen.

Toward mid-morning, people began to drift out of Garabatoon, and soon both banks were lined with spectators. Then General Chonjara and Morgan Hearst were led to the riverbank. Both men were stripped to the waist and had their arms tied behind their backs.

Hearst watched as Chonjara was led out along a gangplank to the floating funeral pyre. He was made to lie down in amongst the high-piled firewood. He almost disappeared in it. The guards withdrew. The Ondrask climbed up to Chonjara, raised a knife high, stabbed down, and hauled out Chonjara's beating heart. The crowd gave a roar of approval.

Even as Hearst was hustled forward by the guards, other guards were putting torches to the firewood. A black cloth had been thrown over Chonjara's body, but the wood around was splattered with gore. Hearst was laid down in amongst the firewood in a coffin-sized indentation. He took his last look at the sky. The Ondrask loomed over him.

The Ondrask spoke briefly. Hearst did not understand, but a guard standing at the Ondrask's shoulder translated.

'Goodbye, Morgan.'

'I speak Ordhar,' said Hearst, using the Collosnon battle language.

'The Ondrask speaks only Eparget,' said the guard, in the Galish Trading Tongue.

There was the sound of the black cloth being twitched away. Hearst could not see the body. The Ondrask bent down, leaning to one side. He was dipping his finger in blood. He anointed Hearst with the blood, and spoke earnestly. The guard translated.

'Morgan, I have to kill you, but I bear you no ill. My religion holds that the soul of the warrior goes to Nazagost, the place of the Testing. Have courage for the Test. Endure.'

Hearst made no answer.

He watched as the Ondrask raised his knife. The blade had not been cleaned. It was still bloodstained. As Hearst watched, a drop fell from the blade. He could smell smoke. He heard the fierce crackle of flames, and knew the wood was well and truly ablaze. He saw the Ondrask grimace, about to stab downwards. Despite himself, Hearst closed his eyes.

He felt a lacerating pain in his chest and heard his own scream. Opening his eyes, he saw the Ondrask holding aloft his beating heart. Then he was falling, his sight failing. He fell through fire, smashed into a barrier, and knew no more.

*   *   *

Morgan Hearst opened his eyes and stared up at a strange sky of blue and green. He tried to speak; a croak came out of his mouth. A stranger, a woman with long hair, fed him water. Honey had been mixed into the water. He drank, and it was good.

'This is Nazagost,' said the woman. 'The place of Testing.'

So it was true. He had died, and had come to the place of Testing. Slowly, he raised his right arm, and saw the articulation of wood and metal that held his hook in place. He was bitterly disappointed to find he had been reincarnated as a cripple.

'I will contend against any man, god or hero if the battle can win me my hand,' said Hearst.

'It can win more than that,' said a familiar voice, as someone sitting behind him spoke. 'It can win you an empire.'

'Yen Olass?' said Hearst.

His chest was hurting. Looking down, he saw a ragged cut in his skin, as if someone had sliced it with a jagged knife. He tried to turn around to see Yen Olass.

'Are you dead too?' said Hearst.

'We'll all be dead if we carry on with this nonsense,' growled a voice.

Hearst propped himself up on an elbow and saw Yen Olass Ampadara and General Chonjara sitting in opposite corners of a . . . a bamboo room? A room on a raft? He glanced up at the ceiling. Loose-woven bamboo, still fresh and green, making a pattern of blue and green as the sky showed through. But he had seen his own heart! He remembered it being dragged out of his body.

'There was a hole in the bottom of the sacrifice raft,' said Yen Olass. 'You were dropped through it. We recovered you. I pulled you out myself—I'm a good swimmer, you know.'

'But my heart—'

'An ox, stupid. He had two great big beefy oxen under that great big black cloth. One for Chonjara, one for you.'

'But I felt my . . . I felt my heart getting torn out. I remember.'

'That's your imagination speaking,' said Yen Olass. 'You were slashed across the chest, that's all.'

'But if the whole sacrifice was a sham,' said Hearst, starting to get angry. 'Then why cut me at all?'

'Because my lover is something of a sadist,' said Yen Olass.

'Your lover?' said Hearst. 'The . . . the Ondrask?'

'Not yet,' said Yen Olass. 'But he will be. Once I'm Kenagek.'

'Kenagek?'

'The Kenagek is the mother of the emperor,' said Yen Olass.

'You're going to try and make yourself Celadric's mother?' said Hearst, feeling confused.

'No,' said Yen Olass. 'Celadric is going to abdicate in favour of Monogail. He doesn't know it yet, of course. But he will.'

'How are you going to persuade him?' said Hearst.

'With a knife,' said Yen Olass. 'A castrating knife, if necessary. He's accepted an invitation to dine with the Ondrask at noon. His brother Meddon's coming too. We'll kill Meddon and kidnap Celadric. Once we get him to the Lesser Teeth, we can make him agree to anything we want.'

'You've left something out of your battle plan,' said Hearst.

'What's that,' said Yen Olass.

'York.'

'Oh, I've killed him already,' said Yen Olass happily. 'I'm famous, don't you know. Hundreds of soldiers are out combing the countryside for me. Celadric always wanted his brother dead, but as a matter of form he's even committed his personal bodyguard to the hunt.'

'You're crazy,' said Hearst scornfully. 'Garabatoon is still swarming with men. What've you got here? Five? Six?'

'About a dozen,' said Yen Olass. 'And the same number of women.'

'You'll all be dead by nightfall,' said Hearst.

'By nightfall, we'll be safely at sea,' said Yen Olass. 'Losh Negis—'

'Who?'

'The Ondrask here,' said Yen Olass. 'There was a banquet last night. Afterwards, he went to Draven's ship, anchored just downriver from Garabatoon. He'd offended the emperor, and did not think it safe to spend the night in Castle Celadric. They spent part of the night plotting. Today, while we seize Celadric, Draven's men will be raiding the marketplace at Garabatoon, to release Watashi and the others.'

'A handful of pirates versus a whole town?' said Hearst. 'That's ridiculous!'

'Draven's got sixty men,' said Yen Olass. 'Some of them have got Collosnon armour. They can pose as Celadric's soldiers.'

'They'll need more than a little amateur acting to cheat the mob of its victims,' said Hearst.

'They're going to burn down the town,' said Yen Olass. 'Start a few fires, and people will be running in all directions— most of them drunk. Draven isn't stupid, you know. Probably there'll be so much confusion that nobody will notice the prisoners are gone until this time tomorrow.'

'Celadric will be missed sooner.'

'Yes, but nobody will know where he's gone. We'll grab him, stuff him into a sack—a wet sack, with dirt and worms and rotten apples in it—then smuggle him down the river in a boat. With someone sitting on him. No, with two people sitting on him! Then we'll put him on Draven's ship.'

'How do you know you can trust the pirate?' said Hearst.

'I don't know if I can trust him at all,' said Yen Olass simply. 'But I don't have much choice. My child's on his ship.'

'Which child is that?'

'What do you mean, which child? Monogail, of course, you ignorant—'

'Monogail! But how—'

'Nan Nulador, that's how. He grabbed her for Celadric. What're your dungeons made of, huh? Ricepaper, perhaps?'

'Where's Nan Nulador now?' said Hearst.

'I was put to the necessity of killing him,' said Yen Olass. 'So I could make good my escape.'

'Really? And tell me, how did you escape?'

'I can walk through walls,' said Yen Olass, not wishing to confess to Hearst that she had been kidnapped and spirited out of the castle by a Yarglat tribesman in the Ondrask's employ.

'That's a very clever trick,' said Hearst. 'You must show it to me one day.'

'One day I will,' said Yen Olass.

'But only if you abandon your crazy scheme to kidnap Celadric,' said Hearst. 'Otherwise you won't live to see nightfall, let alone one day, whenever that may be.'

'Hey, it's not my crazy scheme. It's all these crazy men who thought it up. If you want to argue, you argue with them.'

'I'm not going to argue,' said Hearst. 'I'm going to sleep. Wake me up when it's all over.'

'I haven't finished explaining things to you yet!' said Yen Olass.

'Goodnight,' said Hearst.

And, true, to his word, he laid his head down and went to sleep—or pretended to.

'What does he say?' asked Chonjara, who had been unable to follow this conversation.

'He says he's not going to fight for us,' said Yen Olass. 'He's going to sleep instead.'

'He'll feel better when he's rested,' said Chonjara. 'In fact . . . so will I. Wake me if anything happens.'

And he too laid himself down, and, with the ease of a professional soldier, went to sleep.

*   *   *

Toward noon, the Lord Emperor Celadric came to the Ondrask's raft with his brother Meddon and a mob of fighting men. Some of the soldiers were Meddon's; some were members of Celadric's personal bodyguard, which he had now withdrawn from the womanhunt.

Hearst, Yen Olass and Chonjara watched through cracks in the bamboo walls as the troops came aboard. There was no need for a council of war: they were obviously badly outnumbered. They would not be kidnapping Celadric today.

Losh Negis came into the cabin and silently handed out ceremonial masks, which would obscure their identity if anyone was rude enough to challenge the cabin's privacy. Along with ten of the Ondrask's men, they waited, hoping Celadric and Meddon would not stay too long. Outside, the rest of the Ondrask's people—most of them women—began serving the guests.

With so many people crowded into the cabin and warm sunlight beating down, it was hot. Yen Olass, sweating behind a horsehide mask, peered through a crack in the wall. What she saw was mostly legs, none of which took her fancy.

Outside, the Ondrask was now confronting Celadric, who had brought him a gift.

'What is it?' said Losh Negis, taking the elaborately carved casket his emperor handed him.

'Open it,' said Celadric with a smile.

So Losh Negis opened the casket, and discovered a knife reclining on velvet. A very beautiful knife.

'Do you know what it's for?' said Celadric gently.

'No,' said Losh Negis.

'It's to kill yourself with,' said Celadric, in his oboe-smooth voice. 'Your behaviour last night was less than acceptable. You must understand that such behaviour has consequences.'

Losh Negis hesitated.

Celadric turned to Meddon and said:

'Kill him.'

'With pleasure,' said Meddon, drawing his sword.

Losh Negis dropped the casket and fled. He hurled himself against the door of the cabin, which burst open. He crashed to the floor amongst the bodies inside.

'Eagles!' shouted Meddon.

And in a trice, blades were out and blood was flying. Celadric came running in after Losh Negis. He had been slashed across the face. His panic was masked with blood. Outside, his men were being butchered by Meddon's bravos.

The fight on the raft was brief. Taken by surprise, Celadric's men were easy meat. Most of them, in keeping with the spirit of a river festival, had come unarmed. Meddon, victorious, entered the cabin and looked around. There were fifteen people inside. Every one of them was now wearing a horsehide mask.

'Losh Negis,' said Meddon, 'I've got no quarrel with you. Give me my brother—or my brother's head.'

Losh Negis took off his mask.

'Ah, there you are,' said Meddon. 'Which one's my brother? Come out, Celadric. You can't hide forever!'

'That one,' said Losh Negis, pointing Meddon to the far corner.

'This is treason!' shouted Celadric, tearing off his mask.

'But of course,' said Meddon mildly, advancing on his brother. 'It's your own fault. You shouldn't have had York murdered last night.'

'That woman did it! I never—'

'Skak!' shouted Meddon, less mild as he moved in for the kill.

The next moment he was down on the deck, struggling. Half a dozen men had jumped him as he moved in for the kill.

'Call off your men,' said Chonjara.

'Let me go,' said Meddon, 'Or you're dead.'

Chonjara sliced off one of his fingers.

'Call off your men,' said Chonjara, 'or I'll take your nose off next.'

'Faravaunt!' shouted Meddon, using a code word which meant nothing to anyone inside the cabin.

To his men, it meant retreat.

Instead, they crowded into the entrance.

'Sir—'

'Get out of here, you swine-gutter filth! They're going to cut me to pieces! Go! Horse off!'

Reluctantly, Meddon's men retreated. Hearst took an axe, and, masked, went outside and cut the anchor ropes. The raft began to drift downriver.

'Are they all gone?' said Chonjara.

'They're all gone,' said Losh Negis.

'Good,' said Chonjara.

And he cut Meddon's throat.

Downstream, smoke was rising to the sky as Garabatoon began to burn.

CHAPTER
Forty-seven

They sailed first to the Greater Teeth, and it was there that Yerzerdayla helped Yen Olass put the finishing touches on her plan for taking over the Collosnon Empire.

The original plan, concocted by the Ondrask, had its dubious aspects. Chonjara, having promised to support Monogail as empress, was supposed to rally an army under his own command. The Ondrask thought at least half the Collosnon forces would come to Chonjara's banner.

Morgan Hearst was supposed to raise a mercenary army from his western homeland of Rovac, to support the forces loyal to the Ondrask and Chonjara. Hearst was to be given Monogail's hand in marriage, so that when Monogail attained her maturity she would be wife of the emperor. That guarantee of power and influence was supposed to convince him that it was in his best interests to support their cause.

But, as Yerzerdayla pointed out, this plan had its defects. Initially, it would make Chonjara the most powerful man in Tameran. Given such power, he would be unlikely to relinquish it. And even if he did—what mother in her right mind would want to marry her daughter to Morgan Hearst, a man of no character.

Watashi was the best choice as supreme commander. He was not of the Yarglat, so he would need to come to Tameran as Monogail's general if he was to hope to command the assent of the most powerful Collosnon military commanders, who were all Yarglat clansmen. For Watashi, Monogail would always be indispensable. Stokos was too small and too far away to hope to conquer Tameran, but Stokos was hungry enough and populous enough to provide at least one army to contend against any other powers—such as Onosh Gulkan, the Witchlord—which chose to try for the throne of Tameran.

Hearst, bribed with the prospect of ultimately controlling the west of Argan, could be counted on to provide a second army. If he hesitated, Watashi could offer to bankroll that mercenary army—Stokos was small and hungry, but its gold reserves were substantial.

Yerzerdayla and Yen Olass schemed together, then dickered with Hearst and Watashi, then presented Losh Negis and Chonjara with an ultimatum: they could swear themselves to Monogail's cause, or leave their bones on the Greater Teeth.

They swore their oaths of allegiance.

'But what about you and me?' said the Ondrask. 'What happens between us, now?'

'That,' said Yen Olass, 'remains to be seen.'

She thought about it in the days that followed, as they forced the Lord Emperor Celadric to sign papers formalizing his abdication in favour of Monogail, as they drafted letters demanding that hostages be sent to the Greater Teeth, as they received the garrison commander of Garabatoon and accepted his oath of allegiance.

The Ondrask had changed over the years. Losh Negis was both more and less than the man she had seen so long ago in the cave to the north of the hunting lodge near Gendormargensis. She had seen him compromise his dignity by capering around on all fours, playing a part in a farce organised by Celadric. But then, too, she had seen him attacking Nan Nulador with a battle hammer. A rash act, no doubt, and probably one prompted more by hatred of Celadric than by love of Yen Olass. Still, the fact remained—he had saved the life of her child.

And, as the days went by, he did his best to show his respect for her. He had his hair washed and cut, and his fingernails trimmed and cleaned. He had seven rotten teeth pulled out. His breath came to smell like apples. He courted her assiduously. Yen Olass was flattered by his attentions. But before she could take him seriously, there was one personal defect he would have to remedy—he would have to learn to wash.

She was still trying to think of a tactful way to put it to him when they arrived at the Lesser Teeth. She dropped several hints, but he took none of them—he seemed oblivious to them. So, in the end, she decided to be direct.

The Ondrask met her one afternoon on her direction. He wore his usual stinking clothes and his body stank as always. Yen Olass smiled, kissed him, took him firmly by the hand, and led him, not to the bed which he had been hoping for, but to a large room with a sunken pool in the middle. The pool was filled with steaming water.

There were six hefty washerwomen standing round the pool, waiting. They were armed—no expense had been spared— with sponges, lemons, soap, body oil, body scrapers, cloths, towels and pumice stone. The Ondrask regarded them with some apprehension, then went and took a good look at the pool.

'What's that?' he said.

'A bath,' said Yen Olass.

And she pushed him into it.

*   *   *

While the Ondrask of Noth was enduring the very first bath of his life, Yen Olass went to check on Monogail, to see how she was settling back in. They would be staying on the Lesser Teeth for a little while yet, until they had the ships and the soldiers they needed to move on Tameran.

Yen Olass found Monogail very excited; she had something she wanted to show her mother urgently.

'Mam! Mam! Come and see! Straff's had a baby! So's Ala-manda!'

Yen Olass doubted it, but allowed herself to be dragged along to see. Monogail led the way into her bedroom.

'Here,' said Monogail, drawing her to the big earthenware dish of rocks and weed and water. 'Baby ones! Look!'

Peering into this aqueous paradise, Yen Olass saw a tiny tiny fish sharing the dish with Straff, and a tiny tiny frog occupying a rock with Alamanda. She wondered who had arranged this present for her daughter.

'Baby ones! See!'

'Immaculate conception, huh?' said Yen Olass.

'What's immaculate, mam?'

'We'll say it means perfect,' said Yen Olass, and hugged the child who—no matter who or what the father might be—was most definitely hers.